“[An] imaginative an[illegible] . . . Varley is in top form. *Mammoth* delivers the kind of snappy exposition, clever speculation, and narrative complexity that have made so many of his contributions to the genre so enjoyable and vital . . . He’s a far better science fiction writer than Crichton, though, and he takes pains to make *Mammoth* as unpredictable as possible. He keeps the reader off balance, playing different sets of expectations off one another, and concocts a story that alternates elements from a variety of genres—romance, puzzle story, survival adventure, espionage, and even crime caper. By the time the identity of the mummified caveman is revealed, *Mammoth* has worked through its suspenseful premise with the perfect amount of wit and craftsmanship.”

—*San Francisco Chronicle*

“[A] rollicking, bittersweet tale of time travel and ecology . . . Varley’s sparkling wit pulls one surprise after another out of this unconventional blend of science and social commentary with real people convincingly doing unreal things. Fuzzy, though, is the true hero, an irresistible fifteen-foot-tall reminder of the wonders of nature and imagination. The winner of numerous Hugo and Nebula awards, Varley should garner new laurels with this outstanding effort.” —*Publishers Weekly* (starred review)

“A terrific science fiction thriller with a fabulous final twist that will shock the audience . . . The cast is a delight as the prime players seem real, but it is the science in which John Varley has H. G. Wells meet *Jurassic Park* that hooks the audience.” —*The Best Reviews*

“The author of *Red Thunder* excels in imaginative SF adventure, bringing together an intriguing premise and resourceful characters in a tale of mystery, suspense, and a voyage through time. A good addition to most SF collections.” —*Library Journal*

“Varley’s fans won’t be disappointed.” —*Booklist*

continued . . .

PRAISE FOR
RED THUNDER

"Varley's great strength is in his characterizations, but in *Red Thunder* he also shows a strong sense of place. The novel is also in a sense an elegy: Science fiction readers have long hoped to travel in outer space, and Varley implies that this will be possible only if we discover something radically different from anything now known to physicists. But if you are willing to simply fantasize about fleeing your office cubicle and becoming a heroic space explorer, this novel will fulfill your wishes."

—*The Washington Post*

"The heart-pounding space race is on! [A] riveting SF thriller . . . with hilarious, well-drawn characters, extraordinary situations presented plausibly, plus exciting action and adventure." —*Publishers Weekly* (starred review)

"Fast-paced . . . engaging characters."

—*Rocky Mountain News*

"Full of little gems of wit and intelligence." —*Booklist*

"[A] fun-filled adventure. Varley matches a serious literary style with an outrageous plot and he's one of the few writers in the field who could make it work." —*Chronicle*

"[*Red Thunder*] is unlike anything John Varley has previously written, and yet it bears all the hallmarks of his past work . . . startling ideas, pellucid dreams, amiable characters, a gorgeous specificity of detail, and a sense of honest victories achieved at real costs. Dedicated to the master of such topical tomorrows, Robert Heinlein, this novel also pays allegiance to the comic capers of Carl Hiaasen. Varley lauds the unconquerable human spirit of exploration. But it's just the frosting on the rich cake of practical, visionary comic adventure he's already supplied in full."

—*Science Fiction Weekly*

PRAISE FOR

JOHN VARLEY

"One of science fiction's most important writers."
—*The Washington Post*

"Science fiction doesn't get much better than this."
—Spider Robinson

"Inventive . . . strong and satisfying." —*The New York Times*

"Varley is a mind-grabber." —Roger Zelazny

"Superior science fiction." —*The Philadelphia Inquirer*

"Varley has earned the mantle of Heinlein." —*Locus*

"One of the genre's most accomplished storytellers."
—*Publishers Weekly*

Books by John Varley

THE OPHIUCHI HOTLINE
THE PERSISTENCE OF VISION
PICNIC ON NEARSIDE
(*formerly titled* THE BARBIE MURDERS)
MILLENNIUM
BLUE CHAMPAGNE
STEEL BEACH
THE GOLDEN GLOBE
RED THUNDER
MAMMOTH
RED LIGHTNING

THE GAEAN TRILOGY
TITAN
WIZARD
DEMON

THE JOHN VARLEY READER:
THIRTY YEARS OF SHORT FICTION

MAMMOTH

JOHN VARLEY

ACE BOOKS, NEW YORK

THE BERKLEY PUBLISHING GROUP
Published by the Penguin Group
Penguin Group (USA) Inc.
375 Hudson Street, New York, New York 10014, USA
Penguin Group (Canada), 90 Eglinton Avenue East, Suite 700, Toronto, Ontario M4P 2Y3, Canada
(a division of Pearson Penguin Canada Inc.)
Penguin Books Ltd., 80 Strand, London WC2R 0RL, England
Penguin Group Ireland, 25 St. Stephen's Green, Dublin 2, Ireland (a division of Penguin Books Ltd.)
Penguin Group (Australia), 250 Camberwell Road, Camberwell, Victoria 3124, Australia
(a division of Pearson Australia Group Pty. Ltd.)
Penguin Books India Pvt. Ltd., 11 Community Centre, Panchsheel Park, New Delhi—110 017, India
Penguin Group (NZ), Cnr. Airborne and Rosedale Roads, Albany, Auckland 1310, New Zealand
(a division of Pearson New Zealand Ltd.)
Penguin Books (South Africa) (Pty.) Ltd., 24 Sturdee Avenue, Rosebank, Johannesburg 2196,
South Africa

Penguin Books Ltd., Registered Offices: 80 Strand, London WC2R 0RL, England

MAMMOTH

An Ace Book / published by arrangement with the author

PRINTING HISTORY
Ace hardcover edition / June 2005
Ace mass market edition / June 2006

Cover art by Matt Stawicki.
Cover design by Annette Fiore.

For information address: The Berkley Publishing Group,
a division of Penguin Group (USA) Inc.,
375 Hudson Street, New York, New York 10014.

ISBN: 0-441-01335-X

ACE
Ace Books are published by The Berkley Publishing Group,
a division of Penguin Group (USA) Inc.,
375 Hudson Street, New York, New York 10014.
ACE and the "A" design are trademarks belonging to Penguin Group (USA) Inc.

PRINTED IN THE UNITED STATES OF AMERICA

10 9 8 7 6 5 4 3 2 1

This book is dedicated to John and Doris Varley.

My father, John E. Varley, died on
January 13, 2005, at the age of 79,
in Big Spring, Texas.

He was a very good man who led a good life
and raised two good daughters, and me.
He hated the Notre Dame Fighting Irish,
the New York Yankees,
and the Texas A&M Aggies,
and loved most other Texas teams.
He lived to see the Red Sox humiliate the Yankees,
and a lot of people didn't.

FROM "LITTLE FUZZY, A CHILD OF THE ICE AGE"

Once upon a time in what would one day come to be known as the month of August, many, many years ago, in a place that would one day be known as **Manitoba**, a herd of mammoths came over the low hills to the south and into a gentle green valley rich with the scent of water.

There were twenty or twenty-five mammoths in the herd. Maybe thirty. No one is sure. What we do know is that the herd was made up of females of all ages and males younger than fifteen years old.

Mammoths did not live in families like we do, with a daddy and a mommy and their children, and maybe a granny and a grandpa. Mammoths were like our elephants today, and their families were bunches of sisters and aunts and nieces and young male mammoths.

When the males reached a certain age they became troublesome, bothering the females all the time . . . just like boys do today! When this happened, the older female mammoths ganged up on the youngster and pushed him out of the herd so he wouldn't cause so much trouble. The young male would then find his way to a herd of other males.

The leader of this herd was the oldest and largest female, what scientists call the **alpha cow**. We'll call her Big Mama.

Big Mama was old, maybe forty-five, maybe fifty; no one knows for sure because mammoths didn't have calendars and didn't write down their birthdays like we do, so they didn't know how old they were. But Big Mama had seen many winters and many summers, and she had been the alpha cow for many years. She was the wisest and strongest member of the herd, by far, and all the other females respected her without question.

It had been a hard summer. The places that would one day be called the **Mississippi and Missouri river valleys** had not seen any rain in many months but there had been plenty of lightning. The prairies were dry and there were many fires.

Big animals like mammoths and bison and woolly rhinoceros had to keep moving to find enough food and water. Big Mama had not led her herd this far north in many years, but her memory was good and she kept them moving.

Sure enough, on that fine day in what would be August, they came into a land bursting with green shrubs and grass and trees with tasty leaves just waiting to be pulled down by the clever trunks of the mammoths.

But others were there before them. They were mammoths, but they were strange, completely covered with hair.

To understand why this should be strange to Big Mama and her herd, you should know that there was more than one kind of mammoth, all those years ago. (There were also cousins of mammoths, called **mastodons**, but we don't need to worry about them.)

There were people back then, and they hunted the mammoths, but we don't know what they called them. Today, we call the two types of mammoth that lived in North America the **woolly mammoth** and the **Columbian mammoth**.

The woolly mammoths stayed mostly in the north, in what we now call Canada.

The Columbian mammoths stayed mostly in the south, sometimes as far south as what we now call **Mexico**!

But there were places where you could have found both kinds of mammoth.

Mammoths sometimes traveled great distances in search of food. Scientists call this **migration**. When woolly mammoths and Columbian mammoths met they usually didn't get involved with one another, any more than they concerned themselves with the **giant ground sloths** or **woolly rhinos** or **giant bison** they shared the plains with. You can see a scene very much like this in **Africa** today, with **elephants** and **rhinos** and **giraffes** and **wildebeests** grazing in the same areas peacefully, ignoring each other.

Most of the time the woolly mammoths and Columbian mammoths ignored each other, too.

But sometimes they didn't.

5

THE helicopter flew low over a landscape as barren as any to be found on planet Earth. This was Nunavut. It wasn't a province and hardly a territory though they called it that. As far as Warburton was concerned they could give it all back to the Eskimos—which was exactly what Canada had done, back in 1999. Nunavut was 810,000 square miles of nothing much, one-fifth of Canada's land area.

Warburton looked out his frosty window and was amazed to see a polar bear loping along a few hundred feet below him. Hunting? Fleeing the helicopter? He was tempted to ask the little Inuit with the brown and weather-beaten face, but realized he could never hope to deal with the man's name. He was introduced to Warburton at the Churchill airport as Charlie Charttinirpaaq, which sounded like a man with a bad cough and a severe case of the hiccups.

Warburton hated helicopters. And he hated large helicopters even more than he hated small ones. The one he was sitting in now was a Sikorsky HB-53F, the civilian version of the military Sea Stallion, probably the largest passenger-carrying chopper outside of Russia. It could be configured to carry fifty soldiers with full combat gear. This one had only two rows of seats bolted to the floor up in the front, the rest of the cavernous interior was empty. With so little cargo the Sikorsky's range was enormous, more than enough to make it from Churchill, where the Air Canada flight had dumped him, to the site known to only a handful of people as Mammoth Seven.

It was damn cold inside, but it didn't seem to bother Charlie. The little Inuit had pushed the hood of his parka back, revealing straight black hair that looked to have been groomed with rendered walrus blubber. His gnarled brown hands were bare. His coat had a handmade and hard-used look to it, but his boots looked like L.L. Beans. He seemed to feel Warburton's gaze, looked across the helicopter and smiled, revealing widely spaced but strong, brown teeth. Didn't they chew reindeer hides to soften them? Or was that just the women? Warburton's own outfit, purchased at Abercrombie & Fitch during his layover in Toronto and guaranteed by the salesman to protect him from a polar blizzard, was providing him no more warmth than a Banlon shirt.

He looked out his window and saw the first spot of color he had seen for more than five hundred miles. The heavily insulated modular dwellings that had been flown in dangling from the cargo hook of this very helicopter were almost the same color as the snow. But a short distance from them was a large half-cylinder tent, like a Quonset hut, made of blue and red canvas panels, strongly anchored with yellow poly ropes, near the bottom of a large, bare hill. This was Mammoth Seven.

Warburton saw people emerge from one of the trailers. One looked up and waved. Then they were setting down on a big red X in the middle of a red circle that had been painted on the snow. Warburton and Charlie unfastened their belts and waited for the pilot, another Inuit, to open the door and lower the ramp.

Once outside, Warburton realized he hadn't really been cold at all inside the damn helicopter. *This*, now *this* was cold.

There were two people hurrying out to meet him, all but indistinguishable in their puffed-up nylon and Gore-Tex outfits, hoods over their heads, eyes hidden by big blue sunglasses against the icy glare. Warburton followed them toward the big pressurized tent looming like some high-tech circus big top a hundred feet up the side of the hill. They trudged up the path and entered through a zipper in its side.

Inside, hoods off, Warburton recognized Dr. Rostov, formerly of the St. Petersburg Museum of Natural History, now the head of the Mammoth Seven recovery. They were in a square room about the size of a hotel elevator, which he knew from visits to previous mammoth sites to be a sort of air lock. The tent was held up by internal pressure, so the outer and inner doors of the room could not be opened at the same time.

Rostov started to open the inner door, then cleared his throat. Warburton realized the man was nervous.

"Now, I know what your first reaction is going to be," Rostov said. "It was my first reaction, too. You're going to think this is some kind of joke."

Rostov had just a trace of an accent. He looked the part of a university professor, with an unkempt mane of white hair and a goatee that was more salt and pepper. But his face was almost as weathered as Charlie's, and he had an alarming red nose shaped like a potato. Though his hands were now clad in fur-lined gloves, Warburton knew the doctor had lost the tips of several fingers to frostbite. Being a mammoth hunter in the twenty-first century didn't entail the same risks as it had for our mammoth-hunting ancestors, but it was no picnic, and it took you to climates that could kill just as surely as a wounded and enraged mammoth.

"It never entered my mind that you would bring me up here as part of a joke, Doctor," Warburton said. Now that the green light had come on over the inner door, Rostov ushered the group inside. The interior was well lit, and not nearly as warm as Warburton had hoped, but at least it was out of the wind.

"We keep it heated to only about four degrees below zero to protect the specimen," Rostov said. Warburton translated from the Canadian centigrade scale: high to mid twenties.

In the center of the tent was the excavation into the side of the hill, a rectangular area about twenty by twenty feet. It was well lit by floodlights on tripods. The crew had dug out the mammoth's head and back and most of one side, but those parts were covered with protective cloth. Christian wanted this frozen creature intact, and that meant excavation was a painfully deliberate process, starting with small ice axes, moving to hammers and chisels, getting down to warm brushes and toothpicks before the hairy pelt was reached. And even then, when a section of hide was bared, it was refrozen in distilled water. It would be absurd for this creature to have survived for ten, fifteen thousand years, perfectly preserved to the point that its flesh was probably still edible, and then to have it rot in a few days of digging. The plan was to free the creature from the permafrost and then quickly airlift it to a large refrigerated facility where further actions could be contemplated at leisure.

"Seven is by far the best and the largest *primigenius* we have yet investigated," Rostov said. "In fact, it is so large I have begun to wonder if it might be an actual hybrid, possibly with *Mammuthus imperiori*, which was quite a bit larger than *primigenius*. The flesh is in wonderful shape. The nuclei we've tested so far have yielded promising DNA, though of course we have yet to reach the sexual organs."

Warburton had learned a lot about mammoths in the last four years. He always had to learn things to keep up with his boss's newest manias. He knew *Mammuthus primigenius* was the Latin name for the woolly mammoth. He'd learned a bit about cloning, too, though he had no aptitude for science. But the basic facts were easy enough to absorb. If one wished to re-create a mammoth, one needed some DNA that was reasonably intact. No perfect specimens had ever been discovered, but as the years went by, the criteria for "reasonably intact" had steadily lowered, as new techniques for reassembling genetic material had been discovered and elaborated. Four years ago he had dismissed the whole project as highly unlikely. It hadn't been the first time his boss had pursued a chimera.

The best mammoth cells to use for cloning would be an egg from a female or a sperm cell from a male. The resulting embryo could then be implanted in a female elephant—not an easy project in itself, as the reproductive cycle of elephants was complicated and not completely understood.

But maybe it could be done, and that was why orders had come from Mr. Christian to concentrate on the rear of the giant corpse, to gain access to the testicles. Or, as Christian had put it in a phone call to Rostov that Warburton had overheard, "I want that bull's balls by next Monday, Doctor, or I'll find somebody else to dig 'em out."

This was the following Wednesday, and Warburton presumed he was about to be shown something astonishing concerning mammoth reproduction. It wasn't a prospect he relished, but he'd undertaken tasks much less appetizing in his work for Christian.

One of the things he had not learned was the precise location of mammoth testicles, but he had assumed they were pretty much where they would be on other quadrupeds, like horses, sheep, cattle, and probably elephants, though he had never actually seen an elephant's family jewels. But Rostov didn't take him all the way around the massive beast, but to its left side. The mammoth was sitting more or less upright, with its legs folded under it.

Now Rostov indicated a lump by the hind legs that did not fit with any picture of a mammoth Warburton could come up with, unless its left hind leg was twisted grotesquely out to one side. The lump was covered with the same protective material that concealed the rest of the mammoth.

Warburton looked at Rostov, waiting, and Rostov sighed and pulled back the cover.

The lump was a man.

He was huddled tight against the side of the mammoth, still partly buried. Only his head and torso had been chipped out of the ice. Most of his face and part of his upper arm had been eaten away, gnawed at by animals. Where Warburton could see the chest, the skin was yellow and shriveled and looked like wax.

Warburton looked at Rostov again.

"No joke," the man assured him, with a helpless shrug.

"How old?"

"Around twelve thousand years," Rostov said.

What was left of the man's hair was long and wispy and gray. There were scraps of gray beard lying on his chest. Because of the tissue shrinkage and what Warburton could only think of as an extreme case of freezer burn, it was hard to estimate his age, but he got the impression the man was old. Many of his teeth were missing, or blackened, or brown stumps. But that didn't prove much, did it? Without dental care a young man's teeth could rot out, too, and he supposed the best dental care available where this man had come from was a whack in the mouth with a stone ax.

"I am not an anthropologist," Rostov said. "What I can see of his clothing is consistent with what I know of the era."

Warburton didn't think you'd need a Ph.D. to figure that out. What clothing he could see was made from fur and leather. What else would the man be wearing on a mammoth hunt? Spats and a school tie?

His mind was racing now. He worked for Howard Christian, who was a complex man of many interests, but none of them exceeded his interest in money, so Warburton immediately was thinking of ways to turn this into a lot of cash. A mummified Stone Age man? Good money to be made, no question. Get *National Geographic* out here, have them document the removal, show the film on Discovery Channel or PBS.

"If you lean over just a bit," Rostov said, "you can just see the top of the head of the second person."

Second person? Warburton leaned over the corpse—noting it smelled a little like the inside of his refrigerator when he returned from a long trip—and could just make out what might be the top of a human head through a thin rime of ice.

"You're sure?"

"Oh, yes. When we got this far we stopped and did a close-range sonogram scan. There is a second person between this one and the mammoth. It is somewhat smaller. Possibly a woman, or a child."

Two people? Woman or child? Better and better, Warburton thought. Alley Oop and . . . what was her name? Ooma? Oona? The cartoon strip was a bit before his time, but he had to figure that a Stone Age couple was twice as interesting as a lone mammoth hunter. As for a man and his son or daughter, sheltering behind the massive corpse of a freshly killed woolly mammoth while a savage blizzard froze them solid . . . well, you couldn't do much better than that.

And then, because he was a troubleshooter and not really in the business of turning out made-for-cable documentaries or television movies, he thought about what sort of troubles he might be called upon to shoot.

When you got into the area of North American antiquities there was always the Indian question to consider. A lot of tribes considered the study of any old dead bones, much less a couple of more or less intact corpses, to be grave robbing. What's more, governments lately had begun agreeing with this, and museums were being forced to return bones for proper burial on tribal lands. What was the name of that ten-thousand-year-old skeleton they'd found in Oregon or Washington? Kennebunk Man, something like that? They'd hassled over that one for years. He made a mental note to find out what Canadian law had to say on the subject.

For the first time, he noticed that the other man who had accompanied Rostov and himself into the pit had an Inuit look about him. Warburton looked at him, then at Charlie, and both of them were looking solemn. Could be a problem, definitely could be a problem.

"How many people know about this?" Warburton demanded.

"Just the five of us on the team, Mr. Christian and whoever he told, and you and whoever you told," Rostov replied.

"Nobody else? None of you called home and talked about it?"

They all shook their heads.

"Here's what we do, then. Talk to no one. Not your mom, not your wife. If you think you might make a little money tipping off CNN or *Hard Copy*, forget about it. I promise you I will make it worth your while, you'll all be getting substantial bonuses. If, on the other hand, you do talk to someone, and I find out . . . well, Howard Christian has about forty billion dollars, and he could make your lives miserable in ways you can't even begin to imagine. Do you follow me?"

Charlie and the other Inuit nodded. But Rostov clearly had something else to say.

"What's the problem?" Warburton asked.

Rostov reached out and swept away a bit of cloth that had covered the frozen man's left forearm and hand. Warburton saw a gleam of metal. He leaned closer, and saw the man was wearing a wristwatch.

FROM "LITTLE FUZZY, A CHILD OF THE ICE AGE"

All those many long years ago, the life of a mammoth was not a bad one.

Mammoths were the largest animals that walked on the land at that time. There were no **predators** that could kill them, except when they were very young, and mammoth mothers were very alert to the approach of a big **saber-toothed tiger** or a **lion**. (Oh, yes, there were lions in North America in that time, so many years ago! But they didn't bother mammoths.)

Big Mama's herd were Columbian mammoths, and you may be surprised to learn that they were larger than the woolly mammoths who were their close relatives. They had hair, but it was shorter and lighter than woolly mammoth hair, and they didn't have as much of it. That was because they lived most of their lives in warmer climates, and they had lost the thick pelts their ancestors had. Scientists call this **adaptation**.

They also had large ears, like present-day elephants. Woolly mammoths had very small ears.

Woolly mammoths lived farther north, where it was colder. People think that because we call it the **Ice Age**, everything was covered with thick **glaciers**. It is true that vast ice sheets covered parts of North America, but animals as big as mammoths could not survive there. There wasn't enough to eat!

But there were many places where not much snow fell during the year, and food could be found all the year round. We call these places **tundras** or **steppes**. This was the domain of the woolly mammoth.

Life was not bad for the mammoth females, but for some it was better than for others.

Life was best of all for Big Mama. She had been the leader, or **matriarch**, of the herd as long as she could remember, and she had a long memory! None of her sisters or daughters or cousins or nieces or grandchildren ever gave her any trouble. When a male mammoth reached the troublesome age she drove him out. A few whacks from her trunk were always enough to do the trick!

Life was good for the mammoth children, too. Mammoth mothers loved their children and took care of them for a long time, just as human mothers do. Mammoth children were also looked after and protected by all the other grown-up members of the herd.

Life was good . . . but there was an awkward age for mammoths, just as there is for children, known as **adolescence**. At about the age of fifteen a female mammoth was no longer a child, but not really an adult yet, either.

At that age a female mammoth's thoughts would start to turn to male mammoths, to falling in love, and to having babies.

But mammoth society was arranged according to what scientists call a **social hierarchy**, or what chicken farmers call a **pecking order**. That means that one mammoth was on top of the hierarchy—Big Mama—one was in second place, one in third place, and so on.

And that means somebody was on the bottom. That summer it was a seventeen-year-old female named Temba.

6

MATTHEW Wright sat in his aluminum canoe and tried to think like a trout.

He was on Clear Lake, some dozen or so miles south of Mount Hood, in Oregon. He had been told to relax. Take it easy. Take a few months off, find a hobby, something to take your mind off your work. Because, frankly, Matt, people have been remarking about some of your behavior. No, you haven't stripped naked and painted yourself blue and run through the Student Union shouting about the end of the world, but you have been acting . . . well, a little unusual.

Matthew didn't precisely remember who it was that first suggested trout fishing as a suitable avocation for a scientist on the verge of a nervous breakdown.

"Breakdown? Breakdown?" he muttered. "A long, long ways from a breakdown. I saw *A Beautiful Mind*, too. *That* was a breakdown. All I was having was panic attacks."

One of Matthew's colleagues had commented, after seeing some of his preparations for his future hobby, that if Matt had decided to take up snowboarding, step one would have been to redesign snow, from the molecular level upward, and one day we'd all wake up to find that snow was half as cold and twice as slippery as it had been before. Matthew Wright was just that kind of guy, the kind who always starts from basics and goes logically from there.

Step one, in trout fishing, was to understand trout. How does a trout experience the universe? What does he see? What does he think?

To find out, Matt first went to Safeway and bought a trout, which he then dissected. He learned a lot, including the fact that fish had hard, clear, spherical lenses in the middle of their eyes.

He read what others had learned about trout fishing. Where did they like to hide? What times of day, what water temperature, what atmospheric conditions made the difference between fish that were biting and fish that sulked in deep pools?

Using all the data he had collected he wrote a computer program, a virtual trout, in which he could adjust twenty-seven variables. After a long series of runs on the computer he had charts of optimum conditions. He could then cast a virtual fly into his program, and see if his cyber-trout was interested enough to bite.

After a few weeks he bought a metal canoe, a twenty-five-foot trailer, a tackle box for his specialized flies, and a rod and reel. He set out into the wilderness along a road that used to be part of the Oregon Trail, only in reverse, feeling pleasantly like William Clark or Meriwether Lewis.

At Clear Lake he launched his canoe and paddled out to the middle of the lovely little body of water. He opened his laptop and lowered a thermometer into the water, consulted a dandy little handheld weather station from the Oregon Scientific Company, and entered all the resulting data into his computer. The result immediately appeared on the screen: lure 14. He removed that lure—a gaudy one with two long red feathers and a bit of Christmas tree tinsel, one of his favorites—from the tackle box and tied it to the end of the clear nylon line, and prepared to make his first cast.

He figured that, if he did catch a trout, it would have cost him no more than a few thousand dollars per pound. But that wasn't the point, was it? He was doing this to relax, and he had to admit, just rowing out to the center of the lake was relaxing. Matt was a city boy, not used to such silence, to trees so green and thick, to the sweet smell of the mountain air.

He waved the line back and forth over his head as he'd seen casters do in one of the videos he studied, letting out more and more line. Then he cast it out before him.

The hook caught in the shoulder of his REI canvas fisherman's vest, barely missing his ear. The length of line he'd carefully paid out fell down all around him, like spider silk.

"Story of my life," he muttered. "Great on theory, poor on execution."

He was still trying to untangle himself when he heard the sound of an approaching helicopter. He waited while the noisy machine turned abruptly and hovered over the middle of the lake. He could just make out someone in the back looking at him through a big pair of binoculars. Then the chopper flew off to the east, toward where Matt knew there was a clearing large enough for a helicopter to land. He stowed his rod and reel and started paddling for shore.

The helicopter's engine had died by the time he reached shore, and as he pulled the boat up on the sand, a large, balding, powerfully built man in an expensive-looking gray suit was picking his way through the low shrubs and patches of mud that surrounded the shallow lake. Matt started toward him, indifferent to the mud on his L.L. Bean heavy-duty fishing boots.

"You must be the guy I talked to on the phone, Mr. Warburton," Matt said. "And I'm still not interested."

"Be that as it may," the man said, stopping a few yards from Matt, "I have to make my pitch. You hung up on me."

"Then pitch. I can give you five minutes. As you can see, I'm pretty busy."

Warburton looked momentarily confused. Then he shrugged it off.

"I spoke to some of your colleagues at the university, and it seems you're not that interested in money. You already have your full professorship. So it's a problem, since everybody I ask about finding the top man in the country concerning the physics of time immediately tells me it's Matthew Wright. No second place."

"Then you do have a problem," Matt said.

"I am prepared to offer you your own private lab with a research budget of ten million dollars yearly. No more faculty committees to satisfy, no pressure to publish, no agenda, no hindrance at all to exploring in any direction you choose. After you've addressed the job we're hiring you for, of course."

"I already have most of that," Matt said. "And the project would be . . . ?"

"As I said on the phone, I can't tell you that until you've signed a secrecy agreement. This would be in effect whether or not you took the job. We are prepared to pay you one hundred thousand dollars simply to go with me this afternoon and examine certain artifacts that have come into the possession of the company I work for. Then you take the job or you don't take it; the hundred grand is yours either way."

Matt was going to take the job. He had known he would take it from the moment he hooked his jacket, before Warburton's helicopter even landed. But there was no sense jumping the gun, nor in giving up his negotiating advantage.

"We're not talking about *the* Company, are we? As in the Central Intelligence—"

"No, I can tell you that much. It's a private company."

"And what did you say the salary would be?" He laughed at the expression on Warburton's face. "Who told you I don't need money, anyway? Everybody needs money. That's why they call it money."

"I believe it was Professor Wellburn."

"Of course. Old Wellybelly has hated me since I got the Hawking Chair. I'd like a salary of . . . two million dollars a year."

Warburton, who had been authorized to offer another ten million, tried to look as if the demand was a bitter pill to swallow. After a suitable time frowning, he nodded.

"Done. I have a man aboard who will pack up your gear and drive your—"

"Don't bother with the gear," Matt said. "If I kept it I'd only be tempted to try fishing again."

He flung the brand-new rod and reel out over the water. As it hit, two trout began fighting over the fly, but by then Matt was following Warburton to the helicopter.

FROM "LITTLE FUZZY, A CHILD OF THE ICE AGE"

Temba had first come into season two years before that long dry summer, many thousands of years ago.

Though mammoths and elephants are very much like us in many ways, they are different in other ways.

Mammoth and elephant females become sexually mature about the same time that human females do. But human females are fertile once a month, and elephants and mammoths are only fertile once a year. With elephants that is usually in December or January. We are not completely sure when mammoths came into "season," or as scientists call it, **estrus**, but we think it was in the summer.

The two summers before that, Temba had watched as the male Columbian mammoths joined the herd and started looking for mates.

Another way humans are different from elephants and mammoths is that during mating season male elephants and mammoths go through something called **musth**. No other animals that we know of do this. During musth a male elephant gets very cranky, like human females sometimes do when they are having their **menstrual period**. He will tear up trees and go charging about angrily and attack anything that comes near him. You do not want to get in the way of a bull elephant during musth!

Poor Temba.

She smelled the bull elephants and she wanted to mate with them. But she was at the bottom of the pecking order, and so every time a bull in musth approached her she was shoved rudely aside by one of her older cousins or aunts. She could only watch through two summers as the mature bulls passed her by.

But this summer it would be different.

7

HOWARD Christian stood in the Eagle's Eye at the 140th-floor level of the Los Angeles Resurrection Tower and looked out over the city and saw that it was good.

Christian had conceived the tower as a memorial to the atrocities of September 11, 2001. He had architects design a tower 150 stories high. It was four-sided and square, like the destroyed World Trade Center, but there the resemblance ended. Christian had always felt the original buildings were too boxy. The architects had solved this by making the walls swoop out of the ground in what mathematicians called an asymptotic curve, one that approached a limiting vertical line but would never reach it.

From the moment the plans were unveiled people called him crazy. A tower that tall, in earthquake country? The relevant governing bodies would never approve it. A giant, defiant skyscraper in a world still plagued by horrific terrorist deeds? It would draw zealous maniacs like a rotten apple draws flies.

Those who predicted opposition from politicians and city planners had underestimated the determination of Howard Christian, and the power of money. With a combination of backroom horse trading, numerous quids pro quo, bullying, public relation blitzes, and a lot of old-fashioned bribery, minds were changed, including the important minds that held the power of a yea or nay over the project.

What finally sold it was the stainless steel eagle that perched on the tower's top. Taller than the Statue of Liberty, the eagle's baleful gaze turned continuously, covering all quadrants of the compass hourly, a fearsome bird of prey ever vigilant to find and punish America's enemies. At night, two multimillion-candlepower searchlights beamed from the golden eyes. The tower had weathered the most recent 6.2 quake with only a few cracked windows.

Unfortunately, the tower had never been more than 70 percent full. Even this many years after 9/11, there were many people who would not enter a skyscraper at all. The images of catastrophe were too vivid.

So the Resurrection Tower was a money-loser for Howard Christian. It ate up almost a quarter of a billion dollars of his cash each year. Howard didn't mind. At that rate, to misquote Charles Foster Kane, he'd be broke in . . . 140 years.

Howard Christian was different from most multibillionaires in many respects, and a big one was this: he bought things. Most members of that very small club that never had meetings and mostly couldn't stand one another were content to husband their vast holdings of stock, and if they bought something, it was probably another corporation. What they did, mostly, was to move money around. Money in motion generates more money, as surely as one of Newton's laws.

Christian didn't much care for money movement, for banking, for the stock market. He had bought companies in his time, naturally he had his bankers, and he owned a great deal of stock, but none of that was his main interest.

He liked real estate, he liked building things on his property, just like the Monopoly games he had played as a child. He liked research and development, spent upwards of three billion dollars a year on projects most accountants would estimate as unlikely to return much profit. More often than not, they were wrong. His own fortune came from blue-sky research, and he never forgot it. He had, in fact, made two huge fortunes, though the second triumph wouldn't have been possible without the infusion of vast amounts of money from the first fortune.

Infusion. He liked that. The source of his first fortune was discoveries and patents he held in the field of nanotechnology, specifically in the design and assembly of the kind of molecular transistors currently to be found in the CPUs of almost every computer on the planet, and in outer space, too. He had done the research for these devices in a tiny laboratory, funded with only a few hundred thousand in grant money.

The path to the second fortune was paved and greased with

billions from his first company, Nanobyte. Everybody laughed, all the technobullies had kicked silicon sand in his face and scoffed that it couldn't be done, but in seven years he had the first practical and functioning fusion reactor. It was beneath him now, over a hundred feet below Resurrection Tower, and it was the chief reason that all the lights on all the floors of the tower burned all night, in spite of southern California electric rates so ruinous that even Howard might not have been able to pay the bill year after year. But fusion power was cheap, once the reactor was built. A dozen such reactors were being built all around Los Angeles by his second company, ConFusion, Inc.

But now that all that was done, now that he had revolutionized technology twice, and on a scale no one had equaled since Edison, Howard Christian devoted most of his time to his twin passions: show business and collecting.

He had the means to be a second Hearst, pillaging the world's museums for great art, but he had tried it and found it unsatisfying. He enjoyed some of the old masters of the Renaissance, but most of their work was not for sale or came onto the market so infrequently you could grow old waiting to have a crack at a particular Rembrandt or Titian. He was puzzled by the impressionists, and baffled by everything since then. What was he supposed to do? Hang an ugly mess by Pollock in his office and then stand and stare at it, wondering why anybody spent six dollars on crap like that, much less a million, and feeling like a fool? Pretend he really liked some stupid scrawl by Picasso? He owned quite an extensive collection of original Norman Rockwells, a single Monet that he found pleasant to look at, hanging behind his desk, and that was the extent of his fine art collection.

No, Howard Christian's mania was for things a lot more recent. He collected twentieth-century ephemera, and automobiles and aircraft of any vintage.

His idea of a wonderful day was to drive his silver-gray 1937 Packard V-12 convertible coupe to a toy collectors' convention and spend ten or twenty thousand dollars on a few rare tin robots from Japan. Or even better, to toodle along Melrose Avenue in his Hispano-Suiza H6B, made for Andre Dubonnet by the Nieuport Astra Aviation Company from copper-riveted tulipwood—the only car of its kind in the world—and turn in under the fabulous white gate of the Warner Brothers Studio, which he owned, gate and all.

He also owned a major television network, several cable channels, a chain of theme parks, and Ringling Brothers, Barnum and Bailey Circus.

He stood now in the eagle's right eye and looked out in satisfaction at the entertainment capital of the world, much of which he owned. As the mighty bird turned, he could pick out all the major sites. Over there was Culver City, where MGM once reigned as the big dog of the silver screen. Now its old backlot was full of condominiums. There was CBS Television City. And there, to the west, was the abomination of Century City, and the corpse of 20th Century Fox Studios, now just a depressing collection of uninspired skyscrapers.

He loved standing there. It made him feel like Batman.

A bell sounded discreetly.

"Warburton here, Mr. Christian. I have Professor Wright."

"Good. Bring him right up, please."

MATTHEW Wright was first out of the elevator. "Oh, wow," he said, and strode straight for the eagle's eye, not seeming to see Howard Christian standing there. He looked out over the city, and down the steep side of the tower.

Christian was somewhat taken aback. No more than a dozen people had ever been in the eagle's head, other than the maintenance crew. He brought people up to impress them, of course, and it was a measure of the reputation Matt Wright had in the small world of cutting-edge physics that Christian had known immediately that no other place would do for their first meeting. But he had expected to control it, as he always did, and in a way he couldn't quite put his finger on, he felt he had lost control already, before he could get two sentences out.

"Oh, boy," Matt said, shaking his head as he stepped back from the window. "I'm doing it again. I'm afraid I don't have a lot of social graces, Mr. Christian. I'm Matt Wright." He held out his hand.

Christian took it, slowly, and allowed his hand to be pumped. Christian saw a man who might be in his late twenties, but whose eyes were considerably older. The dossier Warburton had given him pegged his age at thirty-four. He wore hiking boots and heavy canvas pants, a lumberjack shirt, and, absurdly, a khaki vest with dozens of pockets, festooned with the bright tinsel and feathers of trout lures. Christian himself disdained business clothing almost entirely, preferring cheap jeans and western shirts and outrageously expensive hand-tooled cowboy boots made from all manner of exotic leathers. The last time he could recall wearing formal clothing was three years ago, picking up the Academy Award for Best Picture.

"I understand you've accepted my offer, Professor Wright."

"Your man said something about a hundred thousand dollars."

"Of course. Will you take a check?"

"How long would it take to get it in cash?"

Christian looked at Warburton.

"Five minutes," Warburton said, and reached for a telephone.

"Never mind," Matt said. "I just never held that much money all at once."

"Neither have I, come to think of it," Christian said.

"What, you don't have a money bin someplace where you shove tons of coins around with bulldozers?"

Christian's smile became genuine for the first time. "You know Uncle Scrooge McDuck! I'll have to show you my comics collection sometime."

"It would be a pleasure."

Warburton was looking at his wristwatch, and he cleared his throat.

"Ah . . . yes," Christian said. "I'm sorry to have ripped you so abruptly from your fishing trip. But I hope to make it up to you with a late lunch at the Polo Lounge. We have a reservation."

"Okay. But didn't I read that you've said you'd rather eat at Burger King?"

"I grew up eating Burger King," Christian said, with a tight smile. "Never developed a taste for the finer things, I guess."

"Well, I'm not a gourmet, either. You clearly have something you're dying to tell me. Why don't we save time, eat on the way to wherever it is we're going?"

ON the way to lunch, Matt decided he could get used to this way of life.

The helicopter in Oregon had whisked him quickly to PDX, where one of Howard Christian's private jets awaited. It was an all-black vintage Boeing 727 that had once belonged to Hugh Hefner. A bunny head had been painted on the tail. At the tower, he had been swept up into a high place, as Satan had done with Jesus; only, unlike Jesus, Matt had accepted the offer. Not that he intended to fall on his knees and worship at the monetary altar of Howard Christian, but he recognized the billionaire was now his boss, and he knew bosses could turn out to want many things, some of them impossible.

Then down in the private elevator to the fifth subbasement, where there were a dozen fantastic automobiles. Howard Christian didn't believe in letting his toys gather dust—he liked to get them out and play with them. He was probably the richest man in the world who actually drove very much.

Matt paused at a pale yellow convertible with red trim that looked longer, taller, and wider than any car he had ever seen, and yet managed to seat only two people. It had big globe headlamps and four chromed pipes coming out of the hood cowl on each side.

"I see you like this one. It's a '36 Duesenberg Model J, special built with a short wheelbase, standard Deusy V-12 engine."

"This is the *short* version?"

"It was built for Clark Gable. He drove it to and from the studio while he was working on *Gone With the Wind.* Or up and down Hollywood Boulevard with Carole Lombard sitting beside him. Get in, we'll take this one."

CHRISTIAN drove them out of the basement and down Wilshire Boulevard, both of them content to enjoy the soft purr of the engine, the smell of the pale yellow leather, the luxurious suspension and road-handling ability, and the stares of other drivers. Sports car enthusiasts might sneer, but only if they were profoundly ignorant of precision engineering.

Matt asked, “Howard, could I buy this car?”

“It’s not for sale.”

“No, I mean, could I afford it?”

Christian glanced at him.

“What am I paying you?”

“Two million dollars a year.”

“You could make a down payment.”

Christian looked over at Matt again, with a smile that was a bit smug but with enough sense of almost adolescent wonder that Matt could forgive him.

He said, “They say in Los Angeles, you are what you drive.”

“So what does that make you?” Matt asked.

“Anybody I want to be.”

THERE was no one in the drive-thru at the Jack in the Box. Christian pulled up to the window and nearly shut the place down as most of the patrons and employees craned their necks to get a better view.

Warburton got out of one of the two heavily armored Mercedes SUVs that had been preceding and following the Duesenberg, each carrying two heavily armed men, and hurried to Christian as he was about to pull out with the sack of food sitting next to him. He handed Christian a brown envelope and went back to his car, where he would sweat profusely in the plush air-conditioned interior until his employer was back in the relative safety of a building Warburton controlled.

Christian handed the envelope to Matt, who opened it and found one hundred new-minted thousand-dollar bills. At least, he supposed it was a hundred; it wouldn’t seem right to count it just then.

“Now we’ve both held a hundred grand, cash, in our hands,” Christian said.

* * *

ON an impulse Christian drove to the Santa Monica Pier, where he parked in the lot and was instantly hemmed in by his security crew, who were the very best money could buy, and who, to a man, wished Howard Christian had never learned how to drive.

Christian unwrapped a hamburger, studied it critically, removed a dangling string of Bermuda onion, and took a bite.

"Professor Wright," he said, "do you believe time travel is possible?"

"Oh, brother," Matt said. "Howard, stop calling me Professor, and please, tell me you don't want me to build you a time machine."

Christian stopped chewing.

"I had a lot of time to think on the plane ride down," Matt said.

"And what did you think about?"

"What you might be willing to pay me two million dollars a year for, *plus* a large research and development budget. I was pretty sure it wasn't fly-tying lessons, and aside from that, I don't have a lot of special skills other than a knack for mathematics."

"Some knack. I can't follow your papers. Mentioned for the Nobel Prize."

"It's just a beauty contest. And don't feel bad about not understanding the equations. It's only on my best days that I understand them myself. Your reputation precedes you, Howard. I'm not talking of the engineering breakthroughs that made you rich. I mean your . . . enthusiasms. Your penchant for . . ."

" 'Haring off after a wild hair,' that's what somebody once said about it."

"There was that rigid-frame airship you were talking about a while back," Matt said. "What ever happened to that?"

"That's still in development," Christian said, a bit defensively. The neozeppelin project, code-named Zipper, was actually in the prototype stage, and had thus far eaten well over a hundred million of Howard Christian's dollars and returned nothing.

"Twice the length of the Hindenberg, was it?" Matt asked.

"Just about."

"Pretty expensive to fill it with helium."

"We're using hydrogen."

Matt laughed in real admiration.

"That will be a real heavy lifter. So long as you can keep it from exploding."

"Not a problem. There won't be anything aboard that can make a spark. Carbon composite construction, throughout."

"I also heard you're trying to clone a mammoth. Anyway, knowing just these things about you, I asked myself what a man like you would want from a man like me. You offer a lot of money and a ride in a fancy car and a fine meal"—Matt gestured with half a hamburger—"and then you casually ask if I believe time travel is possible. The conclusion I draw is that you may want me to make you a time machine and get you a mammoth. It's wild, but it's all I can think of. Now tell me where I went wrong."

Christian didn't say anything for a few moments.

"First, answer my question. Is time travel possible?"

"Without question."

"You're talking about something on the subatomic level, aren't you?"

"Sure. There's a type of quantum entanglement whereby two particles can influence each other even though they're separated by many light-years of distance and thousands of years of time."

"Okay. Hypothetically, then. Is it possible to build the kind of time machine, the kind that"—Christian spread his hands wryly—"that a man like me would want to buy?"

"You're talking about a fancy bicycle with a crystal handle and rotating thingamabobs and so forth like in a movie."

"More or less. Something that can get a useful mass from Time B to Time A—"

"Without killing it."

"Sure."

"I'd have to say no. See, the theory allows for moving in any direction through time . . . but it forbids the transfer of any information that way, whether the information is a single 1 or 0 bit, or the information in, say, strands of mammoth DNA, or the rather more complex information that is the molecular makeup of a living body. And Howard, I really hate to tell you that, because I was getting to like this lifestyle, and now I have to say I can't take your money. That is, if building a time machine *was* what you wanted to hire me for. Was I right?"

Christian looked at the sea, and the big Ferris wheel, and when he turned back to Matt there was a measure of satisfaction there.

"You were on the right track, but not on the money," he said.

"Excellent. That's where you learn things. So how did I go wrong?"

"Not enough information."

"There's always that danger."

Christian turned the key in the ignition and the V-12 engine rumbled powerfully. He put the Duesenberg in gear.

"I don't want you to make me a time machine, Matt. I already have one. I want you to see if you can fix it."

FROM "LITTLE FUZZY, A CHILD OF THE ICE AGE"

That same summer in what would one day be called Canada there was a male woolly mammoth we will call Tsehe.

Tsehe was in musth in a very bad way.

Just as human females are affected in different ways by their menstrual cycles, male elephants react to musth in different ways. For some women, getting their period is no big deal. For others, it means days spent being sick in bed and getting angry at everyone.

Tsehe was like that.

The long, thick fur on his head was sticky and matted from smelly stuff that oozes from a gland male mammoths have on their temples. It was irritating.

His **penis**, which he normally kept tucked safely away in a **sheath** like horses or dogs do, was now erect almost all the time. Sometimes it dragged on the ground (mammoths had very long penises!), which was irritating.

He urinated constantly and that made a green alga grow on his most sensitive parts, and that irritated him. He took to rubbing himself against rocks and trees because it itched so badly, but this only made it hurt worse.

No wonder mammoths in musth were cranky!

He had a bad headache, like what we would call a **migraine**, so that colors looked too bright and every movement around him made him feel dizzy.

At the same time, he was very sexually aroused.

All around him for many miles were herds of woolly mammoth females coming into season. They were calling out to him. And they were doing it in an amazing way.

Since mammoth females could only become pregnant during four or five days out of the entire year, it was important that males and females get together for courtship and mating during those few days.

But because males and females lived apart and didn't really have that much to do with one another during most of the year, this could be a problem.

Mammoths had very good noses (just look how long they are!), but this was not always enough to bring males and females together at the right time.

Mammoths could bellow very loudly, just as elephants can, but normal sound can only travel so far before it becomes too quiet to hear.

However, evolution had provided mammoths with a way. It was a sort of long-distance telephone, many years before humans invented the telephone. Mammoths could make sounds that would have been below the range of human hearing. Imagine the deepest musical note you have ever heard . . . and then try to imagine a note twice as low as that! (Musicians call this an **octave**.)

Scientists call these very low notes **infrasound**, and it travels much farther than normal sound.

When male mammoths heard these infrasound songs, they became very excited. In mammoth language, the females were singing:

"I'm ready!"

And the males sang back:

"I'm on my way!"

8

LELAND said, “How do you give an enema to an elephant?”

“Diplomatically,” Roger suggested.

Susan Morgan sighed and scowled at them from the other side of Queenie. “Will you boys get serious long enough to get this done? There’s a lot at stake here.”

“Especially for Queenie,” Leland responded. Roger giggled.

Susan didn’t know why she bothered. Leland and Roger were in fact both older than she was. But they were unable or unwilling to repress what she thought of as their frat-boy/med-student tendency toward the gross-out . . . what they would have described as irreverent humor.

The procedure they were about to undertake wasn’t an enema but, as Leland had observed yesterday, it was close enough for rock and roll. What they were getting ready for was the last stage of a process Susan was pretty sure had never been tried on an elephant, in vitro fertilization. If it was successful, in about twenty-two months Queenie would give birth to a baby that was half *Elephas maximus* and half *Mammuthus primigenius*.

In laymen’s terms, half Indian elephant, half woolly mammoth.

SUSAN Morgan had been working for Howard Christian for almost eight years, but had never thought of it that way. She was circus people, third generation, and she worked for the circus. If that circus was owned by a network, which was owned by an Internet service provider, which was owned by some vast tax-evading offshore holding company that was owned by Howard Christian, who gave an elephant fart?

She had worked with elephants all her life, had begun actual training at age six under the stern eye of her grandfather, and there had never really been any question about what she wanted to be when she grew up. To her, the circus really was the greatest show on Earth, that was not just a slogan, and circuses were about elephants. All that other stuff, the wire walkers and trapeze fliers and lions and tigers and bears and clowns and human cannonballs, was just window dressing for the elephants. When twenty elephants came thundering into the big top, when those elephants reared up in their bright silk finery and placed their forefeet on the back of another elephant and curled their trunks up . . . well, that was what living was all about. If that didn't give you goosebumps, you might as well get back to your video game.

Susan was often at the head of that thundering parade, trotting along beside the leader, but she was not a performer. The spotlight never sought her out. She had no stage presence, and didn't want any. There was a Russian known as the Great Kristov who handled the glamorous part of the show, who wore the spangled tights and flashed the perfect teeth. Kristov was touted as the world's greatest animal handler, but the truth was that if it hadn't been for Susan and two big cat behaviorists doing the endless training behind the scenes, Kristov wouldn't have lasted a week in his big finale, which included four elephants, eight lions and tigers, and eight white horses.

There were those who said the day of animal acts was, or at least should be, over. They said it was barbarism to teach our animal cousins unnatural behavior, or to have them in captivity at all. Susan understood their point of view and had witnessed abuses, but as long as she was in charge her twenty-six elephants would lack nothing, and would get only the best treatment while working, and guaranteed care in retirement. She preferred to think of her relationship with her animals as a partnership, as it was with the best mahouts in Thailand and India and Sri Lanka, where she had spent three years teaching and learning after getting her D.V.M. She was the first in her family to go to college, a great source of pride to her grandfather.

She had heard of Howard Christian and his mammoth-cloning project and wasn't sure she approved, though the thought of getting to know an actual mammoth was almost too seductive to contemplate.

When Howard Christian sent out the emergency call for the world's best elephant handler, he was informed that there were many who were about equally good, but he already employed one of the best at the winter headquarters of the circus, in Sarasota, Florida.

A few hours later a man named Warburton picked his way carefully through piles of elephant dung and made Susan an offer she couldn't refuse.

NOW Susan checked the tension on the elephant press as the two mad doctors prepared their diabolical instruments of torture down at Queenie's other end.

The procedure actually would have been more of a discomfort than torture, but it was academic. Queenie wouldn't feel a thing. Susan had administered a dose of azaperone an hour earlier as a calming agent, to assist the sometimes touchy process of getting her into the sling without alarming her. Then she was led into the elephant press, which was basically like a cattle chute with sides that could compress around an elephant and hold her immobile even if she got frisky.

Once in the press, Queenie was attached to an overhead winch that took the weight off her feet but did not lift her free of the ground.

After that, all Susan had to do was administer the big dose of carfentanil and assist the operation by monitoring Queenie's vital signs, standing ready to pump doses of diprenorphine and/or naltrexone into her if she got in any respiratory trouble.

The comedy team of Leland and Roger had been lucky. They were very experienced at the process of in vitro fertilization with cattle and horses. With an elephant, all you'd need was a bigger probe, right?

Wrong. They had made an attempt to inseminate Queenie without the press and the lift and the drugs, and were lucky to be alive. And so the call had gone out for an elephant handler and a vet, and Howard had found both in the person of Susan Morgan.

SUSAN had been flown to Los Angeles in a black private jet. At LAX she was limoed to a helicopter which deposited her at the base of the Resurrection Tower, then whisked to Howard Christian's office. It finally began to seem real to her, shaking hands with the man whose face she had seen on many magazine covers.

"You want to clone a mammoth, right?" she said. Christian sailed a copy of the secrecy agreement over his desk and sat back in his chair. Susan signed.

Howard Christian had driven her to Santa Monica in a car he said was a 1933 Pierce-Arrow Silver Arrow V-12. She had no reason to doubt him. The front looked a lot like a Rolls-Royce to her and the rear was a '30s version of a car of the future. The inside was luxurious enough, with a lot of maple wood trim. Cars didn't do much for her, though she tried to feign interest.

Their destination was a large but ordinary steel-sided warehouse in a district near the airport that had dozens of warehouses just like it. He drove through a big open door and parked beside a dozen trucks making deliveries. Then they dodged guys with hand trucks and dollies and forklifts unloading and stacking an amazing variety of stuff, most of it new in the box. Everybody was in a huge hurry. Howard Christian was used to paying big bonuses for work done *very* quickly.

Christian dug in one of his vest pockets and came up with a laminated I.D. badge with Susan's picture on it. She was pretty sure it was her driver's license photo, probably obtained from the Florida DMV. These people worked fast.

In one corner was a big concrete cube, and in it was a door of the type used on refrigerated meat lockers. It wasn't cold on the other side, but there was a second door at the end of a long room with a dozen heavy parkas on hooks and insulated boots and gloves in cubbies. They donned the cold-weather gear and Christian punched a code into a pad beside the inner door.

In the center of the big room was a dark, shapeless structure lit from inside. It was canvas draped over a framework of scaffolding. Howard Christian held a flap of canvas back for her, but they both had to duck to get inside.

And there it was. Sitting back on its massive haunches, leaning a little to the right against a support that was no longer there, a looming mass of long, tangled, reddish gold hair. The first specimen of *Mammuthus primigenius* Susan had ever been close to, but judging from the many photos she had seen, possibly the most complete carcass ever recovered.

The animal was still largely in situ, reminding her of a museum diorama. The base was wrapped in black plastic, and it looked like they had brought a large chunk of frozen tundra with the animal.

It didn't smell very good. No matter. Susan was used to working in elephant houses, which weren't very sweet, either.

She took in the humps on top of the head and on the shoulders. She moved around the front of the animal and inspected the tusks, which were fifteen feet long and turned like a corkscrew. She had never heard an explanation of why mammoths had needed tusks that big; surely they would be a hindrance in many things.

She took off her glove and ran her hand over the ancient ivory, and smiled.

"The only work we've done on him so far is back here, of course," Christian said, and guided her around the mammoth's left side. Then she was peering into the incisions that had been made to get at the beast's testicles. Mammoths carried them internally.

"We removed one," Christian said. "Left the other in place in case we screw up the first one, then we'd rethink before we took the other. Two men are in charge of recovering and preparing the spermatozoa. They are well versed in animal in vitro fertilization . . . but they don't know elephants. That's where you come in."

Susan took a deep breath, but there was really no sense in beating around the bush. The only question was pretty much as Warburton had expressed it: Did she want to be involved in the experiment of the century?

"How do I join up?" she said.

* * *

THE well-versed men turned out to be Leland and Roger, the Abbott and Costello of veterinary medicine. But they were competent enough when it came to manipulating the genetic material recovered from the mammoth carcass. Very soon they were ready to implant some reconstructed DNA into elephant eggs cells.

But first, you needed to gather the elephant eggs, and these were in the middle of full-grown cow elephants, eight tons of flesh that might not be eager to surrender them.

Leland and Roger read some papers, called some colleagues. They figured they had a handle on it. They explained what they wanted to Queenie's handler, a lad who worked at the game farm in Simi Valley who had been given just enough instruction to lead the animal into a stall or onto a truck. He saw no problem with it; Queenie had never given him any trouble in the nearly three months he had worked with her.

Queenie's previous handler could have told them that Queenie was touchy, and lazy. She would put up with a lot until a brink was reached, and then she would act. So it worked well, in preparation. They carefully inserted the ultrasound probe, which was narrow, unobtrusive, and really could hardly be felt by an animal as large as Queenie.

That first entry was for test purposes, to calibrate the equipment as well as accustom the elephant to the process. Encouraged, the handler and the vets decided to go after eggs the very next day. The extraction process, called transvaginal oocyte retrieval, involved locating the ovaries with ultrasound, then extending a narrow probe through a needle inserted into the interior of the vagina. They had done it countless times with horses and cows, and expected no trouble because there were no nerve endings inside the vagina.

Queenie must have felt *something*, because she turned around and knocked Leland sprawling forty feet over the messy concrete floor with one massive thrust and shake of her head. She picked up the ultrasound machine with her trunk and smashed it on the floor, over and over, until it came apart. Then she went back to her manger and resumed placidly eating the delicious green alfalfa.

"Could have been a lot worse," Susan told them when she heard the story on her first day at work, which was the very next day after her cross-country trip. "Some of them store up their bad feelings. Then one day you do something she doesn't like and she pays you back all at once. Next day, she's fine."

Two days after that, when the quarters and examining and operating rooms were fixed to her satisfaction, they went in again with Queenie in the press and under mild tranquilizers. They harvested six ooctyes that had been primed and ready for ovulation by two weeks of hormone therapy. Under the microscope they looked good, and two of them began to divide after being injected with the mammoth DNA. They decided to try an implant. They were well into the procedure when Howard Christian walked into the lab with a guy wearing a lot of fishing lures stuck into his clothes.

"This is the mammoth-cloning project everybody seems to have heard so much about," Christian said, perhaps a little petulantly. It had not exactly been top secret, but he didn't like his projects to become the object of too much speculation before they showed results. That was because his projects had, fairly frequently, failed to show any results. He introduced Leland and Roger to his guest.

"And this is Dr. Susan Morgan. Susan, Dr. Matthew Wright."

"Just Matt, please."

"And just Susan." *Doctor of what?* she wondered.

"Susan worked for the circus until a few weeks ago. Now, if this fertilization is successful she'll be a nursemaid to this elephant for two years."

"Must be quite a change after the glamour of the circus," Matt said with a smile. Susan thought he might be putting her on.

"I don't know. Shoveling elephant shit is just about as glamorous here as it is under the big top."

"We have a better grade of elephant shit here in California," Leland offered.

"No, that's bullshit you're thinking about," Susan said.

"I knew it was some sort of shit."

It was obvious that Howard Christian was eager to move on, but Matt asked a question, then another, and Christian paused to listen to the answer, and before long he found himself observing the entire implantation procedure. Matt seemed utterly fascinated with every aspect.

The three vets finished the implantation with Matt watching the ultrasound image over their shoulders as they positioned the probe and delicately inserted the tiny mass of tissue that hardly qualified as an embryo, but which in two years might grow to be the wonder of the century.

Leland pulled the probe out of Queenie, sighed, and stretched.

"Was it good for you, Roger?"

"I could use a cigarette."

"Oh, sure," Leland said. "Then you'll turn right over and snooze, when what Queenie wants right now is a little cuddling."

Susan was busy injecting a dose of doxapram to bring Queenie back to full consciousness, but she looked up in time to see Wright and Christian going through a door in the wall that divided the building roughly in half, a door they'd all noticed and whose handle all of them had tried at one time or another, with no result.

Susan wondered what was on the other side.

FROM "LITTLE FUZZY, A CHILD OF THE ICE AGE"

Tsehe heard the song, and he came calling. Even though it was the wrong song.

Woolly mammoths and Columbian mammoths were very much alike, but they were different in some important ways. One of these were the songs they sang during the mating season.

We can't understand the songs whales sing, but a **hump-back whale** knows the difference between a **dolphin** song and a **sperm whale** song. Canaries sing one way, and crows sing another. Usually these different species ignore the songs of other species.

But the two types of mammoth were very closely related, and Tsehe was feeling very confused and out of sorts, so the song sounded okay to him. When he found the female who was singing the song she didn't look quite right, either. She didn't have enough hair, for one thing. Since mammoth females kept growing until they were thirty years old or so, a mammoth could guess another mammoth's age by her size, and since Columbian mammoths were a bit larger than woolly mammoths, Tsehe took the female mammoth to be older than she really was. Aside from her sparse coat, she looked like a real prize to Tsehe!

Tsehe approached the female and began his courtship.

Mammoths liked to stroke each other with their trunks, just like elephants do. They rubbed against each other and smelled each other, paying a lot of attention to the urine. We find this smell unpleasant, but mammoths found it very exciting!

Right away Tsehe noticed this female smelled funny. His eyes told him this was a female mammoth, and his nose told him she was in estrus. His nose also told him there was something different about her.

But it was all too much for his aching head.

Tsehe hadn't been near the herd very long when Big Mama became aware of him and decided to call a halt to the whole business before it got out of hand. The female Tsehe had chosen was a grand-niece to Big Mama, and she wasn't about to let this intruder trifle with the youngster's affections. Big Mama had her standards. No member of her family was going to consort with long-haired, smelly, tiny-eared trash from the wrong side of the tundra!

Even though he was angry, confused, and irritable, Tsehe knew when he was outclassed. Big Mama was by far the largest mammoth he had ever seen, even if she didn't have much hair. Her tusks were enormous, and her ears were huge! They were like the wings of a giant bird. As if that wasn't enough, there were half a dozen other females behind her as she charged at him in a cloud of dust.

He stood his ground only for a moment. One swipe of Big Mama's tusks to his aching head and he turned tail and ran!

The female watched his retreat sadly. Normally, this would have been the end of things. Vanquished males do not mate in mammoth society.

But he had been driven off by females, not by a larger male who would obviously make a better mate.

And it wasn't as if there was a long line of suitors vying for the trunk of this female mammoth. In fact, there hadn't been a single one.

With a guilty look back at Big Mama, still bellowing her triumph, the female started toward the low hill where Tsehe had gone. Soon she was farther from the herd than she had ever been.

As you've probably already guessed, the female was Temba.

9

IT looked like a briefcase.

It was fifteen inches long by twelve inches wide by six inches thick. It was made of aluminum, with two metal latches. The top fit snugly to the bottom, and there was a rubber gasket between the two parts. When it was built, it was probably waterproof. Now, in the shape it was in, all bets were off.

Matt had finally been admitted to the inner sanctum, the holy of holies, after almost an hour touring the facility. The only part of the tour he had enjoyed was the artificial insemination of the elephant, and that had little to do with his own project. Still, it wasn't every day you saw a possible half-mammoth embryo implanted in an elephant.

The object that Christian had assured him was a broken time machine rested on a long lab table in a big room protected by a keypad-locked door. It had been set there on the table and someone with a sense of the dramatic had positioned a baby spot over it, as if it were a bit of sculpture in a museum.

Matt had been looking at it for half an hour now. He had moved all around it, he had repositioned the light several times, he had moved a bit closer and squinted at this or that detail, but he had not touched it. He hadn't been told not to touch it, the thing was his project, after all, and he would have to be allowed to do what he thought best or what was the point of hiring him in the first place? But he didn't want to rush things.

So he looked at it, and tried to think like a time machine.

FIRST there had been the frozen mammoth carcass, and that had been pretty interesting, too. Christian pulled the plastic back and showed him the frozen man, huddled up against the mammoth's flank. It was gruesome.

"Can you imagine?" Howard almost whispered it. "I wish I'd been there. Amazing enough to find the frozen man, *with the mammoth*! Did he shelter up against a mammoth that was already dead, or did he kill it? Or is it possible he domesticated it? But then . . . they see the briefcase. Frozen under ice that had to have formed ten to twenty thousand years ago."

"Or a few weeks ago," Matt said.

Christian nodded, reluctantly.

"It's a possibility I can't completely deny. Rostov knows what a hoax like that would do to his reputation, he'd have to find a new life's work, and I don't think he's ever cared about anything much except prehistoric creatures. He admitted to me that, when he saw the briefcase, his first impulse was to beat a confession out of his workers, but then he saw how scared they were. He's having horrible and wonderful thoughts right now; he knows this could destroy him if he's been swindled somehow."

"Or win him the Nobel Prize, if they had one in archaeology."

"Exactly. It wasn't hard to persuade him to keep quiet about it. As for the rest of the crew"—he smiled with half his face—"some families in Nunavut are driving around in brand-new snowmobiles and Humvees."

"So I won't have to worry about pressure from the media."

"Or the government, so far." Christian held up crossed fingers. "My influence can only work so far in that direction. If some spook agency gets wind of this and wants it, 'in the national interest,' I don't know if I could hang on to it. I'd hire enough lawyers to gag a mammoth, of course, but this is so revolutionary . . ."

"You don't have to convince me. In fact, I wonder if you realize just how revolutionary it could be." Matt was wondering if anyone, anywhere, at any time, would *ever* grasp the revolutionary nature of this thing as well as he did. Like Howard had said, not many people were equipped to do the math.

* * *

"MAYBE we could use a specialist from a museum," Matt said, still contemplating the box. "Someone who knows how to approach the exploration of old artifacts. Things recovered from the bottom of the sea, things that will crumble if exposed to the air. Someone who knows how to remove a layer of unknown substance without damaging whatever layers may be beneath it. I don't know anything about that. I could use some advice."

"Ask Warburton to find out about that," Christian said. He was speaking to the small man with glasses who had been introduced to Matt as "Ralph, who will get you absolutely anything you need, and keep it all organized for you." Ralph reached for his cell phone and spoke quietly into it.

"I'll need a machinist, and a good computer man, naturally, one who knows where to find the right programs or write them if he has to. An engineer, a metallurgist. They'll tell you what they'll need." Matt turned away at last from the box. He shrugged.

"Howard, the truth is, you don't really need me at all for this stage of your project. I know very little about engineering, and rebuilding or duplicating this thing is a job for an engineer. A gadget man. All I can do is look over his shoulder. Then, when we maybe get an idea of what it's supposed to do, and some notion of how it's supposed to do it, maybe I can be useful uncovering the underlying theory behind the thing. But to make it, and to make it work . . ."

Christian thought he was seeing an attack of cold feet. He just wasn't used to dealing with a man like Matt Wright, who told the truth as he saw it most of the time, and always when it came to mathematics.

"I have confidence in you," he said. "We'll have all that you asked for in place by tomorrow morning. In the meantime, you probably want to get to your hotel suite and clean up. I imagine it's been a long day."

Matt looked down at his trout-fishing vest, realized it *had* been a long day, but he didn't feel tired at all. He knew there were some interesting times ahead, and he knew that could be a problem—did Christian know why Matt had been out in the middle of a lake fishing in the first place?

To tackle this problem, he would have to have some insights on the order of those of Einstein when writing his theory of relativity, or Heisenberg with his uncertainty principle. He would need a new way of thinking.

Because in the universe he thought he knew, this thing was impossible.

IT was the following afternoon before Matt felt ready to get started.

Most of what would be needed for analysis was in place, from a complete forensic lab to a mass spectrometer to a fully equipped machine shop. Matt had his engineer, his metallurgist, his computer man, and, most important, his restoration specialist. This was Dr. Marian Carreaux, an intense, fiftyish woman stolen away from the Getty Museum. She was a suspicious woman. The device was being kept in a sealed glove box in a helium atmosphere.

"Is this thing radioactive?" she asked.

It seemed a natural enough thing to ask. So they brought in a Geiger counter and several other instruments. They reported only background radiation.

She cleaned it on the outside. There were scratches all over it, and on the top side three indentations that Marian said had been made by a metal object, not a stone tool. Near the handle, set into the side, were two standard peanut lights, one red and one green.

It was the bottom that was interesting.

When the grime was cleared away they could see a deep puncture that had been sealed up with tar. And someone had scrawled a message on the aluminum surface. Analysis revealed traces of flint in the grooves.

Howard was summoned and they all looked at the writing on a television screen. It had been computer enhanced.

HAD A GOOD LIFE
NO REGRE

There was another mark, about where the crossbar of a T would have been.

"No regrets?" Howard mused. He looked grim. "I have to

say, I cannot imagine a man from our time going back to the Stone Age and having even a tolerable life, much less a good one. God, it must have been a brutal life."

"I agree. Looks like he died before he could finish the sentence."

"He wanted to send a message to someone, if he was ever found."

Matt shivered, thinking of the man from . . . somewhen? Writing out what had become his last testament as his fingers grew too numb to hold the flint arrowhead.

"Any chance it will release anything toxic when we open it?" Marian asked.

"I have no idea. What would you recommend?"

She had a lot of suggestions. By the time they were ready to open it, they were equipped to detect dozens of poisonous gases, and to collect any gas or liquid that might come out of the box. Nothing that might provide a clue as to function or origin would be allowed to get away.

Finally the moment came. Matt and Howard stood back and looked on as Marian reached into the glove box and prepared to open the time machine.

She secured it with padded clamps, then opened the first of two ordinary latches that held the top down. It squeaked as it came free, and a brownish fluid began to leak around the rubber seal.

That fluid was collected, and the various monitors were checked. Nothing dangerous seemed to be coming out, so Marian proceeded to open the second latch and lift the lid, and everyone crowded around for the first look inside.

FROM "LITTLE FUZZY, A CHILD OF THE ICE AGE"

Young Temba got **pregnant** that long-ago summer in what would become Canada. But Canada would not be the young mammoth's home.

Mammoth mothers carried their children for a long, long time.

Human mothers take nine months to make a baby. Elephants and mammoths take almost two years!

Twenty-two months! Ninety-five weeks! Six hundred and sixty-two days!

Temba moved south with the herd and she never saw Tsehe again. We don't know what happened to Tsehe, but we can hope he led a long and happy life up there on the green and grassy steppes.

Temba did not miss Tsehe. Mammoths were not like humans, they did not mate for life, and in fact except at mating season adult males and females did not concern themselves with the opposite sex very much.

This would not be a good way for humans to live, but it was fine for mammoths.

The herd drifted south and west as the summer drew to a close and the rains came. That winter the herd got as far south as the place we now call Arizona. But Arizona was not like it is today, which is to say very hot and dry and barren. Much of the American southwest was lush and green and tree-covered.

The grazing was wonderful, and that was a good thing because mammoths needed a lot of food! Each full-grown mammoth could eat as much as three or four hundred pounds of grass and leaves and fruits every day.

Temba, making a baby, needed even more. She spent most of each day and sometimes into the night, eating. Eating and eating and eating. She had never been so hungry!

Summer came again and the herd moved north, but not so far north as they had the year before. They spent most of the summer in what we would later call Colorado and Nebraska.

Then it was time to move again.

Now the weather turned bad. The herd had to forage hard to find the food it needed, and sometimes went a few days without water.

But Big Mama was old and wise. She had seen hard times before. She had been over this ground, and many other places as well. She knew where the pools and wallows were, the places where the herd could bathe and frolic after a hot and hungry day. And if there were no pools, she knew every spot where a mammoth could dig with her massive feet and find water under the surface, enough for all her sisters and daughters and nieces to drink enough to get them to the next watering hole.

All through the bad winter they moved west, and when spring came they found themselves looking out at more water than any of them but Big Mama had ever seen, so much water that you couldn't see the other side of it.

The water was what we would later call the Pacific Ocean. It wasn't good to drink but it was fun to swim in, and they were in a green and lush valley we would later call the Los Angeles Basin.

The mammoths had come to California.

10

SUSAN Morgan opened the door in the side of the big trailer box and stepped inside to a familiar smell. It didn't surprise her that the hired attendant hadn't been as scrupulous at cleaning out the traveling stall as he should have been. She'd met the man at the elephant retirement ranch up north and judged him to be one of entirely too many elephant keepers who had no business within a mile of a pachyderm. Elephants frightened him. He relied on a hook to control the beasts, and one day one would squash him like a bug.

Not her problem.

This one was a twenty-five-year-old Indian named Petunia-tu. Most elephants that young would still be working, but Petunia-tu had developed a foot infection a few years back that had left her semicrippled, unable to perform, and a behavior problem when the foot was giving her pain. Little chance of that now; she was doped to the eyebrows with painkillers and tranquilizers for the trip to the big city. The tranks had probably not been necessary. She was a circus veteran, used to traveling to two or three cities a week.

Susan had found her at a game ranch in Simi Valley, run by a humane society, where many circus animals were living out their days on rambling grounds that, in some ways, resembled the African savanna. Not that Petunia-tu would have known that. She was captive-born, in Portland, Oregon, and her ancestors hailed from Sri Lanka. It was an undemanding life up there in the pleasant dry heat, having to do little more than stand around behind a cleverly camouflaged barrier and watch the pickups and SUVs drive by, full of moms and dads and kids pretending to be on safari. But Susan didn't doubt

Petunia-tu could perform her old routines at the drop of a ringmaster's whistle. Elephants really did have good memories.

Now she was about to embark on a great adventure, and she would never know it.

The keeper had given Susan one useful bit of information about his charge beyond the basic medical information concerning the missing part of Petunia-tu's left front foot. She had a fondness for watermelon, so Susan had had one cut into bite-sized—for an elephant—chunks in a wicker basket. She approached Petunia-tu slowly, always watching her eyes, reading her body language. Susan felt she could always spot anger in an elephant's eyes, and the animal's movements spoke volumes to those who could read them. Petunia-tu was radiating calm. She might even have been enjoying her return to the road. It was sure a more interesting life than the game park.

Susan held out a chunk of melon and Petunia-tu took it and eagerly jammed it up into her massive jaws, which began their unique grinding motion. She didn't spit out the seeds. She didn't even spit out the rind.

When the watermelon was half gone Susan opened the gate that separated the carrier into two halves. She took the end of the rope looped around Petunia-tu's neck and tugged her gently, and the living gray mountain lumbered forward, her trunk probing into the wicker basket.

Outside, the keeper had lowered the heavy ramp in front, put there so the cargo didn't have to back up, which was always chancy with a beast weighing ten thousand pounds and lacking a rearview mirror.

Petunia-tu balked at the top of the ramp, not wanting to put her weight on her weak foot to come down the ramp. The keeper—Susan thought his name was Barry—stepped forward and, sure enough, there was an elephant hook in his hand. Susan scowled at him and waved him away, and coaxed Petunia-tu carefully to the ground. After that it was a piece of cake to lead her into her stall in the cool interior of the big warehouse. She perked up a little and raised her trunk as soon as she smelled the other inmates, and immediately went to the fence of steel girders that separated her quarters from Queenie's on her left. The cows sniffed each other for a while, and neither seemed upset. Susan was sure Petunia-tu was instantly aware that Queenie was pregnant, though it would be many more months before she showed.

She stayed a while to be sure no conflicts would erupt. Elephants were social animals and could be temperamental about dominance, which they worked out as nicely as the U.S. Senate, but it was mostly the males who were trouble. Females tended to establish the pecking order peacefully. She expected Petunia-tu to fit into her growing herd easily enough.

Outside, as she was closing the door to the warehouse, the truck was pulling away. As it left it revealed the other, more mysterious half of Howard Christian's mammoth obsession, that Matthew Wright fellow she hadn't spoken to more than half a dozen times since his first day at the project when she had given him the short course in artificial insemination. He was sitting at a wrought-iron table Christian had had installed in the parking lot behind the warehouse, next to the ten-foot security fence that hid the whole installation from prying eyes. He was under a big canvas umbrella that seemed a good idea with his pale complexion; the merciless summer sun would no doubt broil him like a lobster in about five minutes. He had spread the wrapper of a huge Subway sandwich on the table and was watching her as he ate it. He gestured toward the closed door with the hand holding the sandwich.

"More godless, cruel, antinature experimentation, I presume," he said. He gestured to the two enormously determined men who had taken it upon themselves to mount an eternal vigil at the driveway leading to the warehouse—if "eternal" could be taken to mean nine to five, Monday through Friday. Susan didn't know their names or who they were affiliated with. She called the tall one with the day's growth of beard and the look of perpetual angelic bliss on his face the Martyr. He stood all day, muttering something over and over which Susan thought might be the Rosary. She had never seen him move, but somehow he migrated during the day within a thirty-yard range on either side of the gate of Cyclone fencing.

The other might have been the Martyr's father. There was a family resemblance in the withered ruins of this old man who, once or twice a week, took his son's place, sitting in a lawn chair of nylon webbing and holding the same sign. He had a case of dowager's hump so bad he couldn't lift his head above the level of his shoulders, and his jowls sagged far below the level of his jaws. She called him Droopy.

The sign they carried read, STOP GODLESS CLONING. NO FRANKENSTEIN ANIMALS. CALL OR WRITE YOUR CONGRESSMAN.

She would have found it a lot easier to ignore them if there hadn't been a tiny bit of doubt in her own mind as to the morality of what she was doing. She was no technological alarmist and hardly religious at all, but sometimes at night she lay awake and wondered if she had the right to pull such a trick . . . such a *stunt*, on innocent beasts.

She wondered what Matt Wright thought about it. Even more to the point, she wondered just what it was he was doing in his sealed-off half of the building. Breeding and keeping elephants, that took some space. What could Wright be up to that took just as much space? Did it have to do with mammoths, too?

She'd never figured out how to ask him.

Now he was gesturing at his sandwich.

"Could I interest you in an Italian bomber with all the trimmings?" he asked.

"No, thanks." She took off her hat and wiped her brow. "But I'd like a sip of that soda if you don't mind."

"I can do better than that." He opened a small blue six-pack cooler and took out an eight-ounce stubby glass bottle of Coke, twisted off the top. A little foamed over the side, and tiny bits of ice clung to it. Not much else in the world looked quite that good on a scorching day, except maybe a beer, which she wouldn't drink until almost sundown. She took it gratefully and drained a third, then sat at the table with him.

"I always order the twelve-incher," he said ruefully. "Then I end up wrapping up half of it." Susan realized he was talking about the sandwich.

"They're okay cold."

"So how many female elephants do you have in there now?" he asked.

"Cows. Female elephants are cows. And Petunia-tu is the fifth."

"And all of them are . . . I mean, except Petunia-tu . . ."

"Pregnant?" She shook her head. "Just Queenie and the second one, Mabel."

"And I guess you haven't figured out any way to rush things."

Susan laughed. "The old-fashioned way is still the only way I know. Twenty-two months. That would probably surprise old Droopy and the Martyr." He knew immediately who she was talking about, and grinned. "They probably think we're going to grow a mammoth in a test tube. Most of it is well-established veterinary practice."

"And he will be . . . a woolly mammoth?"

She shook her head. "He'll be half mammoth."

"Sure, I knew that. But will he have hair?"

"That's a question Howard asks me about three times a week. Hair, hair, hair, that's all he's interested in, that's what this is really all about. Mammoths had a distinctive body profile, *lots* different than any of the three living elephant species, and they had longer tusks, and—"

"I thought there were only two."

"No, for quite a while now we've divided the African genus into savanna and jungle species. It was determined genetically; they don't have a lot of differences you can see. Anyway, I'll tell you what I tell Howard. We don't know. My guess would be he'll be fuzzy, at least. He probably won't have the really long fur coat the frozen sperm donor had. On the other hand . . . that donor did have a long fur coat, and that was a bit of a surprise, when we finally realized just what it was we had."

Matt frowned, and shrugged. "A mammoth, right?"

"Yeah, but what kind of mammoth?" She couldn't stop herself from grinning. "I tell you, Matt, if Howard wasn't so obsessed with cloning, he could already be a celebrity. All he has to do is let Dr. Rostov publish his findings. This frozen mammoth isn't like any that's ever been found before."

"Tell me about it."

She hesitated, then stood and finished her Coke.

"Come on. I'll show you."

FROM "LITTLE FUZZY, A CHILD OF THE ICE AGE"

Temba had grown and grown all the last year. In California she ate even more, and grew even more. When the time of the year we would later call June arrived, she was so big that walking was awkward. She could feel stirrings inside her as the baby kicked and twisted, wanting to get out into the wide world.

And one day she felt a pain like she had never felt before, and she knew it was her time.

The rest of the herd knew it, too. They gathered around her. They pressed against her sides. They stroked her with their trunks and made reassuring sounds. All day and into the night they stayed near, and then the baby's hind legs appeared.

A few minutes later the little mammoth was born.

He was a boy!

But he was not so little! If there had been scales to weigh him, he would have tipped them at about three hundred pounds!

Temba was very busy for a while then. Mammoths were born wrapped up in something called an **amniotic sac**, like dogs and cats and horses. Temba used her trunk to pull this away from her baby, there in the dark night.

Then she lifted the baby to his feet. He tottered for a moment, then fell onto his side. Temba lifted him again, and again he fell. But the third time she set him on his feet he stayed there, swaying and blinking.

The herd gathered around him and his mother and touched him with their trunks. Some of them flapped their ears nervously and shuffled their big, flat feet.

Something was wrong with the baby.

It smelled funny.

It felt funny. The trunks of the herd explored the tiny little ears and gathered clumps of hair that was still wet and smelled of blood from the womb.

And then Big Mama came over. The others made way for her, respectfully.

For a time Big Mama explored the baby. We can't know exactly what she was thinking that day, so long ago, but if we guess it might be something like this:

(He is a male baby. He is a very hairy male baby. And what about those ears? What is the deal with those ears?)

Animals cling to their own kind, just like people do. And animals can be very harsh with those who are not of their own kind. Big Mama's mighty nose and long memory were puzzling over the odd smell of the newcomer. Big Mama was the ruler of the herd, nobody had even tried to challenge her in many years, and nobody had any plans to anytime soon. If she decided the new baby was not right, it was all over, there would be no argument.

Big Mama kept exploring, and kept up her big, slow thoughts. Finally, she wrapped her trunk around the new baby and stroked him.

Well! Did the other mammoths feel relieved that the baby was accepted?

Probably not. Mammoths and other animals don't think like people do. A lot of what they do is governed by **instinct**. And though mammoths and elephants are much smarter than most other animals, they do not think ahead like we do, and they do not worry about the same things we do. They deal with things as they come up, and since Big Mama did not decide to drive the new baby from the herd, no one ever had to deal with it, and so they didn't worry about it. Temba never knew her baby's fate was being decided by Big Mama. Probably Big Mama didn't even know it. She just sniffed the baby, decided it was odd but okay, and then forgot all about it.

The baby himself had no idea what was going on, either. He simply knew he was hungry. His instincts drove him to where he could smell his mother's milk, and he pressed his face into the space behind her front leg and began to nurse.

Temba was content.

And the baby's name?

Well, mammoths did not give each other names like we do, though they could easily recognize one another.

But we can call the baby Fuzzy.

11

HOWARD Christian held up the shrink-wrapped box and regarded the toy robot inside. It was a rare Bandai X-56 MechaMan, one of the earliest plastic toy robots to become really expensive, mainly because of the extremely limited production run. Howard wasn't a big fan of plastic. Like most serious robot collectors he went for the older tin models most of the time. But he liked the X-56, and he didn't have one.

This was the best-known example, and naturally it was sitting on the table of the unquestioned mogul of collectible toys, a man who called himself Radicon.

The table was near the door to a small side room off the main floor of the Anaheim Convention Center that housed the several dozen most exclusive dealers attending the annual National Toy Collectors Convention—the Nat-Toy—a gathering Howard had not missed in fifteen years. To get into this room you had to know someone, or someone had to know your net worth and credit rating. Toys had changed hands in this room for well over one million dollars.

Naturally, Howard Christian was always welcome. These dealers would, in fact, have been happy to grant him a private showing for as long as he wished, but Howard didn't enjoy that. Part of the fun of a convention, swap meet, or even a garage sale was elbowing through the crowds, looking for the undiscovered gem. Of course, he knew there would be no discovery here. Every person in this room could quote the last known price for any of the top one thousand rarities without having to get out a catalog. You would pay top dollar here, but you would get top quality.

He turned the box over in his hand. One of several problems with plastic toys was that they had started showing up at the same time manufacturers began packaging most of their wares in boxes with clear plastic windows so you could actually see the toy inside. Typically, the box would then be either wrapped in cellophane or shrink-wrapped in a more flexible plastic.

This X-56 was NRFB, and bagged in Radicon's own protective wrapper as well, so no fingerprints could mar the original material. Because, though "never removed from box" was not the only criterion for collectability, it was incredibly important. Early in Howard's collecting career he had paid thirty thousand dollars for a 1950s tin toy, took it home, unwrapped it, and threw away the box. He was stunned to learn, a few weeks later, that the value of the item was now about four thousand dollars. Which meant he could now never show it. Not that he minded losing the twenty-six thousand so much . . . but if he *showed* it without the box, people would realize he no longer *had* the box—it was the only possible explanation. And he didn't want to look like a sap.

Most collectors would not view the presence of original wrapping as a drawback to a toy. They would happily put it on their shelf, or more likely in their climate-controlled sealed exhibition case with the laser alarm system, and smugly check the catalogs every few months to see how it was appreciating.

But when a toy is encased in shrink-wrap you can't get it out without running the seal, and if you can't get it out without ruining the seal, and if you can't get it out of the box, you can't . . . well, you can't *play* with it.

Not actually play, Howard thought. Not like children play. There would be no bashing and tossing and stomping, no battles staged, no leaving it out in the rain in the sandbox. It's just that, when he got something like a toy robot, he wanted to put a battery in it, turn it on, and watch it do its thing. Otherwise, why collect? Investment, so important to the majority of his fellow fanatics, was low on Howard's list of priorities.

He did have a curator on his staff who was very clever with these things. When the man was done repackaging an item, very few experts could tell it had ever been tampered with.

But a few could, and many of them were in this room.

It was a pretty problem.

Howard noticed Warburton had approached him as he examined the X-56. He glanced at him, then put down the robot and picked up a Pez dispenser in a clear baggie. It was the 1960's "Psychedelic Eye," one of the more valuable ones. Naturally it was in mint condition, and Radicon wanted $1,500 for it.

"Wright invited Susan Morgan into the gadget lab about an hour ago," Warburton said, following Howard as he moved from Radicon's table to the adjoining one, which held many boxes of comic books. He began leafing through some in the one-to-two-hundred-dollar range.

"Why do you figure he'd do that?"

"Beats me. He knows the penalties."

The "gadget" was what they were calling the presumed time machine, for security purposes. They got it from the Manhattan Project.

Howard pulled out a Justice League comic and examined it critically through the clear plastic sleeve. He got out his digital assistant and punched in the volume and issue numbers. A picture of the comic appeared on the screen, with the notation that it was an issue he had in medium to fine condition. The one in his hand was marked very fine to mint, and cost $150.

"I don't see this as mint," Howard told the dealer. "There's a chip right here on the fold. See? And isn't that a repaired crease in the corner?" To Warburton he said, "Do we have it on tape?"

"That hardly qualifies as a chip."

"Of course, we tape everything. There's a camera right over the door."

"A chip's a chip. I'll give you a hundred for it. File the tape away. If we ever need to take him to court, it could be valuable."

"I already ordered it."

"One hundred twenty-five."

Howard took a roll from the light trench coat he always wore to sales like this and peeled off a hundred and a twenty, laid them on the table. The man scowled, but scooped them up.

"And you pay the tax," Howard said, strolling back to Radicon's table. He put the comic into one of the coat's big pockets. The Pez dispenser had vanished. He took another long look at the X-56 in the sealed box, then shook his head and walked away.

Warburton hurried over.

"Must have slipped his mind," he said. "He's very busy."

"Sure," said Radicon, solemnly, crossing his arms. They'd played this game before, and would probably play it again.

"How much was that dingus, now . . . ?"

"Twenty-five hundred," Radicon said, with a look that dared Warburton to haggle. He needn't have bothered; Warburton would have gone twice that without a peep. But he couldn't help thinking, *Fifteen hundred for a lousy little plastic pillbox with a hand holding an eyeball on top*. If he worked for men like Howard Christian all the rest of his life—and he knew he probably would—he would never understand them.

Then he hurried to catch up with his sticky-fingered boss.

FROM "LITTLE FUZZY, A CHILD OF THE ICE AGE"

At first little Fuzzy stayed close to his mother, like all mammoth babies.

He was the smallest member of the herd . . . but that didn't mean he was small! He got his long reddish-black hair from his father's side of the family, but his size he got from his mother.

Like most little mammal children, Fuzzy loved to play. Two calves had been born the summer before, a male and a female, and they had been slightly smaller than Fuzzy when they were born, but now weighed almost a thousand pounds! Fuzzy played with these two calves, and when another calf was born a few weeks after his birthday, he played with her, too.

Mammoths were great swimmers. They loved to romp and splash in the water. It was Fuzzy's favorite thing, and whenever the herd went to a watering hole he and the other calves joyously slid down the muddy banks and down into the muddy water, where he would churn around with only the tip of his little trunk showing.

Other creatures came to the watering holes. It was there that Fuzzy first saw the great saber-toothed cats that lived in California at that time. These cats had great fangs that they used to rip and tear at their prey and they were bigger than Fuzzy. They could have killed him easily, but when the big cats were near, the rest of the herd bellowed and snorted and stamped at the ground and waved their big flat ears, and the saber-tooths went away. They knew better than to challenge Big Mama and her herd!

Fuzzy was half woolly mammoth and half Columbian mammoth, and this is what scientists call a **hybrid**. That means he was a cross between two species.

Though animals stick to their own kind, sometimes two species are enough alike that they can breed.

When horses breed with donkeys the baby is called a **mule** or a **hinny**.

When a lion breeds with a tiger the baby is called a **liger** or a **tigon**! Ligers are bigger than either lions or tigers. They have stripes only on their hindquarters!

Horses and zebras can breed, and so can cattle and buffalo. Nature is full of examples of **hybridization**.

Usually, the offspring of these matings are sterile. That means they can't have any babies. But not always.

Was Fuzzy born sterile? Maybe so. We don't know. But the jolly little child didn't know and didn't care. He nursed, he frolicked, he swam in the mudholes and in the crashing surf of the Pacific Ocean, and he was happy.

Life was good!

12

MATT was never quite sure why he invited Susan Morgan into the restricted lab. In the end, he supposed, it was because he was lonely.

It had been two months, and progress was maddeningly slow. He was spending time mostly with Jim, the metallurgist, and Anthony, the master machinist. They were all nice enough people, delighted to be so well paid and not inclined to ask a lot of awkward questions. But Matt didn't have a lot in common with any of them.

Truth be told, Matt didn't have a lot in common with anybody.

It was the story of his life. Labeled as the next Einstein early in childhood, he had found his peers to be either confused by his intellect or actively hostile to it. Even his teachers were often intimidated. He had achieved his doctorate at Cal Tech at the age of fifteen, and felt his real studies didn't begin until then. And by then there were precious few who could keep up with him, and even fewer who could guide him.

At the age of twenty-five he had what was pretty close to a mental breakdown. He just . . . stopped talking. He didn't decide to. He found himself unable to speak.

It was almost a week before anyone noticed.

It was not as though he had a social life. Arriving at college at the advanced age—for a prodigy—of twelve was a bit of a social handicap to a boy who hadn't had any real friends since elementary school. The philosophy of mainstreaming, both of the handicapped and of the precocious, pretending everyone had the same gifts and potentials, was then out of fashion at his school. Accelerated programs were back, and the almost equally disastrous current wisdom had become to let students proceed at their own pace, regardless of their social progress.

As for girls, the business of offering Susan half his sandwich actually rated as a pretty good line, by Matt's standards. More often he would utter something awkward or inappropriate, or simply stay silent. His only real liaisons in thirty-four years of life had been with two girls even more studious than himself, and neither he nor they had known how to keep the relationships going.

In a word: lonely.

So here he was, still smelling faintly of elephant dung from his recent tour of the cloning facility, showing Susan Morgan something he had no business showing her and she had no business seeing. And enjoying the hell out of it.

"I'm beginning to think you're actually serious," she said.

"I'm not much of a jokester," Matt admitted. "Setting this up would be way beyond my skills."

"Yeah, but pulling the wool over my eyes as to what it *actually* is . . . that would be pretty easy."

Matt looked at her seriously.

"No, I don't think so. I don't think you'd be that easy to fool, even if I was good at it. And anyway, *look* at it. Can you imagine a mundane use for something like this? And think about Howard Christian, and ask yourself, would he be pouring money into anything less wacky than a time machine?"

She did look at it again, frowning even more than she had the first time.

"Maybe he's designing a super Rubik's Cube. One that only he has the solution to. I think Howard would like that."

"Ah, yes, but I wouldn't help him build one. There are limits to what I'll do, even for money. And there are things mankind wasn't meant to know."

He said it so seriously that Susan had to look up to be sure he was kidding. She laughed, a sound Matt liked at once. He wanted to say something about that, but was afraid she would take it wrong. *Story of my life*. So he turned back to the window in the big glove box and regarded the gadget, for possibly the ten thousandth time.

She got it right the very first time. Inside the aluminum box was a puzzle in three dimensions. Or maybe four . . .

When it was first opened Matt was reminded of a toy he was given when he was three. It was a flat plastic plate containing thirty-five plastic tiles, each with part of a picture printed on it. Since the plate had room for thirty-six tiles, six by six, there was one empty space, and other tiles could be moved into it. By sliding them around properly the puzzle could be solved. Matt had solved it in two minutes. He would have been quicker but for his clumsy child's fingers. His parents looked at him strangely. It was the first time he really knew he was different from other children.

That puzzle showed a kitten when he was done. This puzzle was a bit more complicated. The heart of it was an array of spheres, each one-half inch in diameter, no two looking exactly alike. A box of marbles, but not just dumped in. Stacked together.

Each marble was encased in a cunningly machined cage made of thin stainless steel. Each cage could attach to adjoining cages and slide up or down, left or right, back and forth. When opened they had been arrayed in a polygon ten marbles high, twelve marbles wide, and twenty marbles long, making the dimensions of the entire structure five by six by ten inches. That made a total of 2,400 spheres.

Plus one sphere.

Since there were 2,401 little marbles, there was no way to stack them so that they made a neat ten by twelve by twenty hexahedron. One cube always stuck out. This had mightily offended Matt's sense of order, at first, but he didn't tell Susan that.

This entire contraption could be rotated up and out of the box without ever removing it, and an entire row of ten, twelve, or twenty marbles could be slid out of the array, taken apart, rearranged, and slid back in. Or one could push a row over, say, three or four spaces, then push another row in another dimension, until the thing didn't look like a hexahedron at all, then pushed back together in a new formation.

"Of course, all that came later," Matt said. "For the first week, we just probed it with everything we could bring to bear. This object has been measured more intensely and accurately than just about anything that exists on the planet."

"I'm surprised it lasted so well. I mean, you say it was down there in the ice for thousands of years."

"We cleaned it up a lot. The box had a rubber seal, but naturally that had degenerated. Dirt and water had gotten in. Our conservator took two weeks to wash it out—she wanted to take a year, but Howard couldn't wait that long—and then we were finally able to move it around. Now all the balls will turn in their sockets. There was a bit of lubricant left, which turned out to be ordinary 3-in-One oil, so we've used that to make the rows of balls slide easily." He reached into one of the gloves and pressed on a row at the left side. One ball on the right side clicked out of the stack.

"We had it completely apart for the first time last week, when we were sure we could put it back exactly the way we found it. We had to set up some pretty stringent protocols to make sure we never got one ball exchanged with another without knowing it. If that ever happened, our chances of getting it back the way it was would be slim."

"I can see it would take a long time, trial and error," Susan said.

Matt snorted.

"Trial and error? Susan, there literally would not be enough time to do it. I mean, not enough time before the heat death of the universe. The universe is fifteen billion years old. If we'd started trying out patterns at the Big Bang, and tried out one per second, we would not even have made a beginning on the permutations by now."

"I guess I always thought a time machine would be something you sat in, and pushed a lever or something . . . maybe with a steering wheel." She laughed. "I guess that's pretty silly."

"I don't think so. I felt the same way, when I thought about it at all. Like what Rod Taylor used in that movie, with a big spinning wheel in the back."

"Or a DeLorean with a Mister Fusion on the trunk."

"Sure. And it would have some sort of odometer on it . . . call it a temporometer, maybe, like 'It is now December 4,

54,034 A.D.,' and it's spinning like crazy." He gestured again to the thing in the glove box. "What we got here in the way of instruments instead is a couple of wires attached to the framework, two little lights, red and green, and what turned out to be the remains of two double-A Duracell batteries. All I could figure is, if the light is lighted, that means it is on. So I replaced the bulb and the batteries, and absolutely nothing happened. If there's an on/off switch, I can't find it. And I don't even think it's a time machine . . . most of the time, anyway."

She looked surprised.

"I thought you just told me—"

"I said I was going to show you what Howard thought was a time machine. And I thought he might be right, at first."

"What else could it be?"

Matt threw up his hands, and paced in a small circle.

"We may never know. Look, it seems certain that the man traveled in time. That is, unless Howard is playing a very expensive joke on poor old Warburton and me, because *no one else* knows about it . . . or Warburton is playing a suicidally stupid joke on Howard. I've considered those possibilities long and hard, believe me I have, and concluded I don't have the resources or the will to find out one way or the other. If that's what's happening, I'll end up wasting six months, a year, something like that, and go home with a lot of money. Most of which is already in the bank. I insisted on getting it up front when I realized what he wanted me to do."

"Me, too," Susan said.

"So, why would he want to make us rich? I can't find a reason. And beyond that . . . I see it in his eyes. He *believes* in this thing.

"So. The mammoth man is a time traveler. Furthermore, he probably started off from right around here . . . that is, right around now. The aluminum case is made in Belgium; you can order as many identical ones as you want. I've got three dozen of them. But maybe he got there . . . I don't know, through a 'time gate' of some sort. You've seen those in the movies, too. You step into a big bright noisy thing, and next thing you know you're in the old Roman Empire. Or aliens abducted him and took him through time and dropped him off in the last Ice Age, and left this thing behind, and it's really an alien child's toy, like building blocks. Or it was some sort of natural or occult phenomenon. A rift opens in space-time, and he falls through it. Or a witch puts a curse on him. Take your pick. Rip van Winkle. *A Connecticut Yankee in King Arthur's Court*. Isaac Asimov or Robert A. Heinlein or Steven Spielberg. There must be a thousand ways people have imagined to travel through time, all of them about equally impossible. None of them demand that you take a lunchbox full of marbles to get where you're going."

He realized he had almost been shouting. He stopped himself, deliberately calmed down. Susan didn't seem disturbed by it, but she did glance at her watch.

"It's feeding time. I'll have to go now."

"Sorry about that."

"No, it's not a problem. But really, Queenie'll get cranky if she doesn't get her feed on time. One thing you don't want to deal with is a cranky elephant."

"I guess not."

"Thanks for showing me this." She seemed about to say something else, maybe about the chance she knew he was taking by bringing her here, but she thought better of it. She waved, and started for the door.

When she was almost there, she turned.

"I wouldn't mind sharing a sub sandwich with you again one of these days, though. Maybe you can tell me more."

"Sub sandwich," he snorted. "Listen, I'd like to take you out for a *real* meal. Kentucky Fried Chicken."

"I don't know if I could deal with luxury like that. But I'll try."

"Tomorrow?"

"Tomorrow."

He waited until he was sure the door was closed behind her, and then did something he seldom did. He danced.

FROM "LITTLE FUZZY, A CHILD OF THE ICE AGE"

Life was not all fun and games for the mammoth herd. There were dangerous things, and not just saber-toothed cats.

One day when Temba was browsing in a big tree, pulling down branches with sweet tender leaves on them and thrusting them into her mouth, Fuzzy wandered off a little ways to another tree.

Baby mammoths, like baby elephants, were born knowing how to stand up, how to walk, how to nurse, and they probably know how to swim, too. But they had to learn to use their trunks, just like baby humans have to learn to use their hands. A mammoth's trunk contained many thousands of muscles and a grown-up mammoth could use it to pick up a single leaf or twig!

The way they learned to use their trunks was the same way people or animals learn to use anything: practice!

Fuzzy picked up a branch with his trunk, like he had seen his mother do. He swung it around, hitting things with it.

He hit the trunk of the tree.

He hit a big stone.

He hit a big pile of yellow straw that smelled funny . . .

And the big pile of straw reared up and screamed at him!

It was big! Bigger than Temba, taller than Big Mama! From the tips of its three curved claws to the top of its little, angry head, it was fifteen feet tall.

It was a **giant ground sloth**.

There is nothing alive today that is anything like a giant ground sloth. Its only **living cousin** is small and lives in the trees where it hangs upside down and sleeps almost all day. But the giant ground sloth was huge, and there were many of them in California at the time little Fuzzy was born.

Giant ground sloths were plant eaters, like mammoths, and usually they gave the herd no trouble. But they could be cranky, and they didn't like being rudely awakened any more than most animals do. This one took a swing at Fuzzy with his mighty arms, and sent the poor little mammoth tumbling over the dusty ground.

Fuzzy was very frightened, and he cried out for his mother.

Well! In no time at all not only Temba but all the sisters and cousins and aunts and nieces and the young bulls who had not yet left the herd were thundering toward the ground sloth, trumpeting their rage!

They came between Fuzzy and the giant sloth and stomped and flapped their ears and lifted their trunks. The sloth stood his ground, roaring back, and it could have gotten bloody, but finally the sloth turned around and lumbered away.

The mammoths did not chase him.

Fuzzy cowered in Temba's shadow for a while until everybody was calmed down. He would remember the smell of the giant ground sloth, and he would run away if he ever saw one again!

—

13

THERE was still much work to do.

From the start Matt had decided there were basically two ways to go about this.

One: Repair this machine.

Two: Build another just like it.

On his third day of work he had put the question to Howard Christian. *Which approach do you favor, Howard?*

"Do 'em both," Howard had replied.

Okay . . .

Easier said than done.

NO two of the marbles were alike.

Some of them appeared to be pretty much exactly that: marbles. They were glass, always of a uniform color. Basically silicon, with various impurities. Over a thousand were minerals, almost anything that could be shaped into a sphere and polished to close tolerances. Any geology student in the world would have loved to have these; many were quite beautiful. Among them were precious and semiprecious stones, including a diamond sphere and others of emerald and sapphire. The remainder were metals, sometimes pure and sometimes alloys.

Full analysis of all 2,401 balls took almost a month after the day Matt first invited Susan into his lab. It was quite a job, and nobody could say it was dull.

"Since coming to work for you," said Jim, the metallurgist, "I've run into stuff that sent me running for the textbooks. It's like a final exam, from a sadistic teacher. It's not every day you come across some praseodymium, neodymium, gadolinium, dysprosium, *and* ytterbium. Some guys will go a whole career and never deal with some of those."

That's exactly what Matt was coming to feel, too, that the device was not so much a practical, working *thing* as a one-time assemblage put together just to frustrate him. Something for him to look at, three paper cups for him to study while the real action with the hidden pea was happening somewhere just out of his sight.

Prestidigitation. Misdirection.

Nevertheless, he couldn't proceed on that assumption until he'd ruled out as many other possibilities as possible. What was important here?

"IN a problem like this," he told Susan, "the first thing you do is try to limit the variables. Too many variables, you never get anywhere."

"Like your twenty-four hundred marbles."

"Twenty-four-oh-one."

"Who's counting?"

"Two thousand, four hundred and one is seven to the fourth power."

"Really? Is that important?"

"I wish to hell I knew."

They were sitting on a bench not far from a heart-wrenching scene. Near the edge of a small pond a mammoth bull stood with his child. The baby had his trunk extended toward a full-grown female mammoth with tusks that must have been twenty feet long, submerged to the hindquarters in the water. But the placid surface of the pond was deceiving, Matt knew. Bubbling constantly from the depths was methane—swamp gas—that you could smell when the wind was right. Just beneath the surface lay a nearly bottomless pit of asphalt that was more than adequate to humble even such a mighty beast. The mammoth cow was a goner.

About once a minute the baby mammoth squealed what Matt supposed was the mammoth word for "Mommy!" All three pachyderms waved their trunks helplessly.

They were on the grounds of the La Brea Tar Pits, and the mammoths were robots. Within walking distance was a working excavation. A stone's throw in the other direction, six lanes of traffic whizzed by on Wilshire Boulevard.

There were a thousand very good restaurants within an easy drive of the mammoth warehouse, and he took her to two before she admitted she didn't really enjoy eating in restaurants that much. It turned out that what she liked was picnics.

"I can do picnics," Matt had said, and headed for the mall. He'd been intending to buy something from Sears, but halfway there he remembered he was rich, turned around, and found a shop in Beverly Hills that sold him a beautiful basket complete with Waterford glasses and fine china and linen napery and a chill compartment for white wine for a price that only made him a little light-headed.

Any of the fine restaurants in Santa Monica or Westwood were happy to oblige when Matt dropped the basket off in the evening and told them, "We will be two for lunch. Surprise us."

They ate together two or three times a week while Matt gathered the courage to ask her out on a real date. They tried to visit a different park each time. Today they were on the grounds of the George C. Page Museum, overlooking the tar pit, and Matt was trying to explain the dimensions of his problem.

"Allotropes are different ways the same element can arrange itself, different crystal structures," he said.

"Right, graphite and coal and diamond. All pure carbon, different arrangements."

"Yes. Some of the metals have several allotropes. In the marbles, the zirconium and . . . sorry, Howard wants me to call them temporal spheres."

"Sounds like Howard," Susan laughed.

"Okay, call 'em marbles. Listen, I could explain this easier if I showed you, back at the lab."

"Suits me. I have to get back anyway."

A big table had been set up in one part of the warehouse away from the glove box containing the actual gadget. On it was a very long rack of wooden cubbyholes, set at a forty-five-degree angle for easy access. They had bought the box from a Chinese language typesetter, who often had over five thousand characters to keep sorted. This one was thirty cubbies deep and one hundred wide, and all but the top few rows were full of the marbles they had assembled, marked 0001 to 2401. Each cubby held twenty identical marbles. Matt was going to make ten identical time machines and hope that one of them worked. If not, he'd try a few more things and use the ten spares of each type.

"We didn't want to damage the originals too much," Matt said to Susan, after showing her the setup. "We couldn't drill them for samples. No matter how fine the drill bit is, it would inflict more damage than I'm willing to risk at this point."

It was a problem with no easy solution. Say you have a sphere of zirconium, one-half inch in diameter. How can you be sure it's zirconium clear through? You know the surface is pure zirconium, but that might be a shell covering a layer of iron or copper.

They had probed each marble with X rays, sonic imaging equipment, and magnetic resonance and had found no obvious anomalies. The pure zirconium sphere seemed to be pure right to the center.

"There's no way we could exactly duplicate some of them," he said. "You ever look through a bag of marbles?"

"Sure. Girls can play marbles, too."

"Then you know there are no two cat's-eyes perfectly alike. We've sorted through thousands and found some that are amazingly close . . . but who knows? And the glass of most of them is marked up, scratched, tiny little chips. One of them, number 451, has a fairly large chunk out of it."

"You know them all by number?"

"No, but it feels like I do. And if I never saw another marble in my life I would be a happy man."

THE next evening Matt completed the first assembly and called Howard's office to see if he wanted to take a look at it. Howard did, and showed up that night in another of his vintage automobiles, an olive-green 1939 Talbot-Lago hardtop racer that had barely room for one person in its streamlined cockpit.

Matt led him inside and showed him the opened assembly. Beside it were a few numbered glass dishes containing metal marbles, or temporal spheres, of varying hues. "We wanted to reproduce the gadget *exactly*," Matt said. "Because we don't know just what it does, much less how it does it, assuming it does anything at all . . . we don't know what's important. But if we have to duplicate it at the subsubatomic level, we're screwed. No way we can analyze the neutrons and protons within the spheres for up-quarks and down-quarks, spin, strangeness, charm, all those too-cute words they use to describe properties nobody can really visualize.

"So then there's the nuclear level. Some of the spheres are ninety-nine point nine nine percent pure. But each element has isotopes—you know, different numbers of neutrons with the same number of protons—"

"I understand isotopes. Go on, Matt. If you get beyond me, I'll let you know."

"Sorry, Howard, I keep forgetting . . ."

That I'm smarter than you *are, except in the really rarefied realms of math*, Howard thought. It grated on him, but he kept quiet about it because he needed Matt. Matt was a professor, after all, used to lecturing. And he'd probably been doing a lot of it lately, on his daily dates with Susan Morgan. Was there love in the air?

"Okay. Different isotopes have different weights, per atom. The ratio of isotopes found naturally is fairly standard; a lot of them decay into something else. Almost all the single-element spheres are what you'd expect, not some exotic variation. You follow?"

Howard nodded.

"But a few were a little odd. Take osmium. Atomic number, 76. Atomic weight, 190 and change. Seven stable isotopes, six radioactive ones, but with half-lives so short there'd be almost none in a normal sample. Commonest isotope, Os-192. Seventy-six protons and one hundred sixteen neutrons. A bit over forty percent of osmium ought to be Os-192. But our little ball only has thirty-five percent. To compensate, there's more Os-188 than there should be."

"Is it a radioactive decay thing?" Howard asked. "One form of osmium emits an alpha particle—"

"No, no. Osmium decays into rhenium and iridium, a little tungsten later on. Those are all there, in trace amounts, what we'd expect. No, somebody, the builder, made sure the osmium ball had a different isotopic ratio from normal. So we *have* to duplicate that ratio, because it's so weird it just *has* to be something important." He stopped, and looked at Howard for a moment. "Don't you think?"

Howard laughed. "That's what I'm paying you the big bucks for. If you think it's important, I will, too."

Matt took one of the spheres of the odd osmium, shiny as mercury, and slipped it into a little metal rack, then snapped it into place. He stood back and regarded it.

"There we are," he said. "The Howard Christian Time Machine, Mark One."

Howard looked surprised.

"You mean it's finished?"

"It's assembled. What comes next is anybody's guess."

"I'm paying you to guess."

Matt sighed. "Yes, you are. But I don't have the foggiest idea what to do at this point. I can manipulate it . . ." He flipped the assembly of marbles onto its side and slid a row of them to the left, then pushed another row back. Several other slides, and it was back together, ten by twelve by twenty, but the marbles were in a slightly different arrangement.

"This way leads to madness. The permutations are damn near infinite. There's a little circuit board in there, identical to the one in the original machine. I went out and bought them at Radio Shack, off the rack. It has a small IC chip, a processor, this and that, none of which seems to be connected in a very logical way. I'll experiment with that. It has two batteries and two lights. What it doesn't have is an on/off switch that I can see, any way of setting your destination in time or space, or a user's manual."

Howard clapped him on the shoulder. "You'll figure it out."

"Well, I intend to spend the next year trying, anyway."

"Maybe you should just bash it. That usually works." He thumped the case with his fist. Nothing happened. He shrugged, turned, and started back to his car.

"Oh, by the way . . . ," Matt said. Howard stopped and turned back toward him. "If you're going to take some of the marbles with you, it would be a lot easier on us if you'd let us know which ones you're taking. I mean, so we can restock."

Howard stared at him for a long moment.

"I don't know what you're talking about," he said.

"Oh, it's not a problem, I mean, not a bad one. And you can do what you want, I know that, you already own all the marbles . . . so to speak." Matt laughed, but it sounded a little hollow, even to him. What was the problem here?

Silence from Howard.

"Didn't you just put a couple of marbles in your pocket?" Matt asked.

Howard had learned an important lesson at the age of eight: Never admit anything. His father had sent him into a supermarket with instructions to select a good steak and put it under his winter parka. "If you get caught," his father had said, "don't say anything. Don't answer any questions, and above all, don't admit anything. *Never admit anything.*"

Howard did get caught, and when they found his father in another part of the store and brought his errant child to him, Christian Senior had scolded the boy, threatened to give him a good whipping when they got home, even threatened to tan his hide right there until one of the cops advised him not to. Howard had cried and cried and cried.

They laughed about it when they got back to the ramshackle trailer with no wheels that Howard's father called home. Christian Senior praised the boy for his acting. "Never saw it done so good," the old man chuckled. Howard was glad to hear what he had done was acting; he'd thought he was scared to death.

Howard got better at it, until one day he was too old to pull it off, and his dad sent him back to live with his mom, who hardly noticed.

There was another principle he lived by. *Never defend yourself*. Attack at once. Those two rules would get you through almost any situation, Howard figured.

"How many times have you had Susan Morgan in here?"

Matt was speechless.

"It doesn't matter," Howard said. "Once is enough to invalidate your contract and make you liable for everything I've paid you, plus damages."

"I'm sorry, I thought that since she's right here and . . ."

Howard smiled and relaxed. He had him. Once they apologize, they are lost. Matt had caved in at once. But what did he expect from a little wimp who had spent his entire career in a university, free to research just about anything he wanted, a man who had had his entire top-rank education handed to him while Howard labored and borrowed to put himself through a state university system, first in computer science, then in business.

Howard had never liked Matt very much. No surprise; he hardly liked anybody. But from that moment, he hated him.

"It's all right," he said. "I'm not going to do anything." *But I could, always remember that, Matt.* "Still, you'll have to be more security conscious from now on. And, of course, you must stop bringing Ms. Morgan into the lab. It might even be best if you stopped seeing her."

"We're not—"

"I know, just friends. Don't imagine there is much about these projects I don't know. I could show you pictures of you lunching at the tar pits."

Matt had assumed he was usually on camera while at work. That he might be spied on during his private hours had not occurred to him.

Howard smiled again.

"Yes, I knew when you first brought her in here."

"I thought you didn't mind."

"If you had left it there, I might have ignored it. But you continue to discuss your theories with her. Why not print out a copy of all your work here and give it to her?" Howard smiled again. "As it happens, it's not going to be a problem. We're moving the mammoth operation to a ranch near Paso Robles. I think the elephants will be happier, and I know Susan will. She's never stopped complaining about the L.A. traffic."

He turned on his heel and left.

"WHERE is Paso Robles, anyway?" Susan asked that night.

"I don't know. Up north somewhere." *Too far to drive every day*, Matt thought.

They were in the large, airy Venice apartment Howard had

rented for Susan during her work in southern California. It was the first time Matt had been there, though he had dreamed of visiting under different circumstances. Now he was in a black depression.

"If you don't want to move, you could threaten to quit," he suggested.

"I can't threaten him with anything. In fact, I'm hoping he won't fire me. I'd be easy enough to replace. Not like you."

Matt snorted. "If only Howard knew how little of the special talents he hired me for have come in handy so far. Any competent engineer could have done what I've done. In fact, my engineering team has been responsible for what progress we've made so far."

"Yeah, but that's all been preparation, right? Step one. Now you've got the new machines assembled, you can really get to work . . . right?"

"That's the theory. I only wish I knew what step two is." He hesitated, but was helpless to stop himself. "You could quit."

"I mean to see this through to the end," she said, raising her voice.

"Of course you do. I didn't mean it, I . . . well, yes, I meant it, but I can see now it wouldn't work. I mean, you're dedicated to your work, and all. . . ."

"Matt, I like you," she said, and touched him lightly on the cheek. "I wish I could go on seeing you. But understand this. Unless Howard cans me, I intend to be there when that mammoth is born."

"How about weekends?" he asked. "I could fly up on weekends."

"Sure, you could do that." She smiled. So maybe it wasn't the end of the world. His cell phone rang.

"Yeah?" He listened for a moment. "I'll be right there." He hung up, and looked at Susan. "That was Ramón, the night guard," he said. "There's been a break-in at the laboratory."

FROM "LITTLE FUZZY, A CHILD OF THE ICE AGE"

In little Fuzzy's world, there were not many creatures that went around on two legs. There were birds. There was the giant ground sloth, which sometimes lumbered around on two legs. And there was a troublesome species that went around on two legs all the time. They looked very much like us. They were humans.

But who were these people? Were they **Indians**? Well, they had their own name for themselves, but we don't know what it was, since they didn't have a written language. They were the ancestors of the tribes who would later live in the area and call themselves names like **Chumash**, **Gabrieleno**, **Serrano**, **Luiseno**, and **Cahuilla**. They had crossed over a land bridge that used to exist during the Ice Ages between the places we would later call Siberia and Alaska. Scientists call this land bridge **Beringia**.

What we call these people today is **Clovis hunters**. They made spearheads, called **Clovis points**, out of flint and strapped them to long branches to make spears. These spears were very sharp! One Clovis hunter could easily kill a rabbit or a turkey with one. Two or three hunters working together could kill a deer or a camel. (Yes, there were **camels** in California when Fuzzy lived there!) But it took a lot of the Clovis people to hunt a mammoth . . . and even then, they had better watch out!

One day the herd was munching its way through a big field full of tender green grass and a few scattered, twisted oak trees when suddenly the ground collapsed beneath the feet of Big Mama's younger sister!

Younger Sister trumpeted her alarm, and the rest of the herd came running!

At the same time small, almost hairless creatures began dropping from the trees. They had been hiding in the branches, upwind from the trap they had dug and covered with branches and grass, so the herd would not smell them! They wore the skins of dead animals. They walked on their hind legs, like birds. And they were shouting, making an awful racket, and throwing sticks and rocks!

Fuzzy hurried to Temba's side and cowered there, barely daring to peek around his mother's thick, tree-trunk leg. Some of his aunts herded all the younger mammoths around Fuzzy and Temba and then made a wall of mammoth flesh around them. They bellowed at the chattering two-legs!

Meanwhile, Big Mama and four or five others charged at the two-legs, who quickly turned and scattered and ran away. Big Mama could not chase them all, but she caught one with one of her huge tusks and threw him into the air! When the two-leg fell to the ground again he didn't move. Big Mama trod him into the dirt. The other two-legs retreated to a nearby hilltop and stayed there. They watched the herd.

When things had calmed down the others went to help Younger Sister, who was still struggling in the pit. It was a very nasty thing. It was not very deep, but the Clovis hunters had sharpened tree limbs and set them into the ground at the bottom of it.

Younger Sister had fallen on several of the sharp points. She was struggling, and crying out in pain, and Fuzzy was frightened to see it and hear it. After a while Younger Sister struggled out of the pit. She had several deep wounds on her legs and her belly, and one sharp branch had broken off in her side.

On the hilltop, the two-legs settled in to wait.

14

THE man Susan knew as the Martyr was not what you'd call a man of action.

He was a nervous fellow, never one to thrive in a group. Terribly convinced of his own inadequacies, his shortcomings, his lack of worth as a human being, he had nevertheless found an ecological niche in human society that suited him quite well. There was a vast stillness within him, a devout capacity for contemplation. He would have made a perfect cloistered monk, he would have taken the vow of silence with unfettered joy, and often his heart ached that he had never been allowed that opportunity. If he let himself think about it too much he might even grow resentful, which would have required an act of contrition and an entire evening spent reciting the Rosary. As he already spent nine hours a day reciting the Hail Mary, the Glory Be, the Anima Christi, and the Holy Face, this prospect didn't appeal to him. No, he spent his weekdays doing God's work, and kept his evenings free for himself. In the evenings he really cut loose. The evenings were for Bible study and memorization.

The leader of the duet of pickets at Howard Christian's warehouse of sin was the man in the aluminum lawn chair, the one Susan knew as Droopy. Though these days he looked about as peripatetic as the average barnacle, in his younger days Droopy had been a pistol. He had spent part of his youth in the merchant marine, and part in the pen. He drank a lot and fought a lot, and on his fortieth birthday he found God and devoted himself to God's work with the same energy he formerly brought to a fistfight. In fact, God's work in those days often *did* involve a fistfight. Many a depraved abortionist had spent a lot of money at the dentist's office after a run-in with Droopy . . . and Droopy spent many more nights in jail as a result.

But now the bones of his spine had turned into something as light and hole-ridden as pumice, with the tensile strength of a stick of chalk. His chin practically sat on his chest, and when he turned his head he could hear sounds that more properly should come from a mill making stone-ground wheat than from a human body. All he was good for now was to sit day after day in his lawn chair, the base of a big picket sign jammed between his legs, and hold the sign where passersby could read it.

But Droopy, though a God-fearing man, wasn't big on Hail Marys. As he sat there, and as he had sat over the last five years at many another site of Satan's work, he planned. He plotted. He tried to think of ways to do God's work that would get more attention than sitting there holding a sign rising from his crotch like his pecker used to but hadn't in over twenty years now.

To make any of his plans work, he had to have an accomplice, as his physical condition limited the amount of mayhem he could work against Satan's tools. The Martyr was useless, nothing but a pious pissant, in Droopy's estimation. But every time he had tried to enlist others into his schemes they had turned him down. That was probably because they were pretty stupid plans, on the order of kidnapping the children of abortion butchers and keeping them until the "doctor" swore never to kill an unborn child again.

But sitting outside Mr. Multibillionaire Tool-of-Satan Howard Christian's house of ungodly horrors day after day, he had decided he had to do something. This gene-tampering business was almost as bad as abortion. It had to be stopped.

And this time he had a plan—and an ally, known only as Python. He was a member of the Action Wing of the Soldiers of the Animal Kingdom. SAK was antifur, antimeat, and antivivisection. They specialized in actions like the liberation of lab animals, arson attacks on the property of circuses and rodeos, and even the bombing of butcher shops. They went so far as to oppose horseback riding and the keeping of pets—which they called slaves—of any kind.

In the normal course of events Python and Droopy would

have been unlikely to meet, as SAK had its roots in the liberal side of the political spectrum. Droopy didn't care if every lab rat and monkey in the world died a horrible death. Python and most of his friends championed the murder of children, which they called a woman's right to choose.

Their common ground was cloning, which Python and SAK saw as just one more way to abuse our animal brothers. And their meeting ground was the Internet.

While the Martyr had learned only enough computer skills to access the rich lode of Bible discussions to be found online, Droopy had taken to cyberspace instantly. On the Net, he was a strong, young, active man again. In person it was easy to discount the views of a tired old fart who could no longer raise his voice above a hoarse rattle. In antiabortion chat rooms and newsgroups, he was Swordofthelord, a powerful and well-respected voice in the movement. He met Python on an anticloning message board, they corresponded for a time, and Droopy got the impression of a young man who wasn't too worried someone might get hurt. Droopy had always felt that way. If you didn't hurt them, why would they pay attention to you?

Eventually they had a meeting. Python was disappointed, naturally enough, at the old ragbag who had talked so tough. Droopy knew he had to win Python's respect quickly, so he trotted out some of his best stories of clashes with abortion doctors. Python listened with distaste—he had been the proximate cause of several abortions himself—but remembered the old man's fervent views on this new evil of cloning, and knew that in a holy fight it was sometimes necessary to do business with people you would scorn in a perfect world. After a while, cautiously, Python added a few stories of his own. Droopy didn't mention that he'd hunted deer and rabbits all through his childhood to put food on the table. He hadn't held a gun in fifteen years, but the memories were still fond.

Python resembled that kraut actor, Maximilian Schell, but just missed being handsome. There was a burn scar on the side of his face, and he was missing the pinkie finger from his right hand. A mink had bitten it off while he was freeing her and five hundred of her sisters from a ranch, which he called a concentration camp. Served him right, Droopy thought. Vicious little monsters, minks.

When Droopy mentioned the name of Howard Christian, Python's eyes narrowed with interest. So he went heavy on that angle, and soon was sitting in Python's car on the way to look over the mammoth project warehouse.

Python liked what he saw from the start. The warehouse was in an area of similar warehouses, hardly worth a second glance except for the unarmed guard sitting in a booth beside the door into the building. The whole property was surrounded by a ten-foot chain-link fence topped with coils of razor wire and there was a thirty-foot strip of bare concrete between that and the target. The people who worked inside parked their cars there. They gained access by punching a number into a keypad mounted on a pole, which caused an electric gate to roll back.

Python drove all around the building, then parked his van a hundred feet away and watched the gate for a while. Droopy slumped in the right seat.

"Couldn't sit here too long without that guard getting interested, if he's doing his job," Python pointed out. He looked in the backseat. "That's why you'll come in handy, Lamb." Python, who loved intrigue, had never asked for the names of his companions, and had certainly never given his own. He had code-named them Lamb and Turtle. "You're out here every day?"

"He is, every day," said Droopy/Turtle. "I am, too, on the days my back lets me move around a little."

"By now that guy doesn't notice you any more than he does a rock or a tree," Python said. "Let's do it."

IT didn't take long. Lamb/Martyr stood in his usual spot, calming down gradually when he realized no one noticed him casually lifting a tiny pair of opera glasses to his face whenever someone entered the grounds. The second morning he got the right angle on it. The number was 4-1-5-3-9. He knew, sadly, that they would go in that night.

Python wasn't a smash-and-grab guy, like Droopy. Hit fast, hit hard, don't worry about who gets hurt. Droopy wanted to steal a dump truck and crash right through the gate and the door, knock the guard on the head, and start tossing Molotov cocktails. Then dump a load of cow manure all over the place.

Python liked the cow manure part, but the rest of it sucked. He liked to keep things simple, minimize the violence to bystanders—after all, the guard wasn't cloning monstrosities in test tubes—and maximize the time to do as much damage as possible. Contrary to every Hollywood movie you ever saw, if you started hitting people over the head, sooner or later somebody would be killed.

"The gate is wired," Python pointed out, "otherwise a Cyclone fence is a joke. Pair of wire cutters, and you're through. But if we breach it, an alarm goes off in the guardhouse, and the police are probably called. We get five minutes, tops."

"It doesn't take long to throw a firebomb," Droopy pointed out.

"Yeah, and it's a metal building, and we'd have to be sure we hit something flammable inside. And don't forget, there's half a dozen elephants in there. You want to be the one to clear them out?" Python had already decided that freeing the elephants was out of the question. It was one thing to free a lab full of rats and rabbits or a fur farm full of minks, but he knew even that could go badly wrong. Remembering, he rubbed the stump of his little finger. Who could have known such a little bundle of fur like a mink could be so aggressive, and bite so hard?

"We go tonight, at midnight."

THE first part went smoothly, if slowly. Droopy insisted on going along. He saw it as his swan song, and he wouldn't be denied. Python seethed, slouched down in the anonymous rental van where they had been sitting for almost five hours.

The guard made a slow circuit of the warehouse every half hour, inserting a plastic card in a time clock halfway around to register that he had actually made the trip. It took him about five minutes. That should be just enough time.

So when the guard put down his book and left the small booth at midnight, Python told his troops to get ready. In a few moments the uniformed figure turned the corner and vanished into the darkness.

Python got out of the van and no interior lights came on. He carried a big Maglite flashlight and a crowbar, the all-purpose tool of the serious vandal. He wore a black backpack bulging with cans of paint wrapped in towels. Paint was needed to write slogans on the walls, and could do an amazing amount of damage when sprayed into the delicate innards of scientific equipment. That could be done before getting down to the soul-satisfying work of smashing everything in sight that was smashable. In a biology lab, that was going to be a lot of stuff.

He hurried to the gate and punched in the number Lamb had obtained. The gate immediately began to roll back, not silent, but not very noisy, either. He turned around, itching to go . . .

And they're off! he thought. Lamb and Turtle were almost halfway to the gate, Lamb with his Bible in one hand and his rosary and a crowbar in the other, Turtle jerking his walker ahead one step at a time as fast as he could move it. It was a toss-up which was moving slower, the hot-blooded old man or the reluctant monk.

Python had decided that getting inside in one step would be cutting it too close. His watch read 12:04 when they reached the group of Dumpsters against the warehouse wall. He shoved one out and hurried his accomplices behind it, then pulled it back exactly as it had been.

They heard the guard's footsteps go by, not ten feet away from them, and continue on. They heard him settle down on a squeaky swivel chair. Python edged one eye carefully around the Dumpster and saw the man pick up his paperback book and start reading again.

It didn't smell very good back there. He identified elephant dung, rotting vegetables, and a sour whiff mixed with Old Spice, which he knew was coming from Turtle, as he had smelled it for the last five hours in the van. He heard a sound, like dry sticks cracking. He sighed. If the popping of Turtle's cervical vertebrae didn't bring the guard, they'd be okay, he figured.

The guard left again precisely at 12:30. As soon as he rounded the corner Python's ragtag commandos hurried over to the warehouse door as fast as they were able. They punched in the number and the door opened. Python glanced at the guard's paperback as they passed. It was *Why Me?* by Donald E. Westlake.

There were a few lights on, high overhead. As soon as he turned on his flashlight, he knew a mistake had been made.

Many of his colleagues had never set foot in a laboratory except to destroy it, but Python knew his way around from college classes. He knew the sort of equipment a cloning facility should have, and as he swept the room with his flashlight he saw none of it. The machines he did see were more suited for the practice of metallurgy or physics. There were complicated lathes and drills, a furnace, a mass spectrometer. What was just as important was what he did not see. He didn't see any glassware. He didn't see a gene sequencer.

He didn't see any elephants. Hard to miss elephants, if they were present.

Out in the middle of the half-empty, cavernous room were some ordinary folding cafeteria tables. They were covered with some sort of assemblies, built into aluminum cases. *What the hell?* Python swept his flashlight beam over the array. It would have been beautiful if it hadn't been so puzzling: marbles in every color of the rainbow.

He turned, examining the other item of interest and frustration, a huge rack of hundreds and hundreds of cubbies, or caches, each containing marbles of the same type. At the bottom of each cubby was a number, but looking closer, he could see the numbers had been painted over what looked like Chinese characters. *Chinese?* The whole thing looked like it might be intended to assemble models of molecules, the kind you could see in a high school biochem lab.

Putting aside what he didn't understand, Python swept his light around the room again, and it came to him. Not enough. Not nearly enough space in here.

"Where did they bring the elephants in?" he whispered to Lamb. "Which side of the building?"

But Lamb didn't really hear the question. He was in a state of Rapture.

The concept of Rapture was not, strictly speaking, a Catholic idea, but Lamb/Martyr was not a strict Catholic. He gravitated to a more recent fusion of the traditional Church with more evangelical elements. In the services of this new sect, it was not uncommon for healing to take place, for shouted testimonials and the speaking of strange tongues to be heard.

It was the tension of the break-in and the sensory overload of the thousands and thousands of colorful balls that set him off. His understanding of molecules being extremely limited, he imagined the marbles to be genes themselves, and these tables the very places where the obscenity of cloning was being carried out.

Well, we'd see about that.

"Tools of evil!" he shrieked, and grabbed the Chinese compositor's board by one corner. It was heavy and well braced, but his strength was as the strength of ten because he had become the living, breathing Sword of the Lord. The board tilted and the marbles began to clatter on the floor even before Lamb swung it over to crash on the floor.

The racket was incredible. Python had been on his way to the door connecting what he now knew to be two laboratories when the clattering, clanging, clanking wall of sound rolled over him and made a shiver race up his spine. He turned and watched, frozen, as thousands of marbles rolled noisily all around him. It was like a truckload of cymbals rolling down a slope of broken glass.

"Guide my hand, O Lord!" Lamb cried, and then looked down at the tables. He overturned one, creating a fresh wave of sound. Lamb turned to another table and began flailing with his crowbar, smashing glass bowls with more marbles in them, sweeping everything in his reach onto the floor.

No surprise, Python beat Turtle to the door. He flattened himself against the wall so the door would hide him when the guard swung it open . . . as he did, two seconds after Python got there. The guard swept his flashlight over the room and saw incredible chaos. A wild-eyed man in a baggy trench coat was swinging a crowbar over his head and smashing it down on what remained on the tables; and another fellow, old as anyone the guard had ever seen, was fleeing directly toward him . . . with an aluminum walker. He took a few steps into the building, not quite able to add up the different parts of the scene into anything that made sense. Behind him, Python slipped around the door and gave him a shove. The guard fell forward, dropping the flashlight. He heard the rapidly retreating footsteps of Python behind him.

Lamb had cleared the table of just about everything but one last aluminum briefcase. This one was latched and locked. Lamb was seized with the desire to see what was inside this infernal device. He raised his crowbar and brought it down. There was a dent on the dull silver surface. He hit it twice more . . . and a red light came on.

The resolve left him as quickly as it had come. Suddenly he was sure it was a bomb. The only question in his mind was, *How long do I have?*

Take me in Thy arms, Sweet Jesus.

Sweat broke out on his face. The crowbar clattered to the cement floor. As he had in so many times of stress in the past, he took refuge in his rosary beads, looking at the ceiling as he waited for the Lord to take him.

"Move, you asshole!" Turtle shouted, looking back over his shoulder, pumping his walker forward for all he was worth. It was a bad idea in a room covered in marbles. Turtle stepped on a few and his foot flew out from under him. He bobbled, his hands slipped on the walker, and he came down hard with his left leg bent under him. His knee popped. The good news was he had long since lost most sensation from the thighs down. The bad news was, looking at the unnatural angle of his lower leg, he knew he had surely just taken his last step on Earth. Wheelchairs from now on.

He strained to raise his head high enough to see the door where Python had fled. He saw two more uniformed men enter, these carrying shotguns.

"Well, fuck me," he sighed, and lay down on his back.

FROM "LITTLE FUZZY, A CHILD OF THE ICE AGE"

Younger Sister got very sick.

She stopped eating, and stumbled after the herd for three days. Always, on a ridge a safe distance away, Big Mama could see the two-legs. At night they built fires, which Big Mama hated, but as long as they kept away from the herd she didn't do anything about it.

Once another group of two-legs came wandering by and they stared at the wounded mammoth. The first group of two-legs came charging down the hill, chattering and throwing things. The two groups fought some, but mostly they screamed at each other, and after a while one group went away.

Which group was the winner, the first or the second? Big Mama didn't know and didn't care. She was concerned about Younger Sister, but had no idea what to do about her. Really, there was nothing she could do. Younger Sister would get better, or she would die. That was the harsh rule of nature. The herd would live on.

Other animals began to gather. Sometimes saber-toothed cats would approach, sniffing the air, until Big Mama drove them away. **Dire wolves** and other scavengers were drawn to the scent of sickness. **Vultures** began to circle overhead, and perch in the oak trees.

On the third day Younger Sister sat down and wouldn't get up again, though her relatives tried to help her to her feet. A few hours later she fell onto her side. She lay there in the baking noonday sun as the herd gathered around her, still trying to help her get up. But Younger Sister was too tired.

That evening she stopped breathing.

The herd lingered around her until the sun went down, and into the night. They caressed and smelled her with their trunks. They touched the sharp stick that was still in her side, and smelled the drying blood. They chased away the flies that had gathered around her, but the flies kept coming back.

In the morning they moved on.

As the herd got to the top of a hill Fuzzy stopped and looked back.

The two-legs were coming down from the hill, waving their sharp sticks and throwing rocks and shouting and chattering, driving away the vultures and dire wolves that had already gathered around Younger Sister's body.

They waved burning sticks at the two saber-toothed cats and poked at them with the sharp sticks, and the big cats backed away, screeching angrily.

Then they started to work on Younger Sister.

Fuzzy turned away and followed his mother into the next valley, where there was lots of green grass and leaves and fruit to eat.

15

WHEN Howard Christian arrived at the warehouse—in a red 1950 Crosley Super Sport because it had been closest to hand when the emergency call came in—there were two Santa Monica police cruisers on the scene in addition to three Rapid Response Blazers from Robinson Security. One of the Blazers had a crumpled front fender. Not far away, at the intersection nearest to the warehouse, was a van lying on its side.

He parked next to the blue Ford he knew belonged to Matt Wright. He knew because he had bought it and presented it to Matt, one more perk of the job. He hurried over to the Robinson man with the most braid on his uniform, who was standing with a police sergeant and two men in handcuffs. Warburton and two other bodyguards, seriously out-distanced by the Crosley, parked their bulletproof SUV nearby, got out, and scanned the area nervously, fearing a trap of some sort.

"Evening, Mr. Christian," the security guard said. "I'm Al Kraylow, the night systems manager at Robinson. We got a squeal from the outer warehouse door at 12:34 A.M. We called our man on the scene, Agent Vasquez, as per procedure, and verified that he had not attempted entry, had indeed been where he should have been, on his half-hourly walkaround at the time of the squeal. Two units with two armed agents were immediately dispatched and Vasquez, who as you know is unarmed, was advised to wait for backup. While the unit was en route Vasquez reported some sort of disturbance inside the warehouse. The first of my men arrived at 12:39."

That first unit had been driven by Agent Dawson, an ex-cop who, when he witnessed a dark van leaving the scene at a high rate of acceleration, didn't hesitate to pull up behind it and nudge it on the left side just as the driver was screeching around a corner. The van had lifted up on two wheels, hung there a moment, and crashed onto its side. Dawson had removed the driver at gunpoint as the second Robinson car arrived and apprehended the other two suspects inside the building.

"You say there were three suspects?" Howard asked, looking around.

"Third one was injured in a fall," Kraylow said. "We've got him on the way to the hospital right now."

He examined the remaining suspects. *Suspects?* Hell, no need to think like a cop. They were guilty until they proved their innocence, simple as that. The first one stood there defiantly in his manacles. He had a bloody nose and an old burn scar on one side of his face. But Python was actually feeling anything but defiant. He was thinking about his fingerprints and DNA getting into the system at long last, and about where he might have left those samples of himself in the past.

Calm had returned, belatedly, to the Martyr. He stood in his customary position, feet together, eyes to the heavens, but now in shackles. He was prepared to do time. He was prepared to suffer anything, and intended at all costs not to tell any of these people of the bomb inside, even if it swept him away with everyone else. Perhaps the arch blasphemer, Howard Christian, would be inside when the bomb went off.

HOWARD entered the building and saw Matt Wright and Susan Morgan coming through the connecting door from the elephant compound. As he walked, he kicked some of the scattered marbles and they clattered across the floor. He looked around at the damage, and he knew he had screwed up. And he knew why.

Not too long after making his first fortune, he had watched an old documentary about Michael Jackson on late-night television. At one point Jackson had gone on a shopping spree, in a shop that sold very ugly antiques. The dude had strolled along, pointing to things he wanted. When the bill was totaled, it came to six million dollars.

Howard had bolted from the bed and thrown up before he reached the toilet.

Why? Not long before seeing the program Howard had spent a million dollars for a car, and in fact would within a month or two spend *seven* million dollars on another car, and never have a nervous moment about it, much less a full-blown panic attack.

He viewed psychiatrists and all sorts of counseling as a waste of money, and believed he could work out any emotional problem he had just as he solved scientific or business problems. So he read about it, and thought about it, and decided what was going on here was a tension between his past and his present. Michael Jackson had grown up with unlimited money. He had no more idea of what a dollar was worth than a man from Mars. Howard had grown up with nothing. He was perfectly able to take chances, didn't mind gambling. He had spent three billion dollars buying another company, and he collected expensive things . . . but only after extensive research. Howard *always* knew what the price tag said, and knew if it was an *accurate* price tag, and he *never* paid retail. If he paid seven million dollars for a car, it was with the certainty that he could get seven million dollars for it tomorrow, and probably eight million next year.

What he could not do was pay $2.65 per gallon for gasoline when he could get it a few miles away for $2.63. He would break out in a sweat, his hands would start to tremble. He knew it was stupid, and for that reason he never fueled his own cars anymore, he never bought consumer items of any sort. He had staff that did that, and they never told him the prices. But every once in a while he made a decision on the basis of this ravenous miserliness, something he should have known to be a false economy, such as deciding to go with only one guard at night at the time machine project site, when Robinson had strongly recommended two so one could always remain in the shack just outside the door.

He looked over the chaos again, and knew this was the very picture of false economy.

"The elephants are all okay," Susan was saying. Elephants? God, he'd forgotten all about them. He wondered if Susan had any inkling of just how far onto the back burner he had shoved the cloning project in favor of this incomprehensible mess trying to become a time machine. "Looks like they never got into that part of the building."

"That's good," Howard said.

"They came here because they think cloning is evil," Matt said, with a small smile. "What do you figure they made of all this?" Howard didn't reply. Matt sighed. "The damage isn't as bad as it looks. Give me another week, we can probably be right back where we were."

"Keep at it, then. I'll have all the labor you need out here in the morning to get this cleaned up and sorted out."

"It won't take much. I've got one unit assembled, that one over there, and it wasn't opened. As for the rest . . . might as well wait until the first unit fails before we start assembling the beta version." He stooped over and picked up a clear crystalline sphere from the floor. He tossed it to Howard, who caught it in one hand. "As for the rest, it's mostly just sorting."

Howard's eyes met Matt's for a moment. Both of them knew the incident of the purloined marble would never be mentioned between them again, and that it would affect their relationship forever.

"Do what you have to do," Howard said, turning away. "Call me when you're ready to switch it on."

"I'll call you if I *find* the on switch. *That* would be news."

They watched him leave, slamming the door behind him. Susan looked around.

"All that work . . . ," she said. "I'm so sorry, Matt."

"It's not a big deal. Lucky those idiots didn't let your herd loose. Imagine the mess that would have made. I'm going over to look at the alpha gadget. Looks like somebody whacked it with something."

He went to the table where the alpha unit lay, went around it, and regarded it from the front for the first time.

One of the little lights was on. It was the red one.

"What does that mean?" Susan asked.

"That's what I'd like to know."

He ran his hands carefully over the case, which was cool and smooth to the touch, and now sported three dimples that looked familiar. If he connected the dots with a pen they would form a tall right triangle. As far as he could tell, the three dents were identical to the dents on the original unit recovered with the mammoth and the caveman, now safely stored away in some subterranean vault beneath the Resurrection Tower.

"Is it working?" Susan asked. She stood close, which was probably the only thing that could have distracted him from the gadget at that moment.

"There's a little chip inside, but I never programmed it for anything. Now it looks like it's programmed itself, enough to turn on this light, anyway."

"That's weird."

"That's way beyond weird and right into the occult. Let's take a look inside."

He opened the catches and lifted the lid. Inside was a perfect cube, seven marbles on each edge . . . with one marble sticking out in the dead center of the upper surface. All of the 194 visible marbles were clear as tiny crystal balls. Susan had found a Maglite on the floor where Python had abandoned it as he fled; she turned the beam on the array, just three and a half inches on each side. It sparkled magnificently, and somehow, a little ominously. Something about it didn't look right. Something about it hurt her eyes, like a distorting mirror in a funhouse.

"Can I have that?" Matt took the flashlight from Susan and ducked down, squinting as he shined the beam between the rows. He tentatively prodded the cube here and there. Nothing moved. It was securely attached to the bottom of the case, and the array of little crystal spheres resisted all his efforts to move them. He avoided, for the moment, the conspicuous single marble sitting on the top. He had the weird idea that it might be some sort of trap, that he was *meant* to press that marble, and that whoever had first designed and built this puzzle didn't have Matt Wright's best interests at heart.

"I can't see through it," he said. "Three and a half inches wide, I ought be able to see through the spaces between the rows of marbles and out the other side. But I can't. I just see more light, wherever I look."

"Refraction?" Susan suggested.

"I don't think the light could be scattered that much in such a short distance. Now, what I had assumed, looking at it, was that there would be . . . five cubed, one hundred and twenty-five more marbles inside, in orderly rows. That doesn't seem to be the case. So . . . there are more compact ways of arranging spheres, but if the ones in the center were packed like that, the ones here on the outside would reflect *that* crystalline structure if they were packed as solidly as they seem to be. I think they are packed in there very tightly indeed. And you know why I think so?"

"It's way beyond me, Matt. You're the mathematician."

"Not anymore. Now I'm the student. Because when I locked this box up and went home with you, there were two thousand, four hundred and one marbles in it, arranged in a stack ten high, twelve wide, and twenty long, with one orphan sticking out of the top. I think we can be pretty sure nobody opened the box to play a prank on us.

"Now we've got a cube seven by seven by seven. That's three hundred forty-three."

"So where are the . . ."

"Two thousand fifty-seven." He looked back at the shining cube.

"I think they're all still in that cube, in a multidimensional crystal structure. I think we're seeing just one side of an object folded through space."

HOWARD was walking toward Kraylow with the intent of giving him instructions for the rest of the night, when the man's jaw dropped open in amazement. Howard frowned . . . and something like a big black snake flashed past him, not a foot from his right shoulder. Kraylow saw it coming and dived to his right. The snake hit the ground and popped and hissed for a moment. Howard realized it was a severed power line, now drooping from a pole directly in front of him. He turned around.

The warehouse was gone.

FROM "LITTLE FUZZY, A CHILD OF THE ICE AGE"

Elephants love to splash around in pools and mud. Mammoths were very much like elephants, and they loved to bathe, too. Fuzzy liked it so much that when he smelled a watering hole he got very excited, and wanted to dive in as soon as he could!

Mammoth children were just like any other children. Sometimes they didn't think before they ran. And sometimes they ran off when their mother wasn't looking. That was when they could get into big trouble!

One day Temba and Fuzzy were on the edge of the herd when the sweet heavy smell of a pond came floating over the grassy plain. He flapped his little ears and heard the sound of frogs peeping. He lifted his little trunk and sniffed the air. There was another smell with the water, something Fuzzy had never smelled before. But it wasn't a scary smell, like the smell of a big saber-toothed cat or a two-leg with a spear. Fuzzy set off across the grass in search of the water. Soon he was farther away from Temba than he should have been, but he was excited, and he kept going. The smell of water got stronger.

Then he saw it, a big circle of trees with the shimmer of water in the middle! There was also the smell of mud baking in the sun. Fuzzy loved to roll in the mud! He started walking faster.

About this time Temba noticed that little Fuzzy was nowhere to be seen. She turned in a circle, looking for him. She flapped her ears, listening for him, and lifted her trunk, trying to smell him.

She caught his scent on the wind, and another scent that she remembered, a bad smell that meant death and suffering. She trumpeted loudly!

Come back, little Fuzzy! her cries rang out.

Then she called to the herd. Every ear turned to her at once! She was already moving, walking very fast toward the bad scent.

Fuzzy had come to the pond. It was peaceful and quiet. Ducks were swimming on the water. Fuzzy stood for a moment at the top of a small muddy hill and looked at it.

Maybe, just for a moment, he wondered if he should go back to his mother and tell her about the water and the whole herd could bathe in it.

But the day was hot and many flies were buzzing around his head, and little Fuzzy hated that, like all elephants and mammoths. He wanted a nice cool coating of mud matted into his too-long fur to keep the bugs away. So he started down the slope, and soon he was slipping and sliding, feet out in front of him, down on his knees.

Wheeeee!

He hit the water with a splash . . . and he stuck fast! There was some bad-smelling sticky black stuff beneath the water. He was in it up to his chest. He struggled, he tugged, he pulled, he slapped the water with his trunk and almost got that stuck, too. He was as stuck as Br'er Rabbit with the Tar Baby.

And that was what it was! Little Fuzzy was stuck in a tar pit!

If you go to California even today, to where the city of Los Angeles is now, you can see these tar pits. They look cool and inviting, just as they did that day long ago, but just beneath the surface the tar is still there. Natural gas, what scientists call **methane**, still bubbles out of the water, and that is what Fuzzy and Temba smelled.

Not only mammoths got stuck in the tar. Just about everything that walked or crawled or flew at that time came to the pond to drink, and a lot of them got stuck, couldn't get out, and died. Scientists are still digging out their bones.

So things didn't look good for poor little Fuzzy!

If Fuzzy had been a woolly rhinoceros or a giant elk or a dire wolf, he certainly would have died there in the tar pit. But Fuzzy was a mammoth, even though he was still quite a small mammoth, and mammoths did not abandon members of the herd when they were in trouble.

Temba and Big Mama and the others appeared on the top of

the low hill and saw little Fuzzy struggling and heard him calling out. He was only working himself deeper.

They hurried down the slope, slipping and sliding, and it was a miracle that some of them didn't get stuck, too! But they carefully reached around little Fuzzy with their trunks, and they pulled, and pulled, and pulled, and Fuzzy's legs came free.

Poor little Fuzzy was a mess!

There was sticky tar all over his legs, and under his trunk. Temba and Big Mama and the others picked at it, and they got tar all over their trunks, too. It was matted in their hair. It was awful!

For weeks after that the tar dried out on Fuzzy's legs, and Temba continued to pick at it. It came away bit by bit, with clumps of his hair.

Ow! Ow! Ow!

Little Fuzzy had learned his lesson. He would never step into a tar pit again!

2

MATT and Susan never felt a thing.

The lights flickered briefly, almost too quick for the eye to see. Something changed in the atmosphere and it took a moment for Matt to realize it was the faint, distant sound of the emergency generator coming on. Then he heard something he'd never heard in the building before: the trumpeting of Susan's elephants.

"Why did you push the button?" Susan asked.

Matt held his hands up in a pose of innocence.

"I didn't push anything. That thing just sank into the cube on its own."

They both looked at it, now a perfect cube of small glass spheres. As they watched, the central sphere rose again.

"This is way beyond spooky," Susan said.

"Yeah . . . but what happened?"

"The lights went out, the generator went on."

"Let's go outside and see if Howard felt anything."

"You go. I've got to see what's upsetting my elephants."

Susan headed for the interior door. Matt walked slowly, thoughts of cleaning up pushed aside now. Where did all those other marbles go?

His initial reaction, that they might have been folded through space-time somehow, that they were all somehow still there, packed into a seven by seven by seven volume that looked too small from our three-dimensional perspective but was plenty roomy in, say, five or six dimensions, had quickly paled. He was embarrassed that he'd even mentioned it to Susan. What must she think?

Question: Was there a way to explain the vanished spheres without resorting to extradimensional geometry?

Answer: Ask any magician. Ask any thief. Ask any prankster. Ask the gods of coincidence, chance, error, forgetfulness, and spiteful human nature.

So the box hadn't been opened. So what? The vandals got through the gate. All the data needed to build the structure now in the box was in Matt's computer; maybe he had been hacked.

Howard was pissed at him. Maybe he hired the vandals, arranged all this as a cruel hoax, maybe he liked to toy with men's minds that way. He could afford it.

Matt's mental state, though greatly improved since meeting Susan, was sometimes delicate. Maybe he'd simply replaced the alpha assembly himself while in a fugue state, and forgot.

Maybe he had been kidnapped by flying saucer men from Venus and brainwashed and this whole evening—even the whole last year—was a virtual reality experiment of surpassing cleverness.

Any of those things and many more now seemed more likely than multidimensional gymnastics. Matt felt considerable relief that he had blurted out his first theory to Susan rather than to Howard. It would be a lot easier to live down.

He reached the door, opened it, and saw that Santa Monica was gone.

SUSAN was not as frightened as Matt had feared she would be, at least not at first. The possibility had existed, they had talked about time travel in the abstract, she knew he was working on a time machine. But she had not expected to travel through time. If she did, she might have expected the journey to be more dramatic.

They made a circuit of the building. They felt they had to do at least that much, even before the sun came up. In an unknown situation, Matt said, step one is to establish the parameters of your problem. For all he knew, he could turn the corner of the building and find that Santa Monica was still there . . . or Shangri-La, or an alien spaceship landing on Devil's Tower, or the first steps of the Yellow Brick Road.

Matt carried the Maglite Susan had found on the floor, and

aside from that light beam, there was nothing, until they looked up. Then they saw stars in numbers neither of them had seen before, on the clearest night of their lives. Matt switched the light off for a moment, and they saw even more stars.

"Is that a light over there?" Susan asked. Matt could barely see her hand, pointing toward what he figured must be the Hollywood Hills. He thought he might see the tiniest imaginable orange spark against the blackness.

"Somebody built a fire?" he wondered. "Maybe there's people around here."

Who could tell? But at that moment they got evidence that there was *something* sharing the night with them. It was a blood-curdling screech, very far away, but so powerfully malign that Matt felt his knees begin to shake. He turned the light back on, and they soon found themselves running around the last corner and into the pale but warm square of light, the door leading back inside the steel building.

"Can you get us back home?" Susan asked, breathing hard and afraid to look at him.

"I don't know. I think we'd better put that question aside for a few hours and figure out how long I have to solve that problem. How long we can expect to live."

"What do you mean? You think time traveling is harmful?"

"Not so far as I know. No, I mean how long we can survive."

IT quickly came down to water.

They sat together in the quiet warehouse and batted it around. The first thing that became clear was how utterly dependent people of the twenty-first century had become on the vast, interlinked network of goods and services and transportation that they called civilization. The second thing they recalled was that the Los Angeles Basin was a desert.

The taps were dry, of course. Matt assumed they were cut off abruptly, underground, just like the asphalt and concrete surrounding the building ended about five feet away from the sides.

They did an inventory. It didn't look good. Each of the five elephants had a drinking trough, and they varied from full to half empty. That wouldn't last long and there was no way to refill them. There were four rest rooms, two on each half of the warehouse, with two toilets in the ladies' rooms and one each in the men's. That was a good supply in the six tanks, but it wouldn't last long, either.

"I wish we'd put in one of those water coolers with the ten-gallon jugs," Matt said. "There's always a dozen full ones sitting around."

"How many do you think we'll need?"

"Again, I haven't any idea."

The best news was the Coca-Cola machine. It was a big one, with a curved, lighted front. Looking at it, Matt suddenly felt very thirsty. He searched his pockets and came up empty.

"You have any change?"

"My purse was in the car."

Matt looked around and found the crowbar abandoned by one of the vandals. He set the end of it against the door of the Coke machine and started to pull. The door popped open and he took out a cold can of Coke. "You want something?"

"Is there any Mountain Dew?"

"All we have here that's clear is Sprite."

"That'll do."

They popped the tops and drank, then were silent for a moment. They had worked for several hours on the inventory, not having to talk about the central fact of their dilemma, but Matt knew it was unavoidable.

"Look . . . ," he said, and had to stop. He took a deep breath. "I'm sorry about this. I'm so sorry about it."

"About what?"

"About . . . well, about getting you thrown down a temporal wormhole to what might very well be the year 13,000 B.C."

"Is that what happened? A temporal wormhole?"

"You know what I mean."

"Sure. The part I don't see is why any of this was your fault."

"I thought it was sort of . . . obvious."

"Not to me." She sighed. "Okay, you were trying to build a time machine."

"Trying to duplicate something that was found that might be a time machine."

"Don't get technical. You built it, some ignorant yahoos came in and did something to it—"

"We scientists call that 'whacking the shit out of it.' "

"Getting technical again. Anyway, something happened, which I dearly hope you can somehow make *un*happen . . ." For just a moment her voice got shaky, but she took a deep breath and plowed on.

"I keep elephants. I keep them in strong, secure stockades, and I keep people away from them. But what if those yahoos got in there, opened the gates and the outside doors, and threw a bunch of firecrackers into the paddocks? And the elephants stampeded down Wilshire and hurt a lot of people? Is that my fault?"

"Well . . ."

"Don't think about it too long." There was a tiny edge to her voice.

"No, of course not. Not if you took reasonable precautions. But did I?"

"I don't think anybody could tell what 'reasonable' was, before this happened."

"Maybe. Maybe not. I keep thinking I could have done more."

"Howard sure could have. He could have splurged on two or three guards, around the clock. I think we ought to take that up with him . . . when we get back."

He noticed it was *when*, not *if*, and was grateful for her confidence . . . or was she just whistling past the graveyard?

"I think I will. But there's a larger question. What was I doing fooling around with something as dangerous as time travel in the first place?"

"Satisfying your scientific curiosity. I don't see anything wrong with that."

"That's exactly what Robert Oppenheimer and Enrico Fermi and a few dozen other physicists were doing in the early 1940s."

"So does that make the atomic bomb their fault?"

"People will probably debate that forever. One thing I'm sure of, if they hadn't researched those questions, if they had opted out from fear of the consequences . . . somebody else would have found the same answers."

"No question. It's the same with cloning research. We can try to keep it in control, but the answers *will* come."

"Yes. I know it's foolish to worry too much about the effects of what you might discover. We'd stop discovering anything at all. Still . . ." He leaned back in his chair and sighed, wondering if he needed to get into this. But there wasn't much they could do until the sun came up, which could be hours yet. He went on.

"When I was very young, I discovered science. I couldn't get enough of it. I read everything. I figured I'd continue doing that until I *knew* everything *about* everything. Chemistry, biology, physics, math, astronomy, you name it, it was all the same to me. In fact, I didn't see any distinction."

"Not a bad way to look at it," Susan said.

"That's true. In many ways, there isn't any difference. You can't do biology without chemistry, you can't do astronomy without physics . . . and you can't do any of them without math. That's what I kept coming back to, after I realized there was too much knowledge for any one person to learn in a hundred lifetimes. So when I reached the point where I had to specialize, I asked people what I seemed to be the best at, and they all said math. Which was good, because that's what I thought, too.

"And I'd given some thought to the responsibility of the researcher. Astronomy seemed fairly safe . . . until you started thinking about the power inherent in stars, in neutron stars, black holes, quasars. Same with physics. Biology gets into the realm of really hairy moral questions, like biological or genetic war, which in some ways is scarier than nuclear bombs. I'll tell you, it got to the point, if I'd been any good with the harmonica, I'd have dropped out of school and started a blues band. Unfortunately, I have no talent for music, or sports, or business, or sales, or fishing . . . no talents at all, really, except for memory and logical thinking. So I concentrated on math. Math seemed safe."

"You were how old?"

"Twelve."

Susan smiled. "Prodigies. When I was twelve I was learning how not to fall off when an elephant was lifting me on her trunk."

"I wish I knew how to do that."

"I'll teach you. But go on."

Matt wasn't sure he wanted to, but he'd started down the road.

"Well . . . I got my Ph.D. in mathematics. Even in math you're expected to specialize, but I tried to stay as broadly based as possible. One month I'd be working on the most theoretical things I could find, another I'd get interested in what we call 'real-world' problems. About a year ago I was noodling around some equations concerning superstrings. Do you know what that is?"

"Sure. It's that goop you squirt out of a can at parties. Sticks to stuff."

"Right. But the other sense of the word concerns what quarks are made of."

"Quarks being the particles that make up protons and neutrons and such."

"Yes. So far there is no real evidence of their existence, just some interesting mathematical theories. If they do exist, they are very small. Anyway, superstrings seemed as remote in one direction as quasars are in the other. I didn't think it was likely anything I discovered would have a lot of real-world applications."

"You should have remembered that, in 1939, protons and neutrons seemed incredibly tiny."

"Yes, but Einstein and others knew the potential for great energy release was there, and had some idea of the mechanisms to let it loose. Superstrings are about as close to a totally abstract thing as I can think of. They are so tiny, it was hard to see how they could ever have much relevance to our lives, given quantum constraints. I mean, the fundamental quantum fuzziness of things shows up on a level trillions of times larger than superstrings. At the quantum level, certainty is no longer possible. How much less certain could we be of anything I might postulate concerning a superstring?"

"I gather it didn't work out that way."

"At first, it was fine. Lovely speculation. Good response to the papers I was publishing, interesting feedback from the three or four people around the world looking into the same thing.

"Then I stopped publishing. I didn't even realize I had done it at the time. I thought I was just organizing my thoughts, I'd put them down and send them in later.

"A year went by, and I started sleeping badly. I was getting an inkling of something that was . . . frightening me. I'm still not sure why. It got to be hard to do the math; sort of like writer's block, I guess.

"Then one day I stopped talking." Matt swallowed hard, and suited action to his words. After a minute had gone by, Susan spoke, cautiously.

"That must have been awful."

Matt laughed.

"You'd think so, wouldn't you? Actually, it wasn't so bad, at first. The weird thing was to discover I could get through the day pretty easily without speaking at all. I never had a lot of human contact at work, math is a lonely game sometimes. Casual contact could be handled with a nod or a smile. Hell, it's not like I was the office clown *before* that; people didn't expect a lot of words out of me. But gradually it became clear that I wasn't *choosing* not to speak, but that I *couldn't* speak. I'd open my mouth to say something, and nothing would come out. I wrote notes, memos, and emails to cover myself in most things . . . then I realized I was having trouble writing, too. I knew it was time to get help.

"And that's sort of where I was when Howard found me. I'd spent a month in a very nice, quiet facility in the country, mildly sedated, and after a while I could talk to a therapist. I was advised to take a few months off to think things over. I didn't need a lot of time to decide one thing: I wouldn't publish my results on the superstring research. There was too much potential danger. In fact, I knew I had to destroy the equations."

There wasn't much he could add that wouldn't get into more specificity than Susan could handle, and she seemed to recognize that. They were silent for a while, until Susan looked toward the door they had left propped open, and realized there was pale gray light coming through it.

They approached the door cautiously. Outside, there were entirely unremarkable trees and shrubs. The analytical side of Matt's mind noted there was no sign of whatever trees and shrubs had occupied the ground the time-traveling building now sat on. Were those trees now growing from Howard Christian's land in Santa Monica? Something to think about later, after they had made a plan.

A plan. It was surprisingly hard to do. There was a strong impulse to just bar the doors of the warehouse and huddle inside, let the outside world take care of itself. But time was pressing, events would not wait. So, step one when in new territory was to define the lay of the land. There was a ladder bolted to the side of the warehouse, and Susan started up immediately, followed by Matt.

At the top, they looked out over a primeval Pleistocene landscape, untouched in any way by the hand of man.

To the west, the Pacific was still gray in the morning light. To the north they could see what had to be the Hollywood Hills, surprisingly green and covered with scrub oaks. To the east the sky was orange, the sun about to burst over the horizon . . . and the mountains over there seemed to be frosted with snow. To the south, just rolling country and, far in the distance, what looked like a herd of horses.

"Maybe horses, maybe camels," Susan said. "I can't tell from this far away."

"Camels?"

"Sure, there were several species. And the horses may have three toes."

"And the tigers have big teeth."

"Not really tigers, Matt, they were a lot more like lions."

"You're the expert. But we'd probably better watch out for them. I'll bet they could hide pretty well in all this underbrush."

"If we stick with the elephants, we shouldn't be bothered much by saber-toothed cats."

"Right. The elephants. What are we going to do about the elephants?"

"Water them, obviously."

"And how do we do that?"

"I think we leave it to them." They were silent again as the first rays of the sun reached them. "That is so beautiful," Susan said, with a catch in her voice. "I wish I'd brought my camera."

Matt was thinking about saber-toothed cats and wishing he'd brought a gun . . . a very *large* gun.

"So . . . ," Susan said. "Where did you hide your superstring data?"

"It's in my safe-deposit box, in Portland."

They looked at each other, and laughed.

"Well, I *should* have destroyed it," Matt said.

"You wouldn't be much of a scientist if you did."

Matt looked into the distance again, and decided to say nothing.

"I guess we'd better get to work," Susan said. "I think we've got an interesting day ahead of us."

ABOUT twelve thousand years in the future, Howard Christian was finally at the end of the most interesting day of his life, and one of the more expensive ones.

He had heard somewhere that the New York City police department used to have an informal code for the offering of bribes, a way to avoid the awkwardness of just coming out and saying "Would you take a bribe?" Instead, you could say, "You look like you could use a new hat." What that meant was: "Would twenty dollars make this problem go away?" Sometimes it took a new suit to do the job: one hundred dollars.

Tomorrow a half dozen Santa Monica patrolmen would be driving around in brand-new Land Rovers. Kraylow, Vasquez, Dawson, and probably a few others at Robinson Security had just earned themselves new homes in Simi Valley.

According to Howard's lawyers, there was nothing illegal, in itself, in making a large metal warehouse vanish from the face of the Earth, and that was all the police officers had witnessed. The money they would receive, very discreetly, was simply for not talking about what they had seen. Howard was confident the matter could be buried easily enough, especially since each of the superior officers in the department would be getting the price of two or three Land Rovers.

The price was steeper for the Robinson people because they were the only ones who knew there had been two people inside the building when it ceased to exist.

Howard's lawyers weren't quite so sure of the ramifications of that one. Unless it could be determined just what had caused the warehouse to evaporate it would be difficult to charge Howard or any of his enterprises with anything that might have befallen Matt and Susan . . . and who could even prove they had been harmed? Perhaps they were fine . . . wherever they went. Still, they had been there, and now they were gone, and the Robinson people knew it, and not mentioning it to the police might be seen as negligence, at the very least, and so they had earned the price of a house in Simi Valley, the dream of every Southland cop and ex-cop.

But where *did* Matt and Susan go?

That was a question Howard was determined should never be asked. Everyone who knew that Matt was working on a time machine had either vanished with the building or was in Howard's employ, so that was under control.

It would have been a lot cheaper for Howard if he could have simply stonewalled: My building disappeared, I don't know why, and I don't know where it went. End of story. But there would never be an end to it, and he knew it. Reporters would be all over the story, and soon the bugs would start crawling out of the baseboards. Roswell flying saucer bugs, crop circle bugs, Area 51 bugs. Alien abductees.

Howard wasn't having any of that. The last thing he needed was to be seen as having screwed up again, or having let an experiment get out of control. No, hushing up everyone involved was going to be expensive, but cheap at the price.

It took all morning, but at last he felt he had it under control. He was exhausted, but willed himself to drive back to the scene of the disaster. He took one of the Robinson Blazers this time, not wishing to draw attention to himself in one of his antique cars.

There was another Robinson vehicle parked outside the gate, manned by Kraylow, who nodded at Howard but did not get out. There was a small group of people, mostly men who worked in the area, standing around with puzzled looks on their faces. Luckily, there were not many of them. No explanation would be offered to them, and what were they going to think, anyway? That the building had fallen into a temporal wormhole?

No, they would conclude, sensibly, that somehow Howard Christian, the eccentric billionaire, had had the structure demolished overnight, right down to the concrete pad, and replanted in scrubby-looking oak trees.

Howard drove around to the far side where there were no people. He got out, walked to the chain-link fence, and grabbed it with his hands. He scowled at the trees inside, trees that had obviously grown right where they now stood, for thirty, forty, maybe fifty years. He shook the fence in frustration.

Where did you take my building, Matt?

FROM "LITTLE FUZZY, A CHILD OF THE ICE AGE"

Mammoths did not sleep a lot. Most nights they would sleep only four or five hours, and only for an hour or so at a time. Somebody was always awake, watching for danger.

Sometimes they slept standing up. This wasn't uncomfortable for mammoths, as it would be for us. Many animals sleep standing up. But sometimes they liked to lie down on their sides for a while and sleep that way.

One night a few weeks after Fuzzy got into big trouble at the tar pits, he was sleeping lying down. There were still hard balls of tar clinging to his front legs and he didn't like that. He rubbed his legs against trees and on the ground, trying to get them off. Maybe he dreamed. What would a mammoth dream about? We don't know.

But just after the night was darkest, when the moon had just risen over the hills to the east, Fuzzy was awakened by the urgent touch of Temba's trunk. He opened his eyes to see a strange light.

The herd was all awake, and milling around nervously. Fuzzy got to his feet and huddled close to his mother's side, where he felt warm and safe and secure.

Then the quiet of the night was broken by the high, horrible cries he had heard once before. He remembered them well.

Two-legs!

They came from the south, waving burning sticks that were so bright they hurt the eyes of the mammoths.

Most animals don't like fire, and mammoths were no different. They ran away!

But the two-legs were determined, they kept coming. The mammoths would stop for breath, and once again the two-legs would be almost on them.

And now they were touching their flaming sticks to the ground, and the yellow grass itself began to burn. It raced toward the herd, and the two-legs were close behind.

On and on the mammoth herd ran, into the night, trying to stay one step ahead of the inferno on the ground. Little Fuzzy began to get very tired.

Then he smelled something that made his young heart beat even faster. It was a smell he would never forget, the smell of that awful day when he was almost swallowed up in the thick black goo that lurked just beneath the surface of that quiet, inviting pool.

It was the smell of tar!

Fuzzy wanted to turn back. He looked back at the fire. It was impossible to go that way. Temba and Big Mama and the rest of the herd kept going, onward toward the tar pits.

Then they were joined by other mammoths. These were big bulls, the biggest mammoths Fuzzy had ever seen! They were panicked, too, rushing forward as fast as they could go.

And then a very, very strange thing happened. . . .

3

SUSAN was a list maker. While Matt made a last attempt to make the time machine work again, she sat down at her laptop and listed their assets:

2 laptops
1 tera-mainframe computer
1 generator (diesel fuel for 4 days of operation)

WATER:
about 500 gallons in elephant tanks
about 40 gallons in toilet tanks
97 soft drinks (Coke, 7-Up, root beer)

FOOD:
assorted snacks from machine
8 watermelons
20 cantaloupes
3 sacks apples
elephant feed for 2 days

CLOTHING:
what we're wearing

SHELTER:
1 large warehouse

WEAPONS:
2 fire axes
8 fire extinguishers

1 tranquilizer gun
1 elephant gun

TOOLS:
2 butane lighters
complete machine shop
3 boxes mechanic's tools
1 box woodworking tools
1 electron microscope
1 mass spectrometer

She supposed the laptops might be useful for something other than the list she was currently making, but she couldn't at the moment figure what that might be. As for the state-of-the-art computer Howard Christian had provided to Matt for analyzing the possible permutations of the time machine . . . Matt had told her it would take even that monster millions of years to make a dent in the problem. And, when the generator stopped working, the big computer would become nothing more than a very complex piece of junk. So would the generator itself, and everything inside the warehouse that ran on electricity . . . which was almost *everything*.

The food and water situation could have been better, and it could have been worse. It was too bad there wasn't a commissary of some kind, or a lunch wagon parked on the grounds when the wormhole opened and swallowed them, but there wasn't. On the other hand, the snack and pop machines had only been there a few weeks, and Susan had no idea why they had been installed. She'd never seen anyone buy anything from them, and she'd bet the coin boxes were empty or nearly so. It would stretch for some weeks, with care, though they'd surely get very tired of Pop-Tarts and tiny bags of potato chips.

Every few minutes Susan had to stop herself from asking Matt how long he thought it would take to put the machine into reverse and step on the gas, floor the son of a bitch full-speed into the twenty-first century. If he had any idea, she knew he would have told her, and simply to ask the question was to invite the impossible answer, the answer she didn't think she could bear to hear: *How long? It will be thousands of years before we, or our bones, reach the twenty-first century.*

Clothing could be a problem. They didn't know what time of year it was now. Who could even tell if summer would be hot or winter cold? The climate had changed a lot in thousands of years. Both of them were lightly dressed in what they had thrown on when Matt got the call. It seemed pleasant enough for now, but it had been chilly last night, Susan remembered. What if this was summer? What if the Los Angeles Basin got a lot of snow in December? What about tonight, for that matter? They must find water soon, and that meant that if the elephants didn't find some close by, they would likely be spending the night in the open, on the ground, and they didn't have so much as a blanket.

More frightening than the idea of getting cold, though, was the idea of getting eaten. Susan had spent some time years ago camping out, but Matt had hardly ever slept outside of a building. Neither of them knew much survival lore. And there were sure to be things out there happy to make a meal of them. She looked at the big elephant gun lying there on the table, and almost wanted to laugh.

Five years ago, an ill-treated elephant had run amok in Los Angeles. It killed three police officers and soaked up a ton of LAPD lead before a weapon powerful enough to kill it had been brought to the scene. The city council enacted a law requiring anyone keeping elephants to have such a weapon handy at all times. Susan had scoffed at the time, but dutifully took the thing—she had no idea of the maker or the caliber, except that it fired bullets that seemed almost as big as beer cans—to an indoor range and fired it . . . twice. The first time knocked her down and badly bruised her shoulder. The second shot was to prove to herself she could master it. She had, and never intended to fire it again.

Now she was glad they had it. If it would knock down an elephant, it ought to deal with a saber-toothed cat easily enough . . . if she could hit it. The tranquilizer gun was also required by law, but it was more problematic. She figured a big cat could chew off a pretty big chunk before the drugs took hold.

"How are you doing over there?" she called to Matt.

He glanced up, and shrugged.

"I've got a good program roughed out for the computer to run. But I'm flying blind. Give me another few minutes."

She went back to her list.

The ax would be handy for cutting firewood, if they needed heat. As far as building a shelter, she thought staying in the warehouse would be the best idea, unless water was too far away.

There had not been a vehicle within range of whatever force had taken them through time. She thought a mid-sized SUV would be able to handle most of the primeval terrain of Los Angeles. Hell, with the machines Howard had installed in Matt's lab, he could probably *build* an SUV, given time. She hoped they wouldn't have that much time.

She looked across the room to the door to the giant refrigerator. She wondered if she should add that to her list: FOOD: TEN TONS OF MAMMOTH MEAT. In a few days it would be thawed and rotting.

She couldn't stand it anymore, so she got up and stood behind Matt. He had the case open, and was carefully pushing the hypercube here and there, in different combinations. Nothing was happening, nothing at all. She got the impression he could keep at it for hours, maybe days.

"What do you say we get moving?" she said.

He looked up at her, and closed the case. "You're right. Let's go."

LEARNING to get on the back of an elephant wasn't as easy as Susan had hinted. He had stepped on Queenie's trunk, as instructed, and then felt she was going to toss him right over her back, the ride upward was so swift, his weight so negligible to the giant animal. He ended up sprawled across the elephant's head, which couldn't have been too comfortable for her, but she displayed endless patience as Susan grabbed his arm and helped him get seated behind her. Then, off they went, at the head of a row of pregnant pachyderms that would have made P. T. Barnum proud.

The view was spectacular, and the ride wasn't too uncomfortable. He already preferred it to his one ride on a horse.

He got to enjoy it for almost a mile.

"This is no good," Susan said, giving Queenie the touch command that made her stop. "We're going to have to walk."

"And I was having such a good time. Why not ride?"

"Too many reasons. These are all former circus elephants, but I didn't train them, and they're all rusty. Queenie is responding to most of my commands, but she's slow, I think she's forgotten some. And she's edgy."

It was a new environment, and he imagined it was full of new and exciting and probably disturbing smells. He had noticed all the elephants were raising their trunks frequently. It stood to reason that with ten feet of nose, they smelled things he couldn't even imagine. What if something scared her?

"You've convinced me," he said.

So they got down, and Matt quickly found the elephants set a pace a lot quicker than he had realized. So high off the ground, it didn't seem so fast.

Susan walked alongside Queenie, guiding the great beast with touches of a wooden broom handle, trying to slow her down. But the other elephants weren't having any of it.

"I was hoping they'd accept her as the herd leader," Susan told him. "She's the oldest. But Queenie has never been dominant. They won't follow her."

"So who's the leader of the pack?" Matt asked, already starting to pant from the pace the elephants were setting.

"That would be Becky, the one with the notch in her left ear."

"Why not go to Becky, slow her down?"

"Becky doesn't like me. We never hit it off."

She tried to slow Becky, but soon the great gray moving wall of flesh had had enough, and ignored further commands. She set her own pace, which was too fast for the humans to keep up with.

"They're getting away," Matt observed, bent over trying to catch his breath.

"Probably for the best."

"You think so?"

Susan shrugged, but he could see she was upset.

"Matt, they had to go free sooner or later. I can't feed them, I can't water them. They'll have to fend for themselves. Which shouldn't be hard; this land is full of things they can eat, so long as they find water."

"What about our water?"

She pointed to the retreating tails of her former charges. A fleet of trucks might have just passed, tearing up shrubs, breaking branches off trees, leaving deep indentations in the soil. Tracking a herd of elephants didn't require the services of Tonto.

"I'm pretty sure they're on the scent of it. All we need to do is follow, and hope it's not a three-day trip."

So they set off at a comfortable walking pace. Soon the elephants disappeared over a rise, and when they got to the top of it, the herd was nowhere to be seen.

THEY stopped several hills later and sat down to eat a few bags of peanuts and candy bars and wash it down with cans of warm root beer. Susan kept watch for predators while Matt opened the time machine once again to glare uselessly at the gleaming, frozen innards. There had been no change. He shut it again in disgust.

Susan looked around at the empty landscape. So far they hadn't seen so much as a prehistoric bunny rabbit, but any one of those clumps of trees could conceal a whole herd of saber-toothed cats. Did cats come in herds? Prides? She vaguely remembered reading of a North American lion, which had been bigger than the saber-tooths. Her fingers worked nervously on the stock of the elephant gun. Did the big cats hide in trees and jump down on their prey? Or did they wait in ambush on the ground, or stalk and pounce? Did they hunt at night, or during the day? She didn't know, and didn't think even an archaeologist could have told her. But she'd have given a lot to have one around just then.

"You know, Matt, I could really use some good news here."

He looked up at her. "The red light flickered a while ago."

"It did? Why didn't you tell me?"

"I don't know what it means. I'm hoping it's detecting

something. Some fluctuation in space-time. If the green light comes on, maybe it will work again."

"How do we make it come on?"

"Trial and error, I guess. That's the best I can say. Keep moving."

Susan glanced at the sun, then to the west. She gazed longingly in that direction, then back to the elephant trail, which still led steadfastly eastward. She looked at Matt helplessly, and shrugged.

"First things first," he agreed. "Find a water supply *before* we start to get thirsty. It made sense this morning, and it still makes sense."

So they continued down the path the elephants had beaten for them.

NEITHER of them had a great picture of Los Angeles in their heads. As new arrivals who had spent most of their time working, they knew the neighborhoods where they had lived and worked, and some other places where people of good income went to shop and dine: Santa Monica, Westwood, Hollywood, Beverly Hills, Venice. They had made a few excursions into Valley communities. But except for a trip or two to the airport neither of them had ever driven as far south as Century Boulevard, and in fact had seldom been south of Venice. In the same way, Western Avenue was the eastern limit of their known territory. Neither had ever set foot in downtown Los Angeles, though they knew where it was, had seen its skyscrapers in the distance.

Matt wasn't sure how much good it would have done them, considering that the things an urban dweller would note about his surroundings would be streets and buildings, all of which were now gone . . . that is, none of which were here yet . . . but he didn't see how it could have hurt. Twelve thousand years wasn't enough to have changed the large features of the area. No new mountains had been built in that time, and the canyons would be only slightly less eroded now than they had been in the twenty-first century. The Santa Monica Mountains had been then, and were now, visible from anywhere in the basin, and were basically unchanged as to their gross outlines. Yet even there, his memory was not much help. You looked at those mountains, and what you noticed was the HOLLYWOOD sign, and thus knew your position roughly. With the sign gone, with all roads and houses gone, the Hollywood Hills were fairly nondescript. He could see several low points. Was that one where Laurel Canyon would be, or was it Cold-water Canyon? Without knowing where such prominent features of the terrain were, how could he hope to venture a guess as to their present position?

And did it really matter?

He knew there was something over to the east called the Los Angeles River, but he seemed to recall it was something of a joke. In the twenty-first century it was a wide, flat, concrete ditch, a favorite of Hollywood film directors for staging car chases, dry most of the year except for a trickle down the middle.

Los Angeles was a desert then, and it looked like a desert now. The shallow arroyos they had crossed were all bone dry. That might be seasonal. In some thousands of years a man named Mulholland would dig a long series of aquaducts and L.A. would bloom with imported palm trees and tropical flowers, but right now the dominant vegetation was sagebrush and scrawny live oaks.

He didn't know how far they had come. He had tried counting steps, and quickly lost count as his mind drifted to other things. Maybe he could estimate the length of their journey by time . . . but how many miles could a man walk in an hour? He had only a vague idea of their speed.

And to make it even more hopeless, the path chosen by the elephants was far from a beeline. Susan seemed to think they were on the scent of water, but if they were, the scent must be coming from several directions, maybe shifting with the wind. They had meandered north for a while, then turned back east, then north again, then east. He hoped they knew what they were doing.

ONE good thing: though the trail was growing colder as they fell farther behind, there was little danger of it vanishing overnight, or even over the next two or three days. And Susan said the elephants would surely stop to browse, whether they found water or not. He was wrapped up in thoughts like that when he almost ran into the giant yellow bear.

That was his first thought, anyway. It was a wall of thick fur, and it was so entangled and crusted with bits of twigs and leaves and acorns and clods of dirt as to almost appear a part of the landscape. It had been almost under a tree, and now it stood up . . . and stood up . . .

He stopped in his tracks and Susan ran into him.

"What's the . . ." Then she got a look at it. It must have been twenty feet tall. Susan whispered something.

"What?" Matt whispered back.

"Sloth. Giant ground sloth."

"Sloth? Like those things that hang in trees? You gotta be—"

"Related," she hissed. "Be quiet. I don't think it sees us."

The thing was turning, ponderously. Way, way up there was a head—it had to be a head, it was at the end of a neck like a tree trunk—that was comically small for its gargantuan body. But small is a relative thing. Matt figured the tree branch it held in its jaws was about the size of his thigh, and it didn't look very big there.

About the time he had that thought, the creature bit through the branch like a toothpick, and spit out the remains. It was facing them now, looking down with big, soft brown eyes that held no fear.

"Let's back away," Susan suggested, in a whisper.

"Good idea."

They began a slow retreat, and the sloth watched them. Then it took a step in their direction.

"Should we run?" Matt asked.

"Best not to, unless we have to," Susan decided. "I figure he could catch us if he wanted to."

The animal took another step, then another . . . and Matt realized that it was running toward them. Its huge size made the movements seem slow, but each stride was enormous, and it was suddenly a lot closer to them.

"Run!" Susan hissed. Matt didn't need any prodding. He took half a dozen quick backward steps, afraid to turn away, then he did turn, and ran as fast as he had ever run in his life. Behind him he heard the sloth crashing through brush, and the sound of Susan's footsteps.

Wait a minute. Guys didn't run ahead of girls, that just wasn't done. He half turned as he ran, and Susan nearly ran over him. He was so startled that he tripped over his own feet and hit the ground, hard.

He looked up, fully expecting to see the sloth towering over him. But it was nowhere near. In fact, it had stopped not far from the point where they began their hasty retreat. He heard Susan return to crouch beside him.

"You okay?"

"Skinned my elbow," he said. "Nothing serious."

They watched the sloth, who seemed to have completely lost interest in them.

"Just scaring us off, I guess," Susan said. "It's so big I'll bet it doesn't have any predators, at least not when it's full-grown."

"Looks like it could pretty well crush a saber-tooth."

"No kidding. Did you see the size of the claws on that thing?"

"Three on each hand. Long as my arm."

"He's pretty well tearing up that tree."

They watched, from a good distance, as the giant sloth stripped leaves and bark from a tree.

"Wonder why he came after us?" Matt asked.

"Maybe it's a female, maybe there's a cub nearby."

IN the next two hours they encountered a lot of wildlife, though none as dramatically. Several times they saw what looked to be ordinary jackrabbits darting in and out of bushes. Once a wolf regarded them for a while from a distance of a hundred yards, then trotted off. Twice they encountered small herds of deer. They looked like ordinary deer to Matt. He supposed a man who had spent a lot of time with deer in the crosshairs of his rifle might have spotted differences in these animals and modern ones.

He had never hunted. He might have to learn. Could he figure out how to make a useful bow and arrows? A spear? Could he learn to throw it hard and far enough to bring down a swift, alert deer? He suspected he could get mighty hungry while acquiring that skill. Maybe traps would be better. How did one make a rabbit trap?

Stop it, he told himself. Keep a positive attitude. You *will* figure out how the machine works. We *will* get out of here.

THE sun was still above the horizon when Susan looked around and said this would be a good place to stop. Matt didn't like it.

"Can't we keep on for a while more? We've still got some light."

"You'd be surprised how quickly that will go away," she said. "There's things we need to do, and it's best to be familiar with the immediate area before it gets dark. We need every advantage we can get if there are night-hunting predators around."

Matt still didn't look convinced, so she added, "Do you really want to gather firewood in the dark with saber-tooths prowling around?"

There was plenty of wood lying around, both dead branches blown down by the wind and a couple trees that had been devastated by large herbivores, probably sloths or mammoths. They worked at it for half an hour, and when they were done it was getting harder to see. They arranged a fire and lit it with the lighter they had found in a desk drawer. Soon it was crackling, and Susan's spirits soared with the sparks that leaped into the air. She looked at Matt, who was sweaty, soot-streaked, and grinning.

"Fire is the basic unit of civilization," he said.

"I never thought of it that way . . . but you may be right."

"It's the first thing that really set us off from other animals," Matt said. "And it still does. Other animals have languages, other animals use tools. We're still the only animal that manipulates energy."

Susan had felt something like that before, sitting around a campfire. Out in the woods, just you and your family or some other Girl Scouts . . . you realized that the bad things feared the light, that as long as you were in the light, you were okay. If the fire went out, if the darkness closed in, that was when you were in trouble.

Matt found a few long branches and arranged them with one end in the fire and the other sticking out where they could reach them.

"If we see anything move out there," he said, "grab one of these and throw it toward the movement. Like a torch."

"Good idea."

They ate some of their remaining fruit and a candy bar each.

"Too bad we don't have some—"

"I wish we had some—"

"—hot dogs!" they finished together, and laughed longer than the coincidence really warranted. When they were through with their meager dinner they sat close together and stared into the fire. Susan finished her drink and was about to toss the empty can into the fire, then she frowned at it.

"Say we leave this back here in the past," she said.

"Yeah? Go on."

"Well, what if somebody finds it? Digs it up, back in the future."

"They'd be mighty puzzled, wouldn't they."

"I mean . . . would it cause a paradox, or something?"

"I've always operated on the assumption that there are no real paradoxes."

"I don't get your meaning."

"I mean 'real-world' paradoxes. Sure, they can exist in math, and in logic. The human mind can propose a paradox, but if you examine it you'll find it's either a semantic problem or a hypothetical physical problem that actually doesn't exist in the real world."

"Help me out here."

"Okay. Take a silly paradox, the one Gilbert and Sullivan described in *Pirates of Penzance*. Frederick was apprenticed to the Pirate King until his twenty-first birthday, not his twenty-first year. But he was born in a leap year, on the twenty-ninth of February. Therefore, though he was twenty-one years old, he had only had five birthdays. You see, the paradox only arises because of the way the contract was worded."

"Got it."

"Then there's another classic one, the grandfather paradox. You build a time machine, go into the past, and kill your grandfather when he's a young boy. So your father is never born, and you are never born . . ." He waited.

"So you never built a time machine and never traveled in time and never killed your grandfather."

"Exactly."

"But . . . that is a paradox. Isn't it?"

"It would be, if time travel was possible. Up to now, I would have sworn it wasn't possible, so I didn't spend a lot of time worrying about temporal paradoxes."

"Sounds like you'd better reorder your priorities."

"Sounds like."

They were silent for a long time, listening to the crackling of the fire. Susan tried not to look at it, not wanting to destroy her night vision. Once she thought she saw a movement at the edge of their little clearing and she tossed a flaming brand at it. Nothing happened, and the torch soon burned itself out.

"So," Matt said at last. "You know any good ghost stories?"

MATT sat up for a while, fiddling with the time machine with Susan watching over his shoulder. He didn't learn anything he didn't know already.

"Matt," she said quietly at one point. "We may never get out of here, right?"

He looked at her a long time, trying to find it in himself to give her a reassuring lie. He knew he couldn't do it, so he just shook his head. She scooted closer to him and rested her head on his shoulder. They hadn't found anything like real bedding in their search of the warehouse. The best they could do were several plastic tarps that had been used for various things. They were sitting on one, and each of them had one to wrap up in. They weren't very thick, and he could feel her warmth against him.

"Maybe we should change our names to Adam and Eve," she said.

He looked at her, and for once in his life he didn't even think about it, he just leaned over and kissed her. She responded for a moment, then pushed him gently away.

"I want you to hold me," she said. "Let's get together under both these tarps, we'll be warmer."

"Good idea," he said, breathing hard. They struggled to get it all arranged, and then lay down side by side and he took her in his arms. She hugged him tightly.

"I'm afraid," she whispered.

"So am I."

"I want you to make love to me," she said. "But I guess it would be too dangerous. There's things out there, hunting. We need to stay alert."

"You're right," he said. She let go of him and started squirming around, and he asked, "What are you doing?"

"Getting out of my pants. Wishing, for the first time in a long time, that I'd worn a skirt, so if we have to run for it I wouldn't have to run half-naked."

"Maybe I should get out of my pants, too. So you won't be the only one running away half-naked."

"That's very considerate of you," she said. She raised her knees under the tarp and got her jeans off, then faced him and slipped her hand into the waist of his pants, and squeezed his erection. "Yes, I do think you should take off your pants."

She helped him, then took his hand and pressed it to her belly. He moved it over her hip, down her thigh, and then into curly hair and wetness. She kissed him, and he moved over her.

"I wanted to tell you . . . I've been trying for weeks to tell you that I love you."

She smiled at him. "You don't have to say that. I'm going to fuck you anyway."

"I wouldn't."

"I know," she said. But Matt noticed she didn't say she returned the love. She asked, "When?"

"When did I fall in love with you?"

"Yes."

"You want me to pinpoint a moment?"

"Sure. Can't you?"

"I'm tempted to say it happened over time, as I got to know you. But I think it really happened the first time I saw you."

She looked at him, and grinned. "Really? Love at first sight?"

"I'll have to admit it wasn't the first time it's happened to me. I used to fall in love at first sight several times a week. This was just the first time I've been able to do anything about it."

She laughed. "When did it first happen?"

"My first day of college. But she was an older woman. She was, oh, I'd guess around twenty. And I was twelve."

"You're something else, Matt. My first supergenius."

It was only later that he even thought about that, of other men she might have made love to, or been in love with. She might still be in love with another man, she had never talked about it. So maybe it was despair, surrendering to the idea that they would never go back to the world they knew. Maybe it was fear of the darkness out there and the things hiding in it. Maybe it was the need for human warmth and knowing he was the only one who could provide it. He didn't care. Just then he lived entirely in the moment, in his body and not in his head. Just then she became his entire world.

THEY never did get to sleep that night. The creatures in the dark made themselves known with rustlings, twitterings, and the occasional terrifying roar. Once they saw eyes reflecting the firelight. They threw a torch in that direction and the eyes vanished. They talked about taking watches, but decided against it. They made love again, this time more carefully, if such a thing can be done, Matt kneeling with his back against the tree they sheltered under, Susan on her hands and knees, aware of each other and aware of their surroundings, too.

When dawn came they started walking again. Within a few hours they came to a low hill overlooking a small stream. The Los Angeles River? There was no way of knowing, but they did know it was quite a few miles from the warehouse. And they weren't the first ones there. From the hilltop they could see, half a mile away, a herd of mammoths drinking and splashing.

"My god, they're magnificent," Susan whispered. And they were, too. There were about a dozen of them, with short reddish coats of hair and big curving tusks. "If only we had a camera, or some field glasses."

Matt wanted nothing more than to get away, but he didn't interfere with Susan's pleasure in seeing the beasts. If they were stuck here, and he was beginning to fear they were, being with an expert on elephant behavior was a lot more luck than he felt he deserved. And being in love with her into the bargain. They would have to learn to deal with mammoths, and much more.

"I hadn't thought about that," Susan said. "Naturally, wherever there's water, there will be other animals. We're going to have to learn to approach it cautiously, just like all the other animals. Predators hang around waterholes."

"Like right over there," Matt whispered, and pointed off to their left, where a saber-toothed cat was slowly approaching the river.

"Jesus!" Susan quickly turned and brought her rifle to bear on the cat. It was not quite as large as an African lion, but far larger than Matt would have liked. Its fangs were six inches long and it moved with the easy grace of a born killer.

"Here," Susan said, and thrust the gun toward Matt.

"I don't know anything about shooting!"

"Neither do I, I've fired it twice. It's got a gigantic kick. You're heavier than I am so maybe it won't knock you over. If it comes at us, aim in the general direction and maybe the noise will scare it away. If it doesn't, keep shooting. If you hit it anywhere you'll probably tear it to pieces."

Matt followed the beast as best he could with the sight, wondering if he should tell Susan this was the first time he'd ever held a firearm.

When the cat was no more than fifty yards away it stopped, looked at them for a long moment . . . then dismissed them and resumed his walk down toward the water. Soon it was out of sight in some bushes.

"Let's get out of here," Matt said.

"Which way?"

"Back toward the warehouse."

THEY talked about it on the way back. Their choices were stark. Neither of them wanted to move away from the warehouse; it was their only protection unless they could find a cave. Neither wanted to spend another night away from the safety of steel walls. But this river was too far away to haul water from.

"We'll just have to explore the area of the warehouse," Matt said, with more assurance than he felt. "There's bound to be watering holes. There's plenty of animals around here; they must be drinking somewhere. There might be one just over the next hill from the warehouse."

"Or we could head to the ocean," Susan said. "All rivers join the sea."

"Good idea."

A bit after noon they did find a watering hole . . . and that's when they realized they were lost.

They had been following what they thought was the trail of their elephants, in reverse, but they had apparently crossed a mammoth trail and not noticed they had taken the wrong turning. They looked around, trying to orient themselves, but other than the distant Hollywood Hills there were no landmarks to guide them.

"We should have blazed a trail," Susan said.

"Next time we will. It shouldn't be a problem. We can't lose the ocean, and the warehouse isn't far from that. How many places could it hide?" *Thousands of places*, Matt told himself, and he knew Susan realized that, too. But there was no point in thinking about that yet. They needed to find it before dark.

"I think we're north of where we should be," she said.

"I think you're right."

Now that they were looking for them, though, they noticed dozens of mammoth trails. They followed some until they started to look wrong, then backtracked and tried again, all afternoon. Finally it was getting too dark to see, and they had to admit it was time to start gathering wood and prepare themselves for another night in the open.

"We're not very good at this, are we," Susan said as she watched Matt blow on the twigs and leaves to get the fire going.

"We'll get better. We have to."

They huddled together again, too tired and frightened to make love again, and eventually they fell asleep in each other's arms.

4

"MATT, something's coming!"

He sat up quickly. There was a red glow far away through the trees. He heard the sound of breaking branches and what might have been a trumpeting elephant. Had Susan's herd returned?

"What is it?"

"It sounds like a stampede to me."

They were both standing now, looking in the direction he knew was west because he had seen the sun set over there. A wind had come up, blowing from that direction, and it brought with it the smell of smoke.

"A brush fire," Susan said.

"Los Angeles," Matt groaned. "Always either burning down or shaking apart."

Then the wind brought a sound different from the mammoth's trumpeting. The sound was answered, again and again.

"Tell me that wasn't a human voice," Matt said.

"I think it was. It sure sounded like a war cry."

"Or a hunting cry." He paused. "I think it's coming this way."

They both stared into the west. Part of the land was indeed burning, but there were also isolated points of firelight on the top of the next ridge, moving quickly down. They looked like torches.

"Somebody's herding the mammoths," Susan said in an awed whisper.

It was hard to see. It must be something like being in the heat of battle, Matt thought. He had read that confusion was the norm, that one seldom had a clear idea of what was happening, there was not a godlike perspective like you had in the movies. Night made it worse, and so did unfamiliar terrain.

Everything seemed to be happening at a distance of about a mile. What little they could see of it was on the top of a small rise, and it seemed to be moving down into the draw, getting swallowed up in the vegetation. Beyond that . . . was that a moving shape in the darkness? Was that another? It was hard to see them, though from the trumpeting they knew they must be out there.

"I think we ought to get out of here," Susan said.

"Me, too. Just take the guns, we may not have much time."

He didn't like leaving their gear, but the sounds of the mammoth hunt were getting closer pretty fast. He picked up the tranquilizer gun from the ground, wishing he had more confidence that he could hit anything with it if he needed to, or that it would bring down a mammoth faster than ten or fifteen minutes. But it was better than chucking rocks, he supposed. With the gun in one hand and the time machine in the other, he fled into the night.

Like a nightmare, he didn't know where he was, he didn't know where he was going. He wasn't sure what was behind him. About all that was missing was the sense of running in place, of being stuck to the ground, working hard and not getting anywhere.

And before they had traveled a mile, he had that, too.

He stepped in something sticky and his foot came right out of his sneaker. He didn't want to stop but he knew he had to. He leaned over and pulled at the shoe, which didn't want to come free of the ground. When it did, it trailed ropes of black goo.

"I know where we are," he shouted to Susan.

She was already some distance ahead of him, but she reluctantly hurried back.

"What's that on your shoe?"

"Tar. We're where the intersection of Wilshire and La Brea will be. We're in the tar pits." At that moment a bull mammoth crashed through the trees and faced them across a mirror-smooth pond.

He was enormous. He had to be fifteen feet high at the head, with a big hump behind that. He was covered with short fur, and his tusks extended so far from his face that he could not have pointed his head straight down without poking them into the ground. They flared out, then curved back and almost crossed each other in front of him. He was no more than fifty feet away from them, and there was nothing between them but the pond, which did not look deep.

His surprisingly small ears flared out and he lifted his trunk and bellowed. He turned in a half circle, every massive muscle in his body flexing, knocking over a tree and tearing up the ground. He trumpeted again, and charged at them. Within four steps he was up to his knees, unable to move, and rapidly sinking deeper into the tar that lay just beneath the surface of the pool.

Matt and Susan stood, frozen in place, and watched as the creature's struggles mired him ever deeper in the tar. He bellowed, he raged, he thrashed about, and nothing did any good. Soon his legs were completely below the surface.

"They're driving the mammoths into the tar pits," Matt said, in awe. The hunters could end this bull's struggles with arrows, or spears, or whatever weapons they had, or wait until it died, and carefully climb onto its back and cut away the parts they could use. An animal like this could feed a tribe for a year, if they dried the meat.

He was going to tell Susan this when he happened to glance down at the time machine. The red light was on.

"Susan . . ."

"Matt! Look!"

He looked up, and a herd of mammoths appeared on the other side of the pond. They milled around in agitation, turning back and forth between the fire and the water where the big bull was trapped. One took a tentative step into the water, sank down to her massive ankle, and pulled back out.

Matt thought *her* because, though they were gigantic, none were as big as the doomed bull. Say, ten feet high, tops. One big cow made her decision, and was heading around the water. The others hesitated, not seeming to want to leave the bull, terrified of the fire, pulled to follow what seemed to be the herd leader. But they soon fell into line behind her. In a few moments they would be right on top of Matt and Susan.

"Come on, let's try to keep the pond between us!"

"Susan, there's . . ." He looked again at the time machine. The green light was on.

"What? *What?* We've got to get moving, Matt!"

"It's on," he said, simply.

Susan frowned at him, licked her lips, and raised the elephant gun to her shoulder.

"Do what you can," she said.

Matt squatted down and opened the box.

The seven by seven by seven array of clear marbles was glowing with a pearly internal light. It was hypnotic, and strangely soothing. He could almost forget where he was, what was going on. . . .

He touched the cube with his finger. It was warm, and hummed with energy. He felt his eyes going out of focus, felt the rippling patterns of light playing with his mind. It wasn't an unpleasant feeling . . . but he knew time was running out. Or moving by, or he was moving down time's arrow in a way he couldn't completely understand. What is time? Can it be experienced any other way? There were mathematical systems that said it was possible. He brought those equations to mind, some of them reaching as far back as Albert Einstein, others new and untried.

He thought he was beginning to see a pattern.

"Matt, they're heading this way."

"Quiet. I've got to think."

"Quiet? Damn it, Matt . . ." But she shut up, and aimed the gun toward the approaching mammoths. He looked up in time to see her elevate the barrel and fire over their heads. The report was deafening, and the mammoths stopped in their tracks. But, possibly more important, it broke Matt's concentration.

I'm going crazy, he thought. I'm twelve thousand years from home, kneeling on the edge of a deadly tar pit, a dozen seven-ton behemoths bearing down on us while the land burns and unseen savage hunters lurk somewhere out there ready to kill us and cook us if the mammoths somehow miss . . . and I'm worried about a little box of marbles.

But he knew he was right. It was the little box of marbles that had got them here, somehow, and somehow it would get them out. So he concentrated.

Soon he was back into whatever zone he had started to

enter. He didn't know how to describe it, but it was a place he had learned to access when he was about six. At first it was arithmetic. He could stare at a page full of numbers and see relationships among them. Adding them up or finding percentages was just the start; the longer he stared, the more he saw. He felt the numbers were speaking to him.

A few years later the concepts of algebra and geometry hit him like puberty would in his early teens. The idea that a number could be *anything*, that a series of numbers could describe a shape . . . he was hooked for life. He invented his own form of calculus before he was twelve.

Now this hypercube was speaking to him, not in words, but in patterns that *almost* made sense. His mind whirled, a few steps behind, then a step behind, then half a step.

Without thinking too hard about it, he picked up the cube and twisted it, just like a Rubik puzzle. The top layer rotated easily, and locked into place. The pattern of chasing lights changed, but nothing else did.

This is crazy. But he ignored the small voice, and twisted again.

The cube became filled with light, and Matt felt his eyes crossing as it collapsed in on itself in a way impossible to describe, and suddenly it was six by six by six.

The cube went through another iteration that twisted Matt's stomach. It happened in a series of quick steps, each one of them seeming logical and inevitable, yet when it was done the cube was five marbles on a side, and there simply wasn't any place the . . . six cubed minus five cubed equals ninety-one . . . the ninety-one marbles on the outer surface to have gone. But they were gone, either compressed into the middle of the cube or turned through another dimension to a place his mind couldn't follow.

When Susan fired the gun again, Matt barely heard it. He was committing the events he had just seen to memory, though already he felt them fading, in the manner of a vivid dream losing its grip on reality with the return of consciousness.

"Matt, we've got to run."

"Three more seconds." He wasn't sure where the figure came from, but he knew it was accurate. He hoped it would be enough time.

Twist. Four by four by four. Sixty-four marbles left.

Twist. Twenty-seven left. It had to be getting tight in there.

Twist. Only eight now.

Twist.

He looked up to see a Los Angeles city bus bearing down on him.

16

THE herd of mammoths appeared on the Miracle Mile at 10:18 P.M. on a Thursday night, almost two days after a building belonging to Howard Christian vanished in Santa Monica.

THE matriarch of the herd didn't have a name, but the press would soon dub her Big Mama.

Big Mama was pissed.

First it was the pipsqueak bipeds with their annoying little spears, too small to do much damage to a mammoth but hurtful if one dared get in close enough to jab, carrying the hateful bright hot light, setting the world on fire. Then a long rush through the night, blinded and stumbling and terrified. Then Big Daddy sinking up to his belly in the sticky pit. It was at that point Big Mama began to get angry.

Big Mama wanted to try to help Big Daddy out of the black goo, and would have, even at the risk of getting caught herself . . . but the world was on fire. So for a few minutes she had dithered, swayed back and forth by conflicting duties and impulses and instincts, until something inside her finally broke and she left Big Daddy to his fate. It was a moment that seldom came to domesticated elephants, but trainers dreaded it like nothing else, because when an elephant's normally placid temper broke, she was capable of doing almost anything.

What Big Mama wanted to do was kill a few of these pesky bipeds. As she rounded the tar pit she could actually feel biped bones crushing under her mighty feet. It was a good feeling.

The explosion of sound startled her and stopped her in her tracks. Another member of the herd, the one with the notch in her left ear, mother of the third child to be born last birthing season, actually collided with her, something that would have been unthinkably rude normally, and would have earned her a big cuff on the head. Big Mama hardly noticed it. She had no idea a slug of lead big and fast enough to have torn through her massive skull had passed a few feet over her head. She only knew she *hated* that sound. She didn't want to go toward it.

But what was she to do? Behind her the land still burned, and she could smell the approaching hunters even over the stench of smoke. After another few moments she lowered her tusks, aimed at the two bipeds, and charged.

Before she had taken three steps, everything changed.

SUSAN was between Matt and the bus, with her back to it, her whole concentration on the herd of mammoths bearing down on them. As the brakes of the bus began to shriek, Matt got up and dived at her, his arms extended, and lifted her right off her feet, thrusting her out of the path of the bus. Then there was no time to do more than put out his hands as his feet got tangled under him. He was falling backward when the bus struck him, the bike rack on the front missing him by an inch. The back of his head hit the pavement and his vision was filled with bright points of light for a moment . . . then he looked up to see the bottom of the front bumper of the bus just above his face and, inches from his head, a massive gray foot smelling of urine and tar and elephant shit. Just above that, he had an astonishing worm's-eye view of a full-grown Columbian mammoth as she thrust forward with all the strength in her body. Glittering cubes of safety glass showered down all over him as he closed his eyes, *hard*, and hoped for the best.

SIGHT is the fastest sense, and the first thing that assaulted Big Mama was a scene in which she recognized *nothing*. A human could not have been more baffled if she had been instantly transported to the bottom of the sea.

Sound arrived next, and the only thing familiar in that cacophony was the terrified bleating of the rest of the herd behind her.

Scent information was the last to arrive in her brain with

her first massive inhalation, but it was the most important to her, and the most awful of all, because there were literally thousands of smells in the night air that were perfectly alien to her. In her normal surroundings just one strange scent made for an exciting day, and she might linger over it for many minutes, fixing it in her comprehensive library of smells, far more vast than a human mind could comprehend.

There was a crumpled McDonald's cup lying in the gutter, which had held a strawberry shake; she smelled that, had a pretty good idea where it was, no idea *what* it was, though she knew it was edible as it was related to her mental folders labeled MILK and BERRIES. On the other side of the street a woman was walking a German shepherd on a leash and Big Mama smelled that, too. It was *something* like the dire wolves she had always ignored in her world, puny little animals, but also wildly different, and mixed with a hundred other smells she could separate but not identify: shampoo, his mistress's perfume, dog food containing the cooked flesh of several different animals plus carrots, grains, charcoal, and the metallic smell of the tin the food had come in.

There were dozens of restaurants a short whiff away, each emanating a thousand smells, very few of them pleasant. There were a thousand people on the street each with an odor as distinctive as a face, each wearing clothing made of alien substances, laundered in harsh detergents, and shoes made from canvas and rubber and leather.

There were smells of creosote from phone poles, paint and plaster and brick from the buildings, a monstrous panoply of chemicals used in processing paper and plastic and cloth and electronic devices and metals and ceramics, a phantasmagoric stench that could be summed up in a word no puny Pleistocene biped had yet used in Big Mama's world: civilization.

Over it all, a vast enveloping presence, was the apocalyptic smell she classified as burning tar, the petrochemical miasma humans constantly swam through, as oblivious to it as a fish to water. The burned tar products belched from the tailpipes of the bright, low, shiny animals that darted past her on all sides, sweated off the oil-coated sides of their roaring guts, oozed off the hard asphalt surface she stood on. It was a smell antithetical to everything her heart knew as wholesome, and she hated it. *Hated it.*

Now here came another animal, an animal actually larger than Big Mama, a unique and affronting experience in itself and one she normally would have run from, being at her center a peaceful and cautious beast. But her capacity for caution was gone and there was nothing left but a red and blinding rage. She turned, faced the creature, and lunged at it. Her tusks went right through its eyes, which were hard and brittle and no match for ten feet of ivory. Inside the beast she could see other creatures, more of the damned bipeds, screaming and fleeing toward the back of the thing's bright alien belly. This made no sense, but she was far beyond any concept of sense. She roared again, and tried to flip the creature onto its back. It was too heavy, so she put one huge foot into the broken eye socket and stomped down on it.

MATT rolled through bits of broken windshield glass, rolled and rolled and was facing the bus just in time to see the front end slam down on the pavement hard enough to score deeply into the asphalt beneath it, the asphalt he had been lying on three seconds before. Dazed, overwhelmed by too many things happening too quickly, he lay there and watched the mammoth attack the city bus until he felt a hard tug on his arm, rolled over onto his back again, and looked up at Susan.

"Matt, you've got to get up!"

He scrambled to his feet. He was vaguely aware of people spilling out the back door of the bus, tumbling over each other. Susan pulled him away and they staggered together to the sidewalk and Matt watched as Big Mama did battle. Still backing up, he hit something metal, turned, and realized he was backed up on the iron fence surrounding the tar pit. In addition to the animatronic mammoth that had been mired in the tar for many years, there was now a live one, still struggling and trying to free himself.

How could that be? He had to accept that it had happened, just as the building and its contents had been swept into the past by whatever forces the machine had unleashed . . . but did the tar the mammoth was mired in come along with him—was he stuck in Pleistocene tar, or twenty-first-century tar? *How can I think about a thing like that with half a dozen mammoths raging through modern-day Los Angeles?*

If Susan was being bothered by such questions she gave no sign of it. She raised the elephant gun to her shoulder and fired it at Big Mama. It made a pathetic little *chunk*, with no recoil at all, and Matt realized it was the tranquilizer gun. She must have picked it up when he dropped it. She racked another dart into it and fired again, and then a third time, before lowering the barrel toward the ground.

"I'm afraid any more might kill her," she told Matt.

"Susan . . . you may have to kill her."

"No," Susan said. "If that has to be done, *you* do it."

As he took the gun from her, he noticed for the first time that tears were running from her eyes. He realized with a shock that this must be the realization of an elephant trainer's worst nightmare: one of her charges running berserk, too angry to reason with and too big to be stopped by anything short of deadly force. He imagined she had envisioned this situation in nightmares, on sleepless nights.

He raised the gun and aimed it at the mammoth, then wondered where the brain was in that massive head. Should he try for the heart? And where was *that*?

"A little to the left, Matt," she sighed. "But don't shoot unless you have to."

"I wouldn't dream of it." But if the mammoth turned this way and took . . . what, two steps? . . . he knew he would have to.

Make it three steps. And one more for Susan.

IF the extraordinary events of that night had happened twenty years earlier, the LAPD would have been ill-prepared to deal with them. Back then, a police special .38, a nightstick, and a shotgun were deemed adequate for any situation an officer might be likely to encounter. But several events of the intervening years had stretched the bounds of likelihood, including an encounter with two bank robbers in the Valley armed as well as a third-world nation, the Rodney King riots, several incidents involving gangs and drug dealers packing tank-killers and surface-to-air missiles, and one actual incident of an escaped elephant run amok.

Now all officers carried 9mm Glocks with twenty-cartridge magazines. Most patrol cars had military assault rifles and concussion grenades in the trunk. Stationed around the city were special weapons vehicles that could be anywhere with ten minutes' notice. And if all else failed, if howitzers and helicopter gunships were called for, there were arrangements with National Guard units that could be brought to bear anywhere in no more than half an hour.

A herd of half-crazed mammoths was a problem, but not an insoluble one.

As in any such situation, the first minutes were chaos. The word "mammoth" was never uttered over a police radio until long after the crisis was past; these were not paleontologists who were called upon to be the first line of defense against the creatures, they were police officers, and to a man and woman they referred to the animals as elephants, according to the well-known principle that if you hear hoofbeats your first thought should be *horses*, not *zebras*. If it's gray, twelve feet tall, weighs ten tons, has tusks and a trunk, anyone could be forgiven for calling it an elephant. In the end, it didn't really matter. Mammoths were just as vulnerable as elephants to the firepower the LAPD could bring to bear in an escape situation, and that firepower was being assembled.

To their credit, the responding officers did not immediately set about wiping out the animals. Their first priority was the protection of human life, but a strong second to most of them was to capture the elephants alive, if possible. Protection of property was clearly in third place, so the first officers at the scene stood by as Big Mama demolished the city bus, once it was clear there was no one inside and all nearby pedestrians and motorists had fled the scene.

Roadblocks were quickly established a block away in all directions from the site of the temporal breakthrough, and lines of cops stood behind them pointing shotguns and handguns at what might have been six, might have been eight milling and confused pachyderms. It was hard to tell in the dark, which had been made worse when several streetlight poles were knocked over by confused mammoths.

When two of the animals started to make a charge for freedom the officers in their path first tried firing into the air, and unleashed such a fusillade that the mammoths turned quickly and rejoined the milling herd.

Things remained in a standoff for almost five minutes.

HOWARD Christian was not physically suited to being the only thing he had ever really wanted to be: a superhero. He knew it was childish and so he had never told anyone of his ambition, not even when he actually was a child. What he really wanted to do was swing through the concrete canyons of New York on fibers of mutated spider silk, or grow steel claws like his favorite X-Man mutant, Wolverine.

The only thing that had ever been super about him, however, had been his brain. During one of the periods he had been in school he had been given an IQ test and the teachers had been so impressed with the result they had sent him to another testing agency for a more accurate one. He scored 185. The man giving the test told Howard it was the highest score he had ever seen on that test. For years he had treasured that number, 185, and had almost convinced himself it was the highest score ever . . . but eventually he learned of higher scores, of students who aced the SAT tests on which he had managed only a 1540. So even in that he was not the *best*, not a true mutant, not superhero material.

But what was the Green Lantern without his ring, or Batman without his gadgets? Just guys in spandex suits, that's what. When he finally convinced himself of that he set about playing to his strengths instead of bemoaning his weaknesses. He began building his own Fortress of Solitude, his Bat Cave in the sky.

Now the Dark Lord of Los Angeles, also known as Howard Christian, sat in the control seat of the Eagle of Vigilance and surveyed his realm.

He came here a lot, mostly at night, and most of all when he was upset. It was a good feeling, almost reclining in the soft leather of the chair custom-built to his body, his feet on the pan and tilt controls, no less than three keyboards arrayed in easy reach, the large red joystick with its array of buttons built into the right armrest. Before him were eight large hi-def video screens butted together so that they could display eight separate scenes or one sweeping panorama.

He liked the term Dark Lord, but that didn't mean he was bad. He felt he was up here in the tallest building in the world to do good, not evil. The dark part came from the fact that he was a creature of the night, unknown to the populace that lay spread out below him. But the night meant nothing to the Dark Lord. He had a thousand eyes: L.A.'s armada of traffic helicopters, security cams on almost every light pole in the city, and satellites that could read a newspaper from space.

If that was all he had, he would be nothing but the world's most high-tech voyeur. No, he had his own secret weapon concealed in the basement, known to only a few of his most trusted employees. Its purpose was to shoot down suicide bombers approaching the Resurrection Tower in hijacked airplanes. Travelers arriving and departing LAX didn't know it, but in addition to the FAA and Homeland Security, their planes were being tracked by Howard's secret death ray.

It was, so far as he knew, the world's most powerful microwave laser. If the military had something bigger, they weren't talking about it. It could burn a hole through armor plate, and cut an airplane in half in a microsecond. Of course, it was there only as a last resort. It had never been used. But it gave him comfort to sit here in his chair, following car chases with the crosshairs centered on some fleeing sack of shit, knowing he could vaporize the bastard with one squeeze of the trigger.

Matthew Wright. Matt and Susan and a whole goddamn warehouse full of elephants and the frozen corpse of a mammoth. Where did they go?

Howard turned his thoughts away from that, for the hundredth time that day. That's what he'd come up here to the Eagle of Vigilance for, to get his mind off this insoluble problem.

Matt Wright, whose IQ on the Stanford-Binet maxed out somewhere between 210 and 240 . . . the scale wasn't very useful in that range. . . .

“Stop it,” he said, then was startled that he had spoken aloud.

He roamed the night with his thousand eyes, his finger on the trigger, his ears tuned to the police radio.

17

BIG Mama took considerable satisfaction from stomping the big square animal. It was all sharp edges and hard as rock, and it stank like nothing she had ever encountered, but none of that bothered her. After she had knocked its eyes out she devoted herself to destroying the creature's head. Done with that she hurried to its side and began pushing, meaning to turn it on its side and attack what might be the softer underbelly. The thing might be dead already, but she wanted to make sure.

But something felt wrong.

She didn't feel so good. Her head was swimming. Her massive legs felt wobbly; she swayed for a moment, then shoved again at the big square monster. In her rage, she had not even felt the tiny bites of the tranquilizer darts as they pricked her leathery skin, but the sedatives they had contained were rapidly doing their work.

She heaved again, and the creature almost went over but then it was too much, Big Mama backed off, and the thing rocked back onto its round, smelly feet.

She blinked, and looked around, feeling more exhausted than she had in her long life. She could no longer remember where she was. What were all these new smells? What were these lights up on shiny trees with no limbs on them? What were all these noises? Big Mama was confused. She went down on her knees. Maybe if she could just sleep for a little . . .

In a moment, Big Mama fell onto her side.

THE herd was already way beyond upset. They were separated from the matriarch, huddled and milling together next to a tall, smooth cliff. The cliff was made of something smooth and clear as water, but which seemed to have no smell at all. Several times they had tried to get to Big Mama's side, and each time some of the two-legs with dark blue heads had pointed sticks at them. These sticks weren't sharp, but they were horribly noisy, noisier than anything any of them had ever heard except thunder. There was fire inside the sticks, and smoke, and the smoke smelled awful.

Now Big Mama fell over on her side. The beta female, what humans might have called the master sergeant of the herd, raised her trunk, smelled Big Mama's distress, and bellowed.

SUSAN had tried to fire her remaining tranquilizer darts at the herd of mammoths down the street, while the big matriarch was still occupied in her epic battle with the Los Angeles city bus, but she couldn't see if she hit anything with the three darts she fired. She tried to get closer but was turned back by police, who didn't have time to listen to her explanation that she might be able to sedate the beasts. All her arguments were turned aside, and she saw this wasn't the time to stand on principle. The cops were barely organized, frightened, and anything could trigger a disaster.

By then Big Mama was staggering, looking around in bewilderment. She let out a mighty bellow. Then she fell on her side. Down the street, the herd began trumpeting.

THE first call came from a frantic patrolman crouching behind his car door. He reported a rampaging elephant, then three elephants, and then an entire herd of elephants. Howard's fingers flew over his keyboards as other officers responded, giving their locations and estimated time of arrival at the corner of Wilshire and La Brea.

One of the screens before him promptly displayed the three commercial satellites currently in range of the Los Angeles area. Through long practice, Howard quickly translated the positions and derived their look-down angles in his head, then selected GEOS-324 as the one with the best view down Wilshire. As a normal user he would have to make an appointment or get in line to gain controlling access to one of the satellite's array of five high-res imaging systems, but Howard owned a company that owned a company that owned GEOS-324, so he punched in an override code, and somebody got bumped. A blurred image of five city blocks appeared on another screen, from an angle thirty degrees west off the vertical from the corner of Wilshire and La Brea. He touched another control and the camera zoomed in until only two blocks filled the screen. Available light in the city was usually enough for a pretty good picture, but Howard wasn't satisfied with what he was seeing, so he brought up a program for real-time enhancement, and the picture clarified and brightened considerably.

In the back of his mind was an equation he could not justify, but which nagged him nonetheless on a level that made his hands sweaty: One herd of elephants vanishing in Santa Monica = One herd of elephants appearing on the Miracle Mile. There was a dizzy logic to it that some primitive level of his mind could not dismiss. Those *must* be his lost elephants. He had seen films of what a rampaging elephant could do, and the idea of a herd of them running wild through a city was almost too frightening to contemplate.

The picture on his screen wasn't very clear. It looked as if some streetlights were out in the target area. He brought up an infrared image on a second screen. He enhanced it. He was presented with a view down Wilshire, looking east. Already quite familiar with interpreting the night-vision infrared orbital cameras, he quickly picked out a line of vehicles that weren't moving, out in the middle of the street, the brightest part of them being the unseen engines under the hoods. Near the curb by the park that surrounded the tar pits and the museum was a larger heat source that he quickly identified as a city bus, and right in front of it was a massive, moving object. He clicked up the magnification twice. It sure looked like an elephant, and it was doing battle with the bus. Beyond it, he could see police cars, doors open, with officers crouching behind them.

There was something odd about the elephant. Howard switched back to the visible light lens, and clicked it up two more notches. The resulting picture was grainy and indistinct, even with the real-time enhancement, but he immediately noticed the fantastically long tusks, the hump behind the animal's head, and the incredible size, four or five feet taller than his Indian elephants. Howard was the first person in Los Angeles to realize that the city was facing an invasion of mammoths.

THIS time when the herd charged, the fusillade of shots over their heads had little or no effect. The mammoths emerged at a dead run from the shadows of the building where they had been milling in confusion, and nothing less than the firepower to stop a tank was going to do anything about it. That sort of ordnance was on its way, estimated time of arrival five minutes. But for now the LAPD faced the thundering herd with nothing but handguns and assault rifles. None of the weapons at hand had the punch to reach a mammoth's brain or heart.

They held their fire as the herd reached the prostrate form of Big Mama, but the animals paused only long enough to snuffle at the sleeping mammoth with their trunks. The mammoths could tell from her smell that she was not dead, and they could see the rise and fall of her massive chest, and they might have wondered why she had picked this moment, of all moments, to lie down and snooze, but they didn't linger on the question. What was clear was that something was horribly wrong. The beta female, now the de facto herd leader, made her second command decision, raising her trunk and bellowing, a terrible declaration of frustration and rage that reached right down to the monkey part of the human brain to make every hair on the body stand up. Instantly the whole herd wheeled and charged at the line of police cars stretching across the broad street.

The cops held their positions, and most held their fire, but they couldn't hold it forever. A shot rang out, then another, and the first burst from an automatic rifle set off a fusillade that stopped the mammoths in their tracks.

The bullets from the handguns did little more than irritate the beasts, but the rifles did real damage. One cow fell to her knees, then staggered up, her head streaming blood. The firing continued, and the charge was stopped. The herd wheeled and took off rapidly in the opposite direction, west on Wilshire.

As many police and soldiers have learned when in a firefight, once you have started firing your weapon it can be very hard to stop until it is time to reload. The hail of lead continued as the mammoths ran away from the police line. Now they were being hit from behind.

In all times and in all things there was one prime instinctive directive all mammoths lived by: *The Herd sticks together*. But now herd civilization collapsed, just as human civilization did when a hundred people tried to escape a burning building through a single door. The herd ceased to exist, they no longer pressed together as they ran, but each ran blindly in whatever direction looked best to her overloaded senses. The steel and glass canyon of Wilshire Boulevard channeled them, but some were in the middle of the street, some on the sidewalks, and the one who had gone to her knees was stumbling, bewildered, over rows of parked cars, crushing hoods and trunks.

They went three blocks in a very short time, and found themselves facing another row of police cars, bumper to bumper across the road. This time the order to fire was given quickly, and once more the mammoths came to a halt, not as a group this time, but one by one as the bullets tore into their thick hide. One went down, fell on her side, and though she was breathing, she did not get up. None of the other mammoths came to her, they were far beyond noticing a fallen comrade now. The survivors wheeled once more and headed east. The street was spotted with dark puddles of blood.

Several officers came out from behind their patrol cars and began to advance on the fleeing mammoths, firing as they went. To the east, more officers were doing the same.

"NO!" Susan shouted. *"Stop shooting!"* Matt had to grab her and pull her back against the partially destroyed fence surrounding the tar pit, then force her to the ground as bullets whizzed through the air all around them. They huddled on the ground and watched as the herd fell apart, broke against the western line of cops, turned, and came back toward the original killing ground. One was down, and a second seemed to have injured herself badly, tearing a foreleg open on a jagged piece of metal from a Toyota Land Cruiser she had stomped almost flat.

"Here they come again," Matt said. "Maybe we should get behind the fence here. It won't stop them, but it might channel them away from us."

Susan could only sob as Matt pulled her to her feet and through the hole in the fence, where they crouched a little down the slight slope and watched the slaughter continue.

HOWARD watched with increasing horror as the scene unfolded before his satellite-aided eyes. The big green blobs in the infrared cameras charged west, then east, then west again. One, then two of them ceased to move.

His frustration was growing. Because of the location of the tar pits, even with his situation high in the Resurrection Tower to the south of the unfolding action, he had doubted he would be able to get a look with the telescope in the tower. He could see things happening in the nearby mountains, see into windows on the sides of buildings that faced him, and the roofs of almost any building within fifteen miles, but a two- or three-story building two miles away always blocked his view of the street beyond it. His recollection of the La Brea Tar Pits area was that such buildings stood between him and the disaster unfolding on Wilshire.

But he called up a map of Los Angeles and was surprised to see he might almost have a clear sightline right down Curson Avenue. He might be able to see the herd as they passed that street, for a few seconds.

Bringing the telescope on line, he quickly aimed it north, then aligned it with Curson Avenue in time to see the remainder of the herd, now caught in a murderous crossfire from both ends of Wilshire, turn one by one and thunder in his direction, big as life though almost three miles away. He thought he could see the blood streaming off their heads as they ran. He even fancied he could see the terror in their eyes.

One thing he was sure of. He could see the thin line of police cars, three of them set across Curson, not quite bumper to bumper, with only six officers standing behind them. And not quite a block beyond them, so that Howard was looking over their heads, was a single yellow strip of police tape tied to lampposts, holding back a crowd of several hundred people who had come out of their houses in the residential neighborhood, probably drawn by the sound of gunfire.

The scene unfolded like a bad dream. The mammoths turned south down the street. The police could be seen shouting at each other, unprepared for what was bearing down on them. Two broke away without firing a shot, running toward the crowd of civilians and screaming at them. The other cops fired at the mammoths . . . three, four, five of them, Howard counted . . . then they too turned and ran. Most of the crowd started to run but, incredibly, a few stood their ground, as if they thought they were watching a television show or a really good movie special effect. Only when the mammoths crashed over and through the prowl cars did the reality of the situation completely sink in.

With a flash of heat on his face, Howard realized . . . *This is it.* This is my superhero moment.

Howard had made many important decisions in his life, critical decisions, even momentous decisions. But every once in a while—and it was by no means certain that a particular person would *ever* find himself in this situation—you might find yourself looking at something that you *knew* must be decided in the next two or three seconds, and that the lives of people you could *see* would be affected, not financially, but in the saving or losing of life itself. A situation where a mistake would be expressed in the spilling of innocent blood, and where proper conduct would save that life. Cops and firemen and medical people faced these situations as part of their jobs. Superheroes faced these life-or-death choices two or three times in every issue. And they acted.

Howard acted.

The narrower street had funneled the individual mammoths back into something resembling a herd. They were no more than fifty feet from the first fleeing onlookers. Beyond that there was nothing to stop them all the way to San Vicente Boulevard, where traffic was still flowing normally. If they weren't stopped now, they might rampage for a long time through residential neighborhoods before the LAPD could corner them and bring them to their inevitable end.

That they were doomed seemed beyond argument. So, with a sick feeling in his stomach, Howard Christian brought the crosshairs to bear on the bloodied head of the lead mammoth, and squeezed the trigger.

Down in the bottommost basement of the Resurrection Tower, behind a vault door monitored by a retinal scanner that would recognize and admit only three people in the world, sat the Beam of Death. It wasn't as big as you'd expect it to be, no larger than a standard outdoor garbage can, though the other devices needed to charge it and operate it filled a fair-sized room. Massive cables attached it to the fusion power plant located on the level just above, and when Howard squeezed the trigger electricity flowed through these cables and pumped energy into the laser. For an instant, all the lights of the Resurrection Tower, shining opulently through the southern California night as they always did, dimmed. The energy that had been accumulating leaped forth, straight up through a vacuum pipe running through the center of the building, hit a moveable mirror just behind the eye of the Eagle of Vigilance, and burst forward into the air. The beam spread only slightly in the nanosecond it took to travel from the tower to Curson Avenue, losing no more than 2 percent of its power. Another 1 percent was lost to resistance of the molecules in the air, and for a second there was a corridor of charged particles and steam that might have been visible in the daytime, but which quickly dispersed. Someone below might have heard a faint hiss of the beam's passage, but in most places traffic noise was much louder. Other than that, the Beam of Death was virtually undetectable. There was no blazing streak of red or green or violet light, no Hollywood sizzle or zap or rolling thunder of special-effect sound. Just that little hiss and a momentary tunnel of fog.

The effect when the beam hit the first mammoth was spectacular enough to make up for all that.

THE firing continued for a few more seconds, then an eerie quiet descended over the street, broken almost at once by the arrival of the first police helicopter. Those present were later shocked to learn that only seven minutes had passed from the mammoths' first appearance to their headlong flight down Curson.

As the searchlight beam from the helicopter played over the street in front of the tar pits, officers began to emerge from behind their vehicles, shaken but still very much pumped. Many of them waved to the helicopter pilot, directing him to the street where the mammoths had turned. The blinding pool of light swung down Curson, and the men and women in blue followed, at a run.

WHEN the shooting stopped, Matt and Susan clambered up the slope from the edge of the tar pool and saw the police heading down Curson, right in front of them.

"Come on!" Susan shouted, and started running down the street.

"What are we going to do?" Matt asked when he caught up with her.

"Stop them," she said.

"Stop . . ." He supposed asking her *how* was not the sort of thing a supportive soul mate should do, but he couldn't help wondering. He wasn't sure Susan meant to stop the mammoths or the police, or both, and wasn't sure which would be the easier task, but he had to admire her flat-out, no-questions-asked, no-prisoners-taken *commitment.*

And looking ahead, he began to wonder if stopping the police would even be a good idea, assuming they could do it, because just beyond them the battered and bloodied herd had just swept aside the thin wall of police cars on the narrow side street and were within a few feet of the half-dozen spectators too slow, stunned, or stupid to move out of the way. He saw a young mother holding a crying child, rooted to the spot, and an old man clinging to his aluminum walker. It looked to Matt like there was nothing to stop or even slow down the thundering herd.

That was when the first mammoth exploded.

There was no big bang and no flames. The massive head simply came apart in a shower of blood and meat and bone, and the ten-ton pachyderm hurtling along at fifteen or twenty miles per hour stopped dead and was shoved backward ten feet as if by a giant hand, tumbling onto its back and into the mammoth following it. A stream of blood fountained from the corpse like a high-pressure hose into the face of the second mammoth, which fell over the body, bellowing in terror. Matt thought he could hear a bone snap in the animal's foreleg, but it was struggling to its feet when it, too, blew up. This time Matt heard a sound he later described as a giant hammer hitting a slab of meat on a butcher's block, and huge chunks of the mammoth's body were flying through the air. The air was thick with the smell of burning meat. The animal was almost cut in half, dead before it hit the ground.

The cops had stopped running and simply stood there, weapons pointing at the ground, almost as stunned as the mammoths. Matt and Susan came to a stop a few yards behind the police, breathing hard.

"What is happening, Matt?" she gasped.

"I have no idea." Then he looked down the street, past the traffic at the end, beyond the low buildings, and saw the bright pinnacle of the Resurrection Tower looming through the night. The eyes of the gigantic eagle were looking right at him, and they glowed with bright menace.

Things began sliding into place in Matt's mind, like little marbles sliding around in their metal racks.

HOWARD fired a third time, then a fourth, and now there was only one mammoth left standing. The animal didn't even try to move. All the fight, even all the fear seemed to have gone out of her. Too overloaded with impossible sights and sounds, standing in the middle of the carnage that had been her herd, the only home she had ever known, she simply gave up. Blood seeped from dozens of bullet wounds.

The young woman with her child had finally managed to get moving and was nowhere to be seen. There was no one left within fifty feet of the lone surviving mammoth, in fact, but the old man standing with his walker, looking at least as stunned as the mammoth. He could almost have reached out and touched her.

Then at the bottom of his screen Howard saw two bulky men in black clothing and helmets running north on Curson, their backs to him. They were the first of the special weapons teams to arrive, in full combat gear and bringing something heavy enough that they had to carry it between them. They took a position a hundred feet away and set the weapon down on a tripod. One of the men squatted behind it.

The old man had gotten maybe ten feet away from the mammoth when she began to follow him. She had never been the alpha, beta, or even gamma cow in the herd, she had been following all her life and now, in her extremity, her instinct took over.

There was a flash of light, and Howard realized the special weapons team had fired a warning shot over the cow's head.

"No, don't shoot," Howard muttered through clenched teeth.

But they did. Howard saw fingers of orange light streak from the barrel of the machine gun—

—AND Matt saw a line of big holes stitch themselves across the last mammoth's side and, incredibly, punch out the other. The noise of the gun was stunning. Susan's fingers tightened on his biceps and her fingernails dug in hard enough to draw blood, but he hardly felt it.

The mammoth must have been dead before her knees even touched the pavement. She tottered like that for a moment, then fell onto her side.

FOR Howard, it all happened in a ghastly silence, like watching a horror movie with no sound track. First the awful necessity of killing those magnificent beasts, blood of innocents on his own hands, he accepted that responsibility.

He liked animals; he would never have bought the circus if he hadn't.

Plus, the value of a herd of mammoths was almost beyond calculation.

Plus . . . imagine the liability problems if this incident could somehow be traced back to him.

But that last one, that poor stunned animal could have been stopped, could have been contained, captured, caged, possibly even patched up and trained. If it was permanently maddened from this trauma, it would be a gold mine even in a zoo setting. But trained, performing . . .

In his mind's eye he saw the lights dim in the big top, heard the drum roll, heard the dramatic voice of the ringmaster, his voice echoing over the public address:

"And now, ladies and gentlemen and children of all ages . . . Ringling Brothers, Barnum and Bailey Circus . . . a Howard Christian Company . . . the Greatest Show On Earth for over a century . . . proudly presents . . . after an absence from planet Earth of over ten . . . thousand . . . years! . . . The Columbian Mammoth!" It was an announcement he had been dreaming of for over a decade, and now not only did he not have living mammoths from the past, all his most promising hybrids had vanished to wherever his building, his host-mother elephants, and two of his employees had gone. Howard didn't know where that was, but it was starting to look like it was the Pleistocene Era.

God *damn* them, trigger-happy cops.

He took a last look at the scene of slaughter, the remains of what could have been the biggest circus attraction the world had ever seen, now just heaps of steaming meat with a baffled old man sitting on his ass on the asphalt beside his walker right in the middle of it, and reached for his phone to dial Warburton. Howard sensed there was going to be a *lot* of coverage of this incident, inquiries, commissions, press snooping around, private "advocates" of one stripe or another, most of them looking for somebody to sue for damages, and he needed to alert his senior fixer to get cracking on containment, at whatever cost. Then he spotted Matthew Wright standing there on the street behind the line of police.

Matt Wright, *Doctor* Matthew Wright, with his 1600 SATs, his IQ off the end of the charts, Matt Wright who was able to do without apparent effort things that Howard Christian had worked his ass off all his life to achieve. Matt goddamn Wright who had the temerity, the gall to *accuse* Howard of . . .

He zoomed in on Matt's face. It was a much more battered face than it had been the last time Howard saw it. Blood and dirt were smeared across it in about equal measure. His clothes were tattered, his hair was filthy. Howard nudged the controls of the telescopic sight and now, in addition to dirt and a smear of blood, crosshairs appeared on Dr. Wright's forehead. Howard felt his trigger finger twitch.

Matt was talking to a woman standing next to him. Howard realized it was Susan, the elephant keeper. She didn't look too great, either, and she was crying. He wished he could hear what they were saying.

For a moment, Matt was looking right into Howard's eyes, as if daring him to shoot. He could almost feel the gigawatts of power gathered in the basement, coiled like a snake, ready to lash out at the speed of light with the application of only a few ounces of pressure from Howard's finger.

He took a deep breath, and removed his hand from the trigger. At almost the same moment, Matt turned and, pulling on Susan's hand, hurried away down Curson Avenue, directly away from Howard, almost as if he sensed the danger.

"Warburton!" Howard shouted into his microphone. "Warburton, get up here, you son of a bitch! I need you!"

"SUSAN," Matt said, "I'm going to have to go away for a while."

They had returned to the corner of Curson and Wilshire, walking at first, then running, Matt having to drag Susan. When they reached the sidewalk in front of the tar pit Matt stopped and looked around. It was amazing, the amount of damage done. All the trees in the median strip had been knocked down. Cars had been trampled. Shattered glass glittered in the remaining streetlights. There was the smell of spilled gasoline and gun smoke.

It took a while for Matt's statement to penetrate through the fog of horror in Susan's mind. Finally she looked at him and frowned.

"Go away? Where?"

"I don't know. There are some things I have to work out. It may take . . . a while. I'm not sure how long."

"But how will I—"

"I can't say any more now, there isn't time. I'll try to contact you as soon as possible. Until then . . . it's very important. I hope you'll just trust me for now."

"I trust you, Matt, but—"

"I'm sorry, Susan; I'm truly sorry. But there's no time. I love you." There was no time, no time at all, and he pulled her close to him and kissed her fiercely, then turned and ran, not daring to look back.

Susan stood there for a moment, watching him vanish into the night. Suddenly the reaction set in, all the horror of the worst night of her life, and she sat down on the twisted remains of the fence that had separated the sidewalk from the tar pits and the audio-animatronic mammoths that had been forlornly waving their trunks at the passing traffic on Wilshire for decades. Emergency workers were running up and down the street in front of her, police were setting up more secure barriers to keep out the curious while the scene of the catastrophe was investigated. Not far to her left people were cautiously approaching the huge bulk of Big Mama, still on her side, and apparently still breathing.

Susan got to her feet and was about to move in the direction of Big Mama to see if her life could be saved, when something made her turn around and look at the outdoor diorama behind her. At that moment a helicopter, searching for any animals that might have been missed, swept its high-intensity beam over the rubber mammoths, lingered for a moment, then moved on, apparently satisfied that these were just museum exhibits.

But one of them wasn't. Cowering at the side of the female on the bank of the tar pit, between the cow and her calf, was a second baby mammoth, this one entirely covered in thick, reddish black hair. It saw Susan and took a step toward her, then retreated back into the shadows of its new surrogate mother and attempted to nurse.

18

THE lights dimmed slowly under the big top until the audience in the bleachers, just back from the intermission with their hands full of expensive popcorn and chips and fresh paper cups of beer, was left in darkness broken only by the faint radiance seeping through the glass ring of skyboxes above and behind them, where the corporate sponsors and the very rich dined on prime rib and lobster and caviar and sipped champagne. There was a burst of excited noise that gradually fell away. The sound of the electronic music, when it came, hammered out of suspended planar speakers like a living thing, beginning on an almost supersonic note and plunging rapidly to spaces way, way, way below the bass clef, became a rumble that grabbed at the guts and shook one's entire body.

Then came the voice of the ringmaster.

"Ladies and gentlemen . . . and children of all ages . . ."

A thousand computer-controlled pencil spotlights blazed in a hundred colors and swept crazily around the arena as the music swooped stereophonically from one end of the big top to the other. Fog belched from hidden ducts, and soon the spotlight beams were slicing through it like crazed laser warfare.

". . . Ringling Brothers, Barnum and Bailey Circus . . ."

The spotlights suddenly merged on a gigantic, flat black curtain at the far end of the arena. The curtain opened slowly to each side to reveal . . . a second scalloped curtain of red velvet.

". . . a Howard Christian Company . . ."

The velvet curtain began to rise at a tantalizing creep, the sound of a thousand snare drums beginning what sounded like the world's longest drum roll. Slowly, slowly a massive proscenium arch was revealed: two stylized giant ground sloths carved from ice, thirty feet tall, backed by a stainless steel arch that reached even higher.

". . . the Greatest Show On Earth for over . . . one . . . hundred . . . and . . . thirty . . . years . . ."

Jungle sounds began to enter the mix, a polyglot, nonsensical, multicontinental cacophony of wild animals that might have been cribbed from an old Johnny Weissmuller Tarzan picture: monkeys chattering, macaws cawing, lions and tigers and bears roaring, lizards hissing, kookaburras doing their kookaburra thing.

". . . takes you back to the last Ice Age, when vast sheets of ice covered the very ground we now stand on . . ."

Now the collective gasp of the audience could actually be heard over the hugely pumped sound track as the vast, billowing big top disappeared to be replaced by towering clouds in a sky so impossibly blue it hurt the eyes, the clouds forming and dissolving and whipping by in time-lapse madness, and maybe the guy sitting next to you breathed in an awed voice *How did they do that?* if he wasn't in on the trick, which was that, though the big top looked like a gigantic tent from the outside—it *was* in fact a gigantic tent, outside—the acres of canvas covered an inner layer that was actually the world's largest spread of millimeter-thick hi-def television screens which had cost *millions*, set over an arena that had been dug into the ground deeply enough that the "skyboxes" were in fact slightly below ground level, and the gently billowing shrouds of honey-colored canvas you had been seeing for the last half hour while the lights were up during the intermission was actually only the *picture* of the inside of a big top.

". . . and proudly presents . . ."

And now a wind began to howl, a cold wind thrust from a solid ring of ducts mounted atop the skyboxes, a wind generated from air that had been supercooling for three hours in frosty refrigeration chambers, impelled now into the arena by fans that used to power supersonic wind tunnels. Hats were blown off, hair mussed, and a trillion goosebumps crawled over acres of exposed skin. Children shrieked in delight and women snuggled under the arms of their menfolk and complained of the chill while the men laughed and tried to pretend they weren't cold, too.

"... *after an absence from planet Earth of over ten ... thousand ... years! ...*"

Overhead, night fell rapidly, blazing stars embedded in a sky so dark it shimmered like polished obsidian, a sky presided over by a full yellow moon that had to be five times—no, ten times—wait a minute—*twenty* times as large as the moon ever appeared from the Earth, even in the Ice Age, the moon was no closer then, *was it, Daddy?* of course it wasn't, it's what they call artistic license, sweetheart, or maybe they call it making it up as they go along, but it's a heck of a show, isn't it, sweetie, so why don't you be quiet for a minute and watch it?

And then, silence. Silence and darkness, all the music and animal sounds and air blowers suddenly quiet and all the lights off, only the murmurings of the crowd filling the dark and almost at once that tapered off, too, as everyone knew something big was about to happen ... and then, what was that smell?

Well, it was essence of mammoth, that's what it was, and it was issuing from tiny openings in each and every chair in the joint, angled up at the faces ... and essence was the right word, but it was a slightly edited essence, wasn't it, there was the musky smell of mammoth hide, the dusty smell of mammoth feet, even the slightly rotten odor of masticated hay and pulverized fruits and vegetables that made up the brown stuff that accumulated around mammoth teeth ... but there was the merest whiff of what was actually the dominant olfactory impression one got if one walked even within a city block of any mammoth habitat and that was, not to put too fine a point to it, mammoth shit. But nobody ever said the circus was about realism, the circus was about *super*reality, taking real animals and people and putting them on a wonderful stage and hyping them up and watching them do fantastic things. And the overpowering odor of mammoth dung swamping one's nostrils was definitely definitely *not* on the menu of anybody's concept of entertainment, so the carefully crafted smell had just a whiff, just enough to titillate the noses of the city-bred audience, no worse than strolling through a carefully tended horse barn at the county fair.

And talk about your superreality, now the darkness of the giant screens overhead gave way to shadowy movements, to vast bulks blocking out the stars and being briefly silhouetted against the awesome globe of the moon. Legs thick as skyscrapers rustled through grasses as tall as pine trees all around the arena, and for one brief, stunning moment, a dark phantom seemed to step right *over* the crowd, one gargantuan leg at a time. And just when people were beginning to wonder if the ringmaster was going to speak again or if he had been struck dumb by the wonder of it all, his voice thundered out again with the words they'd all been waiting for . . .

". . . The Columbian Mammoth . . . Big Mama!"

Well, that wasn't *precisely* what they had been waiting for, but it was good enough, it would do for now because everyone knew that what they had all really come to see would be there in his own good time, this was merely setting the stage, and after all, this was the Greatest Show On Earth, an organization that would never disappoint, these were circus people who knew that building the anticipation was almost as important to the show as the main attraction itself.

And what a buildup!

The night sky was suddenly shattered by a meteor shower the likes of which the planet hadn't seen since the last major asteroid strike, first a hundred, then a thousand streaks of blue-white and pale yellow and blazing green, some exploding silently at the end of their trajectories, then larger chunks, some hitting the ground on the far side of the mountains that could now be seen not only by moonlight, but by meteor light. Explosions could be heard (and nobody cared that the speed of sound dictated that most of those impacts wouldn't be heard until whole minutes had passed, this was show business, not science) and it looked like the Earth was on fire over there, and then one hit on this side of the mountains and the entire gigantic building shook, hard enough to spill a few drinks in the skyboxes and to cause gasps of genuine alarm from those who hadn't read the warning in the program books designed to prevent an earthquake panic ("Explosions, bright flashing lights, and harmless seismic effects are included in tonight's show!"). And not one voice was raised in protest that a giant asteroid impact had killed off the *dinosaurs*, sixty million years ago, not the mammoths in the recent past.

And now, here it came . . . well, no, not yet, but once more no one complained, because what did come was the elephants.

The great steel doors beneath the arched icy ground sloths sprang open and they lumbered out, twenty of them, in full circus regalia of red leather harness studded with brass, multicolored drapes big enough to carpet a fair-sized room hanging from their sides, and headdresses of pink feathers. Ten went left and ten went right around the oval arena floor and they spread out evenly, then turned to face the center. Then all twenty elephants reared up on their hind legs and raised their trunks and started trumpeting, a truly amazing sound, considering that their already ear-splitting volume was caught by throat mikes, amplified, and sent to the speakers overhead.

And now, this is it, this is really and truly it. The spotlights converged on the icy arch and slowly, hobbled by a thick chain connecting her front legs, Big Mama lumbered into the center of the floor.

You couldn't say she dwarfed the assembled Indian elephants . . . well, P. T. Barnum probably would have said it, he claimed his famous Jumbo stood thirteen feet high at the crown of his head, but he never let anyone measure him while he was alive . . . but she stood in relation to her attendant pachyderms as a Clydesdale would to an ordinary horse. She was in *fact* thirteen feet tall at her tallest point, which was her massive, humped shoulders, and none of the Indian elephant honor guard topped out at much over ten feet . . . and come to think of it, maybe that *does* qualify as dwarfing them.

But her tusks. Her *tusks*!

They were the crowning glory of the Columbian Mammoth, growing almost straight out from her face, then curving inward until they almost touched, ten feet from her mouth. They had been yellowish in color when she was captured on the streets of Los Angeles, but assiduous dental care had made them gleam white as a toothpaste advertisement.

Big Mama was a show business veteran by now, used to the bedlam, the flashing lights and the noise and the smells that at one time were so alien to her. It also didn't hurt that a tranquilizer pill the size of an apple had been mixed with her feed an hour before showtime because, though the circus didn't like to talk about it much, Big Mama still had a streak of wildness in her, had been known to lash out without warning, had in fact seriously injured her chief trainer a few years ago because, after all, you can't keep an animal in a tranquilized torpor twenty-four hours a day even if, with an animal like Big Mama, you might like to.

But the big cow had never been known to act up when the spotlight was on her, it was almost as if she enjoyed performing, and she was a trooper tonight, following docilely behind her handler, an anonymous woman with a slight limp dressed all in black so as to be as unobtrusive as possible, like those Japanese *Bunraku* puppeteers who manipulated their life-sized mannequins right out in plain sight but were hardly noticed. She lumbered once around the ring to thunderous applause, the crowd on its feet, bringing down the house. On the screens above, dawn broke, and computer-generated mammoths fully as convincing as real ones circled with her, and if you thought that forty or fifty hundred-foot images of mammoths above would somehow detract from the majesty, the massive dignity, the sheer star power of Big Mama, you would have been wrong; this audience had been weaned on huge screens in outdoor stadiums cheering for the Raiders or the Dodgers, they were used to towering images in replay or magnifying the actions that were tough to see from the nosebleed seats, they loved it, they understood it was just a setting, a backdrop, that it made Big Mama *more* of a towering figure.

She made two circuits of the arena with the ring of elephants alternately saluting her or being urged into other tricks by their black-clad handlers—headstands, dances, daisy chains, stand perches—and it helped cover up the fact that Big Mama essentially had only one "behavior" to demonstrate, which was standing on her hind legs with her head aimed up so that the tips of her tusks were thirty feet above the ground, waving her trunk around and bellowing, and few people knew how hard it had been to get a crusty old bitch like her to do even that. Training elephants, like training any large and dangerous animal, relied on the animal accepting the unlikely idea that the human trainer, though demonstrably smaller and weaker, was in fact bigger and stronger than the trained animal, that the human ought, *by natural right*, to be the dominant figure in the social contract, and Big Mama had been the leader of her herd for too long to accept that idea with any regularity or consistency unless lulled by large doses of tranquilizers.

"*And now, ladies and gentlemen and children of all ages . . . ,*" the ringmaster intoned, and blah, blah, blah, the show went on for a full half hour, a strange mix of Las Vegas and the Discovery Channel. Showgirls swung down on ropes from hatches concealed in the overhead screen, clad in a lot of pink feathers and not much else, and landed on the backs of the elephants, who did more tricks . . . sorry, behaviors. At the same time unctuous voices took the audience through the evolution of the order Proboscidae, from the humble little piggish ancestral Moeritherium, up evolutionary backwaters and dead ends to Dinotherium with its peculiar downturned tusks, Platyhelodon with its massive shovel jaw, pausing a moment to ponder the oddities of the Rynchotheres, of Stegodon, Mastodon, Stegomastodon, Zygolophodon, and Archidiskodon, each defunct genus and species faithfully rendered and animated on the heavenly telestrator like moving constellations, until all heads in the audience were swimming in more unwanted Latin gobbledygook than they'd encountered since the classrooms of the ninth grade, right up to what the announcer implied were the three crowning glories of the Probiscideans: Elephas, Loxodonta, and Mammuthus, better known as Indian and African elephants and the family of mammoths: Imperial, Columbian, and Great Woolly. And the narrative left little doubt that of these the greatest of the great was the Great Woolly.

So where *was* the Great Woolly? For the first time, the audience began to get a little restless.

This did not go unnoticed by the producers of the show. Hidden in every tenth seat were electronic devices that functioned pretty much like a lie detector, measuring heart and respiration rate, palm sweat, and the pressure of butts on seats. Lasers were constantly scanning the audience, measuring pupil dilation and analyzing posture. These factors were inserted into a complex entertainment algorithm to produce a satisfaction index, and every night this presentation produced the lowest value. But Howard Christian liked this part of the show, so it stayed in.

Finally the arena was cleared, the lights and the tent screens faded to black, and one spotlight and every eye in the place swung once more to the grand entrance arch. You could practically feel the ringmaster take a deep breath and then announce, in his most grandiloquent manner—which could have taught the Lord God Almighty Himself thundering *"Let there be light!"* a thing or two about pomposity—

"And now, without further ado, the star of the show, the most famous, the most beloved animal in the world, the Great Woolly Mammoth . . . Little Fuzzy!"

19

LITTLE Fuzzy the Great Woolly Mammoth was no longer exactly little, not really fuzzy, and technically not a woolly mammoth, but it was hard to deny his greatness. He was the biggest animal star in history, bigger than Jumbo, bigger than Seabiscuit, Lassie, Flipper, Secretariat, and King Kong. He was bigger than Mickey Mouse.

HOWARD Christian had arrived on that night of carnage five years ago in a 1935 Mercedes roadster, one of the few sights that could have appeared on Wilshire Boulevard that would have distracted anyone's eye from the horrors all around. He was trailed by four Hummers full of Beverly Hills attorneys, public relations people, bodyguards, and general fixers, under the command of Warburton. Some of these people managed to work three cell phones at once, rousting everyone in the Los Angeles area who could help support the premise Howard Christian was determined to establish: that this debacle, all of it, was the responsibility of Howard Christian and no one else, that he would indemnify the city and all the citizens who had suffered damage, that he would in fact begin cleaning up the mess *right now* . . . and that consequently, and as an acknowledgment thereof, salvage rights would devolve upon him, his corporations and representatives and assigns, including the sedated female mammoth lying by the bus, the bull mired up to his ears in La Brea tar, and the heaps of meat that used to be female mammoths lying in the middle of Curson Avenue. That the animals that had appeared suddenly in the night were, in fact, *his*.

Within a few more minutes the police and emergency response commanders were answering their own phones and getting their orders from the very top levels. Many of them resented it, at least at first, until they saw how quickly and efficiently the scene was being managed, and then it occurred to many of them that this could turn out to be the biggest shitstorm to hit L.A. since Rodney King, and did they really want their names written down anywhere near it? Of course they didn't. The killing of the herd had gone out on live television, and it was not going to go down well with animal lovers around the world. Best to let Christian shoulder the blame.

Miraculously, there were no reports of anyone having been killed or even seriously injured in the catastrophe, though the property destruction had been enormous. Crime scene procedures were drastically shortened, as no one could think of any actual crime that had been committed unless someone had deliberately unleashed the animals on an unsuspecting city. So Big Mama and her slaughtered herd were hastily photographed, even as Warburton's trucks were backing up to haul them away. The fate of the male mammoth, eventually to be known as Big Daddy, was handed off to Howard and Warburton with almost audible sighs of relief.

It wasn't until the arrival of a large horse trailer at the edge of the tar pit itself that anyone other than Howard's people even knew there was a third mammoth still alive.

SUSAN witnessed the arrival of Howard's ridiculous car with more relief than she would have believed possible.

Every second for the last half hour she had feared that she and the baby mammoth would be discovered. The bull mammoth was mired no more than a hundred feet from where she stood, his mighty head moving less and less frequently, his trunk lashing wildly, getting stuffed with the thick goo which he would then snort out, each time more fitfully than the last. Many times flashlights swept over him and she heard people shouting about bringing up some big lights, but that was apparently delayed.

The streetlights in the area were mostly knocked down, and the outdoor diorama was in deep shadow. Twice flashlights illuminated the phony bull in the pool and the phony cow and calf standing on the shore, but Susan was standing behind a thick palm tree and whoever had the flashlight either didn't see the real baby mammoth or accepted it as part of the display, even when he moved his little trunk over the plastic flank of his temporary surrogate mother, and the beam moved on.

At first she had doubted her ability to keep the baby concealed. Looking at him, she figured he ran somewhere between three and four hundred pounds; if he wanted to bolt, how was she, at one thirty soaking wet, going to stop him?

But he had proved amazingly tractable. Mostly he seemed content to hover in the shadow of the big statue. If he started to move away Susan moved toward him, and he quickly retreated to what he must have thought of as safety. It seemed reasonable, from his point of view. *If this auntie here isn't afraid of the two-legs, why should I be?*

She had no idea what to do. One thing she was sure of, though, and that was that this baby was not going to be slaughtered like the others, most of which were probably his aunts and one of which was almost certainly his mother. If she had to stand between the baby and the bullets, so be it. She was not going to let this one get away.

And so, for the first time since she had met him, she was happy to see Howard arrive. Whatever else he might be, Howard was power, and power got things done in this world.

It took her a while to get Howard's attention as he strode up and down the sidewalk above her, shouting into his cell phone or at Warburton. The shadows that had protected her now frustrated her in her attempts to flag him down, there was still too much hubbub for her to easily make herself heard, and she was afraid if she made too much noise she might spook the calf. Once Howard almost seemed to hear her hissed words. He looked around and so did one of his bodyguards, but they didn't see her. He strode off up the street and she almost cried.

He was back soon, but this time a helicopter overhead drowned out any sounds she could make. She scrabbled around on the dark ground, looking for a good rock, but all she could come up with were a few clods of dirt. She started throwing them, and the third exploded at his feet. He stared at it dumbly for a moment, then he looked up in the air as if wondering if he was being pelted by meteors, and at last one of his entourage pointed down the slope to where Susan stood with one hand held out and one finger held to her lips, hoping she was getting across *Be quiet, and don't come down here yet!*

Howard gestured to another of his men, this one holding a big Maglite—the great man doesn't even carry his own flashlight, he hires help for that—and in a moment Susan's eyes were dazzled, then the beam swept over the baby mammoth, on past it . . . and she heard a shout even over the racket of the helicopter. Howard stood there with his jaw dropped and his eyes wide, then he shoved the flashlight away and was frantically signaling to his people, all of whom turned their backs, as Howard did, as four Los Angeles uniformed police walked by in the street. He stood there among them, hands clasped behind himself and looking casually at the sky, in what he apparently thought was an innocent attitude. *My god, was he actually whistling, too?* Susan wondered how he ever got away with anything as a kid if that was the best he could do. When the cops had gone by, he casually turned and gave her a broad wink over his shoulder. Her opinion of his ability to handle this mess plummeted.

She needn't have worried. Howard had learned long ago the secret of getting things done, and it was simple: Hire the people who know how to get things done. He was at that moment surrounded by a dozen such types, headed by the very able Mr. Warburton, the ablest of them all. If Warburton didn't know how to get it done, he knew somebody who knew somebody who knew somebody who did. So he turned to Warburton and said:

"Forget all other priorities I just gave you. We need that baby mammoth out of here, and the sooner the better."

Warburton turned to one of his minions and gave his instructions, and more phone calls were made. Ten minutes later a moving van pulled up to the closest police tape on Wilshire, and a dozen very large men got out. They were given their instructions, and proceeded cautiously down the gentle slope to where Susan was standing. They surrounded the little mammoth, ropes were attached, and the squealing infant was unceremoniously wrestled up the slope, over the collapsed fence, and into the back of the van, while a crowd of cops, emergency workers, reporters, and curiosity seekers looked on. Live images of the capture were fed to a worldwide audience by the dozens of news cameras present both on the ground and in the air.

Susan was already working her telephone as the door slammed on the back of the van—and kicking herself for not thinking of it a few minutes ago. She could have called Howard, standing fifty feet away! But things had been a little hectic there, and she hoped she could be forgiven for overlooking it.

She knew all the elephant keepers from the Griffith Park Zoo, and within an hour most of them were on their way to the Miracle Mile.

When Big Mama woke and staggered to her feet, it was to find herself completely immobilized with ropes and nets. She was bullied and prodded until, not without difficulty, she was induced up the ramp of a giant stake-sided flatbed truck to begin her slow progress through streets lined with most of the population of Beverly Hills, Hollywood, and all intervening Los Angeles neighborhoods until she reached the elephant house at the zoo, at three in the morning.

At the same time crews were trying to figure out how to rescue Big Daddy, but it was hopeless. By the time Big Mama arrived at her temporary new home, the bull had ceased to move, and shortly afterward a veterinarian declared him dead, suffocated by the increasing pressure as he sank into the black ooze. The operation was immediately switched from a rescue to one of recovery. Howard did not intend to let twelve tons of mammoth meat and bones—and viable spermatozoa—be swallowed up to emerge in another twelve thousand years as blackened bones. By the time the sun came up a massive crane had been moved into place, stabilized and counterbalanced. A giant claw, normally used for horsing entire giant eucalyptus logs onto truck beds, plunged into the asphalt and clamped around Big Daddy's corpse. Ribs could be heard cracking as the claw plucked the body free like a cork from a bottle of very bad vintage wine.

These three ultradramatic operations drew attention away from a fourth one going on at the same time on Curson Avenue. As helicopter cameras followed the progress of the trucks carrying Big Mama and the calf, other trucks had arrived on the side street, other cranes and forklifts were gathering every scrap of still-steaming mammoth meat and hustling it into refrigerated vans, which sped off to an undisclosed location. There wasn't a news director in the world who would cut away from the frantic attempts to save Big Daddy to shots of bullet-riddled pachyderm corpses with exploded heads, but by the time the big bull was dead the remains of the other adult cows were nowhere to be found, and even the gallons and gallons of blood had been hosed away. It was as if it had all been a dream, the slaughter on Curson Avenue, and if there hadn't been the video to prove it had happened many people would have preferred to leave it that way.

In fact, by the time Big Daddy was hauled off at noon the next day, Wilshire Street and Curson Avenue were already almost back to normal. All the damaged vehicles had been towed away. Glaziers had replaced all the windows either shot out by police or broken by mammoths. Street sweepers had sucked up the shards of broken windshields and the sawdust spread to soak up spilled crankcase oil and gasoline, city crews were replacing or repairing streetlights. The new palm trees to replace the ones in the median strip on Wilshire, their roots wrapped in big burlap bundles, were being lowered into freshly dug holes.

By two that afternoon, not much more than fifteen and a half hours after the arrival of the mammoths, traffic was flowing smoothly again, and Howard Christian, bone weary by now, retired to his aerie in the Resurrection Tower to begin writing the checks to pay for it all.

But he was smiling.

IT was not much later than that before Susan had a chance to catch her breath and realize, with a flush of shame, that she hadn't thought of Matt more than once or twice the entire day. There had just been too much to do, too many places to be at once, trying to see the baby mammoth safely to his temporary new home at the zoo, monitoring and advising during the operations around Big Mama and Big Daddy by cell phone cameras, with barely any time to weep when Big Daddy breathed his last, mighty breath.

But at last she and the zoo veterinarians completed their checkup of the little mammoth, who stood calm and compliant for all the poking and probing, either in shock or unable to fathom what had happened to him and thus ready to accept any friendly attention, and she sat down with a sandwich and a cup of coffee and wondered why Matt had taken off as abruptly as he did. He had said he might be gone . . . how long? "A while." One of those maddeningly inexact English words describing time. A bit. A moment. A tick. A spell, a flash, a jiffy, a shake, a space, a stretch, a breath.

In this case, a while would be five years.

20

CENOZOIC Park had been erected over the next few years in what had once been farmland not far east of Portland, Oregon, along the newly widened Route 26 that went by Mount Hood and across the Cascades toward Bend.

There was not a lot of middle ground when it came to the theme park. Oregonians either loved it or hated it, and were just about equally divided on the matter. The only thing everyone agreed on was that nobody but the planners and builders called it Cenozoic Park from the moment ground was broken. Everybody called it Fuzzyland.

Portland had been fighting urban sprawl for decades, and having better luck with it than many another metropolitan area. When the plans for Fuzzyland were announced, a year to the day after the slaughter in Los Angeles, environmental activists were stunned to discover it was already a done deal. Several millions of Howard Christian's money, discreetly applied, had obtained variances to land-use regulations. The hearings that followed were a formality. In only weeks bulldozers were at work on the much loathed Mount Hood Freeway, something planners had thought dead and buried for forty years. It was almost finished by opening day, the remaining construction just enough to make the traffic delays getting there merely dreadful rather than nightmarish.

But Fuzzyland was promoted as "environmentally sound," so an extension of the local light-rail system, known as MAXX, was built on an elevated track right down the middle of the freeway, stopping at Fuzzyland, Zigzag, and Government Camp, where a funicular railway would take skiers the rest of the way to Timberline Lodge. This MAXX line was no ordinary two-car light-rail system like the one that served the rest of Portland, though. This was a monorail that levitated on a magnetic field, and its ten-car trains reached speeds of 150 miles per hour.

"A shot in the arm for tourism, and the ski industry!" proclaimed all the various chambers of commerce in the affected areas.

"A blight on the Cascades!" the environmentalists sneered.

Though the words "tasteful" and "circus" are not traditionally used in the same sentence, Howard instructed his architects to do the best they could, and they did manage to avoid the worst excesses of Las Vegas and Orlando. You could barely see the place from the highway, camouflaged as it was by hundreds of Douglas firs. (The trees were actually metal frameworks supporting colored Styrofoam bark and easy-to-clean plastic needles, but who cared?)

When you drove through the forest toward the vast underground parking lots you barely got a glimpse of the park just before plunging into the depths. It was mostly low-slung, sprawling, hugging the ground, dominated by the largest plastic and steel geodesic dome ever built, gleaming in the spring sunshine—or, more likely, glistening in the Oregon rain. It wasn't until you took the long escalators to the monorail that circled the park and took you to one of the four themed areas, three resort hotels, two RV parks, and one campground that you got a sense of the scale of the place.

You quickly realized that the dome was a lot bigger than you had imagined. A structure like that, with very little to give it a sense of scale, it could sort of sneak up on you, it took a while to realize you were farther away than you thought. It was *big*.

Placed between the parking lots and the park itself were the hotels, each with its monorail stop.

First was the smallest, the Alpine, on the side of the nearest hill, a Frank Lloyd Wright knockoff of dressed stone and polished wood and glass, cantilevered over a rushing river à la Falling Water, hangout of those who had come mainly to sample the year-round winter sports under the dome or the winter recreation nearby. Ski bums, hotdogging snowboarders, slumming Euro trash tired of the slopes of Aspen and Gstaad, aging snow bunny wannabes from the RV parks there to take their first and only bobsled or luge ride on the short, hair-raising, but guaranteed safe indoor course.

Next was the Timberline II, "the World's Largest Log Cabin," patterned on the WPA structure on nearby Mount Hood, famous from exterior shots in Stanley Kubrick's movie *The Shining*, only TII was ten times as large and seemed from the outside to be made entirely of Lincoln Logs. (More Styrofoam, but who cared?) This was the cheapest of the three, with its retro '30s decor and its bellhops dressed as forest rangers (but not *cheap*; for cheap you had to go to the little town of Zigzag, to the Motel 6s and 8s and Comfort Inns that had sprouted like weeds when Cenozoic Park was abuilding, and take a shuttle bus to the park entrance).

Just before the park itself you came to the hot ticket hotel, the Cave, a place that had sold out a year in advance purely on the strength of artist's sketches of the exterior, lobby, and rooms, and was in fact adding on two new wings before the park even opened. It seemed to be built entirely of stones, *giant* stones, heaped together almost at random (more Styrofoam) in the fashion of the eccentric Madonna Inn in San Luis Obispo, a favorite stopping point for Howard Christian on his drives up the California coast . . . except, of course, much, much bigger. The cavernous lobby and the dark, meandering, random hallways were lit by torches and featured cave paintings cribbed from the walls in Lascaux, France, and the rooms were grottos—plush-carpeted, television-and-telephone-equipped grottos with comfy king-sized beds and stone-surfaced Jacuzzis, but grottos all the same. If you wanted the full Cenozoic Park/Fuzzyland experience you had to stay at the Cave, which quickly came to be almost universally known as the Flintstone Hilton.

The trip wound through lakes and hills, not Styrofoam this time, but not natural, either, having been scooped out and piled up by Howard Christian's devouring earthmoving machines and landscaped by armies of gardeners, here and there getting glimpses of an ever-growing Ice Dome, until finally the entirety of the park was visible.

First the monorail plunged into the dome itself and all the newcomers would gasp as snow began to swirl around them, melting instantly when it hit the glass and metal of the train cars on a summer day, clinging in the winter. It was always snowing in the dome, somewhere, but only when and where the designers wanted it to snow. Promoters liked to boast that the snow removal budget *every week* at the Ice Dome was greater than that of the city of Portland for the entire winter. (Well, sure, but Portland tended to simply spread a little sand around on the rare occasions when it snowed.) In the center was Mount Mazama—which had destroyed itself thousands of years ago in the explosion that created Crater Lake, but who cared?—five times the height of Disney's Matterhorn and just as hollow, with a bobsled ride that ran on real ice. There were the animal exhibits: the polar bears, the musk oxen, the penguins, the arctic foxes, arctic owls, Seal Island, the white wolves, the caribou herd. There was Frosty's Snowman Lane and Toboggan Hill and Snow Fort Country for the little ones. There were *three* ice rinks, and a roller coaster. All the themed areas had roller coasters.

Beyond that was Redwood Empire, Fuzzyland's obligatory nod to the Sierra Club, where you could wander in the perpetual mists among the towering giants—not Styrofoam this time, but plaster so realistic that crews were kept busy patching woodpecker holes—and learn about Mother Earth and endangered species and how to recycle your newspaper, where most people paused long enough to walk around a massive tree trunk, maybe take an educational ride, pretty much like at Epcot, and then hurry on to less earnest amusements.

Which were to be found in Cenozoic Park itself, now called Cenozoic Safari, originally intended to be the heart of the development but now just one of four areas and only the third most popular. Here were more exciting nature rides, on open-topped robotic excursion buses painted in jungle camouflage, down paths with names like the Eocene Trek, the Oligocene Adventure, the Paleocene Expedition, and the Pleistocene Experience. Here you encountered the amazing mammals of the Tertiary and Quaternary periods, so long upstaged by the big reptiles of the Triassic, Jurassic, and Cretaceous.

No longer. Fuzzy and Big Mama had changed all that; extinct mammals were sexy now. And Cenozoic Park worked hard to make them even sexier. Down these jungle and swampland and savanna paths the armchair adventurer could now encounter them in all their cyber-animatronic glory. Here was Gastornis, a seven-foot nightmare top predator (and, okay, a bird, not a mammal) that ate ancestral horses for breakfast, and Phorusrhacos, a *ten*-foot bird that could have had Gastornis for lunch, if they hadn't lived twenty million years apart. Down these dusty Eocene paths Brontotheres did battle like overgrown rhinos on steroids. Dwarfing even these giants were the Indricotheres, the largest land mammals that ever lived, twenty-ton Oligocene behemoths, fifteen feet high at the shoulder, that could have kicked a full-grown elephant through the uprights of a football goalpost. Waiting to spring out at you were Entelodonts, possibly the ugliest mammals that ever slobbered, two-thousand-pound pigs that were all head, jaw, and shoulder, things that made warthogs look as pretty as sea otters.

And you want big? You think dinosaurs were big? Down the swampy ways of the Cenozoic lurked Basilosaurus—a mammal in spite of the reptilian name—an early whale that grew to eighty feet or more, ate great white sharks like minnows, and could lunge onto shore to dine on primitive hippopotami . . . or it did that in the park, anyway, in one of the animated diorama showstoppers that splashed gallons of water on the delighted safari bus passengers.

Ambulocetus, Durodon, Andrewsarchus, Hyaenodon, Amphicyonia, knuckle-walking Chalicotheres, turtle-shelled giant Glyptodonts, Ancylotherium, Deinotherium, Propaleotherium, Moeritherium . . . by now the kids had had about all the *-theriums* they could take, it was time to get to the Pleistocene Promenade, time to get to a place where the animals had names you could pronounce and remember, names like Mammoth, Mastodon, Irish Elk, Cave Bear, Cave Lion, Woolly Rhinoceros, Saber-Toothed Cat, and Giant Ground Sloth (Megatherium, if you wanted to get technical, which nobody but the guides did by that point). Here they were, the fabled creatures of the various ice ages and interregnums, many of which had been hunted, maybe to extinction, by our ancestors, and like all the large cybers in Cenozoic Park, these didn't just stand there and wave their trunks and nod their heads and maybe paw the ground, they *walked!*

But the most popular area, hands down, was the last stop

on the mono-maglev train before it completed its loop back at the parking lot, was Fuzzyland. If you would rather snowboard on real slopes, if you got your fill of environmental indoctrination in junior high school, and if thirty-foot rubber chalicotheres left you cold—and that was the case with virtually all of the teenagers and most of the young adults—Fuzzyland was the place for you.

The theme was Circus. Turn-of-the-century circus (the *twentieth* century, 1901 if you want to get picky), with lots of wood and brass, calliopes playing ragtime and rock and rap, penny-pitches where you actually pitched silver dollars, vast Victorian canvases depicting two-headed women and snake boys lining the midway—which actually featured fire eaters, sword swallowers, contortionists, and other carny acts rather than human freaks—big tents containing virtual reality video games, dance halls, funhouses, and shops selling a million kinds of souvenir and every type of fattening fried food known to humanity.

And rides. Ordinary carnival rides and multimillion-dollar vertiginous coasters that had been the centerpieces of theme parks since Walt Disney opened Space Mountain.

(So how did that fit with winter wonderland, ecology, and paleontology, the naysayers asked? Badly, of course, but Fuzzy himself, the reason for this entire carnival, was intended to be part of Howard Christian's circus from the get-go, and thus Ringling Bros. B&B maintained its only permanent installation outside of its winter quarters in Florida right here, so circus it would be, and circus it *was*.)

The center of Fuzzyland was Fuzzy's Big Top, dwarfing all the others and yet tastefully done, eschewing the gaudy reds and yellows and whites and purples of traditional big tops for wide vertical stripes of khaki and olive with gold trim, like a designer wine label. Big as it was, though, when regarded as a part of the larger edifice of Cenozoic Park and its sculpted environs, it seemed a small tail wagging a very large dog.

But it was true, and everyone agreed on it: Fuzzy the baby mammoth was the reason all this was here, and without him it might very well all dry up and blow away. Everybody had a great time at all the surrounding attractions with all their bells and whistles, they enjoyed the first act of the circus performances, which featured the very cream of lion tamers, clowns, jugglers, and daring aerialists, they got a big kick out of the opening of the second act with its giant overhead hi-def screens and its elephants and Big Mama . . . but what most people came here to see was the world's darling, Little Fuzzy. "Most people" meaning those who could afford it. Fuzzy's show was put on twice a day, except Mondays—separate ticket required, and that ticket was three times what you paid to get in, and *that* wasn't cheap—so not everyone who visited the park on a given day would get in to the show.

The operators went to a two-tiered system within a week of the opening day: reservations and a much higher price for the skyboxes and front rows, and a lottery of park attendees, who won the privilege of paying for the open seats. An hour before showtime scalping was strictly dog-eat-dog, with crying children and parents sometimes coming to blows.

Twelve shows a week, and practically everyone in the world wanted to get in, even the hard-core environmentalists who opposed the park, the circus, and everything it stood for. Everyone, that is, except for Susan Morgan, who had to be at every one of them.

Twelve shows a week.

She had been doing it for one year, and it was starting to look like a life sentence.

SUSAN left the elephant/mammoth compound at eleven P.M., one hour after the end of the final show of the night. She climbed up into the cab of her super-heavy-duty Dodge pickup, emblazoned on the door with a magnetic smiling baby mammoth logo of Fuzzyland. The beast burst into life with a rumble of its huge 6.2-liter diesel engine.

Now she traveled the route visitors took from the entrance and parking lots, but in reverse, and by pathways visitors never saw. Off to her left she could sometimes glimpse the maglev rail perched on its big concrete pylons, but usually it was concealed behind rows of trees or high fences. Cenozoic Park was, for the most part, a world of illusion—that's what the trees and fences were designed to hide, because the magic went out of the trick if you knew exactly how it was done.

Back here, there was no illusion, just utilitarian blacktop and concrete and nondescript cheap sheet-metal buildings that housed the workshops and electrical boards that kept the machines running, pumps that kept plants and animals and visitors watered, and storage warehouses that fed the insatiable appetites of the thousands who entered every day, from cotton candy mix to tons of frozen hamburger patties to bottles of champagne to Cenozoic Park bumper stickers and T-shirts to Little Fuzzy refrigerator magnets and rubber keychains.

As she came to the Cenozoic Safari a red light began flashing and a striped barrier came down, exactly like at a railroad crossing, and a ten-foot gate rolled back, but what came lumbering across the road was not a train but an Indricothere, looking a little like an elephant from its tree-trunk legs and slab sides, a little like a rhino from the thickness of its neck, a little like a giraffe from the length of that neck . . . but looking most of all like a terrible mistake, because the concealed hatch on its back was thrown open and the operator's head and shoulders were sticking out. Susan recognized him, one of her few friends outside the elephant house. His name was Fred Richardson, and his face was red and swimming with sweat. She stuck her head out the window and called out to him.

"Hey, you, how about moving that piece of crap?"

"Friggin' air conditioner broke down again," Fred called out. He stopped the mechanical monster, made it turn and lower its head until it was staring right through her windshield, and then it opened its mouth and roared. There was a little bear in it, and some elephant trumpeting, and maybe even a hint of *Star Wars* Wookiee, something whipped up in the sound labs. It was sure loud enough.

After the Indricothere had slouched across the road and the crossing alarm shut down, Susan drove past the phony redwoods and skirted the Ice Dome, to the employees' gate. The guard waved her through. A short drive through real forest and she passed by the Animal Vigil one hundred yards from the arch of the main park entrance, the closest they could get without being on private property. They had been there round the clock from opening day. This late there were only half a dozen of the hardest of the hard core, but on weekends there were often a hundred or more. They were not allowed to pitch tents—twice temporary encampments had been torn down by park security. They were forbidden to build fires and on a rainy Oregon day they could be a lugubrious sight, but their morale apparently remained high and even tonight they were slowly marching up and down on the dirt path they had beaten down, chanting slogans and carrying signs:

CIRCUS = CRUELTY

MEAT IS MURDER

ANIMALS HAVE RIGHTS

FREE WOOLLY!

Not even the mighty Howard Christian could prevent them from doing that, though he had tried, and they had vowed to stay there until the place closed down. Since Fuzzyland had been pronounced the most successful entertainment extravaganza since Disney World, Susan figured they had a long wait in store. Or maybe not. . . .

The sight of her truck with its Fuzzyland logo on the side set them off, shaking fists and shouting slogans. She sped down the road and through the blossoming commercial strip of Zigzag, then another mile down to a side road and two miles into the hills. Around a bend, up a steep grade, and there it was. Her hideaway.

The realtor called it a cabin, and it was in fact made of logs—not the kind Abe Lincoln split and notched together, but the kind made in a factory that really weren't much more than a facade for the well-insulated walls behind them. A log cabin with a three-car garage, a huge cantilevered deck with a spectacular view of Mount Hood, a vaulted A-frame living room, four bedrooms, four baths, sauna, Jacuzzi, and wine cellar.

She pulled up the short gravel driveway and parked next to her huge fifth-wheel trailer. It was what was called a "garage" model. She could drive up a ramp at the back in her dune buggy. Andrea had suggested she should have something to do, some activity or hobby, on her Mondays off. She had chosen off-roading. Other than that, she didn't have much of a life. She got out and wearily mounted the twenty steps to the deck.

Her weariness went away instantly, though, when she saw the man sitting with his back against the glass wall next to her front door, right there under the porch light.

His clothes were well used, just short of ragged, jeans and high-top sneakers, a blue down vest, and a flannel lumberjack shirt. There was a small backpack sitting beside him, with canteen and bedroll. His hair was long, black streaked with gray, and fell forward around his face. He seemed to be asleep.

He might be one of those animal rights protesters, he had the look. Should she call the sheriff? And wait half an hour or more for them to get here?

The hell with it.

"Hey, get up and get out of here," she said.

Matt Wright looked up and smiled uncertainly.

"Can we talk for a moment first?" he asked.

She just stood there for a moment, then slowly walked the three steps between them and slapped his face as hard as she could.

21

HOWARD Christian reached into his pocket and took out a peanut, cupped it in his palm, and held it through the heavy horizontal steel I-beams toward the most famous animal that had ever lived, the most beloved creature that ever walked on four legs—or maybe even on two, for that matter.

Little Fuzzy. *His* Little Fuzzy.

In the darkness of the far side of the enclosure a darker shadow stirred, as Howard had known it would. This was supposed to be Fuzzy's sleep time, though neither elephants nor mammoths needed a lot of sleep, sometimes having to feed as much as twenty hours per day to support their enormous bulk on the low-energy foods they consumed—and as much as sixty percent of that went right through their sixty-foot guts undigested to emerge as a cornucopia for dung beetles.

Still, Susan Morgan insisted her charge get his rest at night, claiming the two shows a day tired him out, something Howard had seen no signs of, which was why Howard had to sneak into his own building in his own theme park late at night, when Susan was not there, to get a little quality time with his prize pet.

Fuzzy slept lightly and his hearing or sense of smell was uncanny. He always knew when Howard had entered the building, and he always smelled the peanuts.

Now he shambled over to the mammoth-proof fence and the soft, moist tip of his trunk probed Howard's hand with infinite delicacy. There was a snuffling sound and the peanut was sucked up, the nostrils pinched, and the trunk snaked up above the pendulous lower lip and Fuzzy blew the tiny morsel into his mouth and crunched it. Immediately his trunk was held out for more.

Life is good, Howard thought. *Life is very good.*

* * *

THERE had been some dodgy days there at first, five years ago, when Fuzzy and Big Mama and the herd had appeared like magic on Wilshire Boulevard.

The first twenty-four, forty-eight hours had been critical, as he had known they would be right from the moment he shut down the big laser. His claims to ownership of the mammoths were tenuous at best, but that was what lawyers were for. By noon of the second day, with the media maelstrom swirling undiminished, Howard's legal team had filed no fewer than seventeen lawsuits in five separate jurisdictions outlining why the prehistoric creatures belonged to Howard Christian and no one else, under no fewer than three legal theories, each of them contradictory to the other two. His public relations team was hard at work selling the proposition that not only was Howard entitled to the spoils, it would be a travesty of justice, a blight on the free enterprise system, an insidious undermining of the basic principles that made this country the greatest democracy in the world if ownership of these poor defenseless creatures was awarded to anyone other than the man who was responsible for their arrival in the twenty-first century, i.e., the aforesaid Howard Christian.

Unfortunately, that ultimately entailed the revelation of the *means* whereby they had arrived in the twenty-first century, something Howard would very much have liked to have kept close to his vest, but that was the cost of doing business. You never got everything you wanted, so you concentrated on the main attraction and gave a little here and there.

It was a lot sexier story than cloning, and that would have been sexy enough. That was the angle his PR teams took: Howard the time travel pioneer, Howard the techno-wizard, Howard the man who was going to revolutionize the world once again. And that was fine, too. Wasn't a man entitled to the fruits of his labors?

There was also the matter of actual physical possession. Possession is nine-tenths of the law, or something like that. That was how his father had put it, anyway, and Howard could remember the exact circumstances when he'd first heard it, as Dad stuffed a boombox into a gaffed shopping bag and sauntered casually out of a Wal-Mart, "avoiding the unconstitutional state sales tax," as he had put it.

With that in mind, Howard had made sure that neither Fuzzy nor Big Mama spent more than one night in the elephant compound of the Griffith Park Zoo. At dawn on the second day six lawyers and two large trucks appeared at the zoo gates, waving a court order from a judge who was in a tough reelection fight, and one hour after that both trucks were rolling west and north on US 101, the Ventura Freeway, toward their new home in a compound just outside Paso Robles on the central coast, safely out of Los Angeles County. Howard had possession of both animals, and all the carcasses, and that was nine-tenths of the way to ownership.

Six months later he had legal possession as well, over the protests of the Sierra Club, the Fund for Animals, the State of California and County of Los Angeles, and many others. On the day the appeals court issued its ruling Howard gave the go-ahead to his planning team, which had already been working on tentative proposals for the circus that was to display Fuzzy and Big Mama: *Full steam ahead, boys!*

Yes, life was indeed sweet, or as sweet as it ever gets. There's always a little lemon peel in the lemonade, and there are three things you can do about that: minimize it, add more sugar, and/or learn to like a little bitterness. Howard did all three things, at various times.

There was the question of the slaughter of the fleeing mammoths. There was no way simply to make that ugly event just go away; billions of people had seen it on live television. Not that anyone wanted to arrest anybody over it, the animals were clearly out of control, and if somebody had killed them that was more or less all right . . . but how? Exactly what had happened out there that bloody night?

Best answer, five years later: Nobody knew. Leading theory: It was some side effect of the time traveling itself. Some invisible force seemed to have seized them when they got a certain distance from the point of "temporal translation," as one of Howard's experts put it. It worked like this:

Forces are accumulating as a person travels through the temporal continuum. Those forces are strongly localized to what the expert called a "six-dimensional synclastic infundibular space-time nexus" (i.e., the site of the temporal breakthrough), and increased as the cube of the distance from this nexus to the location of the time traveler, decreasing only as the square of the interval between temporal translation and "present" time X, measured in seconds. If not enough time is allowed between temporal translation and movement away from the space-time nexus, this expert testified to five separate investigation boards and a committee of Congress (with a degree of chutzpah that had serious mathematicians chuckling in admiration even five years later), the accumulated forces discharged, with the awful results everyone had seen repeated endlessly on videotape.

Or some such bullshit.

Howard, who was no math slouch, could not follow all the man's equations, but that was what he was being paid for. Obfuscation, smoke and mirrors, intended to make the ordinary viewer, simple congressperson, or even educated layman drop his jaw and say . . . *duuuuuh, okay, if you say so.*

Knowing the public would never be completely comfortable with an explanation like that, Howard's PR firm suggested how the whole bucket of lemons could be sweetened a bit, and so a second expert was hired. This one was a well-known populizer of science with the stature and stage presence of the late, great Isaac Asimov but without Asimov's scruples. That worthy came up with the following analogy:

Picture the "temporal substrate" as a thick carpet, and a time traveler as a person shuffling his feet as he walks across it. Static electricity is building up on that man, and must be discharged somewhere to avoid catastrophic results. If the time travelers, in the case of the mammoth herd, stray too far from the point of entry into the twenty-first century, the charge they've accumulated will erupt, all at once and without warning, like the man walking on the carpet when he reaches for a doorknob.

Ouch!

Well, yeah . . . but why didn't the same thing happen when Big Mama and Fuzzy and the corpse of Big Daddy were removed? Easy. What happens if you don't reach for that doorknob? What if you wait a minute or two before trying to open the door? Why, the static charge bleeds off into the air.

Viola!

This was all said with such conviction, reasonableness, and aplomb that even Howard almost found himself ready to believe it. And the public and the investigatory boards, knowing that there was a solid basis of mathematical gobbledygook underlying this rampant flummery, accepted it, too.

The biggest reason everyone, scientist and layman alike, pretty much had to accept Howard's version of events was that there was absolutely no proof that it was wrong. Other than to reveal that time travel had been accomplished, that a time machine existed, Howard had revealed a sum total of . . . nothing.

He knew there were those who viewed his exploding mammoth hypothesis as the sheer claptrap that it was. There were alternative explanations, of course, some of them wacky enough to make amusing reading, most just stupid. The Internet was rife with websites claiming to have the straight dope on that fateful night, from UFOs to communists to vast conspiracies of animal-hating capitalists to the Wrath of God Himself. There were even a few that got it right, but who was listening? They all faded into that vast babble of nuts that everyone was so used to by now, the online riffraff, the crazies with an ax to grind who drowned each other out in their relentless paranoia.

Then there were the handful of people capable of following the highest of higher mathematics, who knew that a few decimal points had been dropped, a few numbers divided by zero, a few Riemannian terms sneaked into the Lobachevskian continuum presented with such gusto. But how were they going to explain that to those who couldn't even spell continuum, much less understand what it meant?

Better yet, even many of those who could spot the bad shuffle simply assumed it was deliberate disinformation given out not to cover up anything Howard had *done*, but to conceal what he *knew*. So what if somebody had his thumb on the scales of the equations submitted publicly? The incontrovertible fact was that time travel *had* happened, that human beings had gone back in time and returned to the present day with living—and dead—proof that they had been there.

How they had done it was proprietary, far too closely held even to risk applying for a patent. Howard was assumed to be protecting his interests until he had everything sewed up, until he had figured out how to squeeze every dollar out of this revolutionary new technology, until every conceivable piece of it and application for it was wholly owned by Mr. Howard Christian. In short, he was doing exactly what they would have done if they had discovered time travel. And nobody could do a damn thing about it.

If only they knew, Howard thought, as Fuzzy vacuumed another peanut from his open palm. He had sure put one over on them. On *all* of them. Yes, life was sweet, he really couldn't complain too much. Yet in all that sweetness there was one chunk of bitter he had not been able to do a damn thing about, and every night it threatened to overturn all his triumphs, at least in his own eyes.

He didn't have a clue how to make a time machine.

It was enough to make a billionaire weep.

"Howard, darling, it's getting late."

Just like that, all thought of time machines and defeats and that bastard Matthew Wright and that ungrateful bitch Susan Morgan fled from Howard's mind. He turned, smiling, and drank in the face of Andrea de la Terre.

Andrea de la Terre, head of Terra Firma, the conservation group she had founded and nurtured into a force to rival the Cousteau Society or Friends of Nature. Terra Firma was heartily disliked by the semiradical groups, who sometimes viewed her as wishy-washy—Andrea was not a vegetarian, for instance—but they had to deal with her because she got things done and she knew everybody. Everybody that counted, that is, which is to say all the "green" stars in Hollywood and the music business. A dozen phone calls from her could bring out more star power to a rally, and more money into organizational coffers, than a year of hard work by any lobbying group other than the NRA.

Andrea de la Terre, until recently the very definition of Hollywood Liberal, who had turned down a multimillion-dollar cosmetics endorsement over the issue of animal testing, and prevailed in a brand-libel suit brought against her when she publicly burned boxes of eyeliner, lipstick, and rouge. Andrea de la Terre, the former Melba Horowitz of Queens, New York City. Top female box office draw for the last three years, maker of politically and environmentally responsible epics that also made pots of money, much of it for Howard Christian's studio.

Howard had never actually met her until two years ago. He did not mix with movie stars, even when they worked for him. They had ended up facing each other across a long conference table where he had sat down with groups opposed to Cenozoic Park in an attempt to iron out their differences. That was Andrea's stated intent, anyway. Howard viewed it as a wasted afternoon. He had intended to sit politely and smile politely and nod politely, and then go back to doing exactly what he had been doing before. The nerve of the woman, she and her big-shot famous Hollywood idiot friends, people with perfect teeth and skin and chiseled features, the very guys who had hammered him in the playground from the time he was five, the very girls who had sneered openly at his shitty clothes, his big ears, his zits, his stammer. Screw them all.

Until Andrea de la Terre opened her mouth and spoke, and then he was lost.

ANDREA had brought grapes.

Grapes were on Susan Morgan's approved list, though Fuzzy wasn't supposed to get them in the middle of the night, but who owned Fuzzy? Susan, or Howard?

Let's don't get into that, Howard thought.

She stood there, every man's fantasy, every woman's unattainable ideal, and Howard marveled again at a thought he would never express to her: she was not really beautiful. She was attractive, no question about it, and no single part of her face was anywhere near grotesque . . . it's just that the parts were not assembled in a way that would normally qualify a girl as gorgeous. Howard was reminded of Judy Garland, or of Barbra Streisand, though Andrea looked nothing like either of them. If she was sitting in a bus station or on a stool at Schrafft's you'd walk right by her.

But in the same way that, when Streisand began to sing, you forgot all about the nose and she became the most wonderful thing in the universe, when Andrea looked at you, when she spoke, when she moved . . . you were lost. From the moment she started talking, Howard would have given her anything she wanted. (Lucky for him, she never realized that, but he did concede half a dozen points he had not intended to budge on.)

Howard was in love.

He had never expected to be, not at his age, not at this point in his life. He had had the usual crushes on the prettiest girls in school, those times when he had been in school and not self-educating in an anonymous trailer park or a juvenile hall in one state or another. They were purely sexual attractions, since he had seldom exchanged so much as two words with any of those prom queens and cheerleaders. That had lasted right on through college. Then he was working, inventing, devoting himself to his computers, and there was no time for romance, even in the event he believed any of the engineering majors he met in the pathetic thing he called a social life would respond to him.

Then one day he looked around and realized he was rich. It really seemed to happen overnight. And when others realized it, the girls began to show up. He went so far as to marry one, and the divorce a year later had cost him (and he got a lot of satisfaction every month when he wrote her a check that seemed pitifully small to him now, and must have seemed miniscule to her avaricious heart when she saw what he was worth *now*), and he learned the lesson all rich, homely men learn if they intend to stay rich: Your bank balance is the most attractive thing about you.

Then he was a billionaire, and one of the most eligible bachelors on the planet, and everything he had learned applied doubled, tripled, squared, and cubed. When you have billions, the pool of possible women who might actually love you for yourself narrows enormously. Basically, they had to be either rich or famous, or both, and he simply didn't move with any ease in that social milieu.

He had made a few halfhearted moves to spruce himself up, hired an image consultant who gave him a new haircut and chose his wardrobe for him, but he soon drifted back to his old familiar cowlick and comfortable clothes. He even tried plastic surgery, electing to fix, of all the disastrous features the sawbones swore he could tidy up, his unfortunate nose which, he had always thought, could adorn Mount Rushmore with very little alteration in scale if George Washington ever lost his. But he felt the new schnozz didn't look all that much better than the old one, on the one hand, and yet, on the other, he was sure it was enough different that everyone who knew him saw nothing else *but* the nose, and were snickering behind his back.

And so he added one more thing to the—surprisingly long—list of things that money couldn't buy: confidence. Arrogance, yes; confidence, no.

The week after that conference they were dating, and a month after that they were sleeping together and dodging the tabloid photographers because, let's face it, though Howard had never been of much interest to the celebrity-mad masses, being at least as nerdy and homely as Bill Gates and twice as boring, Andrea was right up there with Liz and Di and Michael and Elvis and Jackie, who were all dead now except for Elvis, and maybe Michael, and then there was the Romeo and Juliet angle, not the star-crossed lovers part or the teenage mad infatuation though it sometimes felt that way to Howard, but the fact that they were from warring houses, the putative rapist of the environment versus the Queen of Green.

Now they were to be married, Andrea up to her unlinered eyebrows in preparations for the Wedding of the Century on a remote Pacific atoll whose name and location were the most closely guarded secret since the Manhattan Project, a place the paparazzi couldn't reach if they tried to fly in on a cruise missile, with a guest list part *Billboard* Top Twenty, part *Variety* box office leaders list, part Who's Who in Washington, New York, Paris, and Geneva, and Howard spent a few minutes every day with his lawyers, honing the language of the prenuptial agreement so it would be generous but not profligate, conservative but not insulting, because no matter how infatuated Howard might be, his permanent adolescent doubts lingered in an atavistic corner of his brain and he sometimes woke in the middle of the night silently screaming, *She couldn't possibly love me!*

But it really seemed she did. There she stood in her high-heel sneakers, her red dress, with her wig hat on her head, and over it all a full-length coat of Columbian mammoth fur, one of only twenty such coats on the planet, a gift from Howard valued at well over a million dollars and the subject of endless controversy among animal lovers worldwide (Is fur murder if the animal was already dead? Would a roadkill possum coat be okay? Is it moral to wear a century-old mink?) . . . feeding grapes to Fuzzy.

Fuzzy loved the coat. It was possible that the pelt had come from his mother, though Howard had been adamant about never doing the DNA testing to determine just which Curson Avenue carcass was the mother.

Until the events on Wilshire Boulevard no one had known anything about the skin and possible furriness of a Columbian mammoth. It turned out that Columbians did have hair, three to four inches in length. This was nothing like the luxurious coat of the woolly, up to three feet long in some places, black or reddish brown, but it would do, it would do, and Howard found the very best tanners and furriers in Russia, who worked wonders with the coarse and lifeless material they were given, ending with a small number of coats, hats, and stoles that sold for unbelievable prices.

Now Fuzzy momentarily ignored the offered handful of grapes and reached through the bars of the enclosure to rub the sensitive tip of his trunk over Andrea's coat, from her shoulders down to the hem at her knees . . . and what must he be thinking? Howard wondered.

So who knew what was going through that large brain? Though there could be little of mammoth scent or of mammoth texture on the hairs Fuzzy was so fondly stroking, who knew what Fuzzy's incredibly superior nose and extremely sensitive trunk tip smelled and felt? Howard looked into the old, wise eye—and all mammoth eyes were old and wise, just like elephants, even when they were infants—and he looked at the slight figure of Andrea standing there, looked at the two beings most beloved to him in the universe, and he felt himself smile.

Yes, life was good.

THE feeling persisted out of the mammoth house and into a slow Oregon drizzle, Warburton carefully holding a big umbrella over Andrea and a bodyguard holding open the door of the pearl-gray 1936 Cord Cabriolet convertible. Howard was about to get behind the wheel when Warburton leaned over and said something into his ear, and Howard's mellow mood vanished at once. He got in the car and slammed the door and just sat there for a moment, until his fiancée looked at him with a brow wrinkled in a way only Andrea de la Terre could wrinkle an eyebrow.

"Something wrong, darling?" she asked.

For a moment Howard could only sit there, the oversized steering wheel in his hands. It had been five years, five long frustrating years since that face had loomed in his sights, so close he had felt he could reach out and touch it, and in those five years he had never again felt that feeling of utter omnipotence, never held a man's life in his hands so intimately. And for the first two years he had felt, at best, ambivalence about his decision not to shoot because, after all, there might be answers to secrets locked up in that head, the secrets of how the universe was really put together, if answers there were.

Over the next years, as Matt Wright wandered the globe like some demented Diogenes looking for an honest philosophy, Howard had come to believe the man knew no more than he himself did, that the answers didn't exist. For the last year, Howard had devoted himself to pure and simple hatred.

At last, he sighed and started the car.

"Andrea, Matt Wright has returned."

22

SUSAN had been contrite about the blow. It was inexcusable for one person to hit another except in self-defense, she said, and he told her he figured if anybody ever had good reason to strike another, she was it. She didn't have anything to say to that, but after a long pause during which he felt like a specimen under a microscope, and not a very appetizing one, she unlocked the front door and invited him in.

And then it was . . . awkward.

He had a million things he wanted to tell her and another million things he wanted to ask her, but he had been far from sure he'd even be invited in the door, and, once in, his tongue seemed tied in knots.

So . . . what have you been up to? He knew most of that; Susan's life had been well documented from the time Fuzzy came into her life. She was famous, had been on the television many times in the early years. Hell, she was a character on a Saturday morning animated television show, she had been played by Andrea de la Terre in the movie version of *Little Fuzzy*.

How are you doing? What, you mean after you walked out on me and stayed away for five years? No, let's don't go there just yet.

There was only one question worth asking, and he couldn't just come right out and ask it, certainly not with the cold look in her eye as she sat stiffly on a big cane chair opposite him, one leg curled up under her and the other one, the bad one, carefully extended. No, you'd have to work up to that one, if you ever had the guts to ask it at all, and she sure wasn't giving anything away.

What little conversation there was soon died away, and she

didn't seem to know what to do with her hands and neither did he, so finally she asked, in a tone of voice that sounded to him a little like one you might use if your least favorite uncle had plopped himself down in your living room and just wouldn't go away, if he wanted something to eat. And he wasn't proud, no sir, he'd use any excuse to stretch his time with her until what he was beginning to feel would be the final and inevitable outcome, himself trudging once more down that lonesome road outside.

So he showered, and hacked away at his unruly and scraggly beard until it was almost presentable, dressed in the only change of clothes he had, and descended the stairs again to find her in the kitchen just pouring spaghetti into a colander.

"You know I'm not a cook," she said, wiping the condensed steam from her forehead with the back of her hand in a gesture that made him almost weep with longing. "But there's nobody around here that delivers except a so-so pizza shop, and I did make this sauce—spaghetti sauce is one of the five things I know how to make. Anyway, it's from the freezer, and so is the bread, and there's no salad because I'm hardly ever here and I just can't keep the refrigerator stocked with fresh things." She shrugged, and set the bowl of noodles and the bowl of bubbling red sauce on the simple pine table. "Anyway, here it is. Do you want some wine?"

He did, and she selected a red from a walk-in cellar with rack space for hundreds of bottles, only a dozen of them occupied.

He was hungry, he hadn't had anything since an Egg McMuffin for breakfast, having spent the whole day pacing or sitting on her front deck, and the food was good, when he could bring his attention to it, but most of the time it tasted like nothing in his mouth, just something to choke down until they could move on to the next stage, which was finding out if she was at all interested in listening to his story or if she'd shake his hand on the way out the door.

It was the tensest meal he ever ate, consumed in absolute silence.

Then they retired to the vast living room with glasses of wine and she invited him to sit on a plush couch with some sort of Indian art pattern, facing the fire ring, which was an artful arrangement of native stones, no mortar, set on glistening white beach sand in the center of the room. A copper funnel hung from the ceiling high above to catch the smoke. She struck a long match and touched it to several places around the stack, then sat in the same chair she had been in before she had invited him to dinner.

She reached over to the small table beside her chair and picked up a small stack of postcards, shuffled them idly through her fingers before tossing them onto the small coffee table that separated them, where they fanned out in accusation. He reached out and picked up the topmost card, saw the picture of the Big Sur coast, waves crashing on huge rocks. He turned it over and could barely read his own indecipherable scrawl:

Dear Susan,
I am well, but cannot contact you as yet.
Will explain later.
I love you.
Matt

His face flushed as he flipped rapidly through them. Had anything ever sounded so lame? But he didn't know how else to say it.

He looked up, and saw her drain her glass of wine. He realized it was her third glass, and the bottle sitting beside her was almost empty. She gave him a twisted smile, then tossed her empty glass at the stones, where it shattered.

She laced her fingers around her good knee and leaned back. "So, Matt. What have you been doing with yourself?"

And the words began to spill out of him.

MATT fled the scene of slaughter that night with only one thought in his mind: He had to find a quiet place to gather his thoughts, order the events of the last hour, *write it all down.* His grasp on what he had seen in the depths of the time machine was so tenuous it made the waking residual images of a dream seem as solid as a slap in the face. He needed to retreat from the storm he could see coming. He was standing beside a brand-new pickup truck whose door was wide open, the owner fled who-knew-where. He saw the key was in the ignition.

Ten minutes later he was on the San Diego Freeway, heading north.

He didn't sleep, he didn't dare, he knew it would all go up in smoke and blow away if he slept; the only way he could keep it all in his head was to invent mathematical mnemonics to trick himself into remembering, so he sat there in the parking lot of a McDonald's, the first restaurant he had seen, and when it opened he bought six cups of coffee and drove carefully down the street to a Bank of America and waited for it to open. When it did, he went inside and, not without some difficulty, withdrew a hundred thousand dollars from his account, worrying every minute that Howard or some federal agency would be looking for him, putting a flag on his account or his credit cards. But he walked out with the cash in a canvas bag and, gulping coffee, found a large consumer electronics store and purchased three personal computers for six hundred dollars.

Then he drove around town looking for a used car lot, abandoned the stolen pickup after wiping the steering wheel and door handles and everything else he might have touched. He knew he must have left DNA traces inside, but hoped that for a routine stolen car the police would only dust for fingerprints. He walked to the car lot and paid four thousand in cash for an anonymous gray sedan that looked reliable enough, then drove it to Ventura, where he checked into a Motel 6 at noon under the name of Kevin Moore, paying an extra hundred-dollar bill for the privilege of not showing his driver's license.

He holed up in the motel for three days, and someone looking over his shoulder as he worked his computers would have been utterly mystified as to what he was doing.

At first it was dense with mathematical symbols, as he tried to document and somehow rationalize the things he had seen in that little metal box on that fateful night twelve thousand years ago . . . or was it really fifteen thousand years ago? Was that too linear a way of thinking? It made it sound as if the Pleistocene was in some . . . direction, a place you could point to, or a vector whose length and orientation was the sole possible result of a specific equation.

He knew he had seen something that a human eye is not really equipped to see . . . and yet how could that be? It was a contradiction in terms, but so was everything else from the moment they went into the past. It could not happen, yet it had happened. Which meant that he, Matt Wright, mathematical genius, was missing something.

On the second day he began to get some inkling of a new direction. At first it was no more than an itch at the back of his mind, something he had experienced before when a new idea was struggling to be born. He knew he couldn't force it to come, so he did what he always did at times like that. He went to bed. Maybe his subconscious mind would give him a boost.

But he woke up no wiser, and knew it was time to move on. He was rested, felt up to driving now. So he checked out and drove on up the coast, up US 101, then California Route 1 until he got to Big Sur, where he pulled over and found a place where he could sit and watch the ocean pounding the shore.

After a while he noticed a collection of buildings not too far away from him. There were tents, yurts, a pool, gardens, a large green lawn, odd-shaped buildings with an impromptu, weathered look, all set in the rugged, up and down, rocky and deeply forested surf-battered terrain for which Big Sur was famous. It looked peaceful, secluded, open to the air and the sea. Some sort of resort, maybe. Possibly just the sort of thing he needed to get his thoughts together.

He got back in his car and soon was driving by a sign that said ESALEN INSTITUTE.

IT took a moment to penetrate, then Susan sat forward.

"Esalen?"

"That's right."

"That place where rich people go to get massages and soak in hot tubs?"

"Well, they're not all rich, though it's not cheap. And there are hot tubs and massages, but there are classes, too, and discussions of . . . well, all sorts of things."

Susan sat back again.

"Let me get this straight. While I was . . . while I . . . you were soaking in a hot tub in Big Sur?"

Susan felt she was right on the edge. She had loved him, she had worried about him, she had gotten angry at him as years rolled by with nothing but his maddening monthly postcards. She had briefly thought she hated him, and then she had tried her best to forget him. God knows she had enough to deal with, between Howard, Fuzzy, her unwanted fame, and Big Mama, goddamn Big Mama, who had damn near killed her. Now here he was, and the reason he hadn't come back to her was . . .

Esalen?

In that moment she felt she could hate him again.

"I couldn't just walk right in the door," he was saying. "You have to have reservations. But I got lucky, there was a cancellation. I got in after waiting three days at a motel in Monterey. I enrolled in 'Gestalt and Evolutionary Psychology' and 'An Introduction to Buddhist Philosophy.' "

"What, no massage?"

"Well, yes, in the evenings." He glanced up at her, and hurried on.

"I almost quit after the first day. I had no idea what I was doing there, but I had this persistent feeling that I was on the trail of something important. But the courses were stupid. There was no logic to them. Things were posited with no empirical proof, then accepted as true with no further discussion. Or, none from anyone but me, that is. I began to realize that no one there but myself had any training in math or science . . . or what I think of as science, anyway. It was another culture entirely, couldn't have been more foreign to me if I'd been dropped off in the fourteenth century."

"Which I guess is no longer just a figure of speech."

"What? Oh, sure, I guess we proved it's possible."

"I didn't prove anything, Matt. I was just along for the ride."

"So was I. More than you'll ever know." He sighed heavily, and drank the last of the wine from his glass. "Anyway, I stuck it out, and by the third day I felt I was beginning to get a handle on something."

"What, that Buddhism is the true faith? Did we travel with a Zen time machine?"

She had thought he would laugh, but he merely looked thoughtful, then slowly shook his head.

"I began to see that there was a tool there . . . or maybe a set of tools, that could . . . what I was looking for, you see, was a new perspective. My scientific one, all my mathematical tools, had failed me.

"You ever heard of the guy who proved that a bumblebee couldn't fly? I'm not sure it's a good analogy; his math was bad, or the proper math hadn't yet been developed to expose the flaws in his reasoning. But I was feeling like him. All my figures added up, I couldn't find any flaw . . . but I had seen something, I had been somewhere, or sometime, and the goddamn bumblebee was *flying*. Obviously, the bee knew something I didn't know, and every day I became more convinced that mathematics, or at least mathematics *alone*, could never get me into the air again."

He stared into the fire for a while.

"Go on," she said. "I'm hanging on the edge here. Did you discover the secrets of the universe?"

"Not right then," he admitted. "On the fourth night they came for me."

HE was never entirely sure just who they were.

Oh, he had a general idea. They were Americans. They represented the government . . . which theoretically represented the people, but the people would never be consulted on anything this group did, nor informed of the results of their actions.

He gathered that the people he came into contact with had been assembled from the myriad of law-enforcement and hush-hush and they-don't-exist agencies for the sole purpose of investigating this time travel phenomenon . . . which meant investigating Matt Wright, as he was the only one who seemed to know anything about it.

It began in the middle of the night. He had a vague memory of waking up in a panic, unable to breathe. He'd had dreams like that before, but this time it turned out to be true.

He had a brief glimpse of a face blackened with soot, big white staring eyes and grinning teeth above him in the darkness, a sharp smell, the taste of a rag in his mouth.

Later, he figured it was good old chloroform. The old ways are the best.

When he woke up he might have been a few miles down the road or he might have been in Patagonia. He didn't know how long he had been out. He was in a sparsely furnished room—cot, steel sink with tin cup and a bar of soap, steel toilet, table with three chairs bolted to the floor, no windows to the outside, a steel door with a six-by-six mesh-reinforced window at eye level, a long mirror set into another wall.

A cell, no getting around it. Larger than most cells, he supposed, never having seen one except in the movies, maybe thirty feet square, room for some serious pacing. Only someone who had never seen a television cop show would fail to realize that the big mirror was partially silvered—the infamous one-way mirror. The ceiling was at least twelve feet high. A small camera was mounted in each of the four corners.

It wasn't particularly clean. The linoleum floor was cracked and peeling in a few places, scuffed here and there, in need of mopping. Dust kitties had accumulated in the floor corners, and there were cobwebs in the ceiling corners. There were smudges on the walls that looked like they had been made by hands, as high as hands could reach. Overhead an ordinary fluorescent light fixture flickered and clicked maddeningly. Exploring the entire place, seeing absolutely everything there was to be seen, took a total of ten minutes.

He was dressed in the clothes he had worn the day before, jeans and shirt, low-top Nike running shoes, cotton socks—which he had not been wearing in bed, when he was chloroformed and kidnapped. Someone must have dressed him. There was nothing in his pockets but lint.

He took encouragement from what was not there. No car batteries or generators with genital clamps attached. No manacles, ropes, whips, thumbscrews, vats of boiling oil, rubber hoses, or billy clubs. Any of those things could be brought in, of course.

Only one feature of the room worried him, and that was a dark brown stain on the floor near the table. He tried to convince himself it was spilled food or drink. As the hours went by he kept looking at it, wondering if it was the source of the smell that tickled at his nostrils, over the sourness of the sheets and blanket and the gathering odor of his own fear. Was it blood?

He later estimated they held him there for twenty-four hours before anyone came to question him. He couldn't be sure. The lights never went off. It could have been as little as twelve hours, or as many as forty-eight, he supposed.

They fed him three times. It was the same each time: the door opened and a man in white coveralls and wearing a white bandanna over the lower part of his face entered with a steel tray and set it on the table.

The first time Matt sat up from his reclining position on the cot.

"I want to speak to a lawyer," he said.

The man didn't even glance at him. He slammed the door behind him, and Matt heard a key turning in a lock.

The food was a hamburger steak with gravy, mashed potatoes, peas, bread and butter, a slice of melon, and a cup of coffee. He ate it with the only utensil provided, a plastic spoon. The next two meals were pretty much the same.

THE second time he woke up it was to find two men in suits sitting at the table.

They were fairly unremarkable, with more of the bureaucrat than the cop or the torturer in their appearance and demeanor, perfect FBI types. One was blond, midthirties, tall and clean-cut, the only thing out of place about him being the argyle socks Matt could see above his black wingtips. The other was sixtyish, short and rather portly, with a rim of feathery white hair around a shiny pink dome of baldness, thick glasses, and a look of perpetual puzzlement on his smooth baby face. Matt felt somehow that he should know him. Later, when the questioning began, it was clear he was conversant with the higher mathematics needed to ask intelligent questions about time travel, so it was entirely possible Matt *did* know him; it was a small world. But he could never place the face with a name, and he finally put it down to a slight resemblance to Albert Einstein.

Neither introduced himself and Matt never learned their names, so he quickly started thinking of them as Albert and Argyle. They sat in two bolted-down chairs on one side of the table, and Albert gestured for Matt to sit in the chair across from them.

Argyle went first.

He started by emptying a box he had brought with him. It contained the things that had been in Matt's possession when he was abducted. He spread out the change, took every card and scrap of paper and dollar bill from the wallet, then opened the Swiss Army knife and meticulously opened all the seams of the wallet, searching for things that might be concealed there—a small display of arrogance and power that was not lost on Matt. He dumped the banded stacks of money from the canvas bag, riffled idly through them, and tossed them aside. He set out the three computers and turned them on.

The last item to emerge from the box was an ordinary glass marble, red in color, in a tiny square cage. He held it up to the flickering overhead light and squinted at it, turning it this way and that. At last he put it down and pushed it toward Matt with his index finger, and for the first time looked Matt in the eye.

"What is this?" he said.

"It's a marble in a steel cage," Matt said.

Neither Albert nor Argyle said anything for almost a minute, both of them looking down at the object on the table. Then Argyle looked up again.

"What is this?" he said.

Matt sighed. It was looking like it would be a long day. He had done nothing wrong, but he knew somehow that that would not matter to these people. He didn't really have a lot to hide, either.

Just one small thing. But, of course, that was what they were after.

"It is a component of a device I was hired to re-create for Howard Christian. He believed it would make it possible to travel backward in time. So to speak."

Albert jumped in.

"Explain that last sentence."

"It's hard to. I mean, the phrase 'travel backward in time' is an attempt to put into language a concept that the language is not equipped to describe. 'Travel' is almost certainly not the correct verb, 'backward' may or may not be a useful modifier to the concept of traveling, and 'time' is a concept that I've come to realize is far from adequately defined."

"But you did go somewhere."

"I can't say that for certain. I could say I went 'some*when*,' but I'm not even sure of that. It is possible that I stayed right where I was and everything else went somewhere or somewhen. Though that requires us to define a space-time locus 'where or when I *was*' and set it in opposition to 'where or when I *went*,' or 'where or when everything else went . . . or didn't go,' and I'm afraid I can't make that reconcile, relativistically speaking."

Albert was nodding. Argyle was gazing fixedly at Matt, mouth slightly open, apparently about as sentient as a cow. Argyle took over again.

"Where is the time machine?"

"I don't know." Truth.

There was another pause.

"Where is the time machine?"

"It went somewhere I can't follow." Truth.

"Or somewhen?" Albert asked.

"Possibly."

Another long silence. Matt had never been interrogated before. But no literate human in America could be totally unaware of a few interrogation techniques. He supposed he was meant to feel a kinship to Albert, who at least seemed to know a little math and was conversant with some of the quantum dichotomies present in the idea of time traveling, and it was plain as could be that Argyle intended to be menacing with his silent contempt and simple, repeated questions.

Matt found he was indeed frightened of Argyle, very frightened. The man stank of suppressed violence and Matt felt sure that, if orders came from his superiors, Argyle would do absolutely anything to obtain the location of the missing time machine.

If he was supposed to like Albert, though, the man wasn't doing his job.

Albert spoke again.

"Matthew, are you aware that it is no longer necessary to

hook a man up to a lot of wires and clamps and springs to run a polygraph test on him?"

"No, I wasn't, but I'm not surprised. Everything's high-tech these days, isn't it? I don't guess you need rubber hoses or thumbscrews or anything so primitive to torture a man today, either, do you?"

Albert looked elaborately around the room, as if searching for instruments of torture.

"Have you been threatened in any way?"

Matt laughed.

"I don't know what else you'd call it when you're kidnapped and held incommunicado and you don't even know where you are. By the way, I'm asking again to talk to a lawyer."

"You don't need a lawyer. You haven't been accused of anything. It's all perfectly legal. Haven't you heard of the Patriot Act? We just want you to answer some questions."

"I have. You have more questions?"

"Yes, but there's no point going on with them right now. Your responses have not been entirely forthcoming."

"You mean you think I'm lying?"

"No. You're telling the truth, but not all of it. You're hiding something." He gave Matt a small smile. "I'm afraid I need to regroup a little, too. It's just possible I'm not getting the right answers because I don't know how to ask the right questions."

"Join the club," Matt said.

The inquisitors put everything back into the cardboard box and left.

MATT was not surprised when they drugged him. It was the logical next step.

There was nothing to prevent them from simply tying him down and jabbing a needle into him, but they elected to put it into his food, or his water. And what could he do? He had to eat and drink, so he ate and drank, and then felt the strange feeling of euphoria overcome him.

He laughed.

They let him laugh for an hour, Albert and Argyle, and

then came back in again. All they brought this time was his computers.

"Good morning, Matt," Albert said. "How are you feeling?"

"I'm feeling great," Matt said . . . and then realized he hadn't said anything at all. He had opened his mouth, he had taken a breath, he had sent the signals to his lips and tongue that should have produced words, but something had short-circuited and no words had come out.

He laughed again. It was very funny.

"You know you have to answer these questions, don't you?" Albert said.

"Yes, I know," Matt didn't say, and laughed again. What was so funny was, he *wanted* to answer the questions. Oh, there was a part of him, a part that seemed to have been deeply suppressed by the drugs—and what *was* this stuff? It was very good!—that wanted to keep his secret, that still felt it was important, but most of him was eager to spill everything. He knew it would make him feel very good to tell these fellows everything he knew. But, on the other hand, *not* telling them, not *being able* to tell them, didn't make him feel *bad* . . . so he laughed.

Albert and Argyle didn't laugh.

"Where is the time machine?" Argyle asked.

Matt tried to tell them. Without success.

Albert drummed his fingers on the table, then abruptly got up and left the room.

Matt and Argyle sat there for ten minutes, staring at each other. Argyle had absolutely no expression on his face, and no nervous mannerisms. Somehow, Matt found this scarier than if he had shown overt hatred, hostility, menace, even frustration. He felt Argyle could rip out his guts with absolute indifference.

But he was not capable of worrying about such things at the moment. Thoughts, observations, conclusions entered his mind and were filed away impartially, with no emotional component. If Argyle had told him he intended to cut off Matt's arms and legs he would have filed that way, too, with no fear. Maybe Argyle knew that, and was saving his venom for a time Matt could appreciate it.

Albert came back with a huge stack of paper under one

arm. He slapped it down on the table in such a way that Matt could see what was printed on the front of the file: DR. MATTHEW WRIGHT. More psychology, Matt figured. All that paper could obviously have been put onto a computer and Albert could have consulted that. Albert wanted Matt to see the amount of documentation available to him.

Albert flipped through the file and reached the page he wanted.

"Aphasia," he said. "You've suffered from it before."

Matt nodded.

"He's faking," Argyle said.

Matt shook his head.

"I don't think he is," Albert sighed. "I think he really wants to tell us where it is. Don't you, Matt?"

Matt nodded.

"Then we'll just have to play twenty questions, won't we?" Albert said.

BIG as the dossier with his name on it was, there was still more.

They brought in stacks and boxes of paper, spread things around on the table. They made no attempt to hide any of it from him.

He had to admire their thoroughness. They had re-created his path from Wilshire Boulevard to Esalen in amazing detail. There were transcripts of interviews with everyone he had spoken to. They must have canvassed every business within a mile of US 101 to find them all. The interrogations were thorough, asking every imaginable question, but they all boiled down to "Did you see this man hide anything?"

Results: zero.

The Esalen Institute had been—was still being—searched. When the government was done they'd have to rebuild the place practically from the ground up. Matt regretted bringing all that trouble on them.

Every police force and fire department and National Guard unit and Boy Scout troop and, probably, the Brownies and Bluebirds, were beating the bushes along his entire route from Los Angeles to Big Sur, looking for a steel attaché case. They had been joined by thousands of civilians spurred by a million-dollar reward.

Results: a big pile of garbage. Thus the game of twenty questions.

It can be an effective tool in the hands of a skilled questioner, and Albert was no slouch. But you have to know the right questions to ask, or you never even get on the right track.

First they brought out a map. *Did you leave the time machine here? No? Did you leave it here? Here?* No, no, and no. All the way down the map, town by town.

Albert thought about it.

Well, did you last see it here? No, no, no, no . . . yes.

The yes was Los Angeles. Albert brought out another map. Pointed to the tar pits.

Yes.

"OH, man," Susan said. "That was . . ."

"About a week after our little adventure. I'm not sure precisely, since I didn't have a clock and the drugs screwed up my time sense a bit."

"That was when they sealed off that whole area. A square mile, evacuated and decontaminated because of that dirty bomb."

"I read about it later," Matt said. "It was a while before I added it up."

"You think . . . the government set off the bomb?"

"If there was a bomb."

"Oh, there was a bomb. They showed a helicopter shot of it going off, blowing up that truck it was in—"

"What I meant was, if there was a *dirty* bomb. A radiological bomb, one that would take a while to decontaminate after it went off. The way I'd do it, I'd put some dynamite in a truck, call it a warning so the immediate area can be evacuated. Then I'd blow it up and release a small amount of some relatively harmless radioactive gas, enough to set off the Geiger counters. The story was the terrorists chose that area because of all the publicity with the mammoths. Then seal off and evacuate a square mile and ban all overflights because of the radiation danger, to give yourself a little privacy, and get to work looking. When I heard about it I figured it was too much for coincidence. What was it, three weeks before they let anyone back in? That's long enough to do quite a search."

"Almost four weeks," came a voice. Susan gasped, turned, and saw Howard Christian standing on her deck, looking through her huge front windows.

23

SUSAN had been raised to offer food and drink to any guest, even if she'd really like to leave him out on the front porch looking in like a pathetic waif. But he was with Andrea de la Terre, and Susan liked Andrea. She had liked her before the woman—amazingly!—fell in love with Howard, first as a fan, later as an acquaintance. She knew a lot of famous people now and had learned that, for the most part, they were no better and sometimes a lot worse than your ordinary citizen.

Andrea was different. She was one of those rare ones that could somehow transcend her celebrity, get close to just about anyone quickly, so that in no time at all you felt you'd known her all your life, and might even think of her as a friend. So she'd shown Andrea where to hang that ridiculous mammoth-fur coat in the front closet, and hurried into the kitchen to see if she had anything suitable to serve to a multibillionaire and the most famous movie star on the planet.

Howard was easy. She knew that a handful of stale beer nuts would satisfy him. What she had was a bag of chips that was only three days past the sell-by date and an unopened bowl of pretty good guacamole dip that didn't smell bad.

So what wine goes with chips and salsa, red or white? She dithered a while over the bottles, hearing the vague buzz of conversation from the living room behind her, wondering what the hell they could be talking about, given the fact that Howard hated Matt. But it wasn't her problem, she decided. Screw Howard. She grabbed a bottle of red and went back to the living room.

Everyone had sat down again, Howard and Andrea side by side and facing Matt across a low glass table, the fire crackling off to one side. Susan set the tray down and opened the bottle in dead silence. Nobody reached for any chips. Oh, well, the important thing was to offer it. She poured wine into four glasses.

"What should we drink to?" Andrea asked.

"How about the return of old friends?" Howard suggested, glaring at Matt.

"How about full disclosure?" Susan said.

"Disclosure of what?" Andrea said, brightly. She looked from Susan to Matt to Howard, obviously realizing she was way behind everybody else here, but not seeming too concerned about it.

"I'd go for that," Howard said, looking back to Matt.

"You first," Matt said. "Was that your dirty bomb?"

Howard drained his wine and set the glass down on the table, hard.

"You have entirely too high an opinion of me," he said. "Or too low, depending on how you look at it."

"Can somebody catch me up here, please?" Andrea said.

Matt kept staring at Howard, but finally sighed and looked away.

"Might as well, I guess. Let's see, where was I? Oh, yes. After the people who may have been government agents or may have been employed by a certain Mr. Warburton couldn't get anything out of me with drugs . . ."

CAUSE-and-effect was at the heart of the paradoxes of time travel, and Matt had had occasion to ponder the concept often in his ruminations while trying to construct a time machine for Howard Christian.

A Jew from Germany observes an atom of a heavy metal split into two parts, releasing energy.

Effect: The best minds of a nation are assembled in strict secrecy. A certain rare ore is mined at a fever pitch and trucked to Tennessee, where the infinitesimal fraction of it that is of any use is painstakingly extracted. A city rises out of the sand of the New Mexico desert. A device is constructed and flown first to a remote island in the Pacific, then to a much larger island where, one fine August morning, it is detonated in the air over a city, incinerating eighty thousand Japanese, mostly civilians.

A man sitting at a table in a room points to a particular spot on a map and says, "I last saw it here." In an adjoining room needles on a machine jump and twitch in a way that suggest the man is probably telling the truth.

Effect . . .

Three days later the operation had been planned out and preparations made. A truck was driven into position, a bomb threat was called in. When the local television news eyes in the sky were in place with good camera angles, the bomb in the truck was detonated, right in front of the old May Company building in the neighborhood known as Museum Row. Damage to the building was minimal. A cloud of smoke formed and drifted slowly eastward, toward the area where there had been that big hullabaloo two weeks earlier. Soon the police and special Homeland Security troops in their radiation gear were swarming all over the site, picking up every piece of wreckage.

The first reports of radiation came three hours after the explosion and stated that the levels were low; nothing to be alarmed about. As a precaution people were being evacuated in a three-block radius. The next bulletin was three hours later, and stated that radiation levels were a bit higher than had been initially believed.

But still no cause for alarm. And, oh, yeah, we're evacuating six blocks in every direction now.

No more "official" reports were really necessary after that. The only problem was to keep Angelenos from voluntarily evacuating the whole metropolitan area. Once again, someone had seriously underestimated the fear the public had of radiation, and of government reassurances.

For twenty-four hours the traffic on the freeways was a complete nightmare. Seven people died from natural causes, just sitting there, ambulances unable to get to them. Airplanes arrived at LAX virtually empty and left full. The next day traffic was better than it had been since 1947, at the opening of the Pasadena Freeway. Every hotel room from San Francisco to Reno to Las Vegas to Phoenix to San Diego was taken, some of them double-booked. For a mile in every direction from the point where Matt's finger had touched the map, there was hardly a human soul in residence. There was a cordon around the whole area.

Now there was room to work. The trouble was . . . work on what?

The results of Matt's interrogation had been very frustrating to those in power. The spectrum of drugs known collectively as "truth serum" were very sophisticated these days. Something could be mixed up that would force anyone to spill everything they knew in only a few hours. Thus the interrogators were used to getting the information they needed, pronto, and being able to deny later that any coercive methods had been used. Matt's hysterical aphasia was a new one to the interrogators, and one that drove them to distraction.

There were older, more distasteful ways of getting information, and back in Washington there were those who began to advocate them. What the heck? This guy holds the secret to something that makes the hydrogen bomb seem like a flint arrowhead, we *must* have it, and if a little blood gets spilled, it will be in a good cause. Always bearing in mind, of course, the fable of the goose that laid the golden egg. Because it is well known, it is axiomatic among students of this kind of thing, that *everybody* talks under torture. The only question is how soon, and the answer is that with most people you only have to lay the instruments of torture out there on the table. The tougher cases will sell out mothers, mates, and children after less than an hour of pain. Just give the word, Mr. President, and we will know everything this man knows by this afternoon.

The president was not one to enter into such an enterprise lightly, however, and the decision was not entirely up to him, anyway, and so the searchers were sent back to the transcripts to pore over them for a clue as to the location of the device.

The transcripts were maddening.

Q: When did you last see the device?

A: I have probably not yet seen it for the last time.

(Analysis: He's telling the truth. Probability 90%.)

Q: Where did you last see the device?

A: The question has very little meaning. I showed you on the map where I was the last time I saw it.

(Analysis: True, 90%)

Q: Where did you put it?

A: As I said, the question has no meaning.

(Analysis: True, 55%)

He was waffling, he was concealing something, but not once in his interrogation did he make a statement that could be demonstrated to be false.

And so the search went on.

It was known that he had not had a great deal of time to conceal the device, so most of the analysts figured the device had to be somewhere on the grounds of the park that contained the tar pits and the museum. And so the park was taken apart.

Magnetometers found many, many things buried on the grounds, from water and electric lines to loose change. The walls of the museum were torn out, the plumbing was torn out, the floors torn up, even the mammoth skeletons on display were disassembled and x-rayed, under the theory that the device had been made of many small parts, and they might no longer be hidden as a single unit. Nothing was found.

But all that was easy. The nasty part was draining the tar pits themselves.

The pits went down a long way, but were not bottomless. The problem was that, anything with any weight that was tossed into the pits sank into the goo, just like a trapped mammoth. People had been tossing old wagons and cars and horseshoes and coins and cans and nails and just *endless* junk into the pits for over a hundred years, so a magnetic scan was useless. The only way to search the tar was to bring it out, bucket by bucket, and go through it by hand. They dug down one hundred feet, and found no time machine. Then they had to put it all back.

At the same time the National Guard was searching house to house in a one-mile radius. It was impossible to keep a search like that a secret, of course, with so many soldiers involved. The object of the search quickly leaked out, television stations were soon showing the pictures that had been handed to the searchers, so the public's help was enlisted, with the cover story that the metal briefcase being so urgently sought was thought to contain three pounds of weapons-grade plutonium smuggled by the same terrorists who had set off the dirty bomb.

"If you find this briefcase *do not touch it! Do not attempt to open it!* Call 911 immediately and get out of the area!"

Virtually every field and pond and swimming pool and basement and closet and toolshed in southern California was searched by someone, either in the spirit of public service or in hopes of landing the huge reward. Many thousands of suspicious objects were examined by police. None contained any plutonium, nor a time machine.

MATT knew none of this at the time. He only knew that Albert and Argyle stopped showing up for the twice-daily interrogations. They put in an appearance now and then, at no predictable intervals, and asked some new questions, few of which made much sense to Matt, but never stayed longer than an hour.

Time crawled by, with no way to measure it. It might have been two weeks or it might have been six weeks. Meals arrived, sometimes when he was hungry, sometimes when he was not. After an hour they were taken away, whether he had eaten them or not. He had all the water he needed, and much more light than he desired, as the overhead fixture was never turned off. There was nothing to read, no television to watch, absolutely nothing to do but lie on the bunk or exercise. He jogged around the room, did push-ups and sit-ups, and soon was in the best shape of his life.

He slept a lot at first, and then hardly at all, to the point where he was surprised to wake up lying in the bunk.

Before long he came to actually look forward to the visits from A&A, something he would have sworn would never happen. He realized it meant they were wearing him down, and knew there was not much he could do about it. In spite of himself, he found himself asking *them* questions. Stupid, desperate questions.

How is the weather today?

Where are you from?

Is Susan okay?

Do you have more than one pair of argyle socks, or do you wash those every night?

Matt had always been a loner, but he found to his surprise that he did not seem to actually be hermit material. He found himself hungering for the barest hint of contact, and even though he was aware that Albert was probably doling out these hints with complete calculation, with the goal in mind of making Matt emotionally dependent on him, he soaked up the tiny bits of data like a sponge.

It's warm and sunny. Perhaps you can get out and enjoy it soon. It's entirely up to you, Matt.

I'm from Oregon. Yes, I know you are, too.

Susan is fine. Would you like to write her another postcard, tell her you're okay?

Argyle never answered about the socks. Argyle never answered *anything*. And of course that was calculated, too.

Matt battled it, but there was no denying, he felt more than a little lost.

But about halfway through his ordeal (as he estimated later), he began to adjust. He spent more and more time simply sitting. Sometimes he cleared his mind, went into a state of meditation, inventing for himself the basics of yoga. Other times his mind was very busy indeed, thinking over what had become the central problem of his life: time travel, and how to accomplish it.

It was during these times of meditation that he decided on his future course.

If he ever got out alive.

THEN one day Argyle showed up without Albert. Another well-known fact about prisoners in solitary confinement is that any change in routine, while it may be welcome in some ways, is also upsetting. When you are utterly in the power of someone else, and you don't even know who that someone else is, there is a superstitious feeling that any change is probably going to be for the worse. Matt swallowed hard, and got up from his seat on the bed.

"Am I ever going to learn your name?" he asked, trying to put on a brave face. Argyle ignored the question, as he had ignored every question Matt had ever asked. He walked up to within a pace of Matt and put his hands on his hips.

"I want you to know something," Argyle said. "I know you've been lying, right from day one. I know how to get the truth out of you, I could have you talking in fifteen minutes, tops. I could have you telling me things you didn't even know you knew. I just wanted you to know that." And he hit Matt in the nose with a right hook before Matt was even aware the man was moving. On his way down Matt caught a left jab to the stomach that explosively brought up the powdered eggs and greasy bacon and coffee he had eaten a few hours earlier. After a moment of blackness Matt found himself on his knees staring at a mixture of vomit and blood on the floor between his hands. The vomiting had stopped, but the blood was still spurting.

So this is how it begins, Matt thought. From the first he had been expecting this. In fact, he'd expected it a lot sooner. He had dueled with them for a long time, doing his best to conceal the one nugget of information that might, *might,* be of some use to them, and did it while always telling the truth. *Always,* and it hadn't been easy. He hadn't fooled them—the punch in the nose was proof of that—but he hadn't given them anything useful, either. He wasn't going to give it all up now, not after two punches, not simply because he was petrified at the very concept of torture. He had to hold out longer than that, didn't he?

So what would a movie hero do? What would Indiana Jones do? Come out with a snappy line, that's what he'd do.

Matt stared at the brown wingtips inches from his face, and at the argyle socks he had come to hate so much.

"I get it," he said. "You don't wash them at all." Well, it wasn't *Hasta la vista, baby,* but he wasn't an indestructible machine, either.

One of the brown shoes came up off the floor and Matt cringed . . . but the shoe came down. He felt something wet land on the back of his head, and realized he had been spit on. Then Argyle turned and walked to the door, through it, and, though he didn't know it at the time, out of Matt's life. Matt sat back on his heels and cradled his stomach and waited to see if he was going to throw up again.

The door was still open when Howard came in and stopped

dead in his tracks. His face flushed bright red and he turned on his heel and leaned out the door.

"I want that man charged with assault and battery!" he screamed, so angry his voice came out at the high-pitched squeak that had been the bane of his school years. "I'm a witness! I want him *fired*, and I want him in *prison*!"

Howard came back into the room, shaking with fury, and strode over to the sink, where he grabbed a towel and hurried back to kneel beside Matt. He started to mop at the blood on Matt's face, but Matt pulled away and Howard just handed the towel to him. Matt used it to scrub at the back of his head.

"He spit on me," Matt explained.

There seemed to be two Howards kneeling before him. He realized his eyes were starting to swell up. He squinted one eye closed, which probably gave him the dubious expression he was going for.

"Took you long enough to get here."

"Matt, I . . ."

"Never mind. So what is this? Stage three of the interrogation? Start out soft, go hard, then try sweet reason? Or is there more brutality to come?"

"There was never supposed to be any brutality in the first place. That man was taking out his own frustrations, and I promise you he's going to pay for it. Here, let's go sit down and we'll talk about it." He grabbed Matt under the arm and Matt submitted, letting himself be helped to his feet, where he staggered to the table and fell heavily into a chair. The flow of blood had dried to a trickle but his nose hurt like hell. He busied himself wiping his face, giving himself time to think about this new development.

Was this staged for his benefit? Rough him up, then bring in a familiar, if not exactly beloved face, and go at him again while he's presumably at his most vulnerable?

You could sure make a case for it, but Matt couldn't buy Howard Christian as that good an actor. He looked across the table and saw a man who might be a real bear at a conference table doing a business deal, but who simply didn't have it in him to simulate the shaking hands, the sick expression.

He decided to trust him, tentatively. Matt knew himself to

be a poor judge of character, not having spent a lot of time studying the human species, but he felt he'd learned a lot during his weeks in here when there was nothing at all to do but study his interrogators. He'd certainly read Argyle correctly.

"You asked me what took me so long," Howard said. "It took me two weeks just to find out who had you."

"Who is it?"

Howard grimaced.

"All right, I understand you haven't told any lies, so I won't either. Part of the deal that got me in here is that I can't tell you that. Think of them as the NNSA."

"Americans, right? What's it stand for?"

"The No Name Spook Agency. That's all you need to know about them, because there's absolutely nothing you can do about your detainment here, or the treatment you've received. Have you been physically abused before today?"

"No. Well, they never turn off the lights, and they drugged me."

"I'm not surprised. Again, nothing to be done about it. It took me another two weeks to find out where you were."

Matt raised an eyebrow, and regretted it. It hurt.

"New Jersey," Howard said.

"They kidnapped me in California."

"It's taken me until now to get in to see you. Matt, believe me when I tell you that I've been working on nothing but the mammoths, and your situation, and *my* situation, from the moment this happened."

"Your situation?"

"You think I'm immune? It's possible that the only reason I'm not in your situation is that I didn't run afterward."

"Right," Matt said. "That, and forty billion dollars."

"Probably thirty-nine now, after my expenses since the mammoths showed up." Matt realized it was an attempt at humor, but he didn't find it amusing, and after a moment neither did Howard. He hung his head briefly.

"You're right, of course. My questioning was done with my lawyer at my side. But don't think it was pleasant. My wealth shielded me from all this"—he waved his hand at the room, glanced once more at the pool of vomit and blood—"but make no mistake about it, the government wants the time machine, and they intend to have it. I've convinced them that I don't have it. Hell, I don't have my warehouse, my frozen mammoth, my caveman, or any of the things you were working on. But Matt, I told the government everything. I told the truth, and they tell me they can't prove you ever told them a lie. But we both know you're hiding something. And I'm not sure I can get you out of here unless you tell them."

Out of here? Matt hadn't even been thinking in those terms. He had assumed he would be detained for a long, long time.

"Howard . . . I'm still not sure there is a 'them.' It might be you, keeping me here."

Howard looked Matt straight in the eyes.

"Maybe I deserve that. I can see how you might think it, anyway. There's no way I can disprove it, because the people who do have you are never going to reveal themselves to you, they're not going to come in here and say, 'Howard Christian has had nothing to do with this; in fact, he's been using every ounce of influence he has to stop this travesty.' All I can do is tell you it's not me, it's not my people."

Matt sighed. "Let me go through it all once more. I don't have the time machine. I don't know where it is. I have told you the last place I saw it, but I don't know where it went after that. I might be able to find it if I was out of here, but I'm not even sure of that.

"There is only one hope here. If I am allowed to leave this place, if they cut me loose and don't bother me, I might be able to figure out how it works. Or how it worked, anyway. I am on the track of something . . . but Howard, it is so crazy, it is so *ephemeral*, that it goes away every time I look at it. I haven't even tried to explain this to the questioners, whatever their names are, because I can't explain it to myself. I need time to think. I need time to explore new avenues. The answer will not be where we expect to find it, I know that much. This requires a new way of thinking, and I don't know if my brain, if *any* human brain, is *equipped* to think about it. It needs new tools. Mathematics isn't enough. Science isn't enough. And . . . that's about all I can tell you." Matt spread his hands, and looked toward the one-way mirror.

"So ask them, when you leave here, ask them if I told one single lie just now. Will you do that, Howard? Examine what I said, see for yourself that it's all the truth, and ask yourself . . . *what could I possibly be hiding?*"

Howard studied Matt's face for a while, then glanced over his shoulder at the one-way mirror, and smiled wryly at the unseen observers.

"How about this," he said. "I can set up the lab again. No problem. You know we have tapes of everything you did, we have all the data you stored on our outside servers. You can get right to work on building another time machine."

Matt clucked his tongue and shook his head sadly, until a stab of pain reminded him that wasn't such a great idea.

"Howard, Howard, you've been accusing me of not telling all the truth, and now look at you. That lab is already set up, has been since a few days after the incident, and whoever was your number two choice to build your time machine is hard at work duplicating it with all that data you're talking about. Since I voluntarily gave these government people all the data in my files, they're doing it, too."

Howard didn't even look guilty this time.

"Of course he is. But now you can take over."

"How's he doing?"

"Getting nowhere. Oh, he's built twenty more machines, and we can't turn on a single one of them."

"Have you tried whacking them?"

"What do you mean?"

"Exactly what I said. My machines didn't work, either, until that nut started hitting one of them with a hammer."

"You can't be serious."

"I'm dead serious. The answer, if there is one, may be just that crazy. It might be that this was all a one-time event, impossible to duplicate. Hitting that box may have shifted something temporally, randomly, in a way that couldn't be duplicated in a billion years."

"Do you think so?"

"I don't know! It's one of the things I've been thinking about, when I'm able to think of anything at all. Clearly something odd happened, and it wasn't my doing. I think you're all barking up the wrong tree here, thinking that if you just pressure me enough I'll be able to give you the secret. I don't know the secret! I don't know how many more ways to say that. But, one more time . . . I may be able to find it. *If you leave me alone*."

"Would you go to my lab to work on it if they let you out?"

"Of *course* I'd go. I'd do almost anything to get out of here." He looked again at the mirrored window. "Pay attention in there! Test this statement for truth! I'd go, I'd spend day after day tinkering with your useless boxes. But it would be a total waste of my time and your time. What I need to find out won't be found by playing with a fistful of high-tech marbles with a lot of government monkeys looking over my shoulder. I have to look elsewhere."

Howard shrugged, and spread his hands.

"Where?"

"Esalen was a good start."

"You want to go back to Esalen?"

"No. I want to be let loose. I want to explore new avenues. I want to find new tools. Because the answer, if there is one, will not be found in your lab."

He tapped the side of his head, and winced.

"It'll be found up here. If that thug hasn't damaged it too much."

THE fifth face Matt saw in his cell was a woman who might have been a doctor. She wore no credentials and gave no name or title, but she carried the tools of the trade: stethoscope, blood pressure cuff, reflex hammer, one of those little flashlights with a lens for looking into eyes, ears, nose. She did a routine exam, carefully checking his pupils and telling him he didn't have a concussion. She checked his nose and examined the bruising on his abdomen.

Two things struck him while she worked. One was that it took a relatively short time without them for a prisoner to become almost *astonished* by the very idea of a female. He was acutely aware of the smell of her, the look of her, the feel of her skin when she took his pulse. He fell head over heels in love, though she was not really that attractive, and not even very nice.

The other was not so charitable. What kind of doctor would work in a place like this? Had she had occasion to treat injuries far more debilitating than his? Had there been bodies to dispose of?

She left. Three more meals were delivered. Then Howard returned, possibly twenty-four hours later, with a cardboard box under one arm.

"I've got good news," he said with a big grin.

"For me, or you?"

"Both of us, I hope. You're outta here." He dropped the box on the table and Matt joined him.

"They ruined some of your stuff," Howard said, taking out the wallet which Argyle had torn apart in front of him. "Your computers seem to be intact. I didn't access anything in them, but I turned them on."

"You have all the data anyway," Matt said, and Howard didn't deny it. "That's fine with me. If somebody else finds the answers in there, so be it. I'd welcome the chance to stop thinking about it." He pawed through the remains of his things. "Where's the marble?"

"Marble? Oh, right. They wanted to keep that. I told them it belonged to you." Howard smiled, and reached into his pocket. He came up with the marble encased in its little wire cage. He held it out to Matt, and Matt knew that if he hadn't mentioned it, Howard would have kept it forever. "Keeping it as a souvenir?"

"Sort of," Matt said, taking it and turning it against the light. It was a superb little agate, red in color, with a swirling imperfection in the center that refracted brilliantly. "It's all that's left of the glorious experiment."

"That, and the time machine," Howard reminded him, hopefully.

"Yes, wherever it is," Matt agreed. He looked up at Howard. "So, what's the catch?"

"Catch?"

"What are the conditions? I can't believe I'm simply being cut loose. I expect this will be more like parole."

Howard looked uncomfortable.

"You're probably right. They haven't told me anything about that, but I suspect they'll be keeping an eye on you."

"So that's it, right? I just walk out of here? No releases to sign? No bills to pay for the room and board? No mighty oaths of secrecy to swear?"

"How can they ask for a release when you haven't even been here? As for secrecy, if you start talking about this you will be punished severely; it will make what that monster did to you today seem mild."

"Killed?"

"I honestly don't know, and very much do not *want* to know. My opinion? I doubt it. But they could make you sorry you're alive."

"I already am."

MATT was thirsty, and he didn't want any more wine. He realized he'd done more talking in the last few hours than he'd done in the last few . . . months? Years, even? He stopped, and there was a long silence in the room.

"Most of this is new to me," said Andrea de la Terre.

"I kept meaning to tell you," Howard said, uneasily. "I never could seem to find the right time."

Andrea looked at him skeptically.

"Or how to go about it," she suggested.

"Honey, everything he just said is the truth."

She thought about that. "Okay. But what he said is that you *told* him you had nothing to do with his kidnapping and imprisonment. I can believe that's the truth. What I need to hear now is *you* telling *me* that you didn't have anything to do with it."

Howard looked hurt.

"You don't believe me?"

"Howard, I don't know yet, because you have chosen not to tell me anything about it. I want you to tell me now."

"I had nothing to do with it," Howard said.

Andrea looked at him for a very long moment, then nodded and patted his hand.

"I believe you." She turned to Matt. "Do you?"

"Yes. I still do." He was going to add that it didn't really matter, it was a long time ago, let bygones be bygones, but decided she didn't need to hear any doubt in his voice. He could give Howard that much help. Watching the expression of relief on Howard's face, Matt realized the man really was deeply in love with his movie star girlfriend, just like the tabloid headlines said. For a moment he thought Howard was going to kiss her, but he turned instead to Matt.

"So, Matt, you're back at last. I guess you know what my next question is."

"Should I speak real loud for the NNSA mikes?" Matt asked.

"Doesn't matter much. They're watching me, too. They'll find out what you say."

"All right, then, Albert, or Mister Argyle Socks, or whoever else has this place bugged, I'm sorry to bring bad news . . . but I haven't learned anything."

Howard looked at Matt blankly. The words didn't seem to have any meaning for him. He said what people often do when a statement is unacceptable to them:

"What do you mean, you haven't learned anything?"

"I. Haven't. Learned. Anything. You want me to say it again?"

Howard couldn't seem to come up with a response.

"Howard . . . it was always an iffy thing. I told you I had a . . . a notion. A hint. A glimmering of something, if you will. I thought it might lead somewhere. It didn't. I'm at a dead end. It was either a fluke, an act of God, a cosmic joke, or something that is just beyond the capacity of my poor, abused brain. I'm through. I give up. I quit."

Matt looked theatrically around the room, and held his arms out, wrists together.

"You hear that, Mr. President? Come on, arrest me again, run me through the wringer. *Fuck you all!*"

Matt found himself shaking with rage. He knew he had suppressed it for a long time. Maybe it was being near Susan again, the bitterness of the five years without her that had been lost, gone and impossible to get back, and the very strong possibility that he would never get her back at all, and who could blame her?

He got himself back under control again quickly, sat back and glanced at Susan, who was smiling strangely at him, then at Howard.

Howard was standing, and his face was red and twisted with fury.

"Well, that's just not good enough, goddamnit. I know you're lying."

Matt couldn't think of anything to say to that.

"Howard," Andrea said, gently, "if he hasn't found the answer, it will have to be good enough."

"No, goddamn it! You lost my warehouse, all my pregnant elephants, the original time machine and all the duplicates, my frozen mammoth, my caveman and my cavewoman, my—"

"Cavewoman?" Matt asked. "You never mentioned any cavewoman."

Howard seemed to realize he had said more than he intended. He really *had* been shaken up.

"It was none of your business. After we got the mammoth sperm there wasn't any pressure to deal with the rest of it. The woman had no metal objects on her. So I deferred to Rostov, my mammoth expert, who wanted to do the recovery properly. Very, very slowly. Then Rostov came down with pneumonia from working in the cold, and the work was shut down for a while. Then he died, and I was looking for a new mammoth expert when...well, when the whole project vanished."

"A woman," Matt said.

"Probably a woman."

"You should have told me about that."

"I didn't see it was relevant to your work."

"You should have told me."

Never defend yourself. Attack. "Screw that. I'm telling you I think you're lying, and I'm going—"

"Howard, you owe him an explanation."

He took a moment to calm himself. Andrea was trying to teach him a more forgiving outlook on things and he was trying to learn. He took a deep breath.

"I didn't tell *anybody*, because Indian tribes have been raising such an uproar over the remains of what they claim were their ancestors. They have been burying priceless anthropological specimens, bodies we could learn a lot from, and . . . well, you get in the habit of secrecy."

"It might have had a bearing on my research."

"How?"

"You just don't hamstring a researcher that way. You tell me everything, and you let me decide what's important."

"Okay. I was wrong, I admit it. But now . . . we both know you're lying. And I won't let you quit—you know something and I mean to find out what it is."

"I don't work for you anymore, Howard," Matt pointed out. "And I don't particularly like being called a liar."

"How do I know you haven't been lying right from the start? We all knew you were hiding something but we could never figure out what it was. I've wondered for a long time if those government people were a bit too heavily invested in their lie detection technology. I've been wondering if you just happen to be so good a liar that the machines can't catch you. I've had it researched, it *is* possible to fool them."

"My understanding is that psychotics are best at it," Matt said.

Howard was about to reply to that when Susan stood up.

"That's the third time you've called Matt a liar. Get out of my house."

"*Your* house? This house belongs to me, and you know—"

"It may belong to you, but it's my legal residence, and as long as it is I determine who is welcome in it. Matt is my friend, and I won't have him insulted in my house. If he says he's telling you the truth, he's telling you the truth. Now, please leave."

Howard stood there, stunned. In his youth he had been all too familiar with being ordered around, but it had been quite a long time since anyone had done so, and even longer since someone had told him he couldn't have something once he had set his sights on it. He opened his mouth to say something, then thought better of it. Matt watched him, interested but not particularly afraid of what he would say next, while one phrase went around in his mind: Matt is my friend. *Friend?* Just what did she mean by that?

Andrea stood up and took Howard's hand.

"Howard, let's go," she said quietly. Matt thought she looked a little confused and conflicted. There had been a lot for her to absorb in the last hour, much more than for any of the rest of them. She needed time to think it all over. In the meantime she was shrewd enough to know nothing good could be accomplished here tonight by dragging out an unpleasant scene.

Howard seemed to realize that too, finally, and his posture gradually softened and he looked away from Matt and allowed himself to be led toward the door. But he couldn't resist a parting shot.

"You haven't heard the last of this," he said.

Matt stayed silent until they had gone. Then he stood and turned to Susan.

"Have I cost you your job here?" he asked.

"*Hah!* Doesn't he wish?" She saw his uncomprehending look, and shook her head wearily. "I haven't filled you in on *my* wonderful life yet, have I? No, don't worry, I'm not angry, I was a lot more interested in hearing your story than telling mine. But I'm going to fall asleep right here on the carpet if I have to talk or listen any more tonight. We'll have to save the rest for tomorrow, okay?"

"Okay."

She looked away from him.

"There's a guest room at the end of the hall upstairs. Nobody's used it since I moved in—I don't have much of a life, outside of the park—so there are no sheets on the bed. I'll go up and—"

"It's not a problem, Susan. I've slept on much worse, believe me."

"You'll have to tell me all about it tomorrow." She suppressed a yawn. "Well, are you okay for tonight, then?"

Other than having a broken heart? "I'm fine," he said.

She moved to him a bit awkwardly and gave him a sisterly kiss on the cheek, which hurt more than a punch in the nose. But she lingered for a moment and whispered in his ear.

"You were lying to Howard, weren't you?"

He kissed her cheek, and whispered, "Yes."

MATT stood for almost an hour by the luminous dial of the watch he had worn religiously since the first day of his release from the prison cell in New Jersey, something he had not done in his earlier life. The moment he hit the street he had been seized by a powerful desire to know what time it was, to *always* know what time it was. Eight weeks in a cell where the lights were never turned off could do that to you. It was a Seiko solar-powered radio chronometer with a stainless steel case and embedded electronics; you could drop it from the Resurrection Tower and run over it with a tank and it would still keep perfect time from the Naval Observatory atomic clock.

He spent the time doing what he often did when confronted by a situation he felt inadequate to deal with. He asked himself what the hero of a romantic comedy would do. He remembered Clark Gable erecting a sheet—the walls of Jericho, he called it—in a motel room, and assuring Claudette Colbert that the wall would not be breached, correctly following the mores of the 1930s. But it was Susan who had put up the sheet, hadn't she? And this wasn't the twentieth century.

What would a modern hero do? Probably never have gone meekly to the guest bedroom in the first place, Matt guessed. But if he did he sure wouldn't have slept there. He would have strode confidently down the hallway at some romantic hour of the night to his lover's room, opened the door, and she would either have been eagerly waiting for him or he would have slipped into her bed and she would have been pretending to be asleep, and then pretend to be overpowered. Both of them would have bright, witty, sexy things to say to each other.

Rudolph Valentino would have ridden all night on his camel and sneaked into her tent and ravished her, even if she resisted at first.

Try as he might, he couldn't see Matthew Wright, Ph.D., nondescript and awkward and tongue-tied and the very definition of the stumbling, fumble-fingered, malaprop geek from Central Casting, making his way from his lonely bed to that of his lady without slipping on a roller skate, toppling a priceless Ming vase, and inadvertently setting fire to the drapes. In the movies, he knew he would play Jerry Lewis, not Dean Martin. There was very little Casanova in him, almost no Cary Grant.

Nevertheless, the wee hours of the morning found him making his way carefully over the plush carpeting, his heart throbbing in the back of his throat. What's the worst she could do? Scream and shout? Throw things? He'd slink back to his room, or even out the front door and into the night, humiliated, but at least aware of where he stood.

The door would be locked, he was sure.

It wasn't. It turned easily under his hand. Now the alarm will go off, he told himself. But it didn't. He pushed the door slowly open and a wedge of light gradually widened and fell across the king-sized bed, where the covers had been turned back. Susan was lying there on her side, nude, her back to him. She rolled over and sat up on one elbow, then swung her legs over the side and sat up, facing him.

"Took you long enough," she said.

"THERE seems to be so much we need to talk about," Matt said, later, "and I can't seem to think of a damn thing to say."

"I've visualized it many times," Susan said, as she nestled herself a little more snuggly under Matt's protective arm. "I saw myself screaming and shouting for, oh, hours and hours. Then kicking your miserable ass right out the door. Then crying all night long."

"Did I say I'm sorry yet?"

"I think you did. Several times. I was a bit too busy there for a while to listen very carefully."

"In case I didn't, I'm sorry."

"You don't have to be. In a way, it's a good thing Howard showed up when he did. Just listening to you tell it like you did explained so much. I wondered why you never contacted me but through those damn postcards. I had no idea you'd been arrested."

"I never was, actually."

"You know what I mean. Abducted? Kidnapped? Whatever you want the call the atrocity they put you through. I lost a lot of faith in America tonight."

"You want to know something funny?" Matt said, and laughed quietly. "In a way, it made me feel better about this country."

Susan sat up and stared down at him. "You can't be serious."

"I am. Think about it. There are a lot of places where, if the government thought I knew something they just had to have . . . well, I'd *still* be in that cell, or a lot worse one, and they'd be torturing me every day. Lots of other places they might not torture me, or at least not much, but they'd never let me loose."

"I can't believe this."

"I've had five years to put it in perspective. Don't get me wrong, I'm not defending it. It was wrong, it was immoral. Unconstitutional—though probably not illegal, if you can follow that reasoning. Bad form, poor sportsmanship, nasty and rotten and not fair, all of that. But I'm alive, and I'm out, and I never thought that would happen. Movies and books and television shows have convinced us of that. What I found out is that *some* people in the government have *some* scruples."

"If you have a billionaire on your side," Susan snorted.

"There's that, that sure helped. I also don't doubt that even this NNSA has forms to fill out and oversight of some kind, a bureaucracy to answer to. Nobody operates with total impunity, everyone worries about a paper or electronic trail that may one day bring them in front of a congressional committee."

"Covering their asses."

"Don't knock it. There are lots of ways to cover your ass, but the best one is to not do the crime."

Susan nestled herself back against his chest, nuzzled his neck.

"You've changed, Matt."

"Is that good, or bad?"

"It's just different. I think I like it. I think you've learned a lot."

"I have learned a lot about myself. That's a big part of what this whole crazy journey has been about."

"I've changed some, too," she said, in a different tone.

"I want to hear all about it. Every detail."

"And I want to tell you," she said, then whispered in his ear, "but not here, and not now."

He frowned, then realized what she meant.

"You think they might—"

"Shh. It's best to assume they might be listening." Raising her voice, she said, "Looks like the sun's coming up. It's been a long night, but would you believe it, I don't feel tired at all. How about we go for a walk?"

"Sounds good to me," he said, hoping he sounded casual.

THERE was a dirt trail leading down the hill where Susan's house sat, that soon reached a small stream that bubbled over rocks and snags.

Matt followed Susan, who seemed familiar with the place. He noticed her slight limp more here than he had in the house. She seemed to pick her way over the stones a bit more carefully than he would have.

Last night in the dimness of her bedroom he had felt the puckered scar on her thigh where the bone had been shattered and poked through the skin. Her hand had immediately grasped his and tried to move it away, but he had resisted, and eventually she had let him explore the length of it. She hadn't wanted to talk about it, but eventually he got out of her that there had been three operations to put her leg back together, that there was a titanium rod where most of her femur used to be.

She wouldn't let him look at it with the light on.

Gradually they lost the magnificent view of Mount Hood and the pine forest closed around them. She stopped, and kissed him fiercely. Then she broke away and gestured toward a fallen log. "Let's sit here for a minute, Matt. There are some things I have to tell you."

He waited.

"Matt, you said you have changed. You're not the only one. When I went into this, all I wanted to do was be a part of a great experiment. I don't care about getting my name in the history books. Howard could have that, him and the gene-pushers that fertilized the eggs."

It took Matt a moment to realize that she was talking about the original project, the production of a mammoth/elephant hybrid, the job she had been hired to do. So much, so very much had happened since then; that project was ancient history, supplanted with the arrival of two live mammoths and a supply of fresh egg cells and sperm from the rest of the herd and from Big Daddy.

"I grew up in the circus. I love elephants, I loved training them, I felt I was doing some good keeping the species alive. There aren't many left alive in the wild and I felt—still do feel—that zoos and circuses were doing valuable work breeding, preserving the gene pool. I know a lot of people disagree, but that's what I felt."

"But you've changed your mind."

"Partly. Things happen." She was rubbing her thigh, not seeming to be aware she was doing it, and he wondered if it was just because it was sore from the hike.

"Go on."

She smiled wryly at him, and shrugged.

"I guess there's really no way to do this but to just come out and say it. I'm going to steal Fuzzy. I'm going to do it tonight. Do you want to help?"

There were so many things Matt might have said.

You're going to steal the most famous and valuable animal on the planet.

The animal belongs to a billionaire, one of the most powerful men on the planet, and one who is not always too fussy about his methods.

Fuzzy is rather . . . large. Why not steal the Golden Gate Bridge while you're at it?

There were just about as many questions he could have asked:

How will you hide him?

Where are you going to take him?

What will you do with him?

Are you crazy?

And simply, *Why?*

But what he said was, "Yes."

24

IT was far and away the most amazing show Matt had ever seen.

He was familiar with the magic that could be done with computer-generated imagery. But he had never been to a major theme park, or a big stage show in Las Vegas or Broadway. He was not prepared for the hyperreality that could be created by live performers, clever lighting, smoke, mirrors, and thundering sound. When the giant mammoths strode over his head on the giant screens above him, he felt like an ant. He almost dropped his popcorn.

He had what he figured was one of the best seats in the house. In a football stadium he would be sitting on about the forty-yard line, five rows up from the field. Some would say the skyboxes were better but Matt couldn't believe it. They were way up there at the top of the stadium, right above the cheapest seats. That position would distort the perspective of the overhead screens, like sitting in the front row of a movie theater, and it was as far as you could get from the action on the floor. He supposed it was a status thing, sitting on a comfortable sofa with servants catering to you, surrounded by your rich and beautiful friends, eating fancy food.

But why would you come here to eat French five-star cuisine? It was the *circus*, for crying out loud! A digitized, computer-controlled, steroid-pumped, and amphetamine-boosted version of the circus, but a circus all the same.

One of Matt's earliest memories was of a visit to the circus. He must have been three or four. In retrospect it had been a shabby little thing: a musty tent with rips in the canvas, a lion tamer with three raggedy big cats that had to be coaxed to stand up and roar, aging aerialists who did tricks a good ten-year-old gymnastic student could top. But it was all magic to him, and the highlight was the elephants. Four of them, lumbering ponderously around and around the single ring to the crack of the ringmaster's whip. He still remembered the exciting, animal smell of them, the insistent beat of the marches by John Philip Sousa and Karl King, and the taste of cotton candy and Cracker Jack.

This circus was everything he remembered, to the tenth power, with the sole exception of the cotton candy. They didn't sell it. Probably too hard to clean up the mess from the deeply padded, rocking seats. He crunched down on another mouthful of something called Karamel Kettle Korn that was too sweet but close enough for rock and roll, and made a mental note to speak to Susan about the criminal lack of Kotton Kandy.

Then he remembered this would be her last day here, one way or the other. And he didn't figure they'd be serving a lot of circus snacks in jail.

Now cut that out, he told himself. *Think positive.*

His seat was one of the perks of Susan's job. She had a block of five seats for every performance. She said the practice was called "ice," and it was a long showbiz tradition which she had known from her earlier circus days, though she had never qualified for it. The headliners all demanded a certain amount of ice, and the number of seats you got was a measure of your importance, so they fought for it fiercely, like movie stars measuring the length of each other's Winnebagos. Up to twelve hours before a show she could give or sell them to anyone she chose. After that they went back into the lottery pool and she got the money, which was a nice piece of cash every night since she hardly ever had anyone she wanted to give them to.

Susan's other four seats had gone to a young couple who obviously could hardly believe their luck, not only winning the daily seating lottery but getting some of the best seats in the house. They had a boy named Dwight who was five or six, and a girl, Brittney, around nine years old. Matt couldn't help noting their reactions. They liked the movie on the tent ceiling but it was obvious they had seen things like that before. The children shivered and giggled when the cold air came blasting in. They liked the meteor shower and gasped when the arena shook in the simulated earthquake.

Then came the elephants, and Big Mama. Matt noticed the huge pachyderm's front legs were chained together and she tended to just stand there until prodded by metal-tipped sticks carried by her handlers. This stick, called an ankus, was a traditional tool of mahouts in Asia. Susan said it could cause damage by an unskilled trainer, but was an absolute necessity with even the gentlest, most socialized captive elephant to remind her who was the boss. The key was to apply it sparingly, lightly, and judiciously, and never, never, *never* think that it would protect you if the elephant really decided to do you damage.

Dwight was beside himself with delight when Big Mama appeared, and seemed awed by the girls in their gaudy costumes. Brittney smiled and watched it all with interest, but it was clear what she was waiting for. She was wearing a Fuzzy T-shirt and a Fuzzy hat with a fuzzy trunk sticking out in front and little woolly mammoth ears flapping at the sides, and waving a Fuzzy pennant.

And now here it came . . . no, not quite yet. First there were the baby mammoths.

There were a dozen of them now, all full-blooded Columbians, all the product of Big Daddy's semen and the egg cells harvested from the bodies of the slaughtered herd of cows, born to Indian elephant host mothers. The oldest of them were three years old now, "toddlers" tipping the scales at twenty-five hundred pounds. These came out first, followed in order by smaller and smaller and smaller youngsters, until the final pair, year-old infant twins weighing no more than nine hundred.

"It's Me-tu and U-tu!" Dwight shouted, and Matt realized that superstar Fuzzy had at least some competition in the hearts of the world's children. He knew that many if not most of the kids here could name all twelve of these animals.

Matt found himself on the edge of his seat, almost as agog as the children all around him, as the moment arrived for Fuzzy's appearance. The music swelled and quickened and reached a volume that was almost stunning, but was not loud enough to drown out the shriek from Brittney that almost broke Matt's eardrum.

Fuzzy entered in a typical elephantine lumbering gait, not as fast as he could go but fast enough so that Susan had to trot at a pretty good pace to stay beside him. Matt remembered Susan telling him that elephants—and now mammoths—were the only mammals that could neither run nor jump. Susan's limp was barely perceptible; if you weren't looking for it you'd never notice.

Fuzzy got to the center of the arena and stopped, turning in a circle to acknowledge the thunderous applause. He seemed absolutely calm, totally unimpressed by all the lights and noise. And why shouldn't he be? He was a veteran of show business; he had been performing since his first birthday in the previous incarnation of this big, permanent home: the Ringling Brothers traveling show, booked into.the biggest stadiums and indoors arenas throughout the United States.

He towered over his retinue of youngsters. Susan had told Matt that Fuzzy had recently passed the two-ton mark, and was seven feet tall.

The producers of the show had rejected the glitter and glitz of the elephant corps for Fuzzy and the baby mammoths. There were no jeweled and feathered crowns, no spangled blankets, no howdahs or ankle bracelets or painted toenails for the mammoths. This was better, Matt decided. These creatures from the distant past would have been diminished by circus trappings. The mammoths were as nature had created them . . . albeit a lot cleaner than they would have been in the wild. These were undoubtedly some of the most pampered animals in the world. Their coats were shampooed daily and combed out and conditioned for hours. Their diets were monitored with the care usually reserved for a rocket launch, and they got thorough veterinary exams every week. Circuses in Japan and China and Russia had standing offers of twenty million dollars for any one of them. Howard had told Susan he would have sneered at fifty million. He intended to keep a total monopoly on live mammoths for the foreseeable future.

The Columbian babies were all as cute as could be, with their short yellow-gold fur. But Fuzzy wore a coat that would have made an Italian movie starlet proud. Glossy black with copper highlights, with a gentle wave that Matt supposed was natural—he had a vision of Fuzzy being done up every night with hair curlers the size of oil drums, and had to laugh—it ranged from only four or five inches on his trunk and around his face to a full three feet long on his sides and belly. The whole glorious pelt waved as he walked, and it was hard to imagine a more appealing animal. Elephants, with their thick, wrinkled, dusky hides inspired awe but Matt had never been inspired to reach out and stroke the skin of any of Susan's elephants. Fuzzy, even at this distance, just made you ache to get close to him and run your fingers through all that fur. He was like a two-ton puppy.

Fuzzy's part of the show went on for only about twenty minutes but it seemed timeless. Later, thinking it over, Matt realized that not a lot really happened. The youngsters went round and round the arena, at some points reaching out and grasping the tails ahead of them with their trunks, which delighted the children. Susan led Fuzzy to within ten feet of the crowd, slowly, so that everyone got a fairly close look at him. But as for tricks, neither Fuzzy nor his troop did much. This was again at Susan's insistence. Several times Fuzzy reared up on his hind legs, to wild applause, but there were no handstands, no balancing on platforms or rolling on big balls, no tightrope walking, none of the stunts you would think an elephant or mammoth couldn't do, but actually could.

Nobody seemed to care. It was enough to see Fuzzy. Matt figured the crowd would go wild if he just stood there and ate hay. When one of the youngsters lifted his tail and unceremoniously dropped a steaming load of dung near the center of the ring, the audience, and especially the children, went wild with delight. They liked it even more when a troop of incompetent clowns scurried out and made a hilarious botch of cleaning up the mess. There must be something universal about toilet humor, Matt decided, because he was laughing, too.

When Fuzzy and his entourage finally left the arena the show was essentially over, but nobody moved. The final attraction was about to unfold, the nightly Super Lottery, and Matt realized, with a bit of a shock, that this was the part of the show he was really here for.

Compared to the Super Lottery, a private papal audience was no big deal.

There were certainly a few people sitting around Matt who would be indifferent to the chance to enter Fuzzy's private quarters, get the chance to stroke his big furry flanks, maybe feed him a handful of his specially formulated mammoth treats. But even they wouldn't miss the opportunity to brag to their friends about how they got to hobnob for thirty minutes with the world's most famous animal celebrity.

Obviously the whole throng couldn't pet the animal, all those reaching hands would eventually wear him down like a pencil eraser. Howard had wanted Fuzzy installed in a glass environment so that the entire departing crowd could at least file by and see him on their way out, but Susan had vetoed that. To Matt's considerable surprise, Susan had vetoed a lot of Howard's more intrusive ideas, and he still wasn't sure how she got away with that. But she had given in to the idea of letting a small group—families with children only, she had insisted—spend a short time with Fuzzy after the shows. She had suggested a lottery and the show's producers had eagerly agreed, as just one more way to heighten the excitement.

So now the ringmaster announced the Super Lottery, and asked everyone to get out their tickets. Matt took his from his pocket with a hand that was suddenly moist and shaky. Everything depended on this.

The ticket wasn't a little stub of cardboard, but a souvenir in itself. It was plastic, three by four inches. There was a screen that showed a picture of Fuzzy striding across a grassy plain, and some buttons beneath the screen. After the lottery it became a handheld game, but right now it was a magic talisman. Searchlights began crisscrossing the crowd at random as the music built once again.

"And the first winning family is"—the ringmaster's voice thundered, and the entire huge arena suddenly was quiet enough to hear a pin drop—*"Paul and Claudette Williamson of Naples, Florida, and their children, Sonny and Michael!"*

Even before the names were announced Matt heard loud shouting far above him, and he turned around to see a man and woman and two boys standing and holding their tickets triumphantly above their heads. The tickets were flashing red.

The spotlights converged on them and the rest of the audience applauded. The Williamsons were met by uniformed ushers at the aisle, and led to an exit, still followed by spotlights.

Three more families were announced, one with just a single child, another with six children, the last a family from Japan with three kids who were so astonished Matt wondered if they might pass out. Matt began to worry. They must be reaching capacity now, there could only be one more family chosen.

Matt knew something nobody else in the audience knew, though some suspected, which was that the lottery could be fixed.

It was openly announced that only families with children were eligible, of course. Naturally most people suspected that the families of the rich and powerful had a big edge, but no one had been able to prove it, and Susan had told Matt that it wasn't true.

No, the cheating was only applied in favor of guests of organizations like the Make-A-Wish Foundation, kids with terminal diseases or terrible injuries. This had been Andrea de la Terre's idea, and it *had* been noticed, but who was going to complain? There had never been an outraged editorial or exposé, and there never would be.

But the fact that the lottery *could* be fixed meant that it could be fixed for anyone. It was all up to whoever controlled the lottery computer.

"And the last family of the night . . ."

It seemed the air pressure dropped a bit from all the people inhaling at once.

". . . is Jerry and Melissa Myers, and their children, Brittney and Dwight!"

To Matt's right the Myers family was bathed in light and Brittney was proving, incredibly, that she had hardly begun to demonstrate the power of her lungs earlier in the show. Matt was showered with Karamel Kettle Korn as she threw her half-eaten jumbo box into the air. He glanced at his ticket, which was flashing red, too, then he slipped it back into his pocket and joined in the thunderous applause.

Then in an instant he was engulfed in the biggest human traffic jam he had ever seen, as all the people who had not dared to leave while they still had a chance were suddenly seized by visions of gridlock in the parking lots, long lines for trains, and the tantrums of cross and exhausted children. He sat and waited for a bit as his feet were stepped on by the shuffling mass, then when his aisle was clear he got up and followed the directions Susan had given him.

EVENTUALLY he reached a point where the wide exit corridors branched beneath a sign that read:

SORRY, NO ADMITTANCE WITHOUT A FLASHING TICKET!

The crowd went one way and he went another. At last he had some elbow room. Fifty feet down a hall lined with a plastic jungle filled with capering mechanical monkeys and the standard whoops, caws, roars, and yelps of a 1930s jungle epic he came to a velvet rope barrier manned by a young fellow in safari khakis and helmet, who took Matt's flashing ticket, glanced at it, and handed it back, stifling a yawn. Theme park workers put in long hours for not much pay; this one looked more than ready to ride the train back to Portland.

Around one last bend and there was the inner sanctum. Compared to the rest of the theme park it was rather prosaic. It was a big room, as befitted the big animal Fuzzy had become, divided roughly in half by a stout fence of steel I-beams that would have stymied Big Mama in an escape attempt, much less Fuzzy. Not that Fuzzy showed any signs of discontent. He was close to the fence, facing it, extending his trunk over and over to take the mammoth treats held out in the hands of the lucky lottery children. The kids were on the far side of a less substantial railing, designed to keep them two feet back from their idol; an easy reach for Fuzzy's trunk but too far for a child to reach out and touch his legs or side.

Susan stood beside Fuzzy on the other side of the heavy fence. Between the two fences was the male assistant handler, an old friend of Susan's, who guarded a gate through which he would let groups of two or three children to a caged enclosure where they could actually reach out and stroke Fuzzy's fur. Most of the children did this in absolute, awed silence, so delicately and tentatively that it was as if they feared their tiny hands could somehow hurt the giant beast. Matt noticed that one of the kids, a girl of about seven, was careful to keep her left side turned away from the people she was with. He glimpsed a hideous burn, and a nose that was in the process of being reconstructed. The look of sheer delight on the undamaged side of the girl's face made the back of Matt's throat burn, and he had to turn away.

What am I doing here? Is this a good idea?

But it was too late for that.

Susan caught his eye, and unobtrusively turned her head and gestured toward a door off to Matt's left. He nodded, trying not to glance too obviously at the cameras set high in the walls of the enclosure. Once inside, he switched on the lights.

This was Susan's office, and it was much like any office anywhere, dominated by various data systems. There were a few old-fashioned filing cabinets, a coffeemaker, and a microwave. He noticed there were fluorescent lights in the ceiling but they hadn't come on. Instead, a series of attractive lamps at each work area gave the room a warmth unusual for a place like this.

One wall facing her desk was a grid of screens displaying various parts of the mammoth compound. On one Matt could see the children still gathering around Fuzzy. On another was a view of Big Mama's quarters. Two attendants were shoveling hay and fruit into her gigantic manger, while another used a machine a little like a Zamboni to muck out the floor, spray and mop it, and spread fresh straw, all in one operation. All three workers seemed to be keeping a wary eye on the irascible old matriarch, though she was securely chained.

The other screens showed scenes of very little interest. There were ordinary hallways, and a few that were much larger and concrete-floored, presumably for moving the elephants and Big Mama from their quarters to the arena floor and back. One camera was focused on a big parking lot where lots of vehicles were jockeying for position to get through what looked like a security checkpoint. At first Matt thought it was the remains of the audience heading for their homes and hotels, then realized it was an employee lot. He knew enough of the plan to realize why Susan would be interested in that lot.

He had been coasting along on the pleasurable high he got from watching the circus show, but now the whole improbable plan, which he had been trying not to think about too much, came crashing back into his consciousness.

Could it work?

Well . . . yes, the first part, anyway. He was dubious about their long-term chances, but there hadn't been time to fill him in on every detail of that part. But the parts Susan had laid out for him seemed well thought out, as he would have expected of her.

Once more he asked himself why he was doing this.

One reason was obvious, and that was his love for Susan. If she wanted to do this, if she thought it was the right thing to do, then that was good enough for him. There was a second reason he thought they might succeed, but he hadn't figured out how to tell her that one yet. In fact, he hadn't had time to reconcile himself to the insanity of the idea.

The third reason was simple. Any robbery of this magnitude could only be carried out with help from the inside. Susan herself was the person with the most unquestioned access to Fuzzy, but even that would not have been enough, alone.

There was another insider.

25

WHILE Matt waited and fretted in Susan's office, a confederate he had never met was seated in a room, waiting and fretting, only a hundred yards away, beneath the circus grandstand seats. His name was Jack Elk, which had almost been a problem when he was hired, six months earlier. He had been born Jack Elkins but had changed his name legally ten years before, at the age of eighteen.

Anyone with the name of an animal was automatically flagged by the personnel computers at Fuzzyland as a potential security risk, as it was fashionable among the more radical animal rights groups to adopt names like that. But Jack had always told people he was half Apache, reclaiming his racial heritage, and he could pass for it, with his dark skin and black hair. In fact he was no Indian at all, but his claim was passed on during the clearance process by a subprogram from the legal department, which went to great lengths to avoid any accusation of racial discrimination.

Now as he sat at his big, curving console expertly scanning fifty monitors, he thought it might have been better if he had called himself Jack Mole, because that was what he was. And like a mole suddenly thinking about leaving his nice, safe tunnel and emerging into the sunlight, he was nervous. Way beyond nervous; he was seriously thinking about chucking this whole insane project and just getting the hell out of Oregon.

How had it happened? How did he come to be sitting here, minutes away from setting in motion a series of events that could end up in one of the most spectacular kidnappings of all time? But . . . could you kidnap an animal? Maybe if you held it for ransom. Call it simple theft, then. It still carried a prison term.

And he'd only met Susan once. He had insisted on it, even though they both knew it was a security risk. He had to look in her eyes and know that she had Fuzzy's best interests at heart, that she wasn't doing this as part of some personal vendetta against one of the richest men in the world.

Howard Christian. *Jesus!* He was going up against *Howard Christian.* And he knew for a fact that Christian never forgot, and never forgave. Jack Elk chewed on his tenth cherry-flavored Tums of the night and watched the clock.

MATT was watching the screen that showed the hallway outside Susan's office door when he saw her open it from the outside, then from the inside. It was a little disorienting. He glanced at the screen showing Fuzzy's quarters. All the guests had gone; there was nothing to see but the star himself, placidly stuffing trunkfuls of his specially blended fodder into his mouth.

"It's time," she said simply, and he stood up. They faced each other for a silent moment, Matt waiting for her to say something else, and he realized she was giving him one last chance to back out. Maybe giving it to herself, too. Her eyes seemed to be pleading with him. It almost looked as if she wanted him to talk her out of it. As for himself, all she had to do was say the word and he was out of there. With her, of course. He didn't give much of a damn about Fuzzy, and she knew that, and didn't care, but he knew that her life had revolved around him for five years, and she had undergone a change at least as radical as the one that had overtaken him during his long quest alone. And he knew that he loved her, and would do anything for her. And there was another reason they had to do this, one he hadn't told her about yet.

So he said, "Let's do it." And surrendered himself to Fate.

JACK Elk saw Susan enter her office. The inside was one of the few places in Fuzzyland that he couldn't look into, others being the rest rooms and the offices of some of the top management and, of course, Howard Christian's offices. Earlier he had seen a man enter, keeping his back mostly to the camera, but there was another camera that gave him a better angle and he had called it up, ran it backward a few seconds, froze a frame that gave him a good three-quarter profile, zoomed in digitally, and enhanced it, just for something to do while he waited. This was what he was good at, skills he had honed in some of the bigger casinos in Las Vegas, where he could spot a pickpocket or a bottom-dealer in a crowd of people as easily as an ornithologist could peg a pelican in a flock of sparrows. He called up the face-recognition program. His own face program, the one he carried around in his brain, was excellent, sharpened by years of BOLOs issued by the casinos concerning card counters and dips and high rollers. This guy's face was familiar, one of those faces you felt was somebody who had been famous briefly, but maybe quite a while ago. Like that, but older.

The computer found him in three seconds. Matthew Wright.

Whoa! Of course. He was the guy who went back into the past with Susan. Did this change anything? Jack wondered. He glanced at the box on his screen labeled THREAT LEVEL. This was an innovation of Christian's, who had designed parts of the security programs, and a fairly dumb one, Jack thought. Christian was a hands-on sort of boss, especially when it came to computers, which to Jack translated as "interfering horse's ass." He was liable to show up at any time with some lame suggestion to "improve" systems that had been fine-tuned by generations of Nevada's most devious minds. Howard's threat levels ran from green to red. Green people were "Perfectly okay" and red people were "Do not admit under any circumstances." Trouble was, nobody but Christian seemed to be entirely sure what threat levels blue, yellow, and orange meant. You might get a blue rating if you had ever served time in jail. Orange seemed to mean "Keep an eye on him."

Matt was listed as threat level yellow. Near as Jack could figure out, that meant Howard just didn't like the son of a bitch. Of course, since he was working with Susan, Jack would have let him slide even if he was red . . . unless the reason for the red rating was that he might be a danger to Fuzzy.

Would he be? Of course not, not if he was with Susan. Right?

He was drawn away from his thoughts by the sight of

Susan and Matt coming out of her office. She stared right into Jack's camera and gave a slow nod. The operation was ready to start.

Jack wiped his palms on his jeans and got to work.

"SO what's the deal with this guy you're working with?" Matt asked, simply for something to say to take his mind off the weak feeling in his knees. "Jack . . ."

"Elk. When I first decided to do this, six months ago, I reached out—very cautiously, through a couple hidden Internet accounts—to people I thought might be willing to help. There's an underground network out there and it's not easy to get into. Animal rights fanatics, antifur people, eco-extremists, some of them involved in some very nasty stuff, so naturally they're cautious. But I had somebody I felt pretty sure would talk to me, at least give me a hearing . . . I'll tell you about him later. We're here."

They had been walking down wide, tall, brightly lit corridors, more than big enough to accommodate a herd of elephants, which was exactly what they were for. A few zigs and a couple of zags that Matt had paid little attention to, a few doors that had opened to a key card Susan carried on a chain attached to a belt loop, and now they were in a very large open room with almost no light at all. Large shapes loomed around them. Susan took a flashlight from a hip pocket and clicked it on, then swept it around the room.

The first thing the flashlight beam encountered was a full-grown giant ground sloth, rearing twenty feet above them, standing absolutely still. The thing was missing its left arm at the elbow, and from there to the shoulder the bare metal of gears and tubing of hydraulics stuck out.

"Repair shop," Susan whispered. It made no sense at all to be whispering, of course, because if anybody was in the room with them they were totally screwed, but he understood perfectly why she was doing it.

"Howard has the biggest toys of anybody on the block, that's for sure," Matt whispered back. She giggled, and it delighted him inordinately that he had made her laugh. How many times in the last few years had he had to simply put out of his mind all the little things he loved about her? That, or go crazy. Now, if they could pull off this thing, maybe they could be together forever.

Or serve separate prison terms.

No use thinking like that. He followed her down winding paths between mechanical prehistoric beasts and was amazed, first, at how many of them there were, and second, how many were in for repairs or maintenance. Getting a colossus like a mechanical mammoth to walk realistically, something a baby mammoth could do within an hour of birth, was still a challenging problem in cybernetics and robotics. Howard's tech people were the best in the world, except maybe for the loyal old guard he hadn't been able to hire away from Disney, but there was a lot to go wrong.

Susan led him through the creatures. Matt was taken back to a trip to the Museum of Natural History in New York when he was very young. Many of the rooms had held massive skeletons, but newer ones had lifelike mock-ups made of rubber and plastic and fake fur, many of which moved their heads or opened their mouths. Very primitive stuff, compared to this, but an unforgettable experience for a child. They reached a second set of doors and Susan's flashlight revealed a prominent sign on it:

NO ADMITTANCE WITHOUT "E" CLEARANCE

"Research and development," Susan said. She carded the door and turned the handle, which opened easily with no alarm.

"You're an E clearance, obviously," Matt said.

"Wouldn't have done me any good if Jack wasn't working with me. Somebody else would have noticed this door was being opened, but Jack should be covering that. Did you know that when Disneyland opened, you bought ticket books, and the E tickets were for the best rides?"

"Really?"

"Howard enjoys touches like that. Come on."

They entered the R&D facility, which was as dark and deserted as the repair shop. All they needed to have the thing blow up in their faces was some nerd working late, but Susan said it wasn't a problem, and he supposed the mysterious Jack knew the whereabouts of anyone with access to this room.

The first thing he saw in the flashlight beam was Fuzzy. The second thing he saw was another Fuzzy. They could be identical twins. Just beyond them was a third mechanical mammoth, the same size and shape but naked, like an elephant, and with a service hatch in its side open. And just beyond that was another automaton with no skin, just metal bones and wires and a maze of tubes.

"Matt," Susan said, "meet Fuxxy."

THERE was no turning back now, Jack knew. He had taken steps that he could conceal for some hours, but not forever. A record of his actions would be stored somewhere in computer memory, and he had no idea where, or how to get at it, or how to alter it, if it could be altered at all. He supposed a computer genius could do it, given enough time, but maybe not. Because, of course, one of the biggest weaknesses of any security system was the watchers themselves. They had to be watched, and at Fuzzyland that was done, as in Las Vegas, by the computers. And Jack Elk, though one of the best in the business at operating top-of-the-line security systems, was no computer genius at all.

When the call had gone out over the underground network for a sympathizer with experience and, most importantly, spotless credentials in his particular field, it would have been too much to hope for that the person they turned up would have any hacking skills. Susan had felt incredibly lucky to find any such man at all, and twice blessed to see by his resume that he was one of the tops in his field. Such men were much in demand, and when he quit his job as shift manager of the Eyes-in-the-Sky team (known to the dealers as the Fink Squad) at the Mirage and moved to Oregon, the Fuzzyland chief of security was happy to get him, and started him off, as per union seniority rules, on the night shift, which was just where he needed to be. He quickly learned the system and settled in peacefully.

Meanwhile, the network was searched for a man who didn't have to be anywhere near as clean as Jack Elk, and who *was* a first-rate computer genius. That man was located (and turned out to be a woman, though Jack would never know that), and given the problem of getting into the Fuzzyland security computers.

Jack spent the next three months carrying a credit card-sized digicam in his pocket, snapping pictures of the layout as well as the inputs and outputs and, wherever possible, the internal wiring of the security system. He wrote down the manufacturer and model number of every piece of equipment he could get close to. He took his time, never took chances. He sent the results through the U.S. Mail and a few weeks later got back a two-inch square clear plastic chip and detailed instructions about what to do with it. A week later, in the wee-est of the wee hours of the morning, he plugged the chip into the machine where he had been told to plug it in. A red light flashed briefly on his panel, then quickly went out. He waited one minute, then removed the crystal memory chip, pocketed it, and on the way home put it in an envelope and dropped it in the first mailbox he passed on his way home as eagerly as he would have rid himself of a pound of plutonium.

Then he sat back and waited, doing his job.

Several things could have happened next.

The presence of the tiny spy could have been detected, though it was supposed to protect itself against that. In that case there would have been an investigation which may or may not have led back to Jack Elk. If it did, he would have been quietly dismissed. Nobody noises it around that there has been an attempted breach of their security.

The second possibility was that the hacker genius would be stymied, that the Fuzzyland computers were too well protected for this stunt. Jack could hang around a month or so, then go back to Vegas with his conscience clear: he had done all he could for the Cause.

The third possibility was what had actually happened. He received in the mail a small parcel with nine two-inch plastic cards exactly like the one he had plugged in before, which had explored the system and diagnosed the proper course of action. Each card was clearly numbered with a grease pencil, one through nine. With it was a short list of instructions, telling him where to remove the appropriate recording cards and plug in the new ones. *When the operation has been accomplished,* said the last part of the printed instructions, *replace these cards with the originals, and there will be no evidence left in the system of just what was done, or how.*

At the bottom someone had written in cursive, with a pen, *Piece of cake!*

And now it was time.

He looked around the room, which had fifteen stations similar to his, which was raised and behind the others, as befitted a shift manager. All the stations faced a long wall with every inch covered in surveillance screens, able to display almost every camera in Fuzzyland at one time. The pictures were constantly changing. There was no earthly reason for such a thing, Jack knew, since each operator looked only at his own twenty-four screens, but display screens were cheap and it made impressive wallpaper to show off to big shots getting a behind-the-scenes tour. It looked like a Hollywood version of a high-security installation. People expected it.

In Vegas, all the stations would be manned 24/7, covering every square inch of public area. At Fuzzyland, after the park closed, there was no need for anything like that level of paranoia. Most of the park had coverage, and every inch of Fuzzy's compound, but there was no need to monitor every camera all the time. Most of them showed nothing but cleaning crews, and after about one A.M. even those guys would go home. Motion detectors would key in a particular camera if something larger than a cat moved anywhere in the park, and Jack or one of his two assistants would take a look and deal with the situation. It was very boring work on the night shift, and boredom is the bane of any security system.

He glanced at his two companions for the night, seated at consoles directly in front of him and just below. To work this shift they didn't exactly have to be the two sharpest pencils in the cup, and they weren't. Security work tended to attract two types: retired cops, and guys who liked to wear police-style uniforms and hoped to one day get a job that would let them carry a gun.

Ed Crane was a perfect example of the first type, a veteran patrolman from the Beaverton force, sixtyish, thick around the middle, more than happy to find a job that let him sit in a soft chair all night and exercise his remarkable ability to sleep soundly with his eyes wide open. Darryl Mosely was the wanna-be: a gangly redhead with bad skin who never failed to show up in the crisply pressed khakis his position entitled him to wear, even though the guys in the pit, including Jack, usually wore street clothes. Darryl was a new hire, had worked there for only a week, and clearly had his eye on bigger things, working his way up in the organization. He was earnest and hard-working, and Jack sort of hated to do this to him. If Susan pulled this off, Darryl was forever going to be one of the guys who let a mammoth be stolen right out from under his nose.

Jack sighed and reached down to his left to open a panel on the side of his console. Consulting his list, he punched a button and a plastic recording card was ejected partway. He plucked it out and inserted card 1, punched it home, and quickly did the same with the rest of the new cards. He was about to close the console when Darryl spoke up in his clipped, military fashion, almost making Jack jump out of his skin.

"Got a camera glitch here, chief!"

Jack looked up slowly—*It's no big deal, it's just a little problem; we get one every night, don't act strange!*—and saw that one of Darryl's twenty-four screens was black.

"Ah . . . try keying it in again." *What the hell was going on?*

Darryl did as instructed, and for good measure, flicked the screen a few times with his fingernail on the well-established principle that giving a balky machine a whack or two was apt to fix it. But it didn't.

"Camera's in Fuzzy's compound," Darryl said. "Other two in there look okay, though. Critter's eatin' his way through another bale of hay."

Jack could see that on his own screens.

"How about I go down there and take a look?"

"No!" Jack said, a little too loudly. "Uh . . . you know we aren't supposed to disturb the big boy unless it's an emergency. He's got his night keeper watching him." He realized he was explaining too much. "Let me see if I can do anything from here."

Do something, do something.

Following a corollary of the same principle Darryl had used earlier, Jack pressed his thumb against each of the nine cards he had replaced . . . and felt a click on number 9.

"Oops! There we are, back on line," Darryl said.

Jack let his breath out very slowly. He hadn't realized he had been holding it.

"TELL me about this Jack guy," Matt said. "Why's he doing this?"

"Isn't the better question why am *I* doing this?"

"I've got a feeling that's a much longer story. I just asked because when my mouth is moving my teeth can't chatter."

"I know what you mean." Susan was at a desk, opening and shutting drawers. She found what she needed—one of the ubiquitous plastic cards that a few years ago would have been a CD and a few years before that a floppy disk, and a cobbled-together thing that looked as if it had been started out as a remote control for a model airplane—and they went back to the first Fuzzy. Excuse me, *Fuxxy*. Fuxxy Mark Two, according to Susan.

"I didn't screw him, if that's what you were wondering."

"Never entered my mind." It hadn't. Matt had wondered, from time to time, if Susan had had any male companionship during his long absence. It would only have been reasonable and natural, and he really didn't care and didn't want to know unless she wanted to tell him. He had only cared if she would take him back, and she had. No, he knew she hadn't gone to bed with Jack because she had said she had only met him once, and it wasn't in her nature to use people that way, to get something from a guy with sex. If she *had* screwed Jack, it would have been because she liked him, not to enlist him.

"Jack Elk is a lurker around the edges of the animal rights movement. He's a member of the Audubon Society and several other middle-of-the-road animal and conservation groups . . . pretty much like me. When he was young he went to a few protest marches and such, he was offered the chance to help 'liberate' some minks from a fur farm and declined—which was a good decision, because most of them got arrested and one had a finger bitten off. He's not a joiner and not an activist, at heart."

She lifted the amazingly realistic flap of one of Fuxxy Mark Two's ears and found a slot there to insert the card. When it was in you couldn't even see the slot.

"He is anticircus and antifur and antizoo and a vegetarian, but he's never done much about it, and we were very lucky to find him, because if he'd joined any of the more radical groups he'd never have got past the security checks here. Now hang on a minute here, I only saw this demonstrated once, and I don't want us to get trampled by a mechanical mammoth."

She concentrated on the controller. A green light came on. She punched a few buttons . . . and Fuxxy Mark Two began to breathe.

I swear it, if it wasn't too late already I'd run to my car and not stop driving until I got to the Nevada state line.

But it was far too late. On screen 1 he could see Susan and Matt and that goddamn contraption coming down the hall. He had to stick it out. Half an hour, just half an hour, that's how long she said it would take.

He got up from his chair, idly walked along the back gallery, stretched his arms and cracked his neck as he did a dozen times every shift . . . and casually glanced down at Ed Crane's console where, if things were not working, two people and a mechanical mammoth would come around a corner in about five seconds. Not that Ed was likely to notice it, staring glassy-eyed into space. But Darryl certainly would, and soon.

Nothing happened on the screen, and he went and sat back down. On his own screen he could see Susan and Matt and Fuxxy. He said a silent prayer of thanks to the Unknown Hacker. *Piece of cake, my ass.*

Slowly, as he watched them move from one screen to another, he calmed himself down, reminded himself why he was doing this, reminded himself that it was a *good* thing to do and about time he got up off his lazy, uninvolved ass and did it.

All his life—or since the age of eighteen, anyway, when he had been horrified by the pictures and stories he had seen at a booth at a career fair at his high school—he had hated the exploitation of animals. It had been like a born-again moment for a Baptist; from that day his outlook on life had changed.

His outlook . . . but not his actions. He was basically lazy, didn't interact well with people, and had found the perfect niche for himself in a job that allowed him to sit down all day and spy on people he didn't have to talk to. He figured in another ten years his ass would be a yard wide and he'd have a hard time walking from the car to the front door, but he didn't particularly care. It was the life that suited him.

But he spent his spare time—where else?—sitting at his home computer connecting with some pretty radical groups, following their exploits, cheering them on from his comfortable safe seat in the grandstands of life.

Then one day the word had gone out that an operational group—what the straight media would call "terrorists"—was looking for someone with skills that could have been culled perfectly from a reading of his resume. From some dark well of guilt in his soul, carefully kept covered for the last decade since that almost-debacle with the minks, he felt the sudden urge to stand up and be counted, to put his ass on the line, to *do something* about the terrible evils he read about every day. Cautiously, he sent out a feeler, and, cautiously, an approach was made. One thing led to another . . .

And here he was, participating in what would probably become known as the heist of the century.

"HE'S on what they call 'come-along' mode," Susan said. "He'll follow the controller wherever it goes, never get closer than five feet."

Five feet felt entirely too close for Matt, who kept looking back over his shoulder to see if the damn thing was still back there, and was never quite sure if he was happy or not to see that it was, at a steady, dependable five feet, lumbering along as naturally as any actual living beast he had ever seen.

"So it's for use in the . . . what do they call that part of the park? With all the mechanical critters?"

"No, he's for the center ring . . . maybe."

"You can't be serious. Howard plans to palm off a mechanical substitute for the real thing?"

"I said maybe. There's still a lot of bugs to be worked out. Can't have 'Fuzzy' falling over during the show and just lying there, trying to walk. So they figure they're about a year away from being able to chance it, not with this one, but with Mark Three or Four, which you saw back there being put together."

Susan sighed heavily.

"It's partly my fault. Howard and I have been head-to-head over this thing practically from day one. He wanted three shows a day, I wanted one; we settled on two. I wanted two days off per week, we settled on one. Howard had power over me, because he's sure it would take a *lot* to make me quit here. Fuzzy is . . . like a child to me. It would be very hard to leave him. But I've got some power over him, too."

"What's that?"

Susan grinned.

"Fuzzy won't work for anybody but me."

Matt laughed out loud, then looked nervously at the camera they were just passing. (Not far away, Jack wondered what the hell the idiot found so funny.)

"You're kidding."

"He imprinted on me that night, or he loves me, or he's just ornery, look at it any way you want to. He lost his mother, and never attached to any of the wet nurses we provided for him. In fact, he didn't seem to like elephant milk much. He preferred to suck the stuff that I mixed up from a bottle. He has other handlers who groom him and can lead him around from place to place if they don't get in the way of what he really wants to do, but he only fully cooperates with me. Howard didn't find that out until the first time he fired me, three years ago, and he was apoplectic."

"Fired you 'the first time'?"

"Oh, he's fired me several times since then, but it lasts about an hour or two. Actually, a while after Andrea came along, he stopped firing me. She's been a good influence on him."

"He could use one."

"Sometimes he seems almost human. Anyway, this robot was supposed to take some of the burden off the real Fuzzy.

Do the early show, sub three or four times a week, something like that. But it's one thing to make a titanothere that can walk around a predetermined track with a human operator inside, and something else to make a robot that can do tricks and really fool the eye under bright lights. The project is way behind schedule. I'm sure they'll get it right one day soon . . . and by then I really, *really* hope they'll need it badly . . . because here we are, and this is the last chance to turn back."

JACK watched them on his screen as they opened the gate to Fuzzy's enclosure and Susan entered, alone. Fuzzy had heard her or smelled her, and he turned from his manger and greeted her with his trunk. She patted his big flanks, gentling him, offering him a treat which he snarfed up. Fuxxy had come to a halt when Susan turned off the follow-me button on her controller. Now she turned it on again, and the imposter lumbered through the open gate and into the enclosure, stopping faithfully just behind her.

Fuzzy was fascinated.

He explored the newcomer with his trunk. Jack wondered what the beast was thinking. Surely Fuxxy didn't smell like a mammoth, but he sure looked like one. But when Susan touched his side gently with the ankus, Fuzzy turned and went with her outside the stall, and when she touched him again and spoke to him he stood beside Matt, apparently incurious about this new guy. And why not? Fuzzy met a hundred new people every day, and was friendly to them all. Fuzzy was everybody's friend, but only took orders from Susan.

Susan got the mechanical monstrosity positioned just where Fuzzy usually spent the night. Later, Fuzzy might normally lie down for an hour or two, seldom longer than that. If he didn't lie down—which Fuxxy couldn't do—neither Darryl nor Ed would think anything of it. Jack watched as Susan did something with the controller. Fuxxy began the slow, back-and-forth swaying that was a normal behavior for Fuzzy when he was content, or asleep on his feet. The mechanical trunk curled from time to time. It looked pretty lifelike to Jack. He looked over his board and down at Darryl's. The kid was still getting the tape loop of the real Fuzzy on his screen.

It was very, very close to the real-time picture now on Jack's. He wiped sweat off his brow.

Then Susan jammed the controller deep under a pile of hay, closed the gate behind her, and moved out of camera range with Matt and Fuzzy.

He followed them down several hallways to a point where a right turn would lead them into the arena, and a left turn to a big door to the outside. They turned left. He checked the external camera. No one out there. He got out his cell phone and punched 1, which dialed Susan's phone. He saw her answer. She said nothing, and he punched the number 2, which sent the text message ALL CLEAR. He watched her switch off, and punched the electric door opener. He gritted his teeth, imagining the racket the thing was making. If somebody were to drive into the wrong parking lot right now . . .

They left the building, the door rumbled back down (silently, to Jack), and the unlikely trio headed out across the parking lot to where Susan had parked her big pickup and monster fifth-wheel trailer. Before they even reached it the tailgate was coming down. From his angle Jack couldn't see inside, but he knew there was a dune buggy parked in the garage in back. Susan had been parking the rig there every Sunday night for months now so she could get an early start for the Oregon Dunes near Florence, or some other off-roading destination to spend Monday, her only day off.

The next part was tricky. Jack couldn't see most of it because of the angle, but it seemed to go smoothly. In fifteen minutes Susan climbed into the driver's seat of the pickup, started the engine, and pulled away.

As soon as she was out of camera range Jack punched nine buttons, ejected nine cards into his hands, and replaced them with the proper ones. There wasn't even a flicker on the screens as the recorded views were replaced by the real ones. The Unknown Hacker's magic was still working.

SUSAN pulled the truck up beside the security booth and braked gently to a stop. Harry, the night guard, left his booth smiling. He liked Susan. He wouldn't after tonight, but there was nothing she could do about that.

"Off to the dunes?" he said cheerfully.

"Getting a late start," Susan said. "Probably head east a bit, there's a good place around Bend."

"Don't break your fool neck, okay?" Harry noticed Matt sitting on the other side.

"He's my guest," Susan said.

"Sir, could you give me your visitor card?"

Matt handed it over, and Harry swiped it through a device that agreed that Matt had been legitimately allowed entrance. Susan opened the door and Harry stepped back to let her out. He followed her around back, and Susan keyed the ramp to come down.

"Damn stupid, having to search this damn thing, Miss Morgan, but you know how it is. Rules are rules."

"I don't mind a bit."

Harry stepped onto the ramp and walked up to the dune buggy parked in the back. There was room to walk around it and into the kitchen and living area. He shone his flashlight around, all the way to a narrow hallway where the bathroom was, and three steps leading up to the bedroom. If Susan was stealing office supplies or circus costumes or even computers she could have concealed a lot of them in this place, but why on earth would she? It would be insulting to Miss Morgan to do a thorough search of this rolling Hilton every Sunday night, and nobody had ever asked him to. He was supposed to make sure nobody in a large vehicle absconded with one of the bigger robotic creatures, and there sure as shit wasn't enough room to hide any of them in here.

And Fuzzy, of course. Harry chuckled at that idea. He closed the door, edged around the buggy, and jumped down to the ground beside Susan.

"Wagons ho!" he said. "Head 'er out!"

"Good-bye, Harry," Susan said. She got back in the cab and drove away.

NOT far down the road Susan pulled onto the shoulder, leaped from the cab, bent over, and threw up. Matt came around the front of the cab but she waved him away until she was through. After a moment, she stood up and gestured to the cab.

"You drive. I've only ever driven it from Portland once and to and from work. I *hate* driving this thing."

Matt thought about telling her that he didn't have all that much experience towing, himself, but knew she didn't need to hear that. And he had pulled a trailer, on the very day that his life had changed forever on his great Trout-Fishing Adventure, when Warburton came down in a helicopter and tempted him into the clutches of Howard Christian. It hadn't been that tough.

He only hoped he didn't have to back the damn thing up.

26

"DID you know Houdini made an elephant disappear on stage?" Matt asked.

"Damn right I do. What he did, he led an elephant into a big box, closed it up, had stagehands turn it ninety degrees, and then raised curtains in the front and back. There were two big holes in the box, it seemed like you could look through it and see the back of the stage. No way an elephant could be in there. The thing is, he did it with mirrors. I couldn't figure out a way to make that work with Harry going inside. Take this exit."

They were barreling through the night at a perfectly legal fifty-five miles per hour. The freeway was straight and nearly empty. It was half an hour since Matt had taken over and they were passing through the community of Troutdale. Matt eased the truck onto the exit ramp and followed a city street up and over a railroad track.

They had discussed this leg of the journey. "You're the mathematician," Susan had said, "*you* figure the odds." It was a complex equation.

Howard Christian would discover his most prized possession was missing by about six at the latest, three hours away. That would happen when Fuzzy's morning attendants arrived for work and found the woman they were supposed to relieve, the graveyard watcher, had not been there all night. ("Of *course* Howard would never leave Fuzzy unattended, not even for a minute," Susan had said when Matt asked. "That was the easiest part of this whole deal. There are two girls who work that shift, and I told each of them the other was on duty tonight.") By then they could be almost to their goal.

Almost. If they kept moving they would avoid the morning

rush hour in Portland, but would probably encounter a lot of traffic later on.

Was it better to travel at night, when they were conspicuous, or during the day, when they were one of thousands of big RVs roaring through the scenic Pacific Northwest? Keep moving, and moving fast, or lay low for a bit and lose yourself on the maze of roads that connected I-84 to I-5 to . . . well, to anywhere.

It all hinged, of course, on Howard.

"Turn in there," Susan said.

Taking it slow and easy, Matt turned into a small parking lot and drove up to a sliding chain-link gate next to a small building with a sign reading TROUTDALE MINI-STORAGE. Susan handed him a card and he swiped it through a security device, and the gate slowly rolled back.

"Just up the hill there, turn left. Unit 142."

Matt did as instructed. As the truck was still slowly rolling Susan jumped out and stood by an orange garage door directing him, then held up her hand and he stopped. The ramp was already coming down on its cables as Matt got to the back. Susan hurried inside, tossing him a key on a string. He opened the lock, lifted the garage door. The unit was big enough for a fair-sized boat and trailer, and it was empty.

Susan sat in the dune buggy, released the parking brake, and let it roll backward and down the ramp. She hopped out and steered with one hand as she and Matt rolled it into the garage.

"Nasty thing," she muttered. "I'm glad to see the end of it."

"Did you ever actually drive it?"

"Once. Just so I could talk about the joys of off-roading, if I had to. Let me tell you, it's vastly overrated as well as being environmentally harmful. Come on."

They got into the trailer and Susan released a hidden catch. They struggled to lift the false floor . . . and there was Fuzzy, lying on his side, his big, horny feet toward the rear, his head scrunched up against the top of a wheel well. He was in a space that he fit into almost as snugly as a guitar fit into a guitar case.

"God, I'm glad this part is over. He loves to go bye-bye—*don't* you, sweetie?" Susan patted his hairy cheek. "But I was afraid this would take him back to that box they put him in to transfer him from the truck to the zoo compound . . . never mind. The tranquilizer I gave him did the trick."

Matt had been amazed at how quietly Fuzzy had stood as Susan stuck a big needle in a vein in his ear and injected the drug, and how obediently he had gone down on his side. There was something unnatural-looking about an elephant or mammoth lying on his side, but he knew it was a natural behavior for them. And the space he was in . . . well, Matt was a mathematician and if you had asked him to walk around the trailer and look in the open back door he would have strongly doubted a seven-foot, two-ton mammoth could fit where he was. Susan had had the trailer specially adapted—by a customizer who probably thought she was planning to smuggle a *lot* of pot somewhere—the floor and sides beefed up, the trap door disguised, extra shocks installed.

"You know, one of the leading theories of how Houdini did that vanishing trick was that he simply had the elephant lie down in the box. Most people don't know they even do it, and practically nobody realizes how much *shorter* it makes them."

Matt stood back as Susan coaxed Fuzzy to his feet, where he swayed for a moment, looking a little lost and confused and . . . well, maybe a little drunk.

"In another year, this trick wouldn't have worked," Susan said, stroking his face. She started to coo at him, which he seemed to like. "Look at the *tusks* on this baby boy. Aren't you proud of them, sweetie? Why, in another year they'll be three feet long and starting to curve. . . ."

This was new to Matt. He had seen her handling the big elephants with kindness, touching them, talking to them, but had not detected a personal attachment. He realized he had a real rival in her affections. He tried to tell himself he wasn't jealous . . . and knew he damn well better not be, because he knew Susan wouldn't put up with it.

"Okay, Matt, I'm leaving it up to you, because frankly I'm too tired and too jazzed at the same time to make a decision. Stay, or move on?"

So they were back to Howard.

Everything depended on whether Howard would call the

cops. If he did, they had to go to ground, and do it for a month, at least. Maybe longer. In which case they would head south, where Susan had rented a farm (Matt hoped she had been *very* careful with that) with a barn big enough to hide Fuzzy and the trailer.

But Susan didn't think Howard would put out the alarm. In fact, she admitted she probably never would have got started with this if she thought he would. The farm was a backup, something neither had much faith in. Once the word was out that Fuzzy was . . . mammoth-napped . . . every barn in Oregon and Washington would be examined, by police or a Fuzzy-crazed public, then Idaho, then California, clear to Key West, Florida. She had prepared a hideaway in the barn, but she wasn't Houdini, and had no faith it would stand up to a determined search. No, if the police were called in, their chances were a thousand to one against. A *million* to one.

On the other hand, if Howard *didn't* call the cops . . . Matt figured they had not much better than one in ten odds. Probably worse.

But Matt didn't think that Howard would let the news out until he absolutely had to. Twenty-four hours, minimum. Maybe as long as three days. Howard had had a *lot* of bad publicity during the legal fights over ownership of Fuzzy, and he *hated* that. Howard hated to lose, hated to look like a fool, and would not want to be remembered as the man who let a *mammoth* be stolen out from under his nose.

"We stay," Matt said.

AT just about that moment, Fuxxy fell over.

Only Jack saw it happen. That particular camera was not displaying at Darryl's station at the moment, though it would soon come up in the regular rotation, and a marching band parading through the room would not have been likely to wake up Ed. Jack watched the stinking, lousy, bug-ridden, useless hunk of junk topple in disbelieving horror. Burned-out fuse, busted gyroscope, loose screw . . . *something*.

Jack didn't encourage idle talk with his crew. They were supposed to stay alert, speaking only when there was something to report. But any movement of the star of the show was a reportable event. *Fuzzy's moved to the other side of his pen,* he heard that a dozen times a night. *Fuzzy's taking a nap. Fuzzy just dropped a* big *load, chief.*

A minute passed.

"Looks like Fuzzy's taking his nap, chief," Darryl said. He waited, but Darryl said nothing more. Three minutes passed.

"I don't like the way Fuzzy's looking, chief."

"He's taking a snooze. What's the problem?" But he could see it himself. The damn thing was twitching its legs, jerking around. Not horribly, not an epileptic fucking *fit* or anything, but Fuzzy usually slept like a log, and when he got up it was in one smooth motion, surprisingly graceful. Jack knew that and so did Darryl.

"Where's that night girl?" Darryl said. "Come to think of it, I ain't seen her go through that room once all night." The night girl spent most of her shift in Susan's office, where there were no cameras, just a window to observe Fuzzy.

"Chief, I think I better go down there and see what's up."

Okay, that's it. Jack stood.

"I'll go. Stay where you are and I'll run take a look."

Jack hurried out of the pit, flew up two flights of stairs, tried to walk calmly down the hallway but ended up almost running, slammed into the outside door, walked to his car, got in, headed for the exit at the posted limit of 15 mph, slowed down and waved his gate pass and smiled at Harry, who smiled and waved back . . . then frowned. Jack accelerated down the road and into the suddenly threatening night.

DARRYL was no Einstein, but he wasn't stupid.

He saw the chief walking down the corridors, following him with three cameras in sequence, saw him reach the place where he should have turned to reach Fuzzy's quarters . . . saw him hurry right on past it.

Saw him go into the parking lot, get in his car, and drive away.

Something funny here.

There was a red button on his console that they called the panic button. It was only to be used in the event of fire, explosion, terrorist invasion, earthquake, or the second coming of Jesus. It had a clear plastic cover so you couldn't accidentally punch it. Darryl had wanted to punch that button from the first moment he saw it.

Ed was second in command—what a joke, the man hadn't stirred for hours, could have had a heart attack and died for all Darryl knew. He decided to show some initiative. That's what officers were supposed to do, wasn't it?

He ran all the way to Fuzzy's enclosure. He glanced through the window into Susan Morgan's office. No one there. He looked over the rail at the recumbent mammoth. It was twitching alarmingly now. He had never been this close to the star of the show. Hesitantly, he climbed over the rail and eased up on the beast, thinking about getting kicked by one of those big feet.

One of Fuzzy's eyes had popped out.

He felt a sudden urge to throw up . . . then an even worse feeling as he saw no blood on the eyeball, saw that it was hanging out of the socket on wires, saw metal in the empty eye socket.

What the *fuck*?

He got back to his station in half the time it took him on the way out, flipped up the plastic cover on the panic button, and slammed it with his fist.

The alarm was so loud Ed Crane woke up and fell out of his chair.

IT started to rain as they walked Fuzzy down the ramp. Fuzzy stopped and looked around. The poor thing hasn't been outside in so long he's forgotten what rain is, Matt realized. He got his washing from hoses and his—very clean—wallow tub, and his drinking water from a tank.

Susan got him moving into the second unit she had rented, which was strewn with hay and had a basket of Fuzzy's favorite fruits. Matt drove the truck and trailer out of the storage yard and parked it two blocks away under some tall trees that met over the street, the best they could do to foil aerial surveillance, which was their biggest fear. He hurried back and found Fuzzy had decided to sleep off his drug hangover.

"Snoozing," Matt observed.

"Yeah. Trouble is, so is the other one. I got a call from Jack Elk. Fuxxy went haywire. Jack ran off; nothing he could do about it. The alarm is out by now."

Matt saw she was shivering. He was soaked to the skin but she welcomed his arms around her. She had done so much, so incredibly much, planning it all out, making the contacts, able to do most of it only on Mondays when she wasn't a prisoner of her job, in some ways a slave to her love for Fuzzy. Now she seemed at the end of her rope. She needed reassurance . . . and he was happy that he didn't even have to lie to her.

"Makes no difference," he said, stroking her hair. "Howard gains a couple hours."

"I don't know . . . I feel we should just get him back in the trailer and *run*."

"Big mistake. If the cops are looking for us, we're screwed, we both know that. If we move now, we stand out like a sore thumb. He'll have us before the sun comes up. We stick to the plan, it's the best one we have."

"But it gives him more time to—"

"He'll *expect* us to keep moving. Every minute the circle he has to search gets wider, and he'll concentrate on the circumference of that circle. We stay here, the most intense part of the search spreads away from us, the search gets *harder*."

She smiled up at him. "Okay. You're the guy who can do the math, I guess."

"It's my thing. Trust me."

He hugged her again. The only trouble was, he knew, Howard was no slouch at math himself.

27

THE panic button rang in several places other than Fuzzyland. The nearest fire station and the local police were alerted and were soon on their way.

It also rang in Warburton's bedroom, waking him from a sound sleep. He sat up and looked at the communications console beside his bed. When you worked as the chief troubleshooter for Howard Christian you were never far from the vast machine that protected Howard and Howard's interests. He saw at a glance that there was trouble at Fuzzyland.

He punched a few buttons, heard a phone ring and go unanswered. He frowned, punched a few more keys. He knew that now, in the security pit in Oregon, every single screen on the huge video wall would be displaying his no-doubt groggy face, rumpled hair, and the collar of his orange pajamas.

"Hey!" he shouted. "Somebody pick up the fucking phone!"

Somebody did. The face of a frightened young man appeared on his screen.

"Who are you?" the kid asked.

"My name is Warburton, and I am Howard Christian's personal assistant. What is going on?"

"Sir!" the kid shouted, and actually stood up and saluted.

"Sit down, your face is out of the picture."

"Sir! The . . . the, uh . . . somebody stole the mammoth. *Sir!*"

"Stole Fuzzy?"

"Yes, sir!"

"Okay, hold on." He punched a few more buttons and heard the phone ring in Howard's bedroom. Howard answered on the fourth ring. There was no picture.

"Somebody stole Fuzzy," he said. He listened a moment, heard pretty much what he had expected to hear. He brought the kid back onto his screen.

"Get your supervisor, right now."

"Sir . . . he's . . . uh, he's gone."

"So go get him."

"I mean, sir, he got in his car and drove away. Sir."

Of course. She had help. Warburton rubbed his head. This was going to be no fun at all. He'd catch her, no question, but it wasn't going to be easy.

"What's your name, son?"

"Darryl, sir."

"Listen very carefully, Darryl. Are the police and fire units there yet?"

"No, sir."

"Okay. When they get there, you are going to tell them you hit the button accidentally."

"But, sir, you *can't* hit the—"

"*Listen very carefully*, Darryl. I know you're going to look a little foolish. Don't worry about it. Your job is secure. In fact, you are in for a promotion, starting tomorrow, if you simply tell this harmless little lie. We have the situation under control down here. Darryl, are you still listening?"

"Yes, sir!"

"Tell this little lie, and you are going to be a very, very happy man. You are going to find some money in your bank account. A good deal of money. Okay, Darryl?"

"I understand, sir."

"Good. Now go meet the firemen." Warburton immediately started making more phone calls.

DARRYL hung up the phone and looked at Ed Crane, who had been listening in.

"What about me?" Ed said.

"You, Ed, are going to back my play, and I know Mr. Warburton will take care of you. It's none of our business, right?"

"Right."

Darryl grasped the clear plastic cover that had covered the panic button and twisted it off. He dropped the cover into his pocket and headed out to eat crow in front of the firemen, a big smile on his face.

THE phone woke Andrea first. Howard could sleep through an earthquake. She shivered. She hated staying over at Howard's apartment in his damn tower; she *knew* it would fall over in a quake. But he loved it way the hell up here, and she hadn't talked him out of it. Yet. She shoved him once, twice. That particular phone wouldn't ring with that particular tone unless it was very, very important. He snorted, and sat up quickly.

"What? What?"

"Warburton wants you." She sat back and watched as he punched the speakerphone button.

"Yeah?"

"Somebody stole Fuzzy."

Later, Andrea thought that most men, ambushed by a statement like that, musty-headed with sleep, would have said, *What do you mean, somebody stole Fuzzy?* What Howard said, after only a half-second pause, was . . .

"That *bitch*!"

Howard kept talking. In fact, he continued to pace the room for the next fifteen minutes, seeing nothing, totally focused on the phone pressed to his ear, pausing only to curse steadily as he dialed another number. Andrea didn't need to hear the other sides of the various conversations. She was fairly good at deduction herself.

She went to the big closet and scanned the clothes inside. They would be returning to Oregon, possibly driving down back roads and/or tramping around in the woods. She slipped out of her nightgown and put on a pair of jeans she had paid four hundred dollars for in Switzerland, even though she knew something very similar could be had for twenty dollars at Target. What was money for if you couldn't enjoy shopping? She found a blouse that looked good on her and would be warm. She put on running shoes. Then she followed Howard around, putting her hand on his shoulder to stop him, prompting him to lift first one foot and then the other so she could slip a pair of jeans over the boxer shorts he always wore to bed. She got a shirt on him in similar fashion. She set out a pair of shoes but didn't try to put them on him yet. Then she rang for the night bodyguard and houseboy, and pointed them to the suitcases that were always kept packed. She told them to carry them to the elevator, and call the helicopter pilot to warm up the chopper.

There was nothing in the suitcases or in the closet suitable for the conditions they might be encountering. She would make some calls herself, once they were in the jet, get somebody to have parkas and GoreTex coats and warm wool socks and good hiking boots in their sizes waiting for them when they landed at PDX. It was a little more than two hours to Portland; that ought to be enough time.

She tried not to smile. She had to admit she was glad for the excuse to get back out of this terrorist magnet, this needle on the world's largest seismograph, this damn Resurrection Tower. And she liked an adventure.

I'm amazed at you, Susan, she thought. She liked the woman, and she had just made the biggest mistake of her life, other than carrying a torch for that hopeless nerd Matt Wright. *But look who's talking*, she told herself. She watched affectionately as Howard, supernerd himself, paced the room.

She loved him like this. She loved the intensity of his focus. She herself had a reputation on the set as a perfectionist to the extent that would make Barbra Streisand or Stanley Kubrick seem devil-may-care. But she never threw a temper tantrum. She didn't have to. Her pictures came in on time, on budget, and they made oceans of money. She had one Oscar on her mantel and prospects of another next year. She was so much like Howard it was scary: Howard always got his way, in things that mattered, and so far he had always been right.

And he worshipped her. She was used to that. Millions worshipped her, and it didn't mean much to her anymore. At first, sure, but now she was devoted to her art, and to her causes. She would do anything for those two things, and for Howard.

Howard felt the same about her, and about Fuzzy.

Poor Susan.

And yet, in a part of her mind, she had to admit she was . . . what? Pulling for her? No, certainly not that, if Susan got away with this it would devastate Howard.

But she felt admiration for this incredible stunt. Damn it, the girl had guts.

MICHAEL Bartlett sat in his rented truck in the parking lot of a Goodwill store in the town of Sandy, Oregon, a town that had grown hugely in the last few years because it was just down the road from Fuzzyland. His driver's license was good, there were no warrants on him. He had led a very clean life for the last two years . . . not that it had done him any good. Before, he had not been good at waiting. He always wanted to be moving, always wanted some action. Now, he was an expert at waiting. Three years in jail did that to you. You learned to wait patiently, or you went crazy.

He had waited a long time for this moment. Many times he had despaired that it would ever come—the man was just too powerful, too unreachable. He had imagined a dozen ways to kill him, and he thought a few of them might actually work—the man's security was good but he was often careless. But he didn't want to kill Howard Christian, not really, he didn't think of himself as a killer, only as an avenger, a righter of wrongs, a liberator of the oppressed.

No, what he had been waiting for was the opportunity to kick Howard Christian in the balls, very, very, *very* hard. Michael Bartlett, in what by now seemed almost like a previous life, had once gone by the nom de guerre of Python.

Oddly enough, he was never charged with the destruction he had helped to bring about at the warehouse in Santa Monica. Every shred of evidence had been hurled into the past. The site was excavated but not even a piece of foundation was found. Sometime in the intervening ten to fifteen thousand years the whole structure must have been washed away in a flood or a series of them, buried, and eventually covered by the metropolis. Christian didn't want to prosecute, anyway, he didn't need the possible bad publicity, the demonstrations by animal rights and antiabortion nuts.

He didn't have to. Bartlett/Python was connected to several other incidents and eventually copped a plea: six years, medium security. With good behavior he was paroled in three. That was when his real troubles began.

He came from an upper-middle-class family but his parents were dead, he had spent his small inheritance, and he didn't have much money of his own. He had a college degree but hadn't worked in his field for some years, devoting himself to the cause of animal liberation. He came out of the joint determined to stay away from any criminal activity whatsoever, for all time, end of story, though he intended to keep in contact with old friends from the Movement. But no more action, no more conspiracy. He was well and truly rehabilitated.

Then he found out he couldn't get a job. No, that wasn't quite right. He got hired several times, once went as long as two weeks before being inexplicably fired. No explanation, sorry, man, it just turns out we don't need you after all. Here's your paycheck and there's the door.

At the last place he was fired the boss relented a little. "It was Howard Christian," he admitted. "Somebody working for him. Some . . . pressure was brought to bear. Sorry, Michael, I can't afford to piss that man off. Good luck."

Good fucking luck. He thought about bringing a lawsuit, contact the Equal Opportunity Commission or whatever it was, but knew instinctively there was very little chance, and he had no money. Money talks, and apparently Howard Christian was willing to spend significant money to make Michael Bartlett's life hell.

Shortly after he realized that, he was kicked out of his small apartment.

Howard didn't bother him when he got a job washing dishes or mopping floors, and never approached the landlords of the rattrap single-room-occupancy hotels he stayed at. But he knew that somewhere in the vast Christian organization there was an employee tasked with keeping an eye on Michael Bartlett and making damn sure he was never far from homelessness and hunger. He had, in fact, experienced both of those things several times in a year and a half, before Susan Morgan contacted him.

Yes, sir, just one good, hard kick in the nuts . . .

Headlights turned into the parking lot. Bartlett watched the guy kill his lights and hurry from the car.

"I was supposed to ask you for a code word," the guy said.

"Python," Bartlett replied. "What's wrong? You weren't supposed to be here for three hours."

"Never mind, it all blew up. Let's get the fuck out of here."

"What about Fuzzy? Did they get away with Fuzzy?"

"Yeah, for all the good it'll do them."

Python smiled, and started the engine.

"I heard about him from Andrea," Susan said.

"What's she like?"

She smiled at him. "You're a fan?"

"Who isn't? Actually, I've only seen a couple of her movies, but I thought she was pretty good."

Outside the sun was probably coming up, though they hadn't looked. The cars would be creeping along on I-84. There was no point in moving until nine o'clock. They hadn't talked a lot because the plan was now set and there was no point in hashing it all out again unless one of them had a new thought, and neither of them had. Both were too buzzed to sleep or make love—besides, Fuzzy would be watching, it wouldn't feel right.

Matt thought he could really get to resent Fuzzy, if he let himself.

Of course, they had a lot of catching up to do, much they had to tell each other, but each was a little worried about getting into that.

"I like her," Susan said. "Mostly. I'm not sure if I've ever seen the real Andrea; I'm not sure, in a way, if there *is* a real Andrea, if you know what I mean. I think she's played the part of Andrea for a long time. I can't imagine what she sees in Howard, and yet they are two of a kind, in a way. I've seen little flashes of something . . ."

"Of what?"

"Something that tells me that I wouldn't want to be between her and something she really wants. But I think she's basically a good person. One of the reasons is this guy, this 'Python,' Michael Bartlett. We were talking one day—she likes to come by and visit Fuzzy when she can, sometimes without Howard. We were talking about Howard—she likes to do that, and I try to pretend we don't hate each other, but I don't think I fool her very much—and she admitted he has his failings. He is capable of acting like a big spoiled baby when he doesn't get his way. God, do I ever know that."

"He kept firing you."

"Until he finally conceded Fuzzy won't respond to anybody but me. But he'll always resent me, because I stand between him and his favorite toy. Anyway, she was trying to talk Howard out of this . . . hell, it's almost like a Sicilian vendetta, except Howard isn't a killer. Whenever Bartlett finds work, Howard gets him fired. He once bought an apartment building just so he could kick Bartlett out of it."

"Can he do that? What about tenants' rights?"

"Sure, if he's going to tear the building down, which is what he did. He'll end up making a profit on the deal, can you believe it? Anyway, Andrea thought she about had Howard convinced to let the poor bastard alone. Next she was going to get Howard to *tell* Bartlett about it, shout 'olly-olly-oxen-free,' like a kid on a playground, so he can get back to his life. Right now, Bartlett doesn't even *try* to get a job."

"What's he like? Bartlett."

"I've only seen him once, the same time you did; he was the handcuffed guy with the bloody face. Not the one who was praying; the other one. I've only contacted him by email. Anyway, he was the one who found the hacker who let us get around the security system, and he was supposed to help Jack get away, switching cars in case the police started looking for Jack's. He's made some other arrangements." She paused, and looked at Matt's face in the odd light cast by the Coleman electric lantern on the floor in front of them. "What you're asking is, do I like him, right?"

"Swear to god, Susan, I'm not jealous."

"No, I don't think you are. In his emails, he comes across as a sanctimonious jerk. Maybe what you're asking me is, what's come over me? What made me do this? Have I turned into an animal rights fanatic?"

Matt grinned. "Yeah, I guess that's what I must have been asking."

She punched his shoulder, then rubbed her thigh. He had seen the deep scar tissue there. She had quivered when he first touched it but he had remained firm and she had slowly relaxed. In the course of their lovemaking he had kissed it once, lightly.

"It started when Big Mama almost killed me. My fault. You never, never forget for a moment that an elephant—let alone a mammoth—is a big, powerful, sometimes willful animal. I turned my back on her, and she dug her tusk into my leg and flipped me twenty feet across the stall. I blacked out almost at once, but they tell me she was straining on her leg chain. She would have killed me if she could have reached me."

Matt had been alarmed, years ago, when he was doing some reading on elephants so as to be better able to talk to her, to discover that the occupation of elephant keeper was one of the most hazardous professions in the world, right up there with test pilot. Susan had once told him that the question when working with elephants was not if you would get hurt, but when, and how bad.

"In the hospital I had a lot of time to think. Did you ever see *King Kong*? The original, 1933 or something like that?"

"Yeah. Pretty amazing for its time, I guess."

"I saw it when I was four or five. And sure, it looks phony today, didn't scare me a bit, but it made me cry. I watched it again from my hospital bed. The guy who brings Kong to New York, he walks out on the stage with the poor beast in chains, and he says—and I memorized these lines, he says: 'He was a king and a god in the world he knew. But now he comes to civilization, a show to gratify your curiosity.'

"Can you think of a better description of Big Mama? She was the matriarch of the herd. She ruled everything, as far as her world extended. She was a queen and a goddess in the world she knew. Now she is trotted out into a show ring twice a day in chains. Mondays off. Wouldn't you be pissed?"

"No question."

"I started questioning my life. And no, I haven't joined any radical animal rights groups. I don't think animals can have 'rights,' as I understand the word. I'm against cruelty. I don't like fur farms or trapping, I could never be a hunter, but I'm not against it. I don't like medical research on primates but I try not to think about it too much. I don't eat a lot of red meat but I wear leather shoes and I eat fish and fowl.

"I guess what I feel so strongly now is, there is a difference between domesticated animals and wild animals. I still favor zoos for species survival. But I realized I no longer felt it was right to 'tame' wild animals and make them perform. Working elephants in Burma is one thing, it's not much different from using a horse to pull a carriage. But putting them in show business . . . it's beneath their dignity. And that came very hard to me, Matt, because I grew up in show business, and I'm at the top of the heap right now. And I realized I just can't do it anymore. End of sermon. The congregation will now sing hymn number fifty-two, 'Born Free.' "

Matt had been so fascinated just watching her face as she told the story that it took him a moment to realize she was waiting for a response. Anxiously.

"Amen, sister," he said. "I admit I haven't spent a lot of time thinking about it, but that all sounded right to me. I wince when I see those pictures of rabbits with cosmetics being tested on their eyes, but I don't much care what they do to a lab rat. And I've eaten rabbit. Maybe that makes me a hypocrite, I don't know."

They both looked at Fuzzy, who was swaying happily and slowly chewing a mouthful of hay in that peculiar back-and-forth jaw motion that worked like a grindstone.

"I'm so glad he's so good-natured," Susan said. "You know, he hasn't seen sunshine or breathed open air for three years?"

"That seems stupid."

"The last time he was outdoors was the day some nut flew over in one of those ultralight airplanes and started shooting at him."

You're kidding seemed an idiotic thing to say, so Matt said nothing.

"We were just lucky it was so windy that day he couldn't aim straight, or maybe he was just a miserable shot. The security guard was better. He put a round into the engine and brought the guy down. He was cheerful about the whole thing. Said he wanted to be the only man alive to bag an actual mammoth. Maybe he thought we'd let him have the head, I don't know. He said he didn't mind going to jail. What were we going to charge him with, murder?"

"World's full of nuts."

"That's what Howard said, too. From then on Fuzzy got his exercise running around in a big covered yard with me on his back. I suspect the shooter is living on the streets of skid row in Portland now. I mean, considering what Howard did to Michael Bartlett, what do you think he thought up for *that* asshole?"

"The mind reels. And in his case, I don't mind." They both laughed. It didn't break the tension for long.

"Matt, do you think the plan is stupid? Is this all pointless? Can I ever get Fuzzy to a place where he can roam around outdoors?"

Matt knew a lie wouldn't do.

"Fuzzy can never live a 'normal' mammoth life," he said, slowly.

"I don't mean that, I know that's impossible. Mammoths are social, they live in herds—at least until they reach sexual maturity, if they're male, and if they're like elephants, which I think they are. No . . . I mean . . ."

Matt took her hand.

"The plan is *not* idiotic. If it works, it'll get Fuzzy nearer to a normal life than anything I could think of. So it's *not* pointless. Obviously, I can't tell you if it'll work or not. But I think we have a chance."

"You do?"

"I do."

"That's all I ask for."

She leaned her head on his shoulder and they didn't say anything for a long time.

28

THE security industry was a growth business all through the last half of the twentieth century and showed no signs of slacking off in the first decades of the twenty-first. This was true of both the public and private sectors, but private security usually had the better technology.

There was no lack of private detective agencies if Howard needed manpower on the streets, and plenty of firms that specialized in guards and surveillance equipment stood ready to provide anything from armored personnel carriers to high-altitude robot drones to six-man midget submarines.

He thought briefly about the subs because he'd never been in one. He knew Fuzzy could swim, but where would he swim to? Anyway, a surface boat would do for that. What Howard needed mostly, at first, were helicopters. Before he was done he had chartered over a hundred of them.

Howard, Andrea, and Warburton landed at PDX as the sun was coming up and the rain was tapering off. It was still too cloudy for Howard's needs—satellite technology would be a vital part in the success of this operation, and visible light was often the best medium for a preliminary search, and you couldn't see through clouds—but the forecast was good, with westerly winds moving a high-pressure area over everything from British Columbia to northern California. It should be clear as a bell in a few hours, and into the night, which was far more important.

They didn't even leave the plane. It was Howard's personal jet, a 757 modified into a flying palace and equipped with every electronic device he had back home in the Resurrection Tower. Just about everything but the actual capture could be accomplished right here. Howard was determined to be in at the kill so a helicopter waited a few steps from the plane.

Andrea called for a cook to come to the airport and make meals in the plane's full galley, otherwise Howard would forget to eat. He would have been content to have Domino's deliver breakfast, lunch, and dinner, but Andrea's tastes were a bit more refined. She had eggs Benedict for breakfast.

Things were already well advanced before they even landed. Still, an operation of this scale takes a certain amount of time to get fully in gear, no matter how much money you offer for speed. Not all the chartered choppers were equipped with the electronics needed for the search; that equipment had to be obtained and installed, crews had to be assembled. A computer laid out a search pattern and assignments were made. All in all, it was eleven before everyone was flying toward their assigned zones.

All the way there in the plane Howard and Warburton had discussed the options open to them as Andrea listened but seldom spoke. They worked out a strategy, and Howard was forced to order his priorities and face some bad possibilities.

"Worst-case scenario," Howard said, "we search for a set time, then we call in the authorities. What's the downside?"

Warburton shrugged. He wasn't going to mention that Howard would look like a fool; that was a given, the whole reason for first trying to find the damned beast themselves. Warburton would have sent up all the flares ten seconds after the first phone call, but he wasn't Howard.

"Not much. You'll catch some flack for not reporting it at once, but the search will be nationwide, and they'll be found."

"Okay. Next-worst scenario. We find them, but it's real public and everybody finds out Fuzzy was stolen. I mean, much as I'd like to, we can't just shoot 'em even if we find them isolated out in the country."

"Howard," Andrea said, "you wouldn't shoot them in any case."

"You're right. But we can hold them at gunpoint, make a citizen's arrest, right? They *have* stolen a pretty valuable property. They *have* broken the law."

"As you say, men licensed to carry guns can hold them for

you," Warburton said. "They might get charged with something later, since there is no bounty or warrant out on them; we can handle that. But this may not be possible without people finding out about it. In fact, most of the scenarios I can imagine, it's going to get out that Fuzzy was stolen. It may already have. Working with this many people, there will be leaks."

"Probably," Howard agreed. "But in that case, I want it known that *I* was the guy who tracked them down and brought him back."

"Understood."

"So . . . best-case scenario, we find him in a truck on the road somewhere, stop them, and drive quietly back to Fuzzyland. No publicity, no arrests. Chances?"

"Slim."

Howard sighed. "Okay. I'd settle for the second possibility. But until then we look for him, *hard*, and we work hard to find a way to end this quietly."

"If they've gone to ground in the country, we haven't got a prayer."

"I know that. Every instinct tells me they will stay on the move. They will know they are more conspicuous on lonely country roads, which means they'll stay on the major roads, probably on the freeways. I-84 East and I-5 South get into empty country real fast, so I think they'll head north toward Seattle. Easier to lose yourself in a big city, pull into an RV park or something like that if they need to stop. So our forces on the ground will concentrate on the Seattle metro area. Some of the helicopters will follow every road where they could be, with full electronic enhancement. But I have a feeling we'll catch them with the satellites, tonight."

"Got it. Now, I suggest we set a time frame before we call in the cops. Twenty-four hours."

"From now, or from when he was stolen?"

"The latter."

"Forty-eight hours."

"Split the difference. Noon tomorrow."

"That's not a split . . . but okay."

Andrea was once more conflicted. Part of her was fascinated by the process of the search. She'd learned a lot already. On the other hand, watching two boys playing soldier or spy or something with such enthusiasm was rather boring. It wasn't her sort of picture at all. She tended to tune out, but found herself coming back to the problem and the discussion, wondering if she could contribute.

"Before we set it all in motion, we need to prepare rules of engagement," Warburton said.

"There should be an armed man with every team. They may have guns."

"Don't be ridiculous, dear. Susan wouldn't use a gun."

"Better safe than sorry," Howard insisted. "But I don't want any shooting unless someone is shot at first. No shooting at all if it could endanger Fuzzy."

"Howard . . ."

"Don't worry, Andrea. I don't want to hurt them. Not that way, anyway."

Andrea knew that was the best she could get. She could talk him out of taking his revenge later.

HELICOPTERS fanned out along all the roads leading away from Fuzzyland. With each minute the number of those possible roads and the mileage involved expanded.

A visual inspection was the first step for vehicles on the road. They had a plate number, but most of Howard's advisors expected that to have been changed by now. They ignored the tow vehicle; that could have been changed, too. They were looking, first, for a beige forty-foot 2008 Wilderness fifth wheel with a broad red curving swoosh painted on the side, a fashionable design style for that vintage RV. It had been 3-D computer-modeled from the security videos of its comings and goings at Fuzzyland. There was a three-foot-long dimple on the left side from where Susan had turned too sharply coming home one night and scraped it against a tree. That dimple was still there on the video from just hours ago.

With this information a helicopter could hover over the parking lot of a big shopping center and send pictures back to computers that could pick such a trailer out of thousands of vehicles in seconds. Then the chopper could move in and examine it with infrared.

There were a million holes in the plan, and Howard and

Warburton knew it. There were covered parking garages, but very few high enough to admit an RV. As well as switching tow vehicles, they might have switched trailers. A big horse trailer would do fine, so they were being examined, too, and there were thousands of horse trailers out there on the country roads. But a horse in a trailer gave off a very different infrared signature from a mammoth, and they could be quickly eliminated.

Both Susan's and Matt's bank records had been scrutinized and showed that Susan had bought only one RV in her lifetime, and Matt had bought none. Howard didn't know if they had planned this together, but he was certain they had had outside help. If she was smart, she would have kept her outside contact to a minimum. Howard was willing to bet only three or four others beyond Matt and Susan knew *anything* about this. They would be among the small, clandestine group of animal rights extremists, who as a rule didn't have a lot of money. Of course, one financial angel could have donated another RV for the cause, so if it came to it every RV, horse trailer, and truck for a thousand miles would be examined, but by then it would be in the hands of the police. Howard was going with his instincts, with the percentages, and Susan hadn't had a lot of time to set this all up. She only had Mondays to accomplish the physical parts of the plan, and probably most of the rest, too, since she couldn't risk using her home or office phones or computers at all.

Still, as the hours rolled by he knew his prospects were getting grim. It was just so damn much territory, and if he was guessing wrong about any of the variables he was screwed. All she had to do to beat *him* was to sit tight in a well-covered place . . . and wait to be picked up by the police.

He was feeling more depressed than at any time he could remember as the reports kept coming in. Twenty-three similar trailers had been located so far and examined more closely, and they'd come up empty. He had to wait for night.

That was when Andrea brought him a sandwich for lunch. She sat down beside him and smiled.

"So, have you figured out where she's going yet?" she asked.

"Hell, no. It's a big country." Howard took a bite of the fancy sandwich and wished he could have ordered out for a Big Mac.

"Damn right it is, and that means you're just wasting a lot of money and letting them get farther away, which the police won't appreciate when you are finally forced to call them in."

"Is that what you're saying? Call them in now?"

"No, my dear. I'm saying, let's narrow the search."

"How do you propose to do that?"

"By thinking like Susan. Why did she steal Fuzzy?"

Howard snorted. "Because she objects to him performing like—what was it she said last time we had it out over this?—'a trained seal.' As if she hasn't spent all her life making wild animals perform—"

"Never mind that. She's obviously had a change of heart."

"Unless she just wants to poke me in the eye," Howard said sullenly.

"No, dear, that's your style, not hers."

Howard said nothing. She was right. He was working on it, but knew he'd never entirely get his thirst for revenge under control. That's what they were doing here in the first place, instead of staying back home tending to things he could really do something about.

"What does she want for Fuzzy?" Andrea went on.

"She wants him to roam free and natural and not be 'exploited.' " He couldn't keep the sneer out of his voice.

"Where can she find that for him?"

"Nowhere. Not as long as I own him. Damn it, I don't treat that animal badly. He works twice a day, he is the most pampered animal in the *world*, he is happy—he seems happy to you, doesn't—"

"Yes, I think he's happy. Susan thinks it'd be better if he were in a wild animal park of some kind. She wants him out in the open air. She wants him to browse his own grass and eat leaves off wild trees."

"Impossible. That nut *shot* at him."

"I don't know what her answer to that would be. Still, you're going on the assumption that the only way she can ever hope to keep him is to hide him. Get to some place she has prepared, which could be anywhere in the United States . . . and keep him undercover *forever*. It would be smaller than his quarters back in Fuzzyland. She could never let him out in the sunshine—someone's *bound* to notice a mammoth wandering around—and all she would have gained is that he doesn't have to perform in the circus. I think even Susan would agree that Fuzzy doesn't actually mind performing. He even seems to like it, though I wouldn't pretend to read his mind. All I know for sure that Fuzzy likes is Susan and grapes. He tolerates me because I bring grapes."

"So what's your point?"

"You think Susan is stupid enough to go through all this merely to move him from one prison to another? With a *smaller* jail cell when he gets there?"

"You're going to make me ask the question, aren't you? Okay, where is she taking him?"

"Canada."

Howard laughed. Actually it was more of a snort. Andrea didn't mind.

"Right. With her other troubles, she needs to cross an international border."

"The longest undefended international border in the world. Large parts of it, mostly in Washington and Idaho and Montana, are thickly wooded, sparsely inhabited wilderness, not very well patrolled."

Howard was beginning to look thoughtful.

"But when she's there . . . she's got the same problem. Hide him, or lose him."

"Not necessarily. Circus animal acts are illegal in Canada now. Have been for . . . how many years?"

"Eight or nine, I guess," Howard said, grumpily. It was a sore point with him. There were no longer circuses in most of Western Europe, and a growing but still minority movement wanted to ban animal acts and rodeos in the United States. He had wanted to take Fuzzy on a triumphant world tour, but it was never going to happen. There were plans for an Asian tour. People were still less fussy over there. The Japanese, with their cultural quirk for cuteness, were wild about Fuzzy; he sold more big-eyed Fuzzy soft toys there than anywhere in the world. In China Big Mama was the star, for some reason. Russia felt a cultural identification with mammoths. The huge majority of the frozen ones had been found in Siberia, and there were places where ancient mammoth bones piled up like driftwood. Russians were gaga about *both* of Howard's mammoths.

"So what? He still belongs to me."

"Maybe, maybe not. You remember the court decisions awarding him to you were highly controversial. I suspect you greased some wheels."

"*Me?* Bribe a judge?" He grinned.

"I'm sure it was much more subtle than that. Remember, at the time I was fighting on the other side. We heard rumors. I'm still not sure I shouldn't still be *on* the other side, but like you, I don't believe Fuzzy has been mistreated. Do you think a Canadian court might be persuaded that your ownership is . . . might we say . . . questionable?"

Howard said nothing.

"Once she got him across the border . . . what if she turned herself in? What if a team of lawyers was waiting for her when she got there? Do they call them solicitors up there? Anyway . . . how long do you think they could keep him tied up in court?"

"Years," Howard muttered. He was resting his chin on his clasped hands, frowning. "I don't have a lot of connections in Canada, not like down here."

"I did a little Internet search while I was thinking this over. Canadian public opinion is solidly behind the 'Free Fuzzy' movement. Once he's actually there, I think it would be the rare Canadian who would want to let him go back to the circus."

"But what does Susan gain?"

Andrea ticked off points on her fingers. "Time, first of all. Like you said, maybe years. Two, Fuzzy doesn't have to perform. The Canadian authorities aren't fools; they'll protect him. They could move him far, far north, near where his natural habitat would be, put him in a preserve with no roads leading in while the case is being adjudicated. Every day he stays free, it would be harder for you to get him back."

Howard thought about it for almost a full minute. Then he smiled.

"Darling, I've finally found a woman as smart as me."

"Smarter," Andrea said.

Howard laughed, and picked up the phone. "Captain, we're joining Mr. Warburton at Sea-Tac Airport, as soon as you can get clearance." He punched another button. "Warburton, pull everything you've got out of Oregon and California. Concentrate the search in the Seattle metro area, but most of all along the Canadian border. I want teams at every crossing, and continuous helicopter patrols from Puget Sound to Montana. I'll tell you about it when I get there."

Then he stood up, pulled Andrea from her chair, and kissed her.

THE *lady is pretty smart,* Warburton admitted to himself after Howard called back to explain Andrea's reasoning. Both of them were. He wouldn't have thought of it; his mind didn't work that way. He wouldn't embark on a project knowing he would get *caught* . . . but it seemed the best possible outcome, in Susan's terms. Warburton didn't like Susan, didn't like Andrea even more—she was always getting in his way. Warburton didn't really like anybody very much, not even Howard. He didn't have much of a life outside his job, but the job satisfied him and had made him quite wealthy over the years. He was a born problem solver, that was his thing, and he had very few scruples. Fuck the rules of engagement. He was enough of a realist to know that pointing a gun at two people and shouting *Freeze!* was worse than pointless unless you were prepared to use it. He would shoot to wound, the leg or the foot, if he could. But if worse came to worst he would do what he had to do. Like any cautious cop, he carried an untraceable piece-of-shit throwdown weapon to put in the hand of an awkward corpse. He had killed men twice before—only when he had to; he was not a maniac. He had suffered no nightmares. He knew he could do it.

He was in the control center of a security company with headquarters at Sea-Tac. Howard had chartered virtually the entire firm for the duration. He had two assistants. The aptly named Wesley Blackstone was a big, no-nonsense black guy with a shaved head. Blackstone had been given to him as the best man for knowing the terrain along the border. He was an outdoorsman, was in fact still wearing the plaid flannel shirt and heavy boots he had had on when he got a phone call and was plucked from a backwoods campsite a hundred miles from here. He seemed to know his business.

The other assistant was the owner and operator of the company, a white man fully as big as Blackstone and bald as an egg, though not by choice, by the name of Crowder. He claimed to be the best at urban environments. Warburton wasn't quite so sure about him. They were looking at a wall-sized electronic map of Washington State and lower British Columbia. Locations and unit numbers of all the aerial and ground search teams currently in operation were displayed. There were a lot of them. A whole lot of them. Maybe even enough to do the job . . .

The dots and numbers representing searchers moved every few seconds, adjusted by the GPS units each team carried. Most of the air units and many on the ground were now converging on the border.

"Legal crossing points at Blaine, the big one," Blackstone said. He moved a controller and highlighted as he spoke. "Then here at State Road 539, here at Sumas, and not another until way over here, at Lenton Flat. Pretty rough country through there. I wouldn't want to climb it with a mammoth."

"Hannibal crossed the Alps with war elephants. Patrol it anyway."

"Sure. Then there are seven more before you get to Idaho. You figure they'll try to drive across, or follow one of these roads close to the border and walk it?"

"Hard to say. Either way will be tough."

"Here in the west it's fairly flat, farmland, they'd stick out like a sore thumb. Fewer people in the eastern part, a lot of it's pretty arid. Desert. I wouldn't go that route, myself."

"What would you do?"

"Given what you told me? I'd try to drive up to one of the crossings out here in the boonies, go right up to the customs station and turn myself in."

"They've got to cross first. Do we have a team at all of them yet?"

"We will in fifteen more minutes. Stopping them could be awkward, though. U.S. Customs will probably object if you shoot out their tires this side of the line."

"They can use a knife on the tires. Anyway, if they get to a crossing then Plan A, keeping it all quiet, is pretty much busted. They'll make a citizen's arrest, customs will take a look inside and realize there is only one juvenile mammoth on the *planet* and he belongs to Howard Christian, and the whole thing will be confused long enough for me and Howard and fifty lawyers to get there. Susan will realize that, too. If I was her, I'd try to find a place to get close to the border, and walk it. If we spot them doing that, we land and take them prisoner. And you didn't hear me say this, but if they happen to be a mile or two over the border . . . Christian wants them back. Are you reading me?"

"Loud and clear."

"Crowder, you'll continue looking in the Seattle area on the ground, and we'll give you a few helicopters to screen the freeways, but send most of the teams into the country up north. I want somebody in a four-wheel drive within ten minutes of every logging road in that forest, every dirt trail in that desert. I want at least one cross-country motorbike in the back of every vehicle. They have to leave the trailer on a road somewhere if they try to cross on foot. I don't think they'll try to cross at Blaine, I understand there are traffic jams up there."

"They can stretch for miles," Crowder agreed. "We've got three teams there, and we can stop them before they even *see* the border."

"Good. When it gets dark we'll get the satellites to work, and I'm betting we spot them somewhere out in the wilderness within an hour. We have to be ready to move on them. Anything else?"

"What about ferries?" Crowder said.

"Ferries?"

Crowder touched the keyboard and the map view zoomed in on the waters of the area, from the entrance to the estuary at the Georgia Strait, running between the Olympic Peninsula and Vancouver Island, to Olympia at the south end, and the city of Vancouver to the north. There was a lot of water, and a lot of islands. A spiderweb of lines appeared, running all over the water.

"We've always had good ferries up here."

"Never been on one," Blackstone said with a grin. "I get seasick in the bathtub."

"Last ten years they've been adding more. Federal grants or some shit like that, ease the freeway congestion, not that it did a damn bit of good. There's three times as many ferries now as when I was a kid."

"How many go to Canada?"

Crowder touched the keyboard again, and most of the lines disappeared.

"You got your B.C. ferries, and you got your Washington State ferries. One from Port Angeles, on the peninsula, to Victoria, on Vancouver Island. From here at Anacortes to Sidney and Vancouver. Also from Bellingham to Vancouver, and from Everett to Victoria and Vancouver."

"So you cover Port Angeles, Anacortes, Bellingham, and Everett."

"It'd be a dumb way to go. Sometimes you can wait for hours to get aboard."

"Cover them anyway. It would be a perfect place to catch them quietly."

"Will do."

Warburton leaned back and sighed. He realized he hadn't eaten yet today, and it was almost evening. He asked someone to have a pizza delivered.

We'll catch them tonight. The satellites will find them.

29

MATT left the unit at eight that morning, and saw the rain had stopped and the sky was beginning to clear. Bad luck. He walked to the truck and pulled the trailer around the block and into the storage yard. Susan was waiting to direct him, and they lowered the ramp.

Susan had noticed that most places like this were virtually deserted most of the time. This one had half a dozen rows of buildings with garage doors facing each other. Her two units could not be seen from any road or house in the area. There was always a chance somebody would pick that morning to visit a unit close to theirs, but if that happened they would just have to wait.

Matt walked to the end of the row where he could see the entrance gate. He signaled to Susan, and she opened the garage door and led Fuzzy out and up the ramp, and closed the ramp, then the door. Thirty seconds, total.

Matt hurried back and entered the trailer through the side door. Susan was strapping a leather harness around Fuzzy's middle. She attached it to each side of the trailer with heavy chains.

"He traveled a lot before Fuzzyland opened, you know," she said. "He had his own private train. He's been in the back of trucks, too, going to and from the shows. Pachyderms are pretty good at keeping their balance, a lot better than you'd think. But we always used an arrangement like this as a sort of seat belt. I'd appreciate it if you tried not to stand on the brake, though, okay?"

"I'll keep *way* back from the cars ahead."

They went back outside and carefully peeled off the red contact paper Susan had applied in a big red swoosh after painting the rig a uniform beige. She grimaced as she touched the long indent where a tree branch had scraped the side.

"I did that last week. A computer recognition program would pick that out pretty quick, even from high up, don't you think? I was going to paint over it but then I thought it might be better to leave it that way until I was through the security gate."

"Good thinking. Now they may be looking for it. Did you bring the paint?"

"Have I forgotten anything so far?" She got out a bucket and two brushes, and they quickly slapped on a coat of paint. So maybe the showers stopping was a bit of good luck, after all. They got on I-84 and headed west. Traffic was stop-and-go for a while, especially around the Rose Garden mess where the freeway joined I-5. Lucky thing the Trailblazers didn't play games in the morning.

Over the Interstate Bridge traffic eased up, and they headed north. Just south of Tacoma, traffic backed up again. They crept along, nervously watching the sky.

THEY missed the ferry they wanted in Tacoma, at Point Defiance, which put them an hour behind where they had hoped to be. It was a short hop to Vashon Island, at Tahlequah.

Vashon Island was pretty, still partly rural. They weren't able to make up any time; in fact they missed another ferry. Every minute sitting still in the parking lot was agony, but eventually they were waved aboard and undercover again.

This was a larger ferry and they were on the lower deck. They stayed close to the trailer in case Fuzzy started to bellow—which he hardly ever did, but he was in strange surroundings and, besides, Susan didn't want to get more than about fifty feet from him. Through a wide opening on the starboard side they could see planes on approach to Sea-Tac Airport from the north, then the city of Seattle itself. These waters were teeming with boats, many of them other ferries crisscrossing Puget Sound. They pulled into the terminal at Kingston, far behind schedule, knowing they would not get to the last departure of the ferry they wanted. When they drove past the terminal, they could not even see the departing ferry. It was long gone.

Susan had a backup plan, but she was discouraged. They pulled into a big RV park where Susan had booked a space a week earlier under another name. Matt found their space, was relieved to see it was a pull-through, and they parked as the sun was going down. There were trees around them, but not the complete cover they would have liked. Neither of them was sure if the satellites could spot them through trees, anyway.

But there was nothing for it. They would have to spend the night, and hope the search was, by now, focused far away to the north and east.

THEY made a meal from cans and ate it in silence. They hadn't bothered to hook up anything, not even the electricity, but the refrigerator and stove used propane. There was no reason not to turn on all the lights and have a party—Susan had stocked some beer. But the instincts of the hunted left them huddling beneath a single light over the kitchen table. Susan sat facing the back, where Fuzzy stood, maybe ten feet behind Matt's back. Every once in a while she got up to pet him or feed him a treat. He seemed tired of this whole bye-bye business by now.

"He's restless," she said as she sat back down opposite Matt. "He missed his daily run. Hell, he's probably even missing doing his show."

"He's a creature of habit," Matt said. "He'll get used to new habits. You did the right thing."

"Keep saying that every ten minutes, okay?" She yawned. "I thought I'd never be able to sleep again, but I'm afraid I might drop off right here in the middle of a sentence."

"I hope you can stay awake a little longer. There are some things I have to tell you."

She looked up, more alert.

"The rest of your story?"

He smiled.

"Yeah. The good parts . . . well, the better parts. Anything would have felt good after getting out of that cell. And some things you need to know."

"Why don't we get to that part first? We'll have plenty of

time to catch up on the rest, even if we have to do it by mail from our separate prisons."

"I need to build up to it. I'll keep it as short as possible. I'm pretty sleepy, too."

FOR most of the first year after his release, Matt hadn't been able to do much but dodge reporters and continue his researches with his computer on the Internet.

He tried a few times to elude them, managed to shake them off once in a while, got into the habit of withdrawing money from his bank accounts when he had the chance and never using his credit cards, but they always found him again. It wasn't hard to do in this day and age. Few people had the skills to stay hidden for long, and Matt finally admitted it wasn't worth the effort. He decided to wait them out. He had plenty of money, his needs were modest. He stayed at inexpensive hotels and moved every few nights, just to inconvenience the media. Time travel was a very big story, he was one of only two people known to have done it, and the world wanted to know all about it.

At first there were actual satellite trucks that followed him around as he drove from city to city. Those gradually dwindled to a few pool vehicles with cameras recording him every time he got out of his car or left his hotel. One shot or another of him showed up on most newscasts for almost a month. If he sneezed, it would likely get on the air. A stumble was apt to cause a flash newsbreak.

He tried to go to Europe, which was a mistake. A good percentage of his fellow passengers were reporters, and they weren't shy about crowding around and asking questions. When he got off the plane in London he was facing a whole new set of reporters, even more aggressive than the ones at home. You would have thought he was a rock star or the president of the United States. He walked straight to the airline counter and bought a ticket back to America.

Gradually, as he continued his silence—he learned early that even saying "no comment" only encouraged them—the crowds lessened. It helped that Susan was giving accounts of their adventure—always on tape, never live, and always carefully controlled by Howard's spin doctors. The story she told was the truth, in the sense that she didn't lie about anything, but there was much she did not or would not tell.

"WE were both sort of in moving prisons, I guess," Susan said. "I stayed in places where Howard controlled the security. When I went out I had to sneak around, and I had bodyguards."

"It must have been awful."

"Not as bad as what you went through. I watched them hounding you. I did more interviews than I wanted to so maybe it would take some of the pressure off you."

Matt smiled. "You know, I thought it might be something like that. Thanks."

"I have no idea if it did any good." She looked down at the table. "I have a confession to make." She looked up again. "It was during that first year, after wondering where you were while they had you locked up, and then seeing what they were doing to you . . . it was then that I realized that I loved you."

Matt said nothing. She took his hand.

"I liked you a lot when we were working together. I liked making love to you, it made me less afraid of what was happening to us. But I was always a little afraid of you."

Matt was genuinely shocked.

"How could you be afraid of *me*? I didn't think you were afraid of anything."

"Oh, there's plenty of things that scare me. I just try not to show it. You were just so . . . so damn *smart*. You were so much smarter than me I just couldn't keep up with you. When you started talking about quantum physics and like that, I felt like such a dope."

"Last time I checked, they weren't graduating any dopes from veterinary school. Seems to me you need the same skills as somebody who becomes a doctor, only your patients can't even tell you what's bothering them."

"Wrong word, maybe. I know I'm smart, but it's . . . relative, like Dr. Einstein said. I *felt* like a dope." She smiled briefly. "I'd never met a supergenius."

Matt grimaced. "I've had that trouble all my life. I try not to talk shop, explain what it is I'm researching, but with you, we were both working, and you wanted to know. I probably shouldn't have, but as a conversationalist, I *am* a dope."

"I'm not blaming you, Matt. I wanted to know what you were doing. And you're a good explainer. But you'd lose me."

"Like you say, it's all relative. I happen to have a mind that's quick with numbers. And you know what? There are people with an IQ of 60, people who can't even tie their shoes, who can do anything with numbers I can do."

"Is what you've got to tell me more about the time machine? More quantum theory and chaos theory and stuff like that?"

"Some of it is. But you don't have to follow it, because it's a blind alley." He sighed. "You said when Big Mama attacked you it changed your life. Your point of view. I didn't have a blinding moment of revelation. I had a series of insights that led me to the conclusion that my outlook on the universe was too narrow. That a lot of the things I had learned were . . . not exactly wrong, relativity still works, quanta are still doing their things . . . but *chaos*, chaos doesn't even begin to describe it.

"I began to realize that my point of view was entirely too provincial to explain the universe as I had encountered it."

THE media circus that his life had become gradually abated, though it never entirely folded its tent. There was a flurry of activity at the one-year anniversary and from time to time an enterprising intern for a television show would approach him, usually in restaurants while he was eating, in the vain hope that he'd suddenly decide to spill his guts. But a circus can't go on forever if the trapeze artist won't swing.

Matt deliberately tried to lead as boring a life as possible, in part to discourage the hordes of the curious. In other words, he sometimes realized wryly, he tried to return to the kind of life he led before Howard Christian barged into it. He thought about returning to a university somewhere to continue his researches, plenty of places would have jumped at the chance of having the guy they thought of as "the man who invented time travel" on the faculty, no questions asked, no pressure applied, here's your lab, Matt, and do whatever you want in it . . . but he realized that didn't appeal to him anymore. His quest was taking him in other directions.

He entered a monastery in New Mexico for a while. Partly it was so he could look out the window and see the forlorn press pool, only a handful at that point, forced to stake out the building in the blistering heat. But he really was in need of a quiet, cloistered lifestyle.

This was sort of a Club Med monastery, nondenominational, catering to people with emotional problems to resolve or deep doubts about existence to work out. Matt put himself in the latter category. The quarters were Spartan, the food was plain, the brothers wore robes, and you chanted and sang at appointed hours, but nobody demanded that you believe in God. Sort of religion lite.

Things eased up greatly when the biggest male box office star in the world was arrested for murdering his wife and two children. He claimed to be innocent and there were no eyewitnesses but his story was Swiss cheese. He hired a team of high-powered lawyers—some of them lured away from Howard's school of piranha—and suddenly there was hardly room on the news for coverage of the war in Indonesia, much less a nontalking has-been quasicelebrity like Matt Wright. The news organizations took to checking in on him weekly, then monthly, and then he was gone.

Not lost. They found him again easily enough. And during the brief period when there had been no reporters aware of his whereabouts, Matt noticed that two men he had thought were reporters were still dogging him. One was a very large man with very little fat on him, maybe an ex-marine. The other was wiry, moved smoothly as a lizard, and had eyes like stones. He called them Jarhead and Snake. He decided they were probably Howard's agents, and knew they would never give up, but they never interfered with him so he ignored them.

At one point he was glad they were there. A man walked up to him, drew a knife, and lunged at him. He never completed the thrust. Snake appeared like a genie out of a bottle, efficiently broke the man's arm in two places, and Jarhead sat on him until the police came. There was a minicam in Jarhead's gimme cap, and he had tape of the attack to show the officers when they arrived. Matt thanked Snake, who shrugged.

"He was easy. Some of the ones before him were tougher." He grinned.

"OH, Matt, that's awful."

"Scared me a little, I admit it. He told me they'd 'taken down' three men who were trying to do me harm, and foiled one kidnap attempt. Said they'd heard rumors that one foreign government was thinking about trying to get their hands on me."

"What did you do?"

Matt shrugged. "What could I do? I felt claustrophobic enough with the press corps following me around. I didn't like Jarhead and Snake following me, for that matter, but I never complained after that. I didn't want to lock myself away behind walls. I enjoyed the monastery for a month, but I wouldn't have wanted to stay longer. I decided to take my chances.

"Anyway, it was just about two years before I thought things had cooled off enough that I could move around freely. It wasn't wasted time; I was reading and thinking. I read everything I could find about time travel theories. I read every science fiction story I could get my hands on, from H. G. Wells to some ridiculous thing about taking people off of airplanes that were about to crash. But there were places I wanted to go, people I wanted to talk to, and I needed to travel. . . ."

MATT became a globetrotter. For almost three years he sought out people who might have insights that had been denied him in his education, which had been the best possible in the sciences but quite deficient in everything else.

He wandered India, speaking to the holy men of that country's thousand religions. He bathed in the Ganges. He went to Tibet, to Rome, to Jerusalem, to Mecca. He climbed Mount Fujiyama, sought out eremites in Ethiopia and Egypt. He sat in a sweat lodge in Arizona and chewed peyote and tried LSD.

Since the days of Einstein, scientists had been searching

for a "Theory of Everything," a paradigm that would tie together all the known forces in the universe. Much progress had been made, but every time humanity seemed on the verge of being able to write it all down in an equation as elegant as $E=mc^2$, something else came along that made the results *more* complicated rather than less, requiring more theories to explain the new data.

Matt had begun to wonder if everybody was looking in the wrong direction.

"YOU'RE not going religious on me, are you, Matt?" Susan smiled at him.

"About to the degree that you've become an animal rights nut. Religious? No. Philosophical? Yes. Spiritual . . . maybe. What I've decided is that there is something going on in the universe that will never be explained by math or physics, and you might as well call it the spiritual dimension. As far as I can tell, no one has ever studied it rigorously. Partly it's because it's much harder to pin down than a neutrino, and partly it's because science works. It describes the universe as we experience it . . . commonly. But we had an uncommon experience, to say the least, and I've come to think that it ties in to what Einstein called the 'observer,' which means it may have as much to do with consciousness as it does with physical laws of matter and energy.

"Listen, I know you don't want to hear more about string theory, but bear with me a minute. You'll be relieved when I get through it, I promise you.

"What we call a 'string' is a sort of loop of pure energy. They would be very small. Imagine the sun, one million miles across. Now imagine a proton in the center of the sun. Expand that proton until it is the size of the Solar System, out to the orbit of Pluto. A string within that proton would be the size of the proton before we expanded it."

"Pretty damn small."

"The technical term for it is 'teeny weeny weeny weeny weeny *weeny*.' Now, the thing is, string theory has been around a long time now . . . but no one has come up with any experiment that could prove or disprove it. No one has thought of a way to detect a string, to shine a light on it. There are good theoretical reasons to believe that there *is* no way for us to detect them. We keep fiddling with the theory because the math is intriguing, it works out elegantly . . . but we have no way to know if it connects with reality." Matt snorted. "As if we even had a useful definition of 'reality.' "

Susan frowned. "I need a beer. You want one?"

"Sure."

She got up and walked the few steps to the refrigerator, glad to have a chance to turn her back on him for a moment. What he had said earlier had settled her mind a lot, but she supposed she would never be entirely comfortable when he was in his professorial mode.

You'd better learn to get comfortable with it, girl. A professor is what he is, that's the guy you've fallen in love with, so get used to it.

She popped the tops on two cans of Henry Weinhard's and handed one to Matt, then sat back down in the little lecture hall and tried to look alert.

"So you're saying it could all be just a mental game," she said.

"What we mathematicians call 'jacking off,' " Matt agreed. "Nothing wrong with that. Much of mathematics has nothing to do with the 'real' world. But don't worry about it. String theory has nothing to do with it, I'm just showing you some examples. Say we could prove string theory. Strings are made of pure energy. Okay, but what is the nature of energy? Don't answer that, it doesn't matter."

"You're saying we've reached a dead end."

"Very likely. We've been reaching dead ends all over the realm of physics. Don't get me wrong, there is a *vast* amount still to learn, and if the past is any guide, a lot of what we think we know now is wrong.

"But look at the other end of the scale. We can now see out to the theoretical end of the universe. It's fourteen or fifteen billion light-years away, and it seems we can't see any farther than that because there is no 'farther than that.' Space is curved, and what we see out there *is* what was happening fifteen billion years ago. If somebody is out there, on the edge of the universe, looking at *us* . . . what they are seeing is an infant universe. Quasars, protogalaxies."

"You've lost me again."

"Don't worry about it. The point is, it's another limit. One more example. Black holes. They were postulated a long time ago, and then we found them. A triumph for astrophysics. We can observe their effects, we can make a good stab at describing the conditions that exist around them, we can construct a theoretical model of what might be inside them, if that term has any real meaning with a black hole . . . but we can never, never look into one. Another dead end.

"What I'm saying is, we're reaching end points everywhere in what I have believed in all my life, what you might call rational science. So what's left?"

"Irrational science?"

Matt laughed.

"That's a good term for it. I like it better than mysticism, or pseudoscience, or 'wacko New Age stuff.' There are irrational numbers in math, and they are quite useful.

"Susan, we experienced something that, in a rational universe as I thought I understood it, simply could not happen. Therefore, a lot of my assumptions were wrong. I've been looking for answers in other places."

"And have you found anything?"

Matt spread his hands and sighed. "I'm ashamed to tell you just how little."

"Don't be ashamed. I've got a feeling you've found out more than anyone else would have."

"Maybe so, maybe not. Look . . . we all travel through time. We think of it as a train traveling at a steady speed on a straight track. Somebody buys us a ticket—"

"Are you talking about our mothers, or . . . God?"

"I don't know. We come into existence, we come into consciousness, we ride the train for a while, not knowing what our destination is, and then we get off. Not only do we not know what's outside the train, what's at the station, we don't even know what we are. What is consciousness? Would time exist without consciousness to appreciate it? Could consciousness somehow be the basis of it all? Would there be a universe at all without an aware being to witness it? These are the questions I've tried to answer."

"I'm not surprised you didn't make much progress."

Matt smiled. "Maybe 'finding an answer' was the wrong way to put it. I never expected that. I *was* exploring the concept of a creator, among other things. Different cultures have come up with very different ways of looking at the idea. I just wondered, do any of them have a better way of looking at it than the one I was taught?"

"Do you have a religion? I never asked you that."

"I never asked you, either. I was raised in the Christian world, therefore I see the world through that prism, even if I don't believe in it. Christianity and Islam, the great monotheistic religions, see God as omniscient and all-powerful. With Christianity, God is good and Satan is evil . . . but as I understand it, the game is rigged. At Armageddon a great battle will be fought, and the outcome is already known. I mean, we don't call him God for nothing. Which means that even *God's* fate is predestined. By himself, I guess, though I can't imagine why he'd bother to play the game if he knows the outcome."

Susan laughed. "I hate to say this, but you're losing me even quicker with this stuff than you did with the physics."

"That's exactly how I felt. So I looked around. The older religions, what we look down our noses at and call 'mythology,' like the Romans and Norse and Greeks, had a different worldview. Hindus today still see the universe like that. Their gods duke it out from time to time. They are willful, vain, childish, vindictive, quite willing to play dice with human lives."

"So's the Christian God, in my opinion."

"I couldn't agree with you more. But we put all those attributes into one being. Animists and others give different attributes to different gods." Matt sighed heavily. "What I'm going to tell you is that I've begun to get a . . . a hint of an inkling of an intuition of an enigma. Remember the old fable of the blind men and the elephant? One feels his trunk and says an elephant is like a snake. Another thinks he's like a tree, from feeling his leg. Another thinks an elephant is like a wall.

"What's happened to me is like . . . like I'm blind, deaf, and have no hands, and you gave me one hair off Fuzzy's back and asked me to deduce a mammoth from that."

"At last." Susan laughed. "A metaphor I can understand. How far have you gotten?"

"About as far as you'd expect. How about the railroad metaphor? I thought that one was pretty good."

"You're right: I got that one."

"Then try this. We think time is a long, straight train ride at constant speed. Actually, it can turn into a roller coaster. It's got big loops in it. It turns upside down now and then, and sometimes it goes forward and then backward. Why? I don't know. But it could be that during human history we've been riding on an abnormally straight stretch of track, that what we think of as universal laws concerning time are really only local. Maybe in the next galaxy down the block time runs backward. Maybe out there in empty space there are *lots* of loops, and we have no way to detect them.

"I was struck by something a lot of American Indian tribes share, the deity usually called Coyote. The trickster. He enjoys playing pranks on humans. If there is a god or gods out there, maybe they're just having fun with us, putting us on this ride we think is going to be calm and reasonable, and suddenly the bottom drops out and we fall screaming down the first hill and they laugh and laugh and laugh."

"You've given me a lot of maybes."

"Best I can offer. I've got a million more. Maybe these loops in time open up more often than we let ourselves admit. What if the Loch Ness monster is an aquatic dinosaur that fell through a hole in time and swam around long enough to get spotted a few times, create a legend, and then died? What if the Sasquatch and the Yeti were time travelers? What if some—some, mind you, ninety-nine percent of them are swamp gas—some UFOs are lost astronauts from the future?"

"I've heard some of this stuff before. There are websites devoted to it."

"Sure. And until I traveled in time I dismissed them. I have no proof of any of them now, for that matter. As you say, all I've got is a lot of maybes."

Susan took another drink of her beer and thought it over.

"You're disappointed, aren't you?" Matt asked.

"A little," she admitted. "I was hoping you'd found some answers."

"I'm a long way from that. But I did learn to do a trick, and I did make a discovery. You may like the trick, but I don't think the discovery is going to be easy for either of us to accept. Watch this."

Matt reached into his pocket and took out something she immediately recognized as one of the marbles he had tinkered with five years earlier, when he was trying to duplicate the time machine. It looked like ordinary red glass, in a square cage with ridges that could be interlocked with other cages to slide over each other in any direction.

He held it between thumb and forefinger and started twisting it in the air. Left, right, right some more, forward, left again . . . she soon lost track of the permutations. It was like watching a safecracker twisting the dial, only he turned it through three axes. Then he stopped. Nothing happened.

"Nice trick," she said.

"It doesn't work every time. That's what's so frustrating. In science as I knew it, repeatability is *everything*. With this stuff . . . well, like my grandfather used to say, 'It don't work unless you hold your mouth right.'"

He went through the motions again, and she was amused to see that he actually had screwed up one side of his mouth in an odd way, though she didn't think he was aware that he was doing it. Then he set it down on the table between them . . . and this time the little wire cube with the clear red glass ball in it seemed to be seized by a mysterious energy. It began to spin.

Then it began to grow.

It . . . unfolded itself. Watching it, incredulous, Susan thought each move was as logical as unfolding a paper airplane or taking a flattened box and turning it into an assembled one . . . but neither of those operations hurt her eyes. This was an evolution that she felt instinctively that human eyes were not equipped to witness. Now there was a larger cube, three marbles on a side, now four, now five . . . and in a few eye-popping seconds there was the whole array, and the box that contained it, laid out like an opened suitcase in front of her.

She got up and hurried to the bathroom.

* * *

"FEELING better?" Matt asked when she got back.

"I didn't actually lose the beer," she said. "But for a minute there I felt sick as a dog."

"I told you it was a roller-coaster ride."

"Matt . . . what did you just *do*?"

"The only thing I've learned to do. That night, the night that began with the mammoths about to stomp us, and ended up back in Los Angeles . . . I watched this thing do its stuff. I ended up with that one little glass ball, and then I got hit by a city bus. I knew I had seen something and I thought I could remember it, and I knew I had to get out of there. It wasn't until later that I found the ball in my pocket. I don't remember putting it there. We were sort of busy, if you recall. Later, I figured out that the ball was still somehow attached to the rest of the machine. I did computer simulations on the model I had stored in my computer, and eventually came up with an algorithm that . . . that sort of pries up the lid on the place where the rest of the machine is."

"So you've had it all the time."

"That's right. All through the interrogation. But I didn't know what to do with it. I still don't."

"Why not just give it to Howard?"

Matt sighed. "I would love to do that. I don't want this thing. It's like . . . it's like you own a gun and you know how to fire it, but you haven't figured out how to aim it yet, and it can shoot in any direction, totally at random. How often are you going to shoot that gun? It's even worse, though, because sometimes it just goes off by itself, when it wants to, when the conditions are right, when God or Coyote wills it . . . I don't know."

"All the more reason to get rid of it. Give it to Howard."

"Susan, Howard is a collector. That's what he wanted a time machine for in the first place. He wanted me to get him a mammoth, or the means to get one. We did, accidentally. He was fixated on mammoths at the time . . . but you think he'd be satisfied with that? Why not dinosaurs? He could build a real Jurassic Park."

"Well . . . why not? I wouldn't mind getting more mammoths. Fuzzy ought to have more of his own kind."

"Believe me, if I thought it was that simple I'd go back

with a big-game trapper and bring some more mammoths forward in time. But . . ."

"But what?"

"But I think it might be very dangerous."

Susan chewed it over for a time.

"You're talking about changing the past, right?"

"Yes. I don't know if it's possible. Maybe we could change the past and make a better world. Maybe we could make a worse one. Or maybe the way things have happened, are happening, and will happen is written in stone, and can't be changed. I lean toward that last possibility."

"Predestination."

"If you want to call it that. It could be that free choice is illusion. I don't think I have the right to test it."

"I see what you mean. But there's one question I've been meaning to ask you, ever since, ever since you made that . . . that *thing* appear. Who made it?"

"I made it."

"No, no, I know you made that one. Who made the original one?"

"There is only one. I made it. You watched me."

"But that's . . . that's crazy! The only way you knew how to make it was you took it apart and found *out* how to make it."

"Yeah. It's a puzzler, isn't it? Time travel is full of stuff like that."

"But . . . where did it come from? Why is it here? What's the *point* of it?"

Matt smiled.

"That's the big question, isn't it? *Why?* All my life I've been much more concerned with *what* and *how*. Science in the main doesn't attempt to tackle the meaning of things. I hardly even know how to phrase the questions I need to ask. I'm still learning my ABCs, and I've got a sneaking feeling that nobody, *nobody* has even gotten as far as Z yet, much less learned to read. That's been a comfort to me, trying to understand this, that just about everyone else is almost as ignorant as me.

"I don't even think this 'time machine' is necessary. I think a crystal ball might do it, or tarot cards. A man from the last century might actually use a vehicle like the one in *The Time*

Machine. Cavemen might time-travel just by looking into a campfire and thinking the right thoughts."

"The right thoughts? You mean . . ."

"I think it was my mind that sent us back, and brought us home. But it doesn't work all the time. You have to be in the right place, too. We appear to be on an unscheduled loop on the roller coaster of time.

"But one of the few things I know for sure is . . . that if that loop hadn't happened, we never would have met. That's the most important thing in the world to me."

Susan wondered if she was going to cry. She held it in, because there were still more questions she had to ask. She was starting to be disturbed.

"What else are you sure of? You said you had a trick, which you showed me, and that's good enough, please don't turn it on. And you made a discovery. And . . . I thought the roller-coaster ride through time was over."

Matt looked down at the table, then met Susan's eyes again.

"Not quite. To make the discovery, I had to go back to the beginning. I had to go to northern Canada, to Nunavut."

30

THE place was called Kangiqiniq, formerly Rankin Inlet, and it was located about three-quarters of the way up the western shore of Hudson Bay, which put it in the balmy, sun-kissed southern regions of Nunavut.

Matt had never felt so cold.

It began as soon as he stepped off the small plane from Winnipeg, which had been cold enough. It got worse as he moved around the streets of town. Kangiqiniq was a bustling metropolis, for Nunavut. Population almost five thousand, very few of whom seemed to spend any time on the streets. It made sense. The wind howled down the arrow-straight streets between the mostly modular buildings, direct from the North Pole—which was actually the northernmost point in the territory.

There were a lot of parked snowmobiles. Most of the town was not fancy, but in addition to traditional native ways of making a living there was a thriving tourist industry catering to hunters, fishermen, and eco-touring. People who could afford to indulge in things like that usually didn't like to stay in tarpaper shacks, so there were half a dozen fancy resorts built from imported stone and timber, pretending to be Swiss ski lodges or Colorado vacation mansions. They all had indoor pools and gyms, plush rooms, good restaurants. There was actually a golf course, possibly the northernmost one in the world.

It had taken Matt a lot of effort to track down the members of the old recovery team from the Mammoth Seven site. Rostov was dead. There were only four others and they were all Inuit, and scattered all over the territory—which meant they were really scattered, as Nunavut covered two million square kilometers. That was the bad news. The good news was there were only thirty-five thousand citizens. If it came to it, Matt could question most of them, and there was a complex web of blood relationships that meant he should come across an aunt or uncle or third cousin of any of them sooner or later.

He started down his list alphabetically, with a guy named Charlie Charttinirpaaq.

Charlie had an address in Kangiqiniq. Matt took a taxi there and knocked on the door of a modular home with a lot of junk scattered around it. It looked like Charlie was something of a packrat. There was a Mercedes SUV that had been very fancy when new, about five years ago, sitting on four flat tires, and three snowmobiles parked in the yard amid all the clutter.

There was no answer at the door, so Matt went to a neighbor and was greeted by a short, brown woman with narrow eyes and very little expression on her face. Her yard was very clean, and the room behind her was spotless. She wasn't eager to give out information to this red-nosed, sniffling white man, but Matt said he had some money for Charlie—which was true, he was prepared to pay for his story—and a possible job. The woman looked dubious, but told Matt he could probably find Charlie in a bar called the Blind Walrus.

The Walrus wasn't located in any of the fancy hotels. Matt was the only white face when he came through the door. Everybody looked up and gave him the once-over, but he didn't sense any hostility. There were two guys playing pool, half a dozen sitting around watching a hockey match on an old television, and two men at the bar. The only thing of interest in the room was a stuffed polar bear, rearing almost up to the ceiling. Matt went to the bar and ordered a beer. He considered his approach. Just ask the bartender and patrons if any of them were Charlie Charttinirpaaq? The neighbor lady had showed a trace of a smile when he said the name so he was fairly sure he was mangling the pronunciation.

Later, with all the things to think about concerning fate and free will and time paradoxes and such, he had to wonder at his good luck at finding Charlie so easily. Because after a moment he was pretty sure the guy sitting one stool down from him was the man he was looking for. He took the photo he had printed from the one on file at the Nunavut Department of

Motor Vehicles website out of his pocket and compared it to the face he saw in the bar mirror, and it looked pretty close.

And the man was wearing a watch just like the one on Matt's wrist.

Matt wasn't much of a drinking man, but for once in his life he felt he needed a stiff one. He ordered a shot of Canadian Club and choked it down, chased it with the rest of his beer, and turned to the Inuit man and smiled at him.

"I couldn't help noticing, you've got a watch just like mine."

The man frowned, and just for a moment he looked frightened. Matt could understand the initial hostility—he was Inuit, Matt was a stranger—but why would he be frightened? The man—Matt was sure it was Charlie now—looked around as if he expected someone to come crashing through the door.

"See?" Matt said, turning his wrist and pointing to the timepiece he had worn since his incarceration at the secret government facility. "It's a Seiko Naval Observatory, accurate to a billionth of a second."

Charlie relaxed a little, shrugged, and grinned, showing widely spaced, tobacco-stained teeth.

"Not mine," Charlie said. "Mine don't work. Never has."

Not surprising, Matt thought, *since it's twelve thousand years old.*

"Let me buy you a drink," Matt said.

"CHARLIE said he found the watch," Matt told Susan. "Five years ago. Said he thought it would bring him good luck, and it did for a while, but not so much lately."

"You're saying he got the watch off the man beside the frozen mammoth."

"Yes."

"And Howard didn't tell you about it."

"You know Howard. He hates to lose, and he's secretive as hell. He didn't tell me about the watch because Charlie stole it before he got there. He didn't tell me about the second person frozen with the mammoth because it had nothing to do with building a time machine. I didn't need to know. Howard and his damn secrets."

"I'm starting to see where this is going," she said.

"Yes. Susan . . . from the very first I considered the possibility that the dead man beside the mammoth was . . . me. There was one thing that argued *strongly* against it. I simply cannot imagine that I would be able to survive in the Stone Age long enough to be as old as this man was. But I guess anything's possible. Then, when we went back, I was pretty damn sure it *had* been me. I figured I'd explain it to you later, after we had settled in a bit."

"Break it to me slowly. Because there was just you and the frozen mammoth. I wasn't there. Which meant I must have died before you did."

"I'm sorry. I just couldn't figure out—"

"It's okay, Matt. I had enough to adjust to as it was."

"Okay. Then we came back . . . and it no longer made sense that the frozen man had been me. Then I found Charlie, and the watch.

"I came to your house to tell you that I was now sure I was not only the 'inventor' of the time machine, I was the time traveler. I had figured out that, one way or another, the roller-coaster ride wasn't over yet, for me, anyway. I was trying to figure out how to say good-bye to you for good. Then Howard dropped his bombshell—accidentally, the bastard—and I didn't know whether to laugh or cry. I've been trying to decide which ever since, and how to tell you.

"It seems the dead man was me, the dead woman was you, and the dead mammoth was Fuzzy."

"The dead mammoth was a hybrid? Fuzzy is a hybrid," Susan said.

"Yes."

"Oh my god."

THEY went into the bedroom, got undressed and into bed, and just held each other for a while as Susan absorbed it.

"What if you just tossed it into the sound?" she said after a while.

"I'll do it if you want me to."

"And then what?"

"And then we see, I guess. The reason I'm afraid to is, like

I said, if we don't go back in time, live out our lives, and die up north . . . then I don't see how we will ever meet."

"But we have met. We're here. Together. What happens to this, to all that's happened between us?"

"What happens when we die? I have no answers to those questions. Can we alter reality? If we try, then the universe might simply rearrange itself and make it so that none of this ever happened. You'll live your life in Florida, in the circus, and I'll live my life in Oregon. And I have to say, from my perspective in the here and now, whatever that means in this context, it wouldn't be a life worth living. But then . . . would I know? I don't think so."

She kissed him.

"I feel the same way. I guess we don't dare mess with it." She drew her head back and looked at him. "But you must have a theory. About what would happen if we tried to get rid of the time machine."

Matt sighed. "I think one of two things would happen. If I threw it over the side right here, this RV, the ferry dock, and maybe all of Port Townsend would be hurled backward into the Stone Age. Remember, the warehouse and all the elephants went back with us the first time."

"And the other thing?"

"I think a big fish would swallow it, get netted, cut up, the time machine would get thrown in the trash, fall off the trunk on the way to the landfill, get picked up by a scavenger, sold to an antique shop, and one day we'd walk into that antique shop with Fuzzy on a leash . . ."

"So, if we avoid antique shops we can at least delay the trip a while. That's good—Fuzzy has never been interested in antiques."

He laughed and kissed her nose. "I hadn't thought of that. Let's make a vow. When we buy furniture for our home together, we buy strictly new stuff."

"Our home together?"

"I hope so."

"Me, too." She sighed, and snuggled closer. "I don't much fancy a cave as a first home, though. The Stone Age . . . life wasn't easy back then, Matt. I wasn't even a very good Girl Scout. I don't know how I'll be at picking roots and berries."

"I couldn't catch a trout, the one time I tried. I guess we'd better start studying survival manuals, that sort of thing. How are your teeth?"

"Good. Oh, lord, no medical and dental benefits where we're going."

"Not even any Novocain. But we'll have each other, and we'll have a tame mammoth. Fuzzy will be back in his world."

"I guess that's something. No, I mean, that's *everything*, being with you—"

"I know what you meant."

"I had no idea, when I took Fuzzy, just how far we'd be taking him." She was silent for a while. Matt felt himself begin to stir, wondered if she still felt like sleeping. He touched her, and she proved she wasn't sleepy at all. But first she drew back one more time and looked at him.

"So when does this happen, do you think?"

"When it's time."

31

NIGHT fell, and the satellites opened their infrared eyes.

Howard paid for time on every high-resolution commercial orbiter as they came over the horizon until they sank below it. He stayed on the plane with Andrea, parked at the Executive Terminal, monitoring his bank of screens and listening to incoming reports from units in the field—all negative so far—while Warburton and his team watched similar displays in the war room of the security company only about half a mile away.

Warburton was sure they would try to sneak over somewhere in the wilderness, so he concentrated on the eyes scanning the border, from Blaine to western Montana. They set the system to look for trailers of the right size, and for large animals. The heat-sensitive cameras could pick out a single rabbit but the computers were good at sorting through that. They quickly discarded the garbage and sent the larger hits to the screens for a human to decide if it was worth checking out.

It got boring very quickly.

There was a herd of cattle. Warburton watched as the computer examined several areas that turned out to be nothing but clumps of cows that made an unusually large heat signature. More cows. A group of people hiking along a mountain trail. He could see their arms and legs moving, and the beams of their flashlights. Kind of late to be moving around in the woods. Here was a group of five deer. More deer. More people. Deer, deer, deer, man alone, deer, deer . . . what was that? Bear. Now there was a car, a tent, a campfire, and two people . . . my, that's an interesting position.

It was the last interesting thing Warburton saw for several hours.

* * *

THE clock swung past midnight, eased into the wee hours. Warburton had to stop and rest his eyes every fifteen minutes or so. He hadn't had any idea there were so many deer in the whole country, and this was just a narrow strip of Washington and the tip of Idaho. Not to mention RVs. Those were fairly easy. A mammoth in an RV or a truck would shine like a beacon. They had found hundreds of garage-type fifth wheels, some with a heat source at the back where Fuzzy would be standing, but a quick look always showed it to be the still-warm engines of off-roaders like the one Susan had probably abandoned on the roadside somewhere.

He wasn't discouraged yet, they could be undercover somewhere waiting for the occasional border patrol vehicle to go by, but they had to go across sometime, and he was sure they would be detected. But he had thought to have them by now, he had to admit that. Time to go back over it, question his assumptions. Was he missing something?

He called up an area map and looked at it, tried to make it tell him something. After a few minutes he frowned.

"What's this?" he asked Crowder, pointing to the tip of a little peninsula about ten miles west of Blaine. It was an almost perfect square, two miles on a side. He hadn't noticed it before, but it was a different color from the land above it.

"That's the nipple on the hind teat of Canada," Crowder said, with a chuckle.

Warburton waited.

"It's called Point Roberts. Back when somebody was drawing that straight-line border that starts back in Minnesota, that line nicked that little peninsula. 'Fifty-four, forty, or fight,' or some shit like that. It's part of the U.S. Hardly anybody goes there but Canucks crossing to get bargains on stuff that's more expensive up there."

"So there's a border crossing?"

"Sure."

"Is there a ferry?"

Crowder typed a moment, and the map which had been told to display only ferries that went from the United States to

Canada now showed the whole maze of Washington State ferries. Sure enough, a couple lines went to Point Roberts.

"Another boondoggle, you ask me," Crowder said. "Just north of the border is the great big B.C. ferry slip at Tsawwassen. Who needs another ferry?"

Sawasen? Warburton hated the stupid names up here. Humptulips, Mukilteo, Puyallup . . . why couldn't they speak English?

"The ferries that go there. Where do they come from?"

"Let's see . . . here's one from Anacortes, one from Bellingham, and one from Friday Harbor."

"The first two are covered. Where's Friday Harbor?"

"San Juan Islands." Crowder pointed to a maze of islands, all highly irregular in shape. It looked as if there were three or four big ones and dozens of small ones. "One of the ferries from Anacortes to Sidney, in B.C., stops a couple places in the San Juans, including Friday Harbor."

"But we've got that covered."

"Yeah." Crowder frowned at the map. "But there's one that stops at Friday Harbor before going on to Point Roberts."

"Where does it start?"

"Right here. Port Townsend. Over on the Olympic Peninsula."

All they had over there was one team, at Port Angeles, covering the ferry that went to Victoria. Plus, once they decided Susan was going to Canada, they hadn't been checking the main highway over there, US 101, or much of anything, for that matter. Warburton had thought the only way to Canada via the Olympic Peninsula was through Port Angeles, since he had asked only for international ferries.

It was a serious lapse on Crowder's part—he should have thought of the border crossing at Point Roberts—but Warburton wasn't going to take him to task for it. Not right now, anyway. He addressed Crowder and Blackstone.

"I don't want you to mention this to anybody. Not even Howard, yet. You know we've been picking up chatter, there's been some leaks from some of our employees, naturally, and some notice of what's going on along the border. The news and the police are just starting to get wind that somebody's looking for something the size of an elephant. But I may still have a chance to wrap this up quietly. I'm going out to take a look for myself. If there's a newsman waiting when I get there, I'll know how he found out, understand?"

"Don't worry," Blackstone said. Warburton nodded, and went outside to his helicopter, thinking he would retire after this one was over, and never set foot in another helicopter again. He was getting too old for this shit.

IT didn't take long to get over to Port Townsend. Warburton had the pilot keep it high up. With the optics he had there was no need to move in close and make a lot of noise. He examined two RV parks before he found the likely trailer and truck, the engine glowing brightly through the trees, the water heater plainly visible, what looked like two people in the bedroom, and a large heat source in the back. He told the pilot to set it down on the opposite side of town.

There was a motorcycle in the backseat of the chopper. Warburton wrestled it out, pulled on a warm black leather coat and helmet, and headed out. It had a good muffler on it, making no more than a powerful purr as he moved down the deserted streets. Halfway there it started to rain again, the low-pressure system he had been watching and worrying about all night moving in from the Pacific just now arriving here in the western part of the state. He flipped down his visor.

He arrived at the park, killed the engine, and coasted down a slight slope, going by the office, and laid the bike down in shadows. He walked down the rows of sleeping juggernauts and almost missed the one he was looking for. The red stripe was gone, and the long dimple in the side had been painted over.

Smart girl. He had expected no less.

He raised his infrared glasses and looked at the back wall. It looked like somebody had painted the outline of a seven-foot-tall mammoth on the side of the trailer in bright green. As he watched, the mammoth's trunk curled up toward his mouth.

He scanned along the trailer and when he got to the bedroom, perched out above the bed of the pickup truck he saw, for the second time that night, the infrared figures of a couple making love.

Enjoy it while you can, kids.

He got out his phone and called Howard.

"WARBURTON has found them," Howard said.

Andrea looked up from the magazine she had been reading, trying to stay awake. After she had set them on the right track she had completely lost interest in the search. Again, she was far from sure whose side she was on, though she felt she had owed it to Howard to give him her advice.

"Crossing the border?"

"No, but you were right. They plan to cross in the morning." He explained it to her as they left the plane and walked the short distance to the helicopter. A wind was rising, and she could see storm clouds to the west. Not her idea of a good night to fly, but she wasn't too worried about it. They got aboard and lifted off quickly. They passed out over water and then Howard, sitting beside her in the backseat, looked thoughtful. They were wearing earpiece/mike units so they could talk over the noise of the chopper. Howard keyed the pilot.

"Where is Oak Harbor in relation to Port Townsend?" he asked.

"It's on Whidbey Island, sir. The Admiralty Inlet to Puget Sound lies between them. Say ten air miles."

Howard smiled.

"Let's arrive in style," he said to Andrea, then punched a name into his telephone. "Hello? Frank? It's Howard Christian . . . yeah, I know what time it is. I wouldn't be calling if it wasn't important. What it is, I was wondering if I could borrow your boat?" He held the phone away from his ear and grinned at Andrea. "Okay, charter . . . you *owe* me, Frank, and now I'll owe you . . . okay, you talk to my pilot now, and call the harbormaster, get him out there with the keys. Talk to you later, Frank."

* * *

THE boat was an eighty-foot Bertram with twin 1500 horsepower engines. Howard was not much of a nautical man, though he owned a larger yacht than this at Bahia Mar, Lauderdale, and sometimes puttered around the inland waterways of Florida in it. He knew how to pull away from the dock and he knew how to pull into the dock, what was so tough about that? Besides, this rig could literally drive itself. You could input a destination and it would plot the best course and keep a radar eye out for traffic. No need to look for channel markers or worry about tides or depth or weather. If there was a problem, the boat would tell you about it and tell you what to do.

Howard and Andrea boarded, cast off, and pulled slowly away from the small marina at the north end of Whidbey Island, threaded through a passage marked on the electronic chart as Deception Pass, and then moved into moderately choppy seas down the west side of the island and into the Strait of Juan de Fuca.

Halfway there Warburton called.

"They're moving. I'm behind them, they should get there in five minutes. I'll meet you there."

"See you in twenty minutes."

THEY drove the trailer down a ramp and onto a pier jutting out into the sound. It looked new, or recently refurbished; all that federal money, Warburton guessed. The pier was four lanes wide, paved, and had a stout barrier at the end where the ferry would dock in a few hours. The truck and trailer pulled up to the barrier and cut its lights and engine. The first departure was at six A.M. There were no other vehicles parked on the pavement.

Warburton got off his motorcycle at the top of the ramp and walked slowly down toward the trailer. There were two empty lanes to the left of it, where cars would pull off the ferry. Near the barrier was a stairway leading down to a small dock that should accommodate Howard's boat when it arrived. Warburton wasn't sure the boat was a good idea, but it was better than landing a helicopter here in the middle of the night, which was sure to attract attention. And anyway, this was how Howard wanted to do it, and he was the boss.

The Bertram arrived fifteen minutes later. Warburton was standing on the dock to catch the line Andrea threw him. He tied it off, and helped them ashore. They went up the stairs and over to the trailer, Howard holding an umbrella over Andrea against the increasing rain. Howard seemed to be almost trembling with anticipation. Warburton took out his gun, a Glock automatic.

"Howard . . . ," Andrea said.

"Just a precaution, darling," Howard said. He knocked on the door. There was no answer, so he knocked again. The curtain covering the window in the door was raised, but they couldn't see anything inside. Warburton held up the pistol, pointing toward the sky. The door opened, and steps extended themselves hydraulically.

"Come on out, Susan," Howard said into the darkness.

"What if I call CNN?"

"Then I look foolish for a while, and you both go to jail. Is it worth it?"

Susan snapped on an outside light and an inside one. She and Matt were standing there, hastily dressed, barefoot. Susan was crying. Matt had no expression.

"Can I say good-bye to him?"

"I'll give you one minute."

Susan moved toward the back of the trailer. Howard didn't like the look Andrea was giving him. *Well, what was I supposed to do, let her get away with it?* He had expected to feel a lot better about this, but the sense of triumph of only a few moments ago seemed to have washed away in the rain. *Why did she have to cry? I'm not a bully. I've been bullied, until I got too big to push around.*

Matt came down the steps and stood there, getting wet, giving Susan her privacy. His eyes never left Howard, but he said nothing.

Susan appeared, drying her eyes on her sleeve, and started down the steps.

Fuzzy bellowed.

The whole trailer shook. In the back, the side of the trailer dimpled inward, then sprung back. Another bellow, and again the dimple appeared, and this time it didn't pop back out.

Howard hastily climbed the steps and stuck his head in the

door. The mammoth was agitated, rocking back and forth against his chains, but Howard had seen this arrangement before, he knew even Big Mama could not have torn herself loose. The sides of the trailer were holding. Maybe it would be necessary to let Susan ride back here on the return to Fuzzyland, keep him calmed down until he got back in his familiar quarters.

She was finished with Fuzzy, no question, and if that meant canceling the circus shows until the animal had been brought around to accepting her loss, that was just the way it had to be. He had three elephant trainers lined up who guaranteed Fuzzy could be broken, and none the worse for it, in no less than a month. Andrea didn't have to see it.

Then he saw the time machine, sitting right there on the table with its top open. Suddenly all the excitement he had been feeling came rushing back at him. It was a good day. It was a *damn* good day!

He sat where Matt had been sitting and just stared at it for a moment, visions of *T. rexes* and brontosaurs dancing in his head. Matthew Wright wasn't the only genius in the world, not the only man who could figure this thing out. In fact, according to Matt, he never *had* figured it out. The damn thing just turned itself on, took him somewhere, and then brought him back again.

Matt was the only one who witnessed the thing doing whatever it did, and that might help, so maybe he could work out a deal with him to work on it again, though the prospect made him feel like gagging.

Whatever. It had been demonstrated that the thing worked, that was beyond question, and if it worked once Howard could make it work again.

He closed the lid, noticing the dents made when that maniac hit it that night in the warehouse. He snapped the catches, and stood up. He didn't hear the sound of Fuzzy's harness leather ripping.

The next thing he knew, Fuzzy had wrapped his trunk around his neck and slammed him to the floor on his back. He looked up into two tons of angry, hairy death as Fuzzy rammed his massive head downward. He screamed.

Susan bolted back up the stairs. Fuzzy had Howard pinned

to the floor, one tusk just missing him on the right, the other poking into the aluminum case on Howard's left.

"*Fuzzy! Up, Fuzzy, up! Up, Fuzzy*!"

The mammoth paused, down on his knees.

"Up, Fuzzy! That's a good boy. Up, Fuzzy."

Fuzzy moved back slightly, got to his feet, looked down at Howard as if wondering if he might take just one more poke at the guy who had upset Susan so much . . . then backed up to where he had been and stood there, swaying gently.

"Go, Howard," Susan said quietly. "Just get out of here."

Howard scrambled to his feet, thankful he hadn't wet himself. He brushed himself off, and went outside.

"Are you okay, darling?" Andrea went to him and put her arms around him. She could feel him shaking. He hugged her, and turned to Warburton.

"You drive back. Let Susan stay in back with him to keep him calm. I'll meet you at the park."

"Will do."

Warburton stood there holding the gun, though he knew Matt wasn't going to try anything stupid. He watched Howard and Andrea hurry down the stairs and cast off the line, then scramble aboard the boat. The engine started and the boat began to back up.

Then it vanished. There was nothing on the water but some backwash bubbles that quickly dissipated.

Warburton started running toward where the boat had been. Very near the edge of the pier he slipped on an oily patch and went down, striking his head on one of the pilings. Matt started toward him, and saw him roll over the edge and fall into the water.

"Matt, what's happening?" He turned and saw Susan standing in the door.

"You keep Fuzzy calm. I'll see." He went to the edge and looked. Warburton was floating facedown in the water. Matt cursed and jumped in. It was quite a shock, hitting the cold water.

He was an indifferent swimmer, but he managed to thrash along and turn Warburton over and get his arm around his neck in the vaguely remembered lifesaving position, and he treaded water for a moment, then started for the dock where the boat had been docked until a few seconds ago.

Susan was waiting for him at the dock, and helped him pull Warburton up and lay him out on the wood planks.

"Do you know what to do?" Matt asked.

"Mouth to mouth, I guess." She didn't seem pleased. At that moment Warburton coughed up some water, shook his head, and sat up.

They helped him to his feet, got his arms over their shoulders, and staggered up the stairs with him. Halfway to the trailer, Matt suddenly stopped, dropped Warburton's arm, and ran toward the trailer. He went up the stairs, was gone for only a moment, then he came back down and faced Susan and a very groggy Warburton.

"That son of a bitch stole my watch," he said.

THEY didn't have any clothes to fit big, bulky Warburton, so he sat across from them in the breakfast nook, soaking wet and shivering and wrapped in a blanket as he sipped from a cup of instant coffee Susan had heated in the microwave. While Susan was out, Fuzzy had entered the living area, curious now rather than angry, and had done a little damage.

"Do you have a first name?" Susan asked.

"I never use it. Did you loosen the harness on that animal?"

Susan glared at him, got up, and retrieved the harness from the back of the trailer. She showed him where the material had ripped.

"Satisfied?"

"Sorry. I had to ask."

"I would never have endangered Fuzzy that way."

"Point taken."

They were quiet for a while, each of them digesting what they had just seen, none of them quite sure what to think of it yet. Finally Matt spoke.

"Howard never told me about the frozen woman between the man and the mammoth," he said. "Looks like you had your little secret, too. Howard never heard about the watch the man was wearing, did he?"

"What was I supposed to do?" Warburton said angrily. "I

didn't send a message in the clear, that would have been foolish. I just radioed Howard and told him to get up there where they were digging up his mammoth, there was something he needed to see. Howard knows I wouldn't waste his time. Between the time I made the call and the time I got back to the mammoth, that bastard Charlie had swiped the watch and was over the horizon on his snowmobile. I went up in the chopper and looked for him, and I don't know how he managed to hide in that wasteland, but he did. Some of the other Indians, Eskimos, whatever the hell they were, they said Charlie was a weird one, believed in magic, he must have thought the watch had powerful juju.

"Howard was on his way. Rostov had showed me the box by then. I knew Howard would be so happy about finding that . . . what the hell did it matter if the guy was wearing a watch? It was obvious he had traveled in time and I figured the box was the way he had done it. There were only me and five other people, counting Charlie, who knew about the watch. I figured the box was the important thing, but it cost me, *plenty*, to be sure those other five were quiet about it. One of them's dead now." He looked up, saw the expressions on their faces. "Not me. Rostov worked in a refrigerator, he caught pneumonia, he died. End of story. I'm not a hit man."

Susan grasped Matt's hand and squeezed.

"Don't feel responsible for this, Matt," she said. "We were talking about fate all night. I think you pick your fate. Howard did this to himself."

"What about Andrea?"

"That I don't know. But she's with him, I'm sure of that, wherever they are. And a few hours ago I had to consider whether I'd be happier in the Stone Age with you, or here without you. And I know how I decided."

Matt squeezed her hand.

"It just seems so harsh. Howard is the last man I'd expect to survive hardships like that. And what took him up to the Arctic Circle?"

"I guess we'll never know that. But remember what he wrote on the box." She shivered. "I'm just thinking about Howard up there in Canada, getting off the helicopter, going to look at his mammoth . . . and seeing his own dead body."

Nobody had a comment to make about that. Susan looked at Warburton and sighed. "Okay, when do we start back?"

Warburton shook his head.

"You think I care about that? My boss is gone, and I'm retiring. You saved my life, and I pay my debts. I'll call the search off, I'll tell them I'm on my way back to Oregon with the animal, and that's the end of it as far as I'm concerned."

He got up and walked out into the night.

THE rain let up before sunrise, and the ferry pulled into its slip shortly after that. Half a dozen other vehicles had parked before the gate went up and they all drove aboard. It was the same size as the first ferry they had been on.

The crossing to Friday Harbor was smooth, the day overcast. Quite a few more cars got on, and then they were off to Point Roberts. Susan stayed in the trailer with Fuzzy, who was feeling as close to grumpy as he ever got. Matt stood at the bow of the ship and watched some dolphins rolling in front of them, thinking about many things, rearranging his life. It looked like there was another jail cell in the offing, though Susan thought they wouldn't be in custody for long. He could tolerate it if they turned the lights out at night. He didn't think any Canadian jailers would be punching him in the nose.

Howard, why did you do it? There at the end, when he was dying, Howard could have done something, some small thing, to twist events around so that he never would have gone back into the past to live what must have been a very, very hard life. Why didn't he? Before that, he could have refused to go north.

Had a good life. That was the only explanation Matt was likely to get.

The ferry docked and Susan joined him in the cab for the short drive to the crossing, having given Fuzzy another tranquilizer and laid him down in the back. The next few days were going to be stressful.

They crossed the international boundary and pulled up at the Canadian Customs shack. Standing beside the road a little way ahead of them in the area where Customs could pull you over for a thorough search, they could see Jack Elk, the man who called himself Python, and two men with briefcases.

Matt rolled down his window and looked at the smiling officer.

"Anything to declare?" he said.

Matt and Susan looked at each other, and burst out laughing.

1

THE time traveler pulled the fur robe tighter around himself and tried to nestle a little closer to the dead mammoth as the snow drifted higher around him, and wondered why he bothered. He was hours from death, maybe minutes, and he knew it, he welcomed it. He could no longer feel his feet. The fingers of his left hand weren't moving very well. Only his right arm had any warmth in it, still wrapped around his wife's body where he had jammed it after he killed the mammoth, waited for it to bleed to death, and tucked her tenderly as far as he could under the great hairy body.

He had killed her three days before and she was quite frozen, but somehow she still felt warm to his touch.

Oh, lord, how he missed her, the woman who had redeemed him, who had made his life worth living. He was looking forward to joining her wherever she had gone, heaven or hell or sweet nothingness.

He had the preparation of cyanide in his medicine bag. He could go quickly if he chose. His wife had certainly gone quickly enough, and though it had not been completely painless, she had thanked him as she swallowed the fatal dose.

He would take the poison . . . but there was a nagging feeling of something left undone. He couldn't imagine what it might be, but he knew he wouldn't let go until it came to him.

A dying man's life is supposed to pass before his eyes and he had been having many, many memories, but hardly any from before what they came to call Day One of Year One. It all seemed like a past life now. Cities. Helicopters. Computers, satellites, nuclear bombs, cell phones—*any* sort of telephone. He could easily believe he had dreamed it all.

But not a dream, in retrospect. A nightmare. A nightmare he had once thought had *begun* on Day One, Year One . . . but now realized had *ended* on that horrible day.

THERE they were, floating in Puget Sound in a magnificent eight-million-dollar yacht, and the world went away.

Everything he valued in the world, anyway, except for Andrea. There they were, at the entrance to one of the great metropolitan estuaries on Earth, and all he could see for miles and miles was water, rocks, trees, and a sky without airplanes. Here they were, worth thirty-nine billion dollars, on paper (thirty-nine and a half billion, counting Andrea's money), and unable to buy anything. The real meaning of that phrase, "on paper," had never come home to him until that moment.

They spent most of the first day motoring around the sound, looking for signs of human life, Howard raging, Andrea despairing. Was it 1804, were Lewis and Clark somewhere south on the Columbia? Was it 100,000 B.C.? Was it A.D. 100,000, and all the works of mankind crumbled to dust?

At some point Howard had realized that, whatever the date was, he was unlikely to find a filling station. When his tanks were dry, that was *it*. So he anchored and raged some more, and Andrea despaired some more.

But neither of them were quitters.

They inventoried the Bertram, from the scuppers to the fo'c'sle, or whatever they called it, and found they had quite a lot of stuff. Like Howard himself, the friend he had borrowed the boat from had enjoyed gadgets, and liked to have the best. There was plenty of food. There were tools. There was fishing gear sturdy enough to land a killer whale (Howard had never even baited a hook), and rifles and shotguns and pistols and ammunition and tools. There were several computers, including one Howard had brought himself, pocket-sized and able to run on solar energy.

They got out the manuals and learned to run the ship. They turned off the generator on the second day, to save fuel, sat quietly in the dark at night, grudging even a single candle they could never replace, talking over the possibilities. During the day they learned to fish. The waters were *teeming* with fish. They landed salmon the size of atomic submarines.

And day by day a conviction grew in Howard. He could not explain it and he could not prove it, but he knew what the date was. It was shortly before that horrible, *horrible* man, Matt Wright, and that thieving *bitch*, Susan Morgan, had gone into the past with *his* time machine and come back with a herd of mammoths and *no* time machine.

Nothing could sway him from this, and Andrea didn't even try. She herself didn't much care where she was if there was no place to shop, but if she had to be somewhere, southern California was what she knew, and though she realized that Rodeo Drive wouldn't be built for ten thousand years or so, a sea voyage would be better than sitting around here in the damp, cloudy, moldy, rainy, chilly, fungus-ridden, *depressing* Pacific Northwest.

And who knew? Maybe Howard's obsession was right. Maybe she could get back to where her credit cards worked. Andrea was an environmentalist, but no outdoorswoman. The woods were full of chiggers and mosquitoes and spiders and things.

So Howard made his calculations, found they could just get there on the three thousand gallons of fuel remaining, and they made their way down the coast on just one of the big twin diesels at the most economical rpm setting as determined by the boat's computer.

They had good luck. When a big storm hit they were able to shelter in San Francisco Bay. How very, very odd to sail through it with no bridge overhead. There was nothing on Alcatraz Island, nothing on Yerba Buena, no '49ers boomtown. *Nothing*.

Several times they saw, and were seen by, native peoples. Some were on shore, some in canoes, but none tried to catch the big Bertram. So it wasn't the age of dinosaurs . . . but Howard had known that, the coastline pretty much agreed with the ship's maps—though of course all the fancy GPS stuff was useless with no satellites overhead—and the continent had been very different when *T. rex* stalked the Earth.

They anchored near what Howard figured to be the future

site of Santa Monica. Pulling away from the boat, they noticed for the first time that it had a name painted on the transom (they had learned a lot of boating terms on the way down). She was the *Twist of Fate*. They laughed, for the first time in a long time. They loaded their weapons and shouldered their backpacks and set out for the La Brea tar pits.

Howard had hoped to find his missing warehouse on the way, but found no sign of it. It proved nothing, though he scanned the area from the top of every rise. He hadn't realized how easy it would be to hide a single structure in wilderness like this. It could be in the next shallow ravine, or he could be miles away from it.

Or, maybe it hadn't arrived yet.

They found the tar pits. Again, nothing. They spent the night, sleepless from all the unfamiliar and frightening animal sounds, and hiked back to the ship the next day.

On the shore, a hundred people awaited them.

IT was snowing harder now. Howard kept brushing it away from his face, again wondering why he was bothering.

He remembered something he hadn't thought of for a long time: His first sight of the "caveman" nestled up against the frozen mammoth. He remembered his disgust. Soon, probably before the day was over, something would make a meal of his face. Hell, of most of his head. Not a bear, a bear would certainly drag him away and eat a lot more. Probably not a wolf. Most likely some of the little snow foxes he had seen on his way north. They would gnaw at him a while, then the snow would cover him. He found the prospect held no emotion for him, one way or the other. Though if they came while he was still alive he'd fight them off. Howard Christian was not a quitter.

He looked at his watch . . . and smiled again. At *Matt's* watch. Even after all these years he still did it from time to time. His people felt the watch held very powerful medicine, because the chief looked at it so often, and they had been sorry to see him leave with it, but of course too polite to say so.

And it did have heap powerful juju, or voodoo, or power of *some* sort, though not of a type any of them would ever understand. Nor, he admitted to himself, did *he* have more than the faintest, quasispiritual sense of the watch's power. Hell, it didn't even tell time anymore, hadn't since the radio signal from the Naval Observatory had suddenly winked off on Day One, Year One. Years ago.

Years ago.

How many? He could probably work it out, if it mattered. He had a good memory. There was Year One. There was the Year of Building. There was the year of Many Fish. There was the Year of the First-Born Child. There was the Year of the First Mammoth Kill. There was . . .

He had forgotten the sequence. At some point it had ceased to matter. It was probably around the Year Howard Realized Matt Was Not Coming. At some point he had moved from being a middle-aged man to being an old man, and then a very old man. Probably somewhere between seventy-five and eighty.

Damn it, what else was he forgetting?

A few brave souls had actually been aboard the *Twist of Fate*, but they hadn't ventured inside, and they had done very little damage. One had put a steel fishhook through his hand, but didn't seem angry about it. He seemed to treasure the bright, shiny new thing hanging there.

Howard kept his finger on the trigger, and he and Andrea both smiled a lot, and nodded, and showed open palms, and got into their Zodiac and—startling everyone when they started the engine—motored back out to the *Twist*.

Establishing themselves as White Gods didn't take long. They had a practically unlimited supply of miracles to offer. Soon everyone was friendly and eager to see new things. When Howard and Andrea went back to the tar pits and set up a tent, part of the tribe went with them to protect them, and the rest moved their village three miles north to guard the *Twist* and to fish, which was their main livelihood.

Howard waited.

To pass the time, he read. His computer memories held much of the future worlds' libraries, most of it absolutely useless but some incredibly valuable to them, from the Boy Scout Handbook to paleontology and anthropology texts. Year One passed, meticulously marked off by the internal clock in Howard's computer.

They never called the next one Year Two. When it came to an end, it was the Year of Building. Things just . . . happened.

Howard wasn't capable of just sitting and waiting, and neither was Andrea. They got involved in the affairs of the tribe. He was never going to be able to give them automobiles or rifles, hell, he would never even be able to smelt iron. But he could teach them things. Andrea picked up the language like a sponge, and he learned it almost in spite of himself.

And he began to change things. At first, it was for his own comfort. The food in the *Twist* ran out, and he was sick to death of fish. Howard longed for beef. The People trapped and hunted small game and picked wild fruit and vegetables. They lived in huts made of sticks and the bones of mammoths that had died a natural death. Southern California was a lot cooler now than it would be in Howard's time; the wind blew right through the flimsy things, and his tent had big rips in it and was miserable in the rain.

He taught them to build better shelter.

Andrea had a baby, and they named him Adam.

Howard found out how elephants had been hunted and killed before gunpowder, and taught them to do that.

Andrea had another baby, and they named her Eve. Eve died two months later of some disease, and it almost broke their hearts.

HOWARD couldn't even remember what the year was when he finally abandoned his vigil at the tar pits. There was too much else going on in his life by then. He was a part of the community, the leader, the shaman, the medicine man.

Andrea had a third baby and this one lived, and a fourth, and she lived, too. Dear Howie, beloved Daphne.

The People became the most powerful tribe on the coast for as far as a man could walk in many days. They were the ones who slew the mammoths, who had the white gods, and the sticks that killed at a distance. (Well, they used to. The ammo was gone now.) Howard knew the names of every person living within miles of him, all part of his tribe, his people, his family.

Then came the year that he realized . . . he was happy. He was happier than he had ever been in his life.

That's it! I remember now. . . .

WHEN their first grandchild was born, Howard began to feel a restlessness.

He had thought much about time travel. He had improved the lives of the People, gave them new technology. They still lived in the Stone Age, but it was a cleaner, healthier, more prosperous Stone Age. They used to fight with other tribes, but Howard had put an end to that, first with the guns, later with improved weaponry. He gave them the bow and arrow. But there was a big conundrum. Was he changing the future? Or was what *had* happened *fated* to happen?

It occurred to him that he, Howard Christian, may have been the reason mammoths became extinct in North America. The thought did not please him . . . and he eventually dismissed it. Someone else would have doped it out soon enough. Some genius in Europe or Asia had learned to do it without his help.

He had taught the People primitive agriculture because he never grew to like one of their dietary staples, ground acorns. They had found desiccated tomatoes and potatoes in the larder and nurtured them, and Howard once more enjoyed fries and ketchup. Where had they gone? No book in his library mentioned a native California species of tomato. Lost knowledge, or was he changing the future? He had thought of doing more. He knew where to find copper ore. Why not make metals?

But . . . why? He had revolutionized his old world, and it brought him very little real satisfaction. He spent his billions on toys, or on dominating others, or in meaningless games with money. The People didn't even have money, didn't need it. He had revolutionized their lives, too . . . and his satisfaction was enormous. He had real respect among the people, instead of ass-kissing, fear, or envy. Sure, being a white god didn't hurt when it came to gaining respect, but as the years went by, as his family became their family, he one day came to the realization that he had one thing he had never had before in his entire life. He had friends.

Howard had never had a friend, not really. Next to family,

it was the nicest thing that had ever happened to him. There were those among the People he would trust with his life, *did* trust with his life when they were hunting mammoth, or fighting off a saber-tooth.

Would he jeopardize that by inventing copper or bronze tools? What if he changed history and it turned out that he never came back here, never had his children, his family, his People? It was a thought too awful to contemplate.

And he didn't think it would work that way, that it *could* not work that way. Andrea had learned medicine, surgery, had saved the life of many a child who would have died without her help. The first time she did it he worried, they discussed it . . . and decided that anyone who could stand by and watch a child die simply because saving his life might alter the future, or destroy the universe . . . was not somebody either of them wanted to know.

The conviction grew in him that it would all work itself out in the way it had to be. The tomato and potato plants would die out. His technological innovation would either be forgotten, or the People would be conquered by a more aggressive tribe and some of their skills lost. The mammoths would still go extinct, and he didn't need to concern himself about whether it was his fault; the future would be as he remembered it.

But if that was so, he had some obligations.

AS the snow continued to fall, Howard dug the time machine out from where he had wedged it near his legs. How many hours had he wasted staring at the thing, trying to make it work? It was one of his few regrets, that wasted time. He rubbed his thumb over the hole he had patched with tar, the hole punched when Fuzzy had almost killed him. Then he fumbled a flint arrowhead from a pocket with a hand grown numb from the cold. His left hand, because his right was trapped beneath his beloved Andrea. He smiled again. Of course, being right-handed there was no possibility in the world that, one day, he would recognize his own handwriting. He began to scratch a message on the bottom of the battered aluminum case.

* * *

HE started his mission by domesticating mammoths.

He had a head start by his spying on Susan, preparing for his great coup of finally displacing Susan in Fuzzy's affections. He learned how they did it in Sri Lanka and Burma. He got the People to build the necessary surrounds and pens, to hobble the mammoths and break them to the ankus. He and his family and friends learned to ride them. And they set off across the southwest: his family, some of the best and brightest among the People, and six docile mammoths.

Oh, my, the saga he could have written about that mighty journey. Across country that would one day be home to Apache, Navajo, Zuni, Anasazi, much more hospitable now than it would be then but still harsh, still daunting. The tribes they met stood in awe of the People Who Rode Mammoths. There was never any question of fighting.

They came to the plains, and finally Howard enjoyed a great steak. Well, Pleistocene buffalo, actually, but by then he couldn't have told the difference.

He had noticed that here on the plains there was the occasional hybrid mammoth, part woolly and part Columbian. He assumed they were mules. He captured and domesticated an old one and called him Fuzzy-Tu. Then he sat back and waited, knowing he would understand when the proper time came.

It was a long time. He had many grandchildren when Andrea came to him and said she was certain she had cancer. She had drugs that could help with the pain, but nothing that would cure it. He asked her if she wished she could be back in the twenty-first century, where therapy might cure her. She said the thought never entered her mind.

They were somewhere in the Dakotas at the time, he thought. They said their farewells to their family and to the tribe, and set off northward on the back of Fuzzy-Tu.

Winter closed in. Andrea got weaker. At last she asked him to give her the final gift, and he held her as she died. He continued north until Fuzzy-Tu was near collapse, then he sorrowfully killed the great beast.

He sat down to wait.

* * *

HE didn't try to remember the words. He let his awkward left hand do the writing, etching each line over and over until it was clear:

HAD A GOOD LIFE
NO REGRE

He stopped. He remembered it clearly now. He and Matt had assumed the time traveler had died before he could complete his message, unable to finish the vertical line of the T. But Howard was alive still, and though very weak, he knew he could go on. He could finish the message this way:

NO HARD FEELINGS MATT

How would Matthew Wright read that? Maybe, "No hard feelings, Matt." Maybe "No hard feelings, signed, Matt." Either way, it would surely change his reaction, and thus change history.

For a fractional moment, the old Howard Christian seized his hand. *Write it*, the old Howard said. *Get the bastard. Just finish the T and add the S. NO REGRETS.*

But he knew to the depths of his soul that if he tried to write one more stroke . . . a polar bear would bite his head off. A meteorite would come crashing from the heavens and kill him instantly. An earthquake would open a crack in the soil and swallow him up.

And he wouldn't have it any other way.

He had been thrown involuntarily onto this infernal, inevitable roller coaster, and it had turned into a merry-go-round. He had enjoyed the ride.

HAD A GOOD LIFE.

With the last of his strength, he hurled the flint away into the snow.

He closed his eyes.

Soon, a pair of white foxes approached the mound in the snow and started digging.

FROM "LITTLE FUZZY, A CHILD OF THE ICE AGE"

Well, maybe you can imagine the fuss when they opened the back of the trailer and found Fuzzy inside! And nobody even knew he was missing!

What happened next was confusing, and messy, and not very much fun. Matt and Susan were put in jail for a little while, but were quickly bailed out.

At the same time, Howard Christian, the mean rich man, and Andrea de la Terre, the glamorous movie star, vanished in a big boat that must have sunk somewhere, but nobody ever found it.

And then the lawyers went to work. When a lot of lawyers who are making a lot of money start to fight over something in court . . . oh, my! Things can take just *forever* to get worked out. Howard being missing didn't make any difference to the rest of the people who owned the circus where Fuzzy had been kept prisoner for so long. Oh, no! They fought and fought and fought to get Fuzzy sent back to the United States.

They have been fighting for almost five years now, and Fuzzy is getting bigger and bigger and bigger. The lawyers tried to keep Susan away from him, but poor Fuzzy was so unhappy he wouldn't eat, so they had to let her stay. Now Fuzzy lives in a big **preserve** in the province of **Alberta** while the courts keep hearing his case. He will never have his family back, he will never enjoy the company of other mammoths . . . but he lives with some elephants and seems to enjoy being with them. He is out in the woods and valleys, under the bright blue sky and the lovely sunshine, and people can come and stand on a high observing platform and look at him. Some days they have to use telescopes, since his preserve is *really big* and he likes to wander around. You can see him on one of twenty Fuzzycams right now if you click right **here**.

The last time we at **Friends of Fuzzy** went around and asked people, "What do you think should be done with Fuzzy?" . . . well, 94 percent of Canadians think he should stay right where he is! And what's more, 78 percent of Americans feel the same way!

Right now there is a movement to declare Fuzzy a **political refugee**, which means somebody who would be in big trouble if he or she had to go back to his homeland.

Some people say an animal can't be a political refugee.

Other people say . . . why not?

If you are a Friend of Fuzzy, and you think this is a good idea, why don't you write an email or a letter to your Member of Parliament and Senator and the Prime Minister, or if you're an American, to your Representative and Senators and the President (you can click right **here** to do that) and tell them what you think. Have your mother and or father write, too, and all your friends.

It is now **(4)** days and **(15)** hours until the fifth anniversary of Fuzzy's escape, and there will be big parties in most big cities and many small towns to celebrate what we've started calling "Fuzzy's Birthday." Click **here** to find a party near you. Or, go to **Fuzzyland**! They are having a *very* big party there, and those mechanical mammoths put on quite a show!

So keep coming back to this website every day and we will keep you up-to-date on the very latest of the saga of Little Fuzzy, Child of the Ice Age!

Susan Morgan-Wright, webmaster

–

"VARLEY IS THE BEST WRITER IN AMERICA."
—TOM CLANCY

THE GOLDEN GLOBE

BY

John Varley

Sparky Valentine is an actor on the road, bringing Shakespeare—or at least his version of it—to the outer regions of Earth's solar system. Sparky can transform himself from young to old, fat to thin, even male to female, by altering magnetic implants beneath his skin. Indispensible hardware for an actor—and a con man wanted for murder.

0-441-00643-4

"THIS IS AN ENGROSSING NOVEL BY ONE OF THE GENRE'S MOST ACCOMPLISHED STORYTELLERS."
—*Publishers Weekly*

"AN ACTION-PACKED, CROSS-SOLAR-SYSTEM JOURNEY...COLORFUL...INTRIGUING."
—*Science Fiction Age*